perhaps the most exciting SF writer at work today'
Daily Telegraph

f the most ambitious, startling, dextrous writers the SF
n boast of . . . a mature, distinctive voice arising out of
notonous publishing wilderness' *Asimov's SF Magazine*

Jniverse may be stranger than we can imagine, but its
:o have a tough time outdoing Egan' *New Scientist*

ALSO BY GREG EGAN FROM GOLLANCZ

Axiomatic
Distress
Luminous
Permutation City
Quarantine
Teranesia
Diaspora
Schild's Ladder
Incandescence
Oceanic
Zendegi

OCEANIC
GREG EGAN

The right of Greg Egan to be identified as the author
of this work has been asserted by him in accordance with
the Copyright, Designs and Patents Act 1988.

First published in Great Britain in 2009 by
Gollancz
An imprint of the Orion Publishing Group
Orion House, 5 Upper St Martin's Lane, London WC2H 9EA
An Hachette UK Company

This edition published in Great Britain in 2010 by Gollancz

1 3 5 7 9 10 8 6 4 2

A CIP catalogue record for this book is available
from the British Library

ISBN 978 0 575 08654 8

Typeset at The Spartan Press Ltd,
Lymington, Hants

Printed and bound in the UK by CPI Mackays,
Chatham ME5 8TD

The Orion Publishing Group's policy is to use papers that
are natural, renewable and recyclable products and made
from wood grown in sustainable forests. The logging and
manufacturing processes are expected to conform to the
environmental regulations of the country of origin.

www.gregegan.net

www.orionbooks.co.uk

CONTENTS

LOST CONTINENT

1

Ali's uncle took hold of his right arm and offered it to the stranger, who gripped it firmly by the wrist.

'From this moment on, you must obey this man,' his uncle instructed him. 'Obey him as you would obey your father. Your life depends on it.'

'Yes, uncle.' Ali kept his eyes respectfully lowered.

'Come with me, boy,' said the stranger, heading for the door.

'Yes, haji,' Ali mumbled, following meekly. He could hear his mother still sobbing quietly in the next room, and he had to fight to hold back his own tears. He had said goodbye to his mother and his uncle, but he'd had no chance for any parting words with his cousins. It was halfway between midnight and dawn, and if anyone else in the household was awake they were huddled beneath their blankets, straining to hear what was going on but not daring to show their faces.

The stranger strode out into the cold night, hand still around Ali's wrist like an iron shackle. He led Ali to the Land Cruiser that sat in the icy mud outside his uncle's house, its frosted surfaces glinting in the starlight, an apparition from a nightmare. Just the smell of it made Ali rigid with fear; it was the smell that had presaged his father's death, his brother's disappearance. Experience had taught him that such a machine could only bring tragedy, but his uncle had entrusted him to its driver. He forced himself to approach without resisting.

The stranger finally released his grip on Ali and opened a door at the rear of the vehicle. 'Get in and cover yourself with the blanket. Don't move, and don't make a sound, whatever happens. Don't ask me any questions, and don't ask me to stop. Do you need to take a piss?'

'No, haji,' Ali replied, his face burning with shame. Did the man think he was a child?

'All right, get in there.'

As Ali complied, the man spoke in a grimly humorous tone. 'You think you show me respect by calling me "haji"? Every old man in your village is "haji"! I haven't just been to Mecca. I've been there in the time of the Prophet, peace be upon him.' Ali covered his face with the ragged blanket, which was imbued with the concentrated stench of the machine. He pictured the stranger standing in the darkness for a moment, musing arrogantly about his unnatural pilgrimage. The man wore enough gold to buy Ali's father's farm ten times over. Now his uncle had sold that farm, and his mother's jewellery – the hard-won wealth of generations – and handed all the money to this boastful man, who claimed he could spirit Ali away to a place and a time where he'd be safe.

The Land Cruiser's engine shuddered into life. Ali felt the vehicle moving backwards at high speed, an alarming sensation. Then it stopped and moved forward, squealing as it changed direction; he could picture the tracks in the mud.

It was his first time ever in one of these machines. A few of his friends had taken rides with the Scholars, sitting in the back in the kind with the uncovered tray. They'd fired rifles into the air and shouted wildly before tumbling out, covered with dust, alive with excitement for the next ten days. Those friends had all been Sunni, of course. For Shi'a, rides with the Scholars had a different kind of ending.

Khurosan had been ravaged by war for as long as Ali could remember. For decades, tyrants of unimaginable cruelty from far in the future had given their weapons to factions throughout the country, who'd used them in their squabbles over land and power. Sometimes the warlords had sent recruiting parties into the valley to take young men to use as soldiers, but in the early days the villagers had banded together to hide their sons, or to bribe the recruiters to move on. Sunni or Shi'a, it made no difference; neighbour had worked with neighbour to outsmart the bandits who called themselves soldiers, and keep the village intact.

Then four years ago, the Scholars had come, and everything had changed.

Whether the Scholars were from the past or the future was unclear, but they certainly had weapons and vehicles from the future. They had ridden triumphantly across Khurosan in their Land Cruisers, killing some warlords, bribing others, conquering the bloody patchwork of squalid fiefdoms one by one. Many people had cheered them on, because they had promised to bring unity and piety to the land. The warlords and their rabble armies had kidnapped and raped women and boys at will; the Scholars had hung the rapists from the gates of the cities. The warlords had set up checkpoints on every road, to extort money from travellers; the Scholars had opened the roads again for trade and pilgrimage in safety.

The Scholars' conquest of the land remained incomplete, though, and a savage battle was still being waged in the north. When the Scholars had come to Ali's village looking for soldiers themselves, they'd brought a new strategy to the recruitment drive: they would only take Shi'a for the front line, to face the bullets of the unsubdued warlords. Shi'a, the Scholars declared, were not true Muslims, and this was the only way they could redeem themselves: laying down their lives for their more pious and deserving Sunni countrymen.

This deceit, this flattery and cruelty, had cleaved the village in two. Many friends remained loyal across the divide, but the old trust, the old unity was gone.

Two months before, one of Ali's neighbours had betrayed his older brother's hiding place to the Scholars. They had come to the farm in the early hours of the morning, a dozen of them in two Land Cruisers, and dragged Hassan away. Ali had watched helplessly from his own hiding place, forbidden by his father to try to intervene. And what could their rifles have done against the Scholars' weapons, which sprayed bullets too fast and numerous to count?

The next morning, Ali's father had gone to the Scholars' post in the village, to try to pay a bribe to get Hassan back. Ali had waited, watching the farm from the hillside above. When a single Land Cruiser had returned, his heart had swelled with hope. Even when the Scholars had thrown a limp figure from the vehicle, he'd thought it might be Hassan, unconscious from a beating but still alive, ready to be nursed back to health.

It was not Hassan. It was his father. They had slit his throat and left a coin in his mouth.

Ali had buried his father and walked half a day to the next village, where his mother had been staying with his uncle. His uncle had arranged the sale of the farm to a wealthy neighbour, then sought out a *mosarfar-e-waqt* to take Ali to safety.

Ali had protested, but it had all been decided, and his wishes had counted for nothing. His mother would live under the protection of her brother, while Ali built a life for himself in the future. Perhaps Hassan would escape from the Scholars, God willing, but that was out of their hands. What mattered, his mother insisted, was getting her youngest son out of the Scholars' reach.

In the back of the Land Cruiser, Ali's mind was in turmoil. He didn't want to flee this way, but he had no doubt that his life would be in danger if he remained. He wanted his brother back and his father avenged, he wanted to see the Scholars destroyed, but their only remaining enemies with any real power were murderous criminals who hated his own people as much as the Scholars themselves did. There was no righteous army to join, with clean hands and pure hearts.

The Land Cruiser slowed then came to a halt, the engine still idling. The *mosarfar-e-waqt* called out a greeting, then began exchanging friendly words with someone, presumably a Scholar guarding the road.

Ali's blood turned to ice; what if this stranger simply handed him over? How much loyalty could mere money buy? His uncle had made enquiries of people with connections up and down the valley, and had satisfied himself about the man's reputation, but however much the *mosarfar-e-waqt* valued his good name and the profits it brought him, there'd always be some other kind of deal to be made, some profit to be found in betrayal.

Both men laughed, then bid each other farewell. The Land Cruiser accelerated.

For what seemed like hours, Ali lay still and listened to the purring of the engine, trying to judge how far they'd come. He had never been out of the valley in his life, and he had only the sketchiest notion of what lay beyond. As dawn approached, his curiosity overwhelmed him, and he moved quietly to shift the blanket just enough to let him catch a glimpse through the rear window. There was a mountain peak visible to the left, topped with snow, crisp in the predawn light. He wasn't sure if this was a mountain he knew, viewed from an unfamiliar angle, or one he'd never seen before.

Not long afterwards they stopped to pray. They made their ablutions in a small, icy stream. They prayed side by side, Sunni and Shi'a, and Ali's fear and suspicion retreated a little. However arrogant this man was, at least he didn't share the Scholars' contempt for Ali's people.

After praying, they ate in silence. The *mosarfar-e-waqt* had brought bread, dried fruit and salted meat. As Ali looked around, it was clear that they'd long ago left any kind of man-made track behind. They were following a mountain pass, on higher ground than the valley but still far below the snow line.

They travelled through the mountains for three days, finally emerging onto a wind-blasted, dusty plain. Ali had grown stiff from lying curled up for so long, and the second time they stopped on the plain he made the most of the chance to stretch his legs, wandering away from the Land Cruiser for a minute or two.

When he returned, the *mosarfar-e-waqt* said, 'What are you looking for?'

'Nothing, haji.'

'Are you looking for a landmark, so you can find this place again?'

Ali was baffled. 'No, haji.'

The man stepped closer, then struck him across the face, hard enough to make him stagger. 'If you tell anyone about the way you came, you'll hear some more bad news about your family. Do you understand me?'

'Yes, haji.'

The man strode back to the Land Cruiser. Ali followed him, shaking. He'd had no intention of betraying any detail of their route, any secret of the trade, to anyone, but now his uncle had been named as hostage against any indiscretion, real or imagined.

Late in the afternoon, Ali heard a sudden change in the sound of the wind, a high-pitched keening that made his teeth ache. Unable to stop himself, he lifted his head from beneath the blanket.

Ahead of them was a small dust storm, dancing across the ground. It was moving away from them, weaving back and forth as it retreated, like a living thing trying to escape them. The Land Cruiser was gaining on it. The heart of the storm was dark, thick with sand, knotted with wind. Ali's chest tightened. This was it: the *pol-e-waqt*, the bridge between times. Everyone in his village had heard of such things, but nobody could agree what they were: the work of men, the work of djinn, the work of God. Whatever their origin, some men had learnt their secrets. No *mosarfar-e-waqt* had ever truly tamed them, but nobody else could find these bridges or navigate their strange depths.

They drew closer. The dust rained onto the windows of the Land Cruiser, as fine as any sand Ali had seen, yet as loud as the hailstones that fell sometimes on the roof of his house. Ali forgot all about his instructions; as they vanished into the darkness, he threw off the blanket and started praying aloud.

The *mosarfar-e-waqt* ignored him, muttering to himself and

consulting the strange, luminous maps and writing that changed and flowed in front of him through some magic of machinery. The Land Cruiser ploughed ahead, buffeted by dust and wind but palpably advancing. Within a few minutes, it was clear to Ali that they'd travelled much further than the storm's full width as revealed from the outside. They had left his time and his country behind, and were deep inside the bridge.

The lights of the Land Cruiser revealed nothing but a hand's breadth of flying dust ahead of them. Ali peered surreptitiously at the glowing map in the front, but it was a maze of branching and reconnecting paths that made no sense to him. The *mosarfar-e-waqt* kept running a fingertip over one path, then cursing and shifting to another, as if he'd discovered some obstacle or danger ahead. Ali's uncle had reassured him that at least they wouldn't run into the Scholars in this place, as they had come to Khurosan through another, more distant bridge. The entrance to that one was watched over night and day by a convoy of vehicles that chased it endlessly across the desert, like the bodyguards of some staggering, drunken king.

A hint of sunlight appeared in the distance, then grew slowly brighter. After a few minutes, though, the *mosarfar-e-waqt* cursed and steered away from it. Ali was dismayed. This man had been unable to tell his uncle where or when Ali would end up, merely promising him safety from the Scholars. Some people in the village – the kind with a friend of a friend who'd fled into the future – spoke of a whole vast continent where peace and prosperity reigned from shore to shore. The rulers had no weapons or armies of their own, but were chosen by the people for the wisdom, justice and mercy they displayed. It sounded like paradise on Earth, but Ali would believe in such a place when he saw it with his own eyes.

Another false dawn, then another. The body of the Land Cruiser began to moan and shudder. The *mosarfar-e-waqt* cut the engine, but the vehicle kept moving, driven by the wind, or the ground itself. Or maybe both, but not in the same direction: Ali felt the wheels slipping over the treacherous river of sand.

Suddenly there was a sharp pain deep inside his ears, then a sound like the scream of a giant bird, and the door beside him was gone. He snatched at the back of the seat in front of him, but his hands closed over nothing but the flimsy blanket as the wind dragged him out into the darkness.

Ali bellowed until his lungs were empty. But the painful landing he was braced for never came: the blanket had snagged on something in the vehicle, and the force of the wind was holding him above the sand. He tried to pull himself back towards the Land Cruiser, hand over hand, but then he felt a tear run through the blanket. Once more he steeled himself for a fall, but then the tearing stopped with a narrow ribbon of cloth still holding him.

Ali prayed. 'Merciful God, if you take me now please bring Hassan back safely to his home.' For a year or two his uncle could care for his mother, but he was old, and he had too many mouths to feed. With no children of her own, his mother's life would be unbearable.

A hand stretched out to him through the blinding dust. Ali reached out and took it, grateful now for the man's iron grip. When the *mosarfar-e-waqt* had dragged him back into the Land Cruiser, Ali crouched at the stranger's feet, his teeth chattering. 'Thank you, haji. I am your servant, haji.' The *mosarfar-e-waqt* climbed back into the front without a word.

Time passed, but Ali's thoughts were frozen. Some part of him had been prepared to die, but the rest of him was still catching up.

Sunlight appeared from nowhere: the full blaze of noon, not some distant promise. 'This will suffice,' the *mosarfar-e-waqt* announced wearily.

Ali shielded his eyes from the glare, then when he uncovered them the world was spinning. Blue sky and sand, changing places.

The bruising thud he'd been expecting long before finally came, the ground slapping him hard from cheek to ankle. He lay still, trying to judge how badly he was hurt. The patch of sand in front of his face was red. Not from blood: the sand itself was red as ochre.

There was a sound like a rapid exhalation, then he felt heat on his skin. He raised himself up on his elbows. The Land Cruiser was ten paces away, upside down, and on fire. Ali staggered to his feet and approached it, searching for the man who'd saved his life. Behind the wrecked vehicle, a storm like the one that the mouth of the bridge had made in his own land was weaving drunkenly back and forth, dancing like some demented hooligan pleased with the havoc it had wreaked.

He caught a glimpse of an arm behind the flames. He rushed towards the man, but the heat drove him back.

'Please God,' he moaned, 'give me courage.'

As he tried again to breach the flames, the storm lurched forward to greet him. Ali stood his ground, but the Land Cruiser spun around on its roof, swiping his shoulder and knocking him down. He climbed to his feet and tried to circle around to the missing door, but as he did the wind rose up, fanning the flames.

The wall of heat was impenetrable now, and the storm was playing with the Land Cruiser like a child with a broken top. Ali backed away, glancing around at the impossible red landscape, wondering if there might be anyone in earshot with the power to undo this calamity. He shouted for help, his eyes still glued to the burning wreck in the hope that a miracle might yet deliver the unconscious driver from the flames.

The storm moved forward again, coming straight for the Land Cruiser. Ali turned and retreated; when he looked over his shoulder the vehicle was gone and the darkness was still advancing.

He ran, stumbling on the uneven ground. When his legs finally failed him and he collapsed onto the sand, the bridge was nowhere in sight. He was alone in a red desert. The air was still now, and very hot.

After a while he rose to his feet, searching for a patch of shade where he could rest and wait for the cool of the evening. Apart from the red sand there were pebbles and some larger, cracked rocks, but there was no relief from the flatness: not so much as a boulder he could take shelter beside. In one direction there were some low, parched bushes, their trunks no thicker than his fingers, their branches no higher than his knees. He might as well have tried to hide from the sun beneath his own thin beard. He scanned the horizon, but it offered no welcoming destination.

There was no water for washing, but Ali cleaned himself as best he could and prayed. Then he sat cross-legged on the ground, covered his face with his shawl, and lapsed into a sickly sleep.

He woke in the evening and started to walk. Some of the constellations were familiar, but they crossed the sky far closer to the horizon than they should have. Others were completely new to him. There was no moon, and though the terrain was flat he soon found that he lost his footing if he tried to move too quickly in the dark.

When morning came, it brought no perceptible change in his surroundings. Red sand and a few skeletal plants were all that this land seemed to hold.

He slept through most of the day again, stirring only to pray. Increasingly, his sleep was broken by a throbbing pain behind his eyes. The night had been chilly, but he'd never experienced such heat before. He was unsure how much longer he could survive without water. He began to wonder if it would have been better if he'd been taken by the wind inside the bridge, or perished in the burning Land Cruiser.

After sunset, he staggered to his feet and continued his hopeful but unguided trek. He had a fever now, and his aching joints begged him for more rest, but if he resigned himself to sleep he doubted he'd wake again.

When his feet touched the road, he thought he'd lost his mind. Who would take the trouble to build such a path through a desolate place like this? He stopped and crouched down to examine it. It was gritty with a sparse layer of wind-blown sand; beneath that was a black substance that felt less hard than stone, but resilient, almost springy.

A road like this must lead to a great city. He followed it.

An hour or two before dawn, bright headlights appeared in the distance. Ali fought down his instinctive fear; in the future such vehicles should be commonplace, not the preserve of bandits and murderers. He stood by the roadside awaiting its arrival.

The Land Cruiser was like none he'd seen before, white with blue markings. There was writing on it, in the same European script as he'd seen on many machine parts and weapons that had made their way into the bazaars, but no words he recognised, let alone understood. One passenger was riding beside the driver; he climbed out, approached Ali, and greeted him in an incomprehensible tongue.

Ali shrugged apologetically. 'Salaam aleikom,' he ventured. 'Bebakhshid agha, mosarfar hastam. Ba tawarz' az shoma moharfazat khahesh mikonam.'

The man addressed Ali briefly in his own tongue again, though it was clear now that he did not expect to be understood any more than Ali did. He called out to his companion, gestured to Ali to stay put, then went back to the Land Cruiser. His companion handed him two small machines; Ali tensed, but they didn't look like any weapons he'd seen.

The man approached Ali again. He held one machine up to the side of his face, then lowered it again and offered it to Ali. Ali took it, and repeated the mimed action.

A woman's voice spoke in his ear. Ali understood what was happening; he'd seen the Scholars use similar machines to talk with each other over great distances. Unfortunately, the language was still incomprehensible. He was about to reply, when the woman spoken again in what sounded like a third language. Then a fourth, then a fifth. Ali waited patiently, until finally the woman greeted him in stilted Persian.

When Ali replied, she said, 'Please wait.' After a few minutes, a new voice spoke. 'Peace be upon you.'

'And upon you.'

'Where are you from?' To Ali, this man's accent sounded exotic, but he spoke Persian with confidence.

'Khurosan.'

'At what time?'

'Four years after the coming of the Scholars.'

'I see.' The Persian-speaker switched briefly to a different language; the man on the road, who'd wandered halfway back to his vehicle and was still listening via the second machine, gave a curt reply. Ali was amazed at these people's hospitality: in the middle of the night, in a matter of minutes, they had found someone who could speak his language.

'How did you come to be on this road?'

'I walked across the desert.'

'Which way? From where? How far did you come?'

'I'm sorry, I don't remember.'

The translator replied bluntly, 'Please try.'

Ali was confused. What did it matter? One man, at least, could see how weary he was. Why were they asking him these questions before he'd had a chance to rest?

'Forgive me, sir. I can't tell you anything, I'm sick from my journey.'

There was an exchange in the native language, followed by an awkward silence. Finally the translator said, 'This man will take you to a place where you can stay for a while. Tomorrow we'll hear your whole story.'

'Thank you, sir. You have done a great thing for me. God will reward you.'

The man on the road walked up to Ali. Ali held out his arms to embrace him in gratitude. The man produced a metal shackle and snapped it around Ali's wrists.

2

The camp was enclosed by two high fences, topped with glistening ribbons of razor-sharp metal. The space between them was filled with coils of the same material. Outside the fences there was nothing but desert as far as the eye could see. Inside there were guards, and at night everything was bathed in a constant harsh light. Ali had no doubt that he'd come to a prison, though his hosts kept insisting that this was not the case.

His first night had passed in a daze. He'd been given food and water, examined by a doctor, then shown to a small metal hut that he was to share with three other men. Two of the men, Alex and Tran, knew just enough Persian to greet Ali briefly, but the third, Shahin, was an Iranian, and they could understand each other well enough. The hut's four beds were arranged in pairs, one above the other; Ali's habit was to sleep on a mat on the floor, but he didn't want to offend anyone by declining to follow the local customs. The guards had removed his shackles then put a bracelet on his left wrist – made from something like paper, but extraordinarily strong – bearing the number '3739'. The last numeral was more or less the same shape as a Persian nine; he recognised the others from machine parts, but he didn't know their values.

Every two hours, throughout the night, a guard opened the door of the hut and shone a light on each of their faces in turn. The first time it happened Ali thought the guard had come to rouse them from their sleep and take them somewhere, but Shahin explained that these 'head counts' happened all night, every night.

The next morning, officials from the camp had taken Ali out in a vehicle and asked him to show them the exact place where he'd arrived through the bridge. He'd done his best, but all of the desert looked the same to him. By midday, he was tempted to designate a spot at random just to satisfy his hosts, but he didn't want to lie to them. They'd returned to the camp in a sullen mood. Ali couldn't understand why it was so important to them.

Reza, the Persian translator who'd first spoken with Ali through the machine, explained that he was to remain in the camp until government officials had satisfied themselves that he really was fleeing danger, and hadn't merely come to the future seeking an easy life for himself. Ali understood that his hosts didn't want to be cheated, but it dismayed him that they felt the need to imprison him while they made up their minds. Surely there was a family in a nearby town who would have let him stay with them for a day or two, just as his father would have welcomed any travellers passing through their village.

The section of the camp where he'd been placed was fenced off from the rest, and contained about a hundred people. They were all travellers like himself, and they came from every nation Ali had heard of, and more. Most were young men, but there were also women, children, entire families. In his village, Ali would have run to greet the children, lifted them up and kissed them to make them smile, but here they looked so sad and dispirited that he was afraid the approach of even the friendliest stranger might frighten them.

Shahin was a few years older than Ali, but he had spent his whole life as a student. He had travelled just two decades through time, escaping a revolution in his country. He explained that the part of the camp they were in was called 'Stage One'; they were being kept apart from the others so they wouldn't learn too much about the way their cases would be judged. 'They're afraid we'll embellish the details if we discover what kind of questions they ask, or what kind of story succeeds.'

'How long have you been here?' Ali asked.

'Nine months. I'm still waiting for my interview.'

'Nine months!'

Shahin smiled wearily. 'Some people have been in Stage One for a year. But don't worry, you won't have to wait that long. When I arrived here, the Centre Manager had an interesting policy: nobody would have their cases examined until they asked him for the correct application form. Of course, nobody knew that they were required to do that, and he had no intention of telling them. Three months ago, he was transferred to another camp. When I asked the woman who replaced him what I needed to do to have my claims heard, she told me straight away: ask for Form 866.'

Ali couldn't quite follow all this. Shahin explained further.

Ali said, 'What good will it do me, to get this piece of paper? I can't read their language, and I can barely write my own.'

'That's no problem. They'll let you talk to an educated man or woman, an expert in these matters. That person will fill out the form for you, in English. You only need to explain your problem, and sign your name at the bottom of the paper.'

'English?' Ali had heard about the English; before he was born they'd tried to invade both Hindustan and Khurosan, without success. 'How did that language come here?' He was sure that he was not in England.

'They conquered this country two centuries ago. They crossed the world in wooden ships to take it for their king.'

'Oh.' Ali felt dizzy; his mind still hadn't fully accepted the journey he'd made. 'What about Khurosan?' he joked. 'Have they conquered that as well?'

Shahin shook his head. 'No.'

'What is it like now? Is there peace there?' Once this strange business with the English was done, perhaps he could travel to his homeland. However much it had changed with time, he was sure he could make a good life there.

Shahin said, 'There is no nation called Khurosan in this world. Part of that area belongs to Hindustan, part to Iran, part to Russia.'

Ali stared at him, uncomprehending. 'How can that be?' However much his people fought among themselves, they would never have let invaders take their land.

'I don't know the full history,' Shahin said, 'but you need to understand something. This is not your future. The things that happened in the places you know are not a part of the history of this world. There is no *pol-e-waqt* that connects past and future in the same world. Once you cross the bridge, everything changes, including the past.'

With Shahin beside him, Ali approached one of the government officials, a man named James, and addressed him in the English he'd learnt by heart. 'Please Mr James, can I have Form 866?'

James rolled his eyes and said, 'Okay, okay! We were going to get around to you sooner or later.' He turned to Shahin and said, 'I wish you'd stop scaring the new guys with stories about being stuck in Stage One for ever. You know things have changed since Colonel Kurtz went north.'

Shahin translated all of this for Ali. 'Colonel Kurtz' was Shahin's nickname for the previous Centre Manager, but everyone, even the guards, had adopted it. Shahin called Tran 'The Rake', and Alex was 'Denisovich of the Desert'.

Three weeks later, Ali was called to a special room, where he sat with Reza. A lawyer in a distant city, a woman called Ms Evans, spoke with them in English through a machine that Reza called a 'speakerphone'. With Reza translating, she asked Ali about everything: his village, his family, his problems with the Scholars. He'd been asked about some of this the night he'd arrived, but he'd been very tired then, and hadn't had a chance to put things clearly.

Three days after the meeting, he was called to see James. Ms Evans had written everything in English on the special form, and sent it to them. Reza read through the form, translating everything for Ali to be sure that it was correct. Then Ali wrote his name on the bottom of the form. James told him, 'Before we make a decision, someone will come from the city to interview you. That might take a while, so you'll have to be patient.'

Ali said, in English, 'No problem.'

He felt he could wait for a year, if he had to. The first four weeks had gone quickly, with so much that was new to take in. He had barely had space left in his crowded mind to be homesick, and he tried not to worry about Hassan and his mother. Many things about the camp disturbed him, but his luck had been good: the infamous 'Colonel Kurtz' had left, so he'd probably be out in three or four months. The cities of this nation, Shahin assured him, were mostly on the distant coast, an infinitely milder place than the desert around the camp. Ali might be able to get a labouring job while studying English at night, or he might find work on a farm. He hadn't quite started his new life yet, but he was safe, and everything looked hopeful.

*

By the end of his third month Ali was growing restless. Most days he played cards with Shahin, Tran, and a Hindustani man named Rakesh, while Alex lay on his bunk reading books in Russian. Rakesh had a cassette player and a vast collection of tapes. The songs were mostly in Hindi, a language that contained just enough Persian words to give Ali some sense of what the lyrics were about: usually love, or sorrow, or both.

The metal huts were kept tolerably cool by machines, but there was no shade outside. At night the men played soccer, and Ali sometimes joined in, but after falling badly on the concrete, twice, he decided it wasn't the game for him. Shahin told him that it was a game for grass; from his home in Tehran, he'd watched dozens of nations compete at it. Ali felt a surge of excitement at the thought of all the wonders of this world, still tantalisingly out of reach: in Stage One, TV, radio, newspapers and telephones were all forbidden. Even Rakesh's tapes had been checked by the guards, played from start to finish to be sure that they didn't contain secret lessons in passing the interview. Ali couldn't wait to reach Stage Two, to catch his first glimpse of what life might be like in a world where anyone could watch history unfolding, and speak at their leisure with anyone else.

English was the closest thing to a common language for all the people in the camp. Shahin did his best to get Ali started, and once he could converse in broken English some of the friendlier guards let him practise with them, often to their great amusement. 'Not every car is called a Land Cruiser,' Gary explained. 'I think you must come from Toyota-stan.'

Shahin was called to his interview. Ali prayed for him, then sat on the floor of the hut with Tran and tried to lose himself in the mercurial world of the cards. What he liked most about these friendly games was that good and bad luck rarely lasted long, and even when they did it barely mattered. Every curse and every blessing was light as a feather.

Shahin returned four hours later, looking exhausted but satisfied. 'I've told them my whole story,' he said. 'It's in their hands now.' The official who'd interviewed him had given him no hint as to what the decision would be, but Shahin seemed relieved just to have had a chance to tell someone who mattered everything he'd suffered, everything that had forced him from his home.

That night Shahin was told that he was moving to Stage Two in half an hour. He embraced Ali. 'See you in freedom, brother.'

'God willing.'

After Shahin was gone, Ali lay on his bunk for four days, refusing to eat, getting up only to wash and pray. His friend's departure was just the trigger; the raw grief of his last days in the valley came flooding back, deepened by the unimaginable gulf that now separated him from his family. Had Hassan escaped from the Scholars? Or was he fighting on the front line of their endless war, risking death every hour of every day? With the only *mosarfar-e-waqt* Ali knew now dead, how would he ever get news from his family, or send them his assistance?

Tran whispered gruff consolations in his melodic English. 'Don't worry kid. Everything okay. Wait and see.'

Worse than the waiting was the sense of waste: all the hours trickling away, with no way to harness them for anything useful. Ali tried to improve his English, but there were some concepts he could get no purchase on without someone who understood his own language to help him. Reza rarely left the government offices for the compound, and when he did he was too busy for Ali's questions.

Ali tried to make a garden, planting an assortment of seeds that he'd saved from the fruit that came with some of the meals. Most of Stage One was covered in concrete, but he found a small patch of bare ground behind his hut that was sheltered from the fiercest sunlight. He carried water from the drinking tap on the other side of the soccer ground and sprinkled it over the soil four times a day. Nothing happened, though. The seeds lay dormant, the land would not accept them.

Three weeks after Shahin's departure, Alex had his interview, and left. A week later, Tran followed. Ali started sleeping through the heat of the day, waking just in time to join the queue for the evening meal, then playing cards with Rakesh and his friends until dawn.

By the end of his sixth month, Ali felt a taint of bitterness creeping in beneath the numbness and boredom. He wasn't a thief or a murderer, he'd committed no crime. Why couldn't these people set him free to work, to fend for himself instead of taking their charity, to prepare himself for his new life?

One night, tired of the endless card game, Ali wandered out from Rakesh's hut earlier than usual. One of the guards, a woman named Cheryl, was standing outside her office, smoking. Ali murmured a greeting to her as he passed; she was not one of the friendly ones, but he tried to be polite to everyone.

'Why don't you just go home?' she said.

Ali paused, unsure whether to dignify this with a response. He'd long ago learnt that most of the guards' faces became stony if he tried to explain why he'd left his village; somewhere, somehow it had been drummed into them that nothing their prisoners said could be believed.

'Nobody invited you here,' she said bluntly. 'You want to live in a civilised country? Go home and build one for yourself. You've got a war back there? *My ancestors* fought wars, they died for their freedom. What do you expect - five hundred years of progress to be handed to you on a plate? Nobody owes you a comfortable life. Go home and earn it.'

Ali wanted to tell her that his life would have been fine if the meddlers from the future hadn't chosen Khurosan as their fulcrum for moving history, but his English wasn't up to the task.

He said, 'I'm here. From me, big tragedy for your nation? I'm honest man and hard worker. I not betray your hospitality.'

Cheryl snickered. Ali wasn't sure if she was sneering at his English or his sentiments, but he persisted. 'Your leaders did agreement with other nations. Anyone asking protection gets fair hearing.' Shahin had impressed that point on Ali. It was the law, and in this society the law was everything. 'That is my right.'

Cheryl coughed on her cigarette. 'Dream on, Ahmad.'

'My name is Ali.'

'Whatever.' She reached out and caught him by the wrist, then held up his hand to examine his ID bracelet. 'Dream on, 3739.'

James called Ali to his office and handed him a letter. Reza translated it for him. After eight months of waiting, in six days' time he would finally have his interview.

Ali waited nervously for Ms Evans to call him to help him prepare, as she'd promised she would when they'd last spoken, all those months before. On the morning of the appointed day, he was summoned again to James's office, and taken with Reza to the room with the speakerphone, the 'interview room'. A different lawyer, a man called Mr Cole, explained to Ali that Ms Evans had left her job and he had taken over Ali's case. He told Ali that everything would be fine, and he'd be listening carefully to Ali's interview and making sure that everything went well.

When Cole had hung up, Reza snorted derisively. 'You know how these clowns are chosen? They put in tenders, and it goes to the lowest bidder.' Ali didn't entirely understand, but this doesn't sound encouraging. Reza caught the expression on Ali's face, and added, 'Don't worry, you'll be fine. Fleeing from the Scholars is flavour of the month.'

Three hours later, Ali was back in the interview room.

The official who'd come from the city introduced himself as John Fernandez. Reza wasn't with them; Fernandez had brought a different interpreter with him, a man named Parviz. Mr Cole joined them on the speakerphone. Fernandez switched on a cassette recorder and asked Ali to swear on the Quran to give truthful answers to all his questions.

Fernandez asked him for his name, his date of birth, and the place and time he'd fled. Ali didn't know his birthday or his exact age; he thought he was about eighteen years old, but it was not the custom in his village to record such things. He did know that at the time he'd left his uncle's house, twelve hundred and sixty-five years had passed since the Prophet's flight to Medina.

'Tell me about your problem,' Fernandez said. 'Tell me why you've come here.'

Shahin had told Ali that the history of this world was different from his own, so Ali explained carefully about Khurosan's long war, about the meddlers and the warlords they'd created, about the coming of the Scholars. How the Shi'a were taken by force to fight in the most dangerous positions. How Hassan was taken. How his father had been killed. Fernandez listened patiently, sometimes writing on the sheets of paper in front of him as Ali spoke, interrupting him only to encourage him to fill in the gaps in the story, to make everything clear.

When he had finally recounted everything, Ali felt an overwhelming sense of relief. This man had not poured scorn on his words the way the guards had; instead, he had allowed Ali to speak openly about all the injustice his family and his people had suffered.

Fernandez had some more questions.

'Tell me about your village, and your uncle's village. How long would it take to travel between them on foot?'

'Half a day, sir.'

'Half a day. That's what you said in your statement. But in your entry interview, you said a day.' Ali was confused. Parviz explained that his 'statement' was the written record of his conversation with Ms Evans, which she had sent to the government; his 'entry interview' was when he'd first arrived in the camp and been questioned for ten or fifteen minutes.

'I only meant it was a short trip, sir, you didn't have to stay somewhere halfway overnight. You could complete it in one day.'

'Hmm. Okay. Now, when the smuggler took you from your uncle's village, which direction was he driving?'

'Along the valley, sir.'

'North, south, east, west?'

'I'm not sure.' Ali knew these words, but they were not part of the language of everyday life. He knew the direction for prayer, and he knew the direction to follow to each neighbouring village.

'You know that the sun rises in the east, don't you?'

'Yes.'

'So if you faced in the direction in which you were being

driven, would the sun have risen on your left, on your right, behind you, where?'

'It was night time.'

'Yes, but you must have faced the same direction in the valley in the morning, a thousand times. So where would the sun have risen?'

Ali closed his eyes and pictured it. 'On my right.'

Fernandez sighed. 'Okay. Finally. So you were driving north. Now tell me about the land. The smuggler drove you along the valley. And then what? What kind of landscape did you see, between your valley and the bridge?'

Ali froze. What would the government do with this information? Send someone back through their own bridge, to find and destroy the one he'd used? The *mosarfar-e-waqt* had warned him not to tell anyone the way to the bridge. That man was dead, but it was unlikely that he'd worked alone; everyone had a brother, a son, a cousin to help them. If the family of the *mosarfar-e-waqt* could trace such a misfortune to Ali, the dead man's threat against his uncle would be carried through.

Ali said, 'I was under a blanket, I didn't see anything.'

'You were under a blanket? For how many days?'

'Three.'

'Three days. What about eating, drinking, going to the toilet?'

'He blindfolded me,' Ali lied.

'Really? You never mentioned that before.' Fernandez shuffled through his papers. 'It's not in your statement.'

'I didn't think it was important, sir.' Ali's stomach tightened. What was happening? He was sure he'd won this man's trust. And he'd earned it: he'd told him the truth about everything, until now. What difference did it make to his problem with the Scholars, which mountains and streams he'd glimpsed on the way to the bridge? He had sworn to tell the truth, but he knew it would be a far greater sin to risk his uncle's life.

Fernandez had still more questions, about life in the village. Some were easy, but some were strange, and he kept asking for numbers, numbers, numbers: how much did it weigh, how much did it cost, how long did it take? What time did the bazaar open? Ali had no idea, he'd been busy with farm work in the mornings, he'd never gone there so early that it might have been closed. How many people came to Friday prayers in the Shi'a mosque? None, since the Scholars had arrived. Before that? Ali couldn't remember. More than a hundred? Ali hesitated. 'I think so.' He'd never counted them, why would he have?

When the interview finished, Ali's mind was still three questions behind, worrying that his answers might not have been clear enough. Fernandez was rewinding the tapes, shaking his hand formally, leaving the room.

Mr Cole said, 'I think that went well. Do you have any questions you want to ask me?'

Ali said, 'No, sir.' Parviz had already departed.

'All right. Good luck.' The speakerphone clicked off. Ali sat at the table, waiting for the guard to come and take him back to the compound.

3

Entering Stage Two, Ali felt as if he had walked into the heart of a bustling town. Everything was noise, shouting, music. He'd sometimes heard snatches of this cacophony wafting across the fenced-off 'sterile area' that separated the parts of the camp, but now he was in the thick of it. The rows of huts, and the crowds moving between them, seemed to stretch on for ever. There must have been a thousand people here, all of them unwilling travellers fleeing the cruelties of their own histories.

He'd moved his small bag of belongings into the hut allocated to him, but none of his new roommates were there to greet him. He wandered through the compound, dizzy from the onslaught of new sights and sounds. He felt as if he'd just had a heavy cloth unwound from around his head and his unveiled senses were still struggling to adjust. If he was reeling from this, how would he feel when he stepped onto the streets of a real city, in freedom?

The evening meal was over, the sun had set, and the heat outside had become tolerable. Almost everyone seemed to be out walking, or congregating around the entrances of their friends' huts, taped music blaring through the open doorways. At the end of one row of huts, Ali came to a larger building, where thirty or forty people were seated. He entered the room and saw a small box with a window on it, through which he could see an oddly coloured, distorted, constantly changing view. A woman was dancing and singing in Hindi.

'TV,' Ali marvelled. This was what Shahin had spoken about; now the whole world was open to his gaze.

An African man beside him shook his head. 'It's a video. The TV's on in the other common room.'

Ali lingered, watching the mesmerising images. The woman was very beautiful, and though she was immodestly dressed by the standards of his village, she seemed dignified and entirely at ease. The Scholars would probably have stoned her to death, but Ali would have been happy to be a beggar in Mumbai if the streets there were filled with sights like this.

As he left the room, the sky was already darkening. The camp's floodlights had come on, destroying any hope of a glimpse of the stars. He asked someone, 'Where is the TV, please?' and followed their directions.

As he walked into the second room, he noticed something different in the mood at once; the people here were tense, straining with attention. When Ali turned to the TV, it showed an eerily familiar sight: an expanse of desert, not unlike that outside the camp. Helicopters, four or five, flew over the landscape. In the distance, a tight funnel of swirling dust, dancing across the ground.

Ali stood riveted. The landscape on the screen was brightly lit, which meant that what he was watching had already happened: earlier in the day, someone had located the mouth of the bridge. He peered at the small images of the helicopters. He'd only ever seen a broken one on the ground, the toy of one warlord brought down by a rival, but he recognised the guns protruding from the sides. Whoever had found the bridge, it was now in the hands of soldiers.

As he watched, a Land Cruiser came charging out of the storm. Then another, and another. This was not like his own arrival; the convoy was caked with dust, but more or less intact. Then the helicopters descended, guns chattering. For a few long seconds Ali thought he was about to witness a slaughter, but the soldiers were firing consistently a metre or so ahead of the Land Cruisers. They were trying to corral the vehicles back into the bridge.

The convoy broke up, the individual drivers trying to steer their way past the blockade. Curtains of bullets descended around them, driving them back towards the meandering storm. Ali couldn't see the people inside, but he could imagine their terror and confusion. This was the future? This was their sanctuary? Whatever tyranny they were fleeing, to have braved the labyrinth of the *pol-e-waqt* only to be greeted with a barrage of gunfire was a fate so cruel that they must have doubted their senses, their sanity, their God.

The helicopters wheeled around the mouth of the bridge like hunting dogs, indefatigable, relentless in their purpose. Ali found the grim dance unbearable, but he couldn't turn away. One of the Land Cruisers came to a halt; it wasn't safely clear of the storm, but this must have seemed wiser than dodging bullets. Doors opened and people tumbled out. Weirdly, the picture went awry at exactly that moment, clumps of flickering colour replacing the travellers' faces.

Soldiers approached, guns at the ready, gesturing and threatening, forcing the people back into the car. A truck appeared, painted in dappled green and brown. A chain was tied between the vehicles. Someone emerged from the Land Cruiser; the face was obscured again, but Ali could see it was a woman. Her words could not be heard, but Ali could see her speaking with her hands, begging, chastising, pleading for mercy. The soldiers forced her back inside.

The truck started its engines. Sand sprayed from its wheels. Two soldiers climbed into the back, their weapons trained on the Land Cruiser. Then they towed their cargo back into the storm.

Ali watched numbly as the other two Land Cruisers were rounded up. The second stalled, and the soldiers descended on it. The driver of the third gave up, and steered his own course into the mouth of the bridge.

The soldiers' truck emerged from the storm, alone. The helicopters spiralled away, circling the funnel at a more prudent distance. Ali looked at the faces of the other people in the room; everyone was pale, some were weeping.

The picture changed. Two men were standing, indoors somewhere. One was old, white-haired, wizened. In front of him a younger man was talking, replying to unseen questioners. Both were smiling proudly.

Ali could only make sense of a few of their words, but gradually he pieced some things together. These men were from the government, and they were explaining the events of the day. They had sent the soldiers to 'protect' the bridge, to ensure that no more criminals and barbarians emerged to threaten the peaceful life of the nation. They had been patient with these intruders for far too long. From this day on, nobody would pass.

Behind the men there was a huge banner. It bore a picture of the face of the younger man, and the words KEEPING THE PAST IN THE PAST.

'What about the law?' someone was asking. An agreement had been signed: any traveller who reached this country and asked for protection had a right to a fair hearing.

'A bill has been drafted, and will be introduced in the House tomorrow. Once passed, it will take force from nine o'clock this morning. The land within twenty kilometres of the bridge will, for the purposes of the Act, no longer be part of this nation. People entering the exclusion zone will have no basis in law to claim our protection.'

Confused, Ali muttered, 'Chi goft?' A young man sitting nearby turned to face him. 'Salaam, chetori? Fahim hastam.'

Fahim's accent was unmistakably Khurosani. Ali smiled. 'Ali hastam. Shoma chetori?'

Fahim explained what the man on the TV had said. Anyone emerging from the mouth of the bridge, now, might as well be on the other side of the world. The government here would accept no obligation to assist them. 'If it's not their land any more,' he mused, 'maybe they'll give it to us. We can found a country of our own, a tribe of nomads in a caravan following the bridge across the desert.'

Ali said nervously, 'My interview was today. They said something about nine o'clock—'

Fahim shook his head dismissively. 'You made your claim months ago, right? So you're still covered by the old law.'

Ali tried to believe him. 'You're still waiting for your decision?'

'Hardly. I got refused three years ago.'

'Three years? They didn't send you back?'

'I'm fighting it in the courts. I can't go back, I'd be dead in a week.' There were dark circles under Fahim's eyes. If he'd been refused three years before, he'd probably spent close to four years in this prison.

Fahim, it turned out, was one of Ali's roommates. He took him to meet the other twelve Khurosanis in Stage Two, and the whole group sat together in one of the huts, talking until dawn. Ali was overjoyed to be among people who knew his language, his time, his customs. It didn't matter that most were from provinces far from his own, that a year ago he would have thought of them as exotic strangers.

When he examined their faces too closely, though, it was hard to remain joyful. They had all fled the Scholars, like him. They were all in fear for their lives. And they had all been locked up for a very long time: two years, three years, four years, five.

In the weeks that followed, Ali gave himself no time to brood on his fate. Stage Two had English classes, and though Fahim and the others had long outgrown them, Ali joined in. He finally learnt the names for the European letters and numbers that he'd seen on weapons and machinery all his life, and the teacher encouraged him to give up translating individual words from Persian and reshape whole sentences, whole thoughts, into the alien tongue.

Every evening, Ali joined Fahim in the common room to watch the news on TV. There was no doubt that the place they had come to was peaceful and prosperous; when war was mentioned, it was always in some distant land. The rulers here did not govern by force, they were chosen by the people, and even now this competition was in progress. The men who had sent the soldiers to block the bridge were asking the people to choose them again.

When the guard woke Ali at eight in the morning, he didn't complain, though he'd had only three hours' sleep. He showered quickly, then went to the compound's south gate. It no longer seemed strange to him to move from place to place this way: to wait for guards to come and unlock a succession of doors and escort him through the fenced-off maze that separated the compound from the government offices.

James and Reza were waiting in the office. Ali greeted them, his mouth dry. James said, 'Reza will read the decision for you. It's about ten pages, so be patient. Then if you have any questions, let me know.'

Reza read from the papers without meeting Ali's eyes. Fernandez, the man who'd interviewed Ali, had written that there were discrepancies between things Ali had said at different times, and gaps in his knowledge of the place and time he claimed to have come from. What's more, an expert in the era of the Scholars had listened to the tape of Ali talking, and declared that his speech was not of that time. 'Perhaps this man's great-grandfather fled Khurosan in the time of the Scholars, and some sketchy information has been passed down the generations. The applicant himself, however, employs a number of words that were not in use until decades later.'

Ali waited for the litany of condemnation to come to an end, but it seemed to go on for ever. 'I have tried to give the applicant the benefit of the doubt,' Fernandez had written, 'but the overwhelming weight of evidence supports the conclusion that he has lied about his origins, his background, and all of his claims.'

Ali sat with his head in his hands.

James said, 'Do you understand what this means? You have seven days to lodge an appeal. If you don't lodge an appeal, you will have to return to your country.'

Reza added, 'You should call your lawyer. Have you got money for a phone card?'

Ali nodded. He'd taken a job cleaning the mess, he had thirty points in his account already.

Every time Ali called, his lawyer was busy. Fahim helped Ali fill out the appeal form, and they handed it to James two hours before the deadline. 'Lucky Colonel Kurtz is gone,' Fahim told Ali. 'Or that form would have sat in the fax tray for at least a week.'

Wild rumours swept the camp: the government was about to change, and everyone would be set free. Ali had seen the government's rivals giving their blessing to the use of soldiers to block the bridge; he doubted that they'd show the prisoners in the desert much mercy if they won.

When the day of the election came, the government was returned, more powerful than ever.

That night, as they were preparing to sleep, Fahim saw Ali staring at the long white scars that criss-crossed his upper arms and chest. 'I use a razor blade,' Fahim admitted. 'It makes me feel better. The one power I've got left: to choose my own pain.'

'I'll never do that,' Ali swore.

Fahim gave a hollow laugh. 'It's cheaper than cigarettes.'

Ali closed his eyes and tried to picture freedom, but all he saw was blackness. The past was gone, the future was gone, and the world had shrunk to this prison.

4

'Ali, wake up, come see!'

Daniel was shaking him. Ali swatted his hands away angrily. The African was one of his closest friends, and there'd been a time when he could still drag Ali along to English classes or the gym, but since the appeal tribunal had rejected him, Ali had no taste for anything. 'Let me sleep.'

'There are people. Outside the fence.'

'Escaped?'

'No, no. From the city!'

Ali clambered off the bunk. He splashed water on his face, then followed his friend.

Dozens of prisoners had gathered at the south-west corner of the fence, blocking the view, but Ali could hear people on the outside, shouting and banging drums. Daniel tried to clear a path, but it was impossible. 'Get on my shoulders.' He ducked down and motioned to Ali.

Ali laughed. 'It's not that important.'

Daniel raised a hand angrily, as if to slap him. 'Get up, you have to see.' He was serious. Ali obeyed.

From his vantage, he could see that the mass of prisoners pressed against the inner fence was mirrored by another crowd struggling to reach the outer one. Police, some on horses, were trying to stop them. Ali peered into the scrum, amazed. Dozens of young people, men and women, were pushing against the cordon of policemen, and every now and then someone was slipping through and running forward. Some distance away across the desert stood a brightly coloured bus. The word 'freedom' was painted across it, in English, Persian, Arabic, and probably ten or twelve languages that Ali couldn't read. The people were chanting, 'Set them free! Set them free!' One young woman reached the fence and clung to it, shouting defiantly. Four policemen descended on her and tore her away.

A cloud of dust was moving along the desert road. More police cars were coming, reinforcements. A knife twisted in Ali's heart. This gesture of friendship astonished him, but it would lead nowhere. In five or ten minutes, the protesters would all be rounded up and carried away.

A young man outside the fence met Ali's gaze. 'Hey! My name's Ben.'

'I'm Ali.'

Ben looked around frantically. 'What's your number?'

'What?'

'We'll write to you. Give us your number. They have to deliver the letters if we include the ID number.'

'Behind you!' Ali shouted, but the warning was too late. One policeman had him in a headlock, and another was helping wrestle him to the ground.

Ali felt Daniel stagger. The crowd on his own side was trying to fend off a wave of guards with batons and shields.

Ali dropped to his feet. 'They want our ID numbers,' he told Daniel. Daniel looked around at the mêlée. 'Got anything to write on?'

Ali checked his back pocket. The small notebook and pen it was his habit to carry were still there. He rested the notebook on Daniel's back, and wrote 'Ali 3739 Daniel 5420.' Who else? He quickly added Fahim and a few others.

He scrabbled on the ground for a stone, then wrapped the paper around it. Daniel lofted him up again.

The police were battling with the protesters, grabbing them by the hair, dragging them across the dirt. Ali couldn't see anyone who didn't have more pressing things to worry about than receiving his message. He lowered his arm, despondent.

Then he spotted someone standing by the bus. He couldn't tell if it was a man or a woman. He, or she, raised a hand in greeting. Ali waved back, then let the stone fly. It fell short, but the distant figure ran forward and retrieved it from the sand.

Daniel collapsed beneath him and the guards moved in with batons and tear gas. Ali covered his eyes with his forearm, weeping, alive again with hope.

DARK INTEGERS

'Good morning, Bruno. How is the weather there in Sparseland?'

The screen icon for my interlocutor was a three-holed torus tiled with triangles, endlessly turning itself inside out. The polished tones of the male synthetic voice I heard conveyed no specific origin, but gave a sense nonetheless that the speaker's first language was something other than English.

I glanced out the window of my home office, taking in a patch of blue sky and the verdant gardens of a shady West Ryde cul-de-sac. Sam used 'good morning' regardless of the hour, but it really was just after ten a.m., and the tranquil Sydney suburb was awash with sunshine and birdsong.

'Perfect,' I replied. 'I wish I wasn't chained to this desk.'

There was a long pause, and I wondered if the translator had mangled the idiom, creating the impression that I had been shackled by ruthless assailants, who had nonetheless left me with easy access to my instant messaging program. Then Sam said, 'I'm glad you didn't go for a run today. I've already tried Alison and Yuen, and they were both unavailable. If I hadn't been able to get through to you, it might have been difficult to keep some of my colleagues in check.'

I felt a surge of anxiety, mixed with resentment. I refused to wear an iWatch, to make myself reachable twenty-four hours a day. I was a mathematician, not an obstetrician. Perhaps I was an amateur diplomat as well, but even if Alison, Yuen and I didn't quite cover the time zones, it would never be more than a few hours before Sam could get hold of at least one of us.

'I didn't realise you were surrounded by hot-heads,' I replied. 'What's the great emergency?' I hoped the translator would do justice to the sharpness in my voice. Sam's colleagues were the ones with all the firepower, all the resources; they should not have been jumping at shadows. True, we had once tried to wipe them out, but that had been a perfectly innocent mistake, more than ten years before.

Sam said, 'Someone from your side seems to have jumped the border.'

'*Jumped* it?'

'As far as we can see, there's no trench cutting through it. But a few hours ago, a cluster of propositions on our side started obeying your axioms.'

I was stunned. 'An isolated cluster? With no derivation leading back to us?'

'None that we could find.'

I thought for a while. 'Maybe it was a natural event. A brief surge across the border from the background noise that left a kind of tidal pool behind.'

Sam was dismissive. 'The cluster was too big for that. The probability would be vanishingly small.' Numbers came through on the data channel; he was right.

I rubbed my eyelids with my fingertips; I suddenly felt very tired. I'd thought our old nemesis, Industrial Algebra, had given up the chase long ago. They had stopped offering bribes and sending mercenaries to harass me, so I'd assumed they'd finally written off the defect as a hoax or a mirage, and gone back to their core business of helping the world's military kill and maim people in ever more technologically sophisticated ways.

Maybe this wasn't IA. Alison and I had first located the defect – a set of contradictory results in arithmetic that marked the border between our mathematics and the version underlying Sam's world – by means of a vast set of calculations farmed out over the internet, with thousands of volunteers donating their computers' processing power when the machines would otherwise have been idle. When we'd pulled the plug on that project – keeping our discovery secret, lest IA find a way to weaponise it – a few participants had been resentful, and had talked about continuing the search. It would have been easy enough for them to write their own software, adapting the same open source framework that Alison and I had used, but it was difficult to see how they could have gathered enough supporters without launching some kind of public appeal.

I said, 'I can't offer you an immediate explanation for this. All I can do is promise to investigate.'

'I understand,' Sam replied.

'You have no clues yourself?' A decade before, in Shanghai, when Alison, Yuen and I had used the supercomputer called Luminous to mount a sustained attack on the defect, the mathematicians of the far side had grasped the details of our unwitting assault clearly enough to send a plume of alternative mathematics back across the border with pinpoint precision, striking at just the three of us.

Sam said, 'If the cluster had been connected to something, we could have followed the trail. But in isolation it tells us nothing. That's why my colleagues are so anxious.'

'Yeah.' I was still hoping that the whole thing might turn out to be a glitch – the mathematical equivalent of a flock of birds with a radar echo that just happened to look like something more sinister – but the full gravity of the situation was finally dawning on me.

The inhabitants of the far side were as peaceable as anyone might reasonably wish their neighbours to be, but if their mathematical infrastructure came under threat they faced the real prospect of annihilation. They had defended themselves from such a threat once before, but because they had been able to trace it to its source and understand its nature, they had shown great forbearance. They had not struck their assailants dead, or wiped out Shanghai, or pulled the ground out from under our universe.

This new assault had not been sustained, but nobody knew its origins, or what it might portend. I believed that our neighbours would do no more than they had to in order to ensure their survival, but if they were forced to strike back blindly, they might find themselves with no path to safety short of turning our world to dust.

Shanghai time was only two hours behind Sydney, but Yuen's IM status was still 'unavailable'. I emailed him, along with Alison, though it was the middle of the night in Zürich and she was unlikely to be awake for another four or five hours. All of us had programs that connected us to Sam by monitoring, and modifying, small portions of the defect: altering a handful of precariously balanced truths of arithmetic, wiggling the border between the two systems back and forth to encode each transmitted bit. The three of us on the near side might have communicated with each other in the same way, but on consideration we'd decided that conventional cryptography was a safer way to conceal our secret. The mere fact that communications data seemed to come from nowhere had the potential to attract suspicion, so we'd gone as far as to write software to send fake packets across the net to cover for our otherwise inexplicable conversations with Sam; anyone but the most diligent and resourceful of eavesdroppers would conclude that he was addressing us from an internet café in Lithuania.

While I was waiting for Yuen to reply, I scoured the logs where my knowledge miner deposited results of marginal relevance, wondering if some flaw in the criteria I'd given it might have left me with a blind spot. If anyone, anywhere had announced their intention to carry out some kind of calculation that might have led them to the defect, the news should have been plastered across my desktop in flashing red letters within seconds. Granted, most organisations with the necessary computing resources were secretive by nature, but they were also unlikely to be motivated to indulge in such a crazy stunt. Luminous itself had been decommissioned in 2012; in principle, various national security agencies, and even a few IT-centric businesses, now had enough silicon to hunt down the defect if they'd really set their sights on it, but as far as I knew Yuen, Alison and I were still the only three people in the world who were certain of its existence. The black budgets of even the most profligate governments, the deep pockets of even the richest tycoons, would not stretch far enough to take on the search as a long shot, or an act of whimsy.

An IM window popped up with Alison's face. She looked ragged. 'What time is it there?' I asked.

'Early. Laura's got colic.'

'Ah. Are you okay to talk?'

'Yeah, she's asleep now.'

My email had been brief, so I filled her in on the details. She pondered the matter in silence for a while, yawning unashamedly.

'The only thing I can think of is some gossip I heard at a conference in Rome a couple of months ago. It was a fourth-hand story about some guy in New Zealand who thinks he's found a way to test fundamental laws of physics by doing computations in number theory.'

'Just random crackpot stuff, or . . . what?'

Alison massaged her temples, as if trying to get more blood flowing to her brain. 'I don't know, what I heard was too vague to make a judgement. I gather he hasn't tried to publish this anywhere, or even mentioned it in blogs. I guess he just confided in a few people directly, one of whom must have found it too amusing for them to keep their mouth shut.'

'Have you got a name?'

She went off camera and rummaged for a while. 'Tim Campbell,' she announced. Her notes came through on the data channel. 'He's done respectable work in combinatorics, algorithmic complexity, optimisation. I scoured the net, and there was no mention of this weird stuff. I was meaning to email him, but I never got around to it.'

I could understand why; that would have been about the time

Laura was born. I said, 'I'm glad you still go to so many conferences in the flesh. It's easier in Europe, everything's so close.'

'Ha! Don't count on it continuing, Bruno. You might have to put your fat arse on a plane sometime yourself.'

'What about Yuen?'

Alison frowned. 'Didn't I tell you? He's been in hospital for a couple of days. Pneumonia. I spoke to his daughter, he's not in great shape.'

'I'm sorry.' Alison was much closer to him than I was; he'd been her doctoral supervisor, so she'd known him long before the events that had bound the three of us together.

Yuen was almost eighty. That wasn't yet ancient for a middle-class Chinese man who could afford good medical care, but he would not be around for ever.

I said, 'Are we crazy, trying to do this ourselves?' She knew what I meant: liaising with Sam, managing the border, trying to keep the two worlds talking but the two sides separate, safe and intact.

Alison replied, 'Which government would you trust not to screw this up? Not to try to exploit it?'

'None. But what's the alternative? You pass the job on to Laura? Kate's not interested in having kids. So do I pick some young mathematician at random to anoint as my successor?'

'Not at random, I'd hope.'

'You want me to advertise? "Must be proficient in number theory, familiar with Machiavelli, and own the complete boxed set of *The West Wing*?"'

She shrugged. 'When the time comes, find someone competent you can trust. It's a balance: the fewer people who know, the better, so long as there are always enough of us that the knowledge doesn't risk getting lost completely.'

'And this goes on generation after generation? Like some secret society? The Knights of the Arithmetic Inconsistency?'

'I'll work on the crest.'

We needed a better plan, but this wasn't the time to argue about it. I said, 'I'll contact this guy Campbell and let you know how it goes.'

'Okay. Good luck.' Her eyelids were starting to droop.

'Take care of yourself.'

Alison managed an exhausted smile. 'Are you saying that because you give a damn, or because you don't want to end up guarding the Grail all by yourself?'

'Both, of course.'

'I have to fly to Wellington tomorrow.'

Kate put down the pasta-laden fork she'd raised halfway to her lips and gave me a puzzled frown. 'That's short notice.'

'Yeah, it's a pain. It's for the Bank of New Zealand. I have to do something on-site with a secure machine, one they won't let anyone access over the net.'

Her frown deepened. 'When will you be back?'

'I'm not sure. It might not be until Monday. I can probably do most of the work tomorrow, but there are certain things they restrict to the weekends, when the branches are off-line. I don't know if it will come to that.'

I hated lying to her, but I'd grown accustomed to it. When we'd met, just a year after Shanghai, I could still feel the scar on my arm where one of Industrial Algebra's hired thugs had tried to carve a data cache out of my body. At some point, as our relationship deepened, I'd made up my mind that however close we became, however much I trusted her, it would be safer for Kate if she never knew anything about the defect.

'They can't hire someone local?' she suggested. I didn't think she was suspicious, but she was definitely annoyed. She worked long hours at the hospital, and she only had every second weekend off; this would be one of them. We'd made no specific plans, but it was part of our routine to spend this time together.

I said, 'I'm sure they could, but it'd be hard to find someone at short notice. And I can't tell them to shove it, or I'll lose the whole contract. It's one weekend, it's not the end of the world.'

'No, it's not the end of the world.' She finally lifted her fork again.

'Is the sauce okay?'

'It's delicious, Bruno.' Her tone made it clear that no amount of culinary effort would have been enough to compensate, so I might as well not have bothered.

I watched her eat with a strange knot growing in my stomach. Was this how spies felt, when they lied to their families about their work? But my own secret sounded more like something from a psychiatric ward. I was entrusted with the smooth operation of a treaty that I, and two friends, had struck with an invisible ghost world that coexisted with our own. The ghost world was far from hostile, but the treaty was the most important in human history, because either side had the power to annihilate the other so thoroughly that it would make a nuclear holocaust seem like a pin-prick.

Victoria University was in a hilltop suburb overlooking Wellington. I caught a cable-car, and arrived just in time for the Friday afternoon seminar. Contriving an invitation to deliver a paper here myself would have been difficult, but wangling permission to sit in as part of the audience was easy; although I hadn't been an academic for almost twenty years, my ancient PhD and a trickle of publications, however tenuously related to the topic of the seminar, were still enough to make me welcome.

I'd taken a gamble that Campbell would attend – the topic was peripheral to his own research, official or otherwise – so I was relieved to spot him in the audience, recognising him from a photo on the faculty website. I'd emailed him straight after I'd spoken to Alison, but his reply had been a polite brush-off: he acknowledged that the work I'd heard about on the grapevine owed something to the infamous search that Alison and I had launched, but he wasn't ready to make his own approach public.

I sat through an hour on 'Monoids and Control Theory', trying to pay enough attention that I wouldn't make a fool of myself if the seminar organiser quizzed me later on why I'd been sufficiently attracted to the topic to interrupt my 'sightseeing holiday' in order to attend. When the seminar ended, the audience split into two streams: one heading out of the building, the other moving into an adjoining room where refreshments were on offer. I saw Campbell making for the open air, and it was all I could do to contrive to get close enough to call out to him without making a spectacle.

'Dr Campbell?'

He turned and scanned the room, probably expecting to see one of his students wanting to beg for an extension on an assignment. I raised a hand and approached him.

'Bruno Costanzo. I emailed you yesterday.'

'Of course.' Campbell was a thin, pale man in his early thirties. He shook my hand, but he was obviously taken aback. 'You didn't mention that you were in Wellington.'

I made a dismissive gesture. 'I was going to, but then it seemed a bit presumptuous.' I didn't spell it out, I just left him to conclude that I was as ambivalent about this whole inconsistency nonsense as he was.

If fate had brought us together, though, wouldn't it be absurd not to make the most of it?

'I was going to grab some of those famous scones,' I said; the seminar announcement on the web had made big promises for them. 'Are you busy?'

'Umm. Just paperwork. I suppose I can put it off.'

As we made our way into the tea room, I waffled on airily about my holiday plans. I'd never actually been to New Zealand before, so I made it clear that most of my itinerary still lay in the future. Campbell was no more interested in the local geography and wildlife than I was; the more I enthused, the more distant his gaze became. Once it was apparent that he wasn't going to cross-examine me on the finer points of various hiking trails, I grabbed a buttered scone and switched subject abruptly.

'The thing is, I heard you'd devised a more efficient strategy for searching for a defect.' I only just managed to stop myself from using the definite article; it was a while since I'd spoken about it as if it were still hypothetical. 'You know the kind of computing power that Dr Tierney and I had to scrounge up?'

'Of course. I was just an undergraduate, but I heard about the search.'

'Were you one of our volunteers?' I'd checked the records, and he wasn't listed, but people had had the option of registering anonymously.

'No. The idea didn't really grab me, at the time.' As he spoke, he seemed more discomfited than the failure to donate his own resources twelve years ago really warranted. I was beginning to suspect that he'd actually been one of the people who'd found the whole tongue-in-cheek conjecture that Alison and I had put forward to be unforgivably foolish. We had never asked to be taken seriously – and we had even put prominent links to all the worthy biomedical computing projects on our web page, so that people knew there were far better ways to spend their spare megaflops – but nonetheless, some mathematical/philosophical stuffed shirts had spluttered with rage at the sheer impertinence and naïveté of our hypothesis. Before things turned serious, it was the entertainment value of that backlash that had made our efforts worthwhile.

'But now you've refined it somehow?' I prompted him, doing my best to let him see that I felt no resentment at the prospect of being outdone. In fact, the hypothesis itself had been Alison's, so even if there hadn't been more important things than my ego at stake, that really wasn't a factor. As for the search algorithm, I'd cobbled it together on a Sunday afternoon, as a joke, to call Alison's bluff. Instead, she'd called mine, and insisted that we release it to the world.

Campbell glanced around to see who was in earshot, but then perhaps it dawned on him that if the news of his ideas had already reached Sydney via Rome and Zürich, the battle to keep his reputation pristine in Wellington was probably lost.

He said, 'What you and Dr Tierney suggested was that random processes in the early universe might have included proofs of mutually contradictory theorems about the integers, the idea being that no computation to expose the inconsistency had yet had time to occur. Is that a fair summary?'

'Sure.'

'One problem I have with that is, I don't see how it could lead to an inconsistency that could be detected here and now. If the physical system A proved theorem A, and the physical system B proved theorem B, then you might have different regions of the universe obeying different axioms, but it's not as if there's some universal mathematics textbook hovering around outside space-time, listing every theorem that's ever been proved, which our computers then consult in order to decide how to behave. The behaviour of a classical system is determined by its own particular causal past. If we're the descendants of a patch of the universe that proved theorem A, our computers should be perfectly capable of *disproving* theorem B, whatever happened somewhere else 14 billion years ago.'

I nodded thoughtfully. 'I can see what you're getting at.' If you weren't going to accept full-blooded Platonism, in which there *was* a kind of ghostly textbook listing the eternal truths of mathematics, then a half-baked version where the book started out empty and was only filled in line by line as various theorems were tested seemed like the worst kind of compromise. In fact, when the far side had granted Yuen, Alison and I insight into their mathematics for a few minutes in Shanghai, Yuen had proclaimed that the flow of mathematical information *did* obey Einstein locality; there was no universal book of truths, just records of the past sloshing around at light-speed or less, inter-mingling and competing.

I could hardly tell Campbell, though, that not only did I know for a fact that a single computer could prove both a theorem and its negation, but depending on the order in which it attacked the calculations it could sometimes even shift the boundary where one set of axioms failed and the other took over.

I said, 'And yet you still believe it's worth searching for an inconsistency?'

'I do,' he conceded. 'Though I came to the idea from a very different approach.' He hesitated, then picked up a scone from the table beside us.

'One rock, one apple, one scone. We have a clear idea of what we mean by those phrases, though each one might encompass ten-to-the-ten-to-the-thirty-something slightly different configurations of matter. My "one scone" is not the same as your "one scone".'

'Right.'

'You know how banks count large quantities of cash?'

'By weighing them?' In fact there were several other cross-checks as well, but I could see where he was heading and I didn't want to distract him with nit-picking.

'Exactly. Suppose we tried to count scones the same way: weigh the batch, divide by some nominal value, then round to the nearest integer. The weight of any individual scone varies so much that you could easily end up with a version of arithmetic different from our own. If you "counted" two separate batches, then merged them and "counted" them together, there's no guarantee that the result would agree with the ordinary process of integer addition.'

I said, 'Clearly not. But digital computers don't run on scones, and they don't count bits by weighing them.'

'Bear with me,' Campbell replied. 'It isn't a perfect analogy, but I'm not as crazy as I sound. Suppose, now, that *everything* we talk about as "one thing" has a vast number of possible configurations that we're either ignoring deliberately, or are literally incapable of distinguishing. Even something as simple as an electron prepared in a certain quantum state.'

I said, 'You're talking about hidden variables now?'

'Of a kind, yes. Do you know about Gerard 't Hooft's models for deterministic quantum mechanics?'

'Only vaguely,' I admitted.

'He postulated fully deterministic degrees of freedom at the Planck scale, with quantum states corresponding to equivalence classes containing many different possible configurations. What's more, all the ordinary quantum states we prepare at an atomic level would be complex superpositions of those primordial states, which allows him to get around the Bell inequalities.' I frowned slightly; I more or less got the picture, but I'd need to go away and read 't Hooft's papers.

Campbell said, 'In a sense, the detailed physics isn't all that important, so long as you accept that "one thing" might not *ever* be exactly the same as another "one thing", regardless of the kind of objects we're talking about. Given that supposition, physical processes that *seem* to be rigorously equivalent to various arithmetic operations can turn out not to be as reliable as you'd think. With scone-weighing, the flaws are obvious, but I'm talking about the potentially subtler results of misunderstanding the fundamental nature of matter.'

'Hmm.' Though it was unlikely that anyone else Campbell had confided in had taken these speculations as seriously as I did, not only did I not want to seem a pushover, I honestly had no idea whether anything he was saying bore the slightest connection to reality.

I said, 'It's an interesting idea, but I still don't see how it could speed up the hunt for inconsistencies.'

'I have a set of models,' he said, 'which are constrained by the need to agree with some of 't Hooft's ideas about the physics, and also by the need to make arithmetic *almost* consistent for a very large range of objects. From neutrinos to clusters of galaxies, basic arithmetic involving the kinds of numbers we might encounter in ordinary situations should work out in the usual way.' He laughed. 'I mean, that's the world we're living in, right?'

Some of us. 'Yeah.'

'But the interesting thing is, I can't make the physics work at all if the arithmetic doesn't run askew eventually – if there aren't trans-astronomical numbers where the physical representations no longer capture the arithmetic perfectly. And each of my models lets me predict, more or less, where those effects should begin to show up. By starting with the fundamental physical laws, I can deduce a sequence of calculations with large integers that ought to reveal an inconsistency, when performed with pretty much any computer.'

'Taking you straight to the defect, with no need to search at all.'

I'd let the definite article slip out, but it hardly seemed to matter any more.

'That's the theory.' Campbell actually blushed slightly. 'Well, when you say "no search", what's involved really is a much smaller search. There are still free parameters in my models; there are potentially billions of possibilities to test.'

I grinned broadly, wondering if my expression looked as fake as it felt. 'But no luck yet?'

'No.' He was beginning to become self-conscious again, glancing around to see who might be listening.

Was he lying to me? Keeping his results secret until he could verify them a million more times, and then decide how best to explain them to incredulous colleagues and an uncomprehending world? Or had whatever he'd done that had lobbed a small grenade into Sam's universe somehow registered in Campbell's own computer as arithmetic as usual, betraying no evidence of the boundary he'd crossed? After all, the offending cluster of propositions had obeyed *our* axioms, so perhaps Campbell had managed to force them to do so without ever realising that they hadn't in the past. His ideas were obviously close to the mark – and I could no longer believe this was just a coincidence – but he seemed to have no room in his theory for something that I knew for a fact: arithmetic wasn't merely inconsistent, it was *dynamic*. You could take its contradictions and slide them around like bumps in a carpet.

Campbell said, 'Parts of the process aren't easy to automate; there's some manual work to be done setting up the search for each broad class of models. I've only been doing this in my spare time, so it could be a while before I get around to examining all the possibilities.'

'I see.' If all of his calculations so far had produced just one hit on the far side, it was conceivable that the rest would pass without incident. He would publish a negative result ruling out an obscure class of physical theories, and life would go on as normal on both sides of the inconsistency.

What kind of weapons inspector would I be, though, to put my faith in that rosy supposition?

Campbell was looking fidgety, as if his administrative obligations were beckoning. I said, 'It'd be great to talk about this a bit more while we've got the chance. Are you busy tonight? I'm staying at a backpacker's down in the city, but maybe you could recommend a restaurant around here somewhere?'

He looked dubious for a moment, but then an instinctive sense of hospitality seemed to overcome his reservations. He said, 'Let me check with my wife. We're not really into restaurants, but I was cooking tonight anyway, and you'd be welcome to join us.'

Campbell's house was a fifteen-minute walk from the campus; at my request, we detoured to a liquor store so I could buy a couple of bottles of wine to accompany the meal. As I entered the house, my hand lingered on the doorframe, depositing a small device that would assist me if I needed to make an uninvited entry in the future.

Campbell's wife, Bridget, was an organic chemist, who also taught at Victoria University. The conversation over dinner was all about department heads, budgets and grant applications, and despite having left academia long ago, I had no trouble relating sympathetically to the couple's gripes. My hosts ensured that my wine glass never stayed empty for long.

When we'd finished eating, Bridget excused herself to make a call to her mother, who lived in a small town on the south island. Campbell led me into his study and switched on a laptop with fading keys that must have been twenty years old. Many households had a computer like this: the machine that could no longer run the latest trendy bloatware, but which still worked perfectly with its original OS.

Campbell turned his back to me as he typed his password, and I was careful not to be seen even trying to look. Then he opened some C++ files in an editor, and scrolled over parts of his search algorithm.

I felt giddy, and it wasn't the wine; I'd filled my stomach with an over-the-counter sobriety aid that turned ethanol into glucose and water faster than any human being could imbibe it. I fervently hoped that Industrial Algebra really had given up their pursuit; if I could get this close to Campbell's secrets in half a day, IA could be playing the stockmarket with alternative arithmetic before the month was out, and peddling inconsistency weapons to the Pentagon soon after.

I did not have a photographic memory, and Campbell was just showing me fragments anyway. I didn't think he was deliberately taunting me; he just wanted me to see that he had something concrete, that all his claims about Planck scale physics and directed search strategies had been more than hot air.

I said, 'Wait! What's that?' He stopped hitting the PAGE DOWN key and I pointed at a list of variable declarations in the middle of the screen:

$$\textbf{long int i1, i2, i3;}$$
$$\textbf{dark d1, d2, d3;}$$

A 'long int' was a long integer, a quantity represented by twice as many bits as usual. On this vintage machine, that was likely to be a total of just sixty-four bits. 'What the fuck is a "dark"?' I demanded. It wasn't how I'd normally speak to someone I'd only just met, but then, I wasn't meant to be sober.

Campbell laughed. 'A dark integer. It's a type I defined. It holds four thousand and ninety-six bits.'

'But why the name?'

'Dark matter, dark energy . . . dark integers. They're all around us, but we don't usually see them, because they don't quite play by the rules.'

Hairs rose on the back of my neck. I could not have described the infrastructure of Sam's world more concisely myself.

Campbell shut down the laptop. I'd been looking for an opportunity to handle the machine, however briefly, without arousing his suspicion, but that clearly wasn't going to happen, so as we walked out of the study I went for plan B.

'I'm feeling kind of . . .' I sat down abruptly on the floor of the hallway. After a moment, I fished my phone out of my pocket and held it up to him. 'Would you mind calling me a taxi?'

'Yeah, sure.' He accepted the phone, and I cradled my head in my arms. Before he could dial the number, I started moaning softly. There was a long pause; he was probably weighing up the embarrassment factor of various alternatives.

Finally he said, 'You can sleep here on the couch if you like.' I felt a genuine pang of sympathy for him; if some clown I barely knew had pulled a stunt like this on me, I would at least have made him promise to foot the cleaning bills if he threw up in the middle of the night.

In the middle of the night, I did make a trip to the bathroom, but I kept the sound effects restrained. Halfway through, I walked quietly to the study, crossed the room in the dark, and slapped a thin, transparent patch over the adhesive label that a service company had placed on the outside of the laptop years before. My addition would be invisible to the naked eye, and it would take a scalpel to prise it off. The relay that would communicate with the patch was larger, about the size of a coat button; I stuck it behind a bookshelf. Unless Campbell was planning to paint the room or put in new carpet, it would probably remain undetected for a couple of years, and I'd already prepaid a two-year account with a local wireless internet provider.

I woke not long after dawn, but this un-Bacchanalian early rising was no risk to my cover; Campbell had left the curtains open so the full force of the morning sun struck me in the face, a result that was almost certainly deliberate. I tiptoed around the house for ten minutes or so, not wanting to seem too organised if anyone was listening, then left a scrawled note of thanks and apology on the coffee table by the couch before letting myself out and heading for the cable-car stop.

Down in the city, I sat in a café opposite the backpacker's hostel and connected to the relay, which in turn had established a successful link with the polymer circuitry of the laptop patch. When noon came and went without Campbell logging on, I sent a message to Kate telling her that I was stuck in the bank for at least another day.

I passed the time browsing the newsfeeds and buying over-priced snacks; half of the café's other patrons were doing the same. Finally, just after three o'clock, Campbell started up the laptop.

The patch couldn't read his disk drive, but it could pick up currents flowing to and from the keyboard and the display, allowing it to deduce everything he typed and everything he saw. Capturing his password was easy. Better yet, once he was logged in he set about editing one of his files, extending his search program to a new class of models. As he scrolled back and forth, it wasn't long before the patch's screen shots encompassed the entire contents of the file he was working on.

He laboured for more than two hours, debugging what he'd written, then set the program running. This creaky old twentieth-century machine, which predated the whole internet-wide search for the defect, had already scored one direct hit on the far side; I just hoped this new class of models were all incompatible with the successful ones from a few days before.

Shortly afterwards, the IR sensor in the patch told me that Campbell had left the room. The patch could induce currents in the keyboard connection; I could type into the machine as if I was right there. I started a new process window. The laptop wasn't connected to the internet at all, except through my spyware, but it took me only fifteen minutes to display and record everything there was to see: a few library and header files that the main program depended on, and the data logs listing all of the searches so far. It would not have been hard to hack into the operating system and make provisions to corrupt any future searches, but I decided to wait until I had a better grasp of the whole situation. Even once I was back in Sydney, I'd be able to eavesdrop whenever the laptop was in use, and intervene whenever it was left unattended. I'd only stayed in Wellington in case there'd been a need to return to Campbell's house in person.

When evening fell and I found myself with nothing urgent left to do, I didn't call Kate; it seemed wiser to let her assume that I was slaving away in a windowless computer room. I left the café and lay on my bed in the hostel. The dormitory was deserted; everyone else was out on the town.

I called Alison in Zürich and brought her up to date. In the background, I could hear her husband, Philippe, trying to comfort Laura in another room, calmly talking baby talk in French while his daughter wailed her head off.

Alison was intrigued. 'Campbell's theory can't be perfect, but it must be close. Maybe we'll be able to find a way to make it fit in with the dynamics we've seen.' In the ten years since we'd stumbled on the defect all our work on it had remained frustratingly empirical: running calculations, and observing their effects. We'd never come close to finding any deep underlying principles.

'Do you think Sam knows all this?' she asked.

'I have no idea. If he did, I doubt he'd admit it.' Though it was Sam who had given us a taste of far-side mathematics in Shanghai, that had really just been a clip over the ear to let us know that what we were trying to wipe out with Luminous was a civilisation, not a wasteland. After that near-disastrous first encounter, he had worked to establish communications with us, learning our languages and happily listening to the accounts we'd volunteered of our world, but he had not been equally forthcoming in return. We knew next to nothing about far-side physics, astronomy, biology, history or culture. That there were living beings occupying the same space as the Earth suggested that the two universes were intimately coupled somehow, in spite of their mutual invisibility. But Sam had hinted that life was much more common on his side of the border than ours; when I'd told him that we seemed to be alone, at least in the solar system, and were surrounded by light-years of sterile vacuum, he'd taken to referring to our side as 'Sparseland'.

Alison said, 'Either way, I think we should keep it to ourselves. The treaty says we should do everything in our power to deal with any breach of territory of which the other side informs us. We're doing that. But we're not obliged to disclose the details of Campbell's activities.'

'That's true.' I wasn't entirely happy with her suggestion, though. In spite of the attitude Sam and his colleagues had taken – in which they assumed that anything they told us might be exploited, might make them more vulnerable – a part of me had always wondered if there was some gesture of good faith we could make, some way to build trust. Since talking to Campbell, in the back of my mind I'd been building up a faint hope that his discovery might lead to an opportunity to prove, once and for all, that our intentions were honourable.

Alison read my mood. She said, 'Bruno, they've given us *nothing*. Shanghai excuses a certain amount of caution, but we also know from Shanghai that they could brush Luminous aside like a gnat. They have enough computing power to crush us in an instant, and they still cling to every strategic advantage they can get. Not to do the same ourselves would just be stupid and irresponsible.'

'So you want us to hold on to this secret weapon?' I was beginning to develop a piercing headache. My usual way of dealing with the surreal responsibility that had fallen on the three of us was to pretend that it didn't exist; having to think about it constantly for three days straight meant more tension than I'd faced for a decade. 'Is that what it's come down to? Our own version of the Cold War? Why don't you just march into NATO headquarters on Monday and hand over everything we know?'

Alison said dryly, 'Switzerland isn't a member of NATO. The government here would probably charge me with treason.'

I didn't want to fight with her. 'We should talk about this later. We don't even know exactly what we've got. I need to go through Campbell's files and confirm whether he really did what we think he did.'

'Okay.'

'I'll call you from Sydney.'

It took me a while to make sense of everything I'd stolen from Campbell, but eventually I was able to determine which calculations he'd performed on each occasion recorded in his log files. Then I compared the propositions that he'd tested with a rough, static map of the defect; since the event Sam had reported had been deep within the far side, there was no need to take account of the small fluctuations that the border underwent over time.

If my analysis was correct, late on Wednesday night Campbell's calculations had landed in the middle of far-side mathematics. He'd been telling me the truth, though; he'd found nothing out of the ordinary there. Instead, the thing he had been seeking had melted away before his gaze.

In all the calculations Alison and I had done, only at the border had we been able to force propositions to change their allegiance and obey our axioms. It was as if Campbell had dived in from some higher dimension, carrying a hosepipe that sprayed everything with the arithmetic we knew and loved.

For Sam and his colleagues, this was the equivalent of a suitcase nuke appearing out of nowhere, as opposed to the ICBMs they knew how to track and annihilate. Now Alison wanted us to tell them, 'Trust us, we've dealt with it,' without showing them the weapon itself, without letting them see how it worked, without giving them a chance to devise new defences against it.

She wanted us to have something up our sleeves, in case the hawks took over the far side, and decided that Sparseland was a ghost world whose lingering, baleful presence they could do without.

Drunken Saturday-night revellers began returning to the hostel, singing off-key and puking enthusiastically. Maybe this was poetic justice for my own faux-inebriation; if so I was being repaid a thousandfold. I started wishing I'd shelled out for classier accommodation, but since there was no employer picking up my expenses, it was going to be hard enough dealing with my lie to Kate without spending even more on the trip.

Forget the arithmetic of scones; I knew how to make digital currency reproduce like the marching brooms of the sorcerer's apprentice. It might even have been possible to milk the benefits without Sam noticing; I could try to hide my far-sider trading behind the manipulations of the border we used routinely to exchange messages.

I had no idea how to contain the side-effects, though. I had no idea what else such meddling would disrupt, how many people I might kill or maim in the process.

I buried my head beneath the pillows and tried to find a way to get to sleep through the noise. I ended up calculating powers of seven, a trick I hadn't used since childhood. I'd never been a prodigy at mental arithmetic, and the concentration required to push on past the easy cases drained me far faster than any physical labour. *Two hundred and eighty-two million, four hundred and seventy-five thousand, two hundred and forty-nine.* The numbers rose into the stratosphere like bean stalks, until they grew too high and tore themselves apart, leaving behind a cloud of digits drifting through my skull like black confetti.

'The problem is under control,' I told Sam. 'I've located the source, and I've taken steps to prevent a recurrence.'

'Are you sure of that?' As he spoke, the three-holed torus on the screen twisted restlessly. In fact I'd chosen the icon myself, and its appearance wasn't influenced by Sam at all, but it was impossible not to project emotions onto its writhing.

I said, 'I'm certain that I know who was responsible for the incursion on Wednesday. It was done without malice; in fact the person who did it doesn't even realise that he crossed the border. I've modified the operating system on his computer so that it won't allow him to do the same thing again; if he tries, it will simply give him the same answers as before, but this time the calculations won't actually be performed.'

'That's good to hear,' Sam said. 'Can you describe these calculations?'

I was as invisible to Sam as he was to me, but out of habit I tried to keep my face composed. 'I don't see that as part of our agreement,' I replied.

Sam was silent for a few seconds. 'That's true, Bruno. But it might provide us with a greater sense of reassurance, if we knew what caused the breach in the first place.'

I said, 'I understand. But we've made a decision.' *We* was Alison and I; Yuen was still in hospital, in no state to do anything. Alison and I, speaking for the world.

'I'll put your position to my colleagues,' he said. 'We're not your enemy, Bruno.' His tone sounded regretful, and these nuances *were* under his control.

'I know that,' I replied. 'Nor are we yours. Yet you've chosen to keep most of the details of your world from us. We don't view that as evidence of hostility, so you have no grounds to complain if we keep a few secrets of our own.'

'I'll contact you again soon,' Sam said.

The messenger window closed. I emailed an encrypted transcript to Alison, then slumped across my desk. My head was throbbing, but the encounter really hadn't gone too badly. Of course Sam and his colleagues would have preferred to know everything; of course they were going to be disappointed and reproachful. That didn't mean they were going to abandon the benign policies of the last decade. The important thing was that my assurance would prove to be reliable: the incursion would not be repeated.

I had work to do, the kind that paid bills. Somehow I summoned up the discipline to push the whole subject aside and get on with a report on stochastic methods for resolving distributed programming bottlenecks that I was supposed to be writing for a company in Singapore.

Four hours later, when the doorbell rang, I'd left my desk to raid the kitchen. I didn't bother checking the doorstep camera; I just walked down the hall and opened the door.

Campbell said, 'How are you, Bruno?'

'I'm fine. Why didn't you tell me you were coming to Sydney?'

'Aren't you going to ask me how I found your house?'

'How?'

He held up his phone. There was a text message from me, or at least from my phone; it had SMS'd its GPS coordinates to him.

'Not bad,' I conceded.

'I believe they recently added "corrupting communications devices" to the list of terrorism-related offences in Australia. You could probably get me thrown into solitary confinement in a maximum security prison.'

'Only if you know at least ten words of Arabic.'

'Actually I spent a month in Egypt once, so anything's possible. But I don't think you really want to go to the police.'

I said, 'Why don't you come in?'

As I showed him to the living room my mind was racing. Maybe he'd found the relay behind the bookshelf, but surely not before I'd left his house. Had he managed to get a virus into my phone remotely? I'd thought my security was better than that.

Campbell said, 'I'd like you to explain why you bugged my computer.'

'I'm growing increasingly unsure of that myself. The correct answer might be that you wanted me to.'

He snorted. 'That's rich! I admit that I deliberately allowed a rumour to start about my work, because I was curious as to why you and Alison Tierney called off your search. I wanted to see if you'd come sniffing around. As you did. But that was hardly an invitation to steal all my work.'

'What was the point of the whole exercise for you then, if not a way of stealing something from Alison and me?'

'You can hardly compare the two. I just wanted to confirm my suspicion that you actually found something.'

'And you believe that you've confirmed that?'

He shook his head, but it was with amusement, not denial. I said, 'Why are you here? Do you think I'm going to publish your crackpot theory as my own? I'm too old to get the Fields Medal, but maybe you think it's Nobel material.'

'Oh, I don't think you're interested in fame. As I said, I think you beat me to the prize a long time ago.'

I rose to my feet abruptly; I could feel myself scowling, my fists tightening. 'So what's the bottom line? You want to press charges against me for the laptop? Go ahead. We can each get a fine *in absentia*.'

Campbell said, 'I want to know exactly what was so important to you that you crossed the Tasman, lied your way into my house, abused my hospitality and stole my files. I don't think it was simply curiosity, or jealousy. I think you found something ten years ago, and now you're afraid my work is going to put it at risk.'

I sat down again. The rush of adrenalin I'd experienced at being cornered had dissipated. I could almost hear Alison whispering in my ear, 'Either you kill him, Bruno, or you recruit him.' I had no intention of killing anyone, but I wasn't yet certain that these were the only two choices.

I said, 'And if I tell you to mind your own business?'

He shrugged. 'Then I'll work harder. I know you've screwed that laptop, and maybe the other computers in my house, but I'm not so broke that I can't get a new machine.'

Which would be a hundred times faster. He'd re-run every search, probably with wider parameter ranges. The suitcase nuke from Sparseland that had started this whole mess would detonate again, and for all I knew it could be ten times, a hundred times, more powerful.

I said, 'Have you ever wanted to join a secret society?'

Campbell gave an incredulous laugh. 'No!'

'Neither did I. Too bad.'

I told him everything. The discovery of the defect. Industrial Algebra's pursuit of the result. The epiphany in Shanghai. Sam establishing contact. The treaty, the ten quiet years. Then the sudden jolt of his own work, and the still-unfolding consequences.

Campbell was clearly shaken, but despite the fact that I'd confirmed his original suspicion he wasn't ready to take my word for the whole story.

I knew better than to invite him into my office for a demonstration; faking it there would have been trivial. We walked to the local shopping centre and I handed him two hundred dollars to buy a new notebook. I told him the kind of software he'd need to download, without limiting his choice to any particular package. Then I gave him some further instructions. Within half an hour, he had seen the defect for himself, and nudged the border a short distance in each direction.

We were sitting in the food hall, surrounded by boisterous teenagers who'd just got out from school. Campbell was looking at me as if I'd seized a toy machine gun from his hands, transformed it into solid metal, then bashed him over the head with it.

I said, 'Cheer up. There was no war of the worlds after Shanghai; I think we're going to survive this, too.' After all these years, the chance to share the burden with someone new was actually making me feel much more optimistic.

'The defect is *dynamic*,' he muttered. 'That changes everything.'

'You don't say.'

Campbell scowled. 'I don't just mean the politics, the dangers. I'm talking about the underlying physical model.'

'Yeah?' I hadn't come close to examining that issue seriously; it had been enough of a struggle coming to terms with his original calculations.

'All along, I've assumed that there were exact symmetries in the Planck scale physics that accounted for a stable boundary between macroscopic arithmetics. It was an artificial restriction, but I took it for granted, because anything else seemed . . .'

'Unbelievable?'

'Yes.' He blinked and looked away, surveying the crowd of diners as if he had no idea how he'd ended up among them. 'I'm flying back in a few hours.'

'Does Bridget know why you came?'

'Not exactly.'

I said, 'No one else can know what I've told you. Not yet. The risks are too great, everything's too fluid.'

'Yeah.' He met my gaze. He wasn't just humouring me; he understood what people like IA might do.

'In the longterm,' I said, 'we're going to have to find a way to make this safe. To make everyone safe.' I'd never quite articulated that goal before, but I was only just beginning to absorb the ramifications of Campbell's insights.

'How?' he wondered. 'Do we want to build a wall, or do we want to tear one down?'

'I don't know. The first thing we need is a better map, a better feel for the whole territory.'

He'd hired a car at the airport in order to drive here and confront me; it was parked in a side street close to my house. I walked him to it.

We shook hands before parting. I said, 'Welcome to the reluctant cabal.'

Campbell winced. 'Let's find a way to change it from reluctant to redundant.'

In the weeks that followed, Campbell worked on refinements to his theory, emailing Alison and me every few days. Alison had taken my unilateral decision to recruit Campbell with much more equanimity than I'd expected. 'Better to have him inside the tent,' was all she'd said.

This proved to be an understatement. While the two of us soon caught up with him on all the technicalities, it was clear that his intuition on the subject, hard won over many years of trial and error, was the key to his spectacular progress now. Merely stealing his notes and his algorithms would never have brought us so far.

Gradually, the dynamic version of the theory took shape. As far as macroscopic objects were concerned – and in this context, 'macroscopic' stretched all the way down to the quantum states of subatomic particles – all traces of Platonic mathematics were banished. A 'proof' concerning the integers was just a class of physical processes, and the result of that proof was neither read from, nor written to, any universal book of truths. Rather, the agreement between proofs was simply a strong, but imperfect, correlation between the different processes that counted as proofs of the same thing. Those correlations arose from the way that the primordial states of Planck-scale physics were carved up – imperfectly – into subsystems that appeared to be distinct objects.

The truths of mathematics *appeared* to be enduring and universal because they persisted with great efficiency within the states of matter and spacetime. But there was a built-in flaw in the whole idealisation of distinct objects, and the point where the concept finally cracked open was the defect Alison and I had found in our volunteers' data, which appeared to any macroscopic test as the border between contradictory mathematical systems.

We'd derived a crude empirical rule which said that the border shifted when a proposition's neighbours outvoted it. If you managed to prove that $x+1=y+1$ and $x-1=y-1$, then $x=y$ became a sitting duck, even if it hadn't been true before. The consequences of Campbell's search had shown that the reality was more complex, and in his new model the old border rule became an approximation for a more subtle process, anchored in the dynamics of primordial states that knew nothing of the arithmetic of electrons and apples. The near-side arithmetic Campbell had blasted into the far side hadn't got there by besieging the target with syllogisms; it had got there because he'd gone straight for a far deeper failure in the whole idea of 'integers' than Alison and I had ever dreamt of.

Had Sam dreamt of it? I waited for his next contact, but as the weeks passed he remained silent, and the last thing I felt like doing was calling him myself. I had enough people to lie to without adding him to the list.

Kate asked me how work was going and I waffled about the details of the three uninspiring contracts I'd started recently. When I stopped talking, she looked at me as if I'd just stammered my way through an unconvincing denial of some unspoken crime. I wondered how my mixture of concealed elation and fear was coming across to her. Was that how the most passionate, conflicted adulterer would appear? I didn't actually reach the brink of confession, but I pictured myself approaching it. I had less reason now to think that the secret would bring her harm than when I'd first made my decision to keep her in the dark. But then, what if I told her everything, and the next day Campbell was kidnapped and tortured? If we were all being watched, and the people doing it were good at their jobs, we'd only know about it when it was too late.

Campbell's emails dropped off for a while, and I assumed he'd hit a roadblock. Sam had offered no further complaints. Perhaps, I thought, this was the new status quo, the start of another quiet decade. I could live with that.

Then Campbell flung his second grenade. He reached me by IM and said, 'I've started making maps.'

'Of the defect?' I replied.

'Of the planets.'

I stared at his image, uncomprehending.

'The far-side planets,' he said. '*The physical worlds*.'

He'd bought himself some time on a geographically scattered set of processor clusters. He was no longer repeating his dangerous incursions, of course, but by playing around in the natural ebb and flow at the border, he'd made some extraordinary discoveries.

Alison and I had realised long ago that random 'proofs' in the natural world would influence what happened at the border, but Campbell's theory made that notion more precise. By looking at the exact timing of changes to propositions at the border, measured in a dozen different computers worldwide, he had set up a kind of . . . radar? CT machine? Whatever you called it, it allowed him to deduce the locations where the relevant natural processes were occurring, and his model allowed him to distinguish between both near-side and far-side processes, and processes in matter and those in vacuum. He could measure the density of far-side matter, out to a distance of several light-hours, and crudely image nearby planets.

'Not just on the far side,' he said. 'I validated the technique by imaging our own planets.' He sent me a data log, with comparisons to an online almanac. For Jupiter, the furthest of the planets he'd located, the positions were out by as much as a hundred thousand kilometres; not exactly GPS quality, but that was a bit like complaining that your abacus couldn't tell north from north-west.

'Maybe that's how Sam found us in Shanghai?' I wondered. 'The same kind of thing, only more refined?'

Campbell said, 'Possibly.'

'So what about the far-side planets?'

'Well, here's the first interesting thing. None of the planets coincide with ours. Nor does their sun with our sun.' He sent me an image of the far-side system, one star and its six planets, overlaid on our own.

'But Sam's timelags,' I protested, 'when we communicate—'

'Make no sense if he's too far away. Exactly. So he is *not* living on any of these planets, and he's not even in a natural orbit around their star. He's in powered flight, moving with the Earth. Which suggests to me that they've known about us for much longer than Shanghai.'

'Known about us,' I said, 'but maybe they still didn't anticipate anything like Shanghai.' When we'd set Luminous on to the task of eliminating the defect – not knowing that we were threatening anyone – it had taken several minutes before the far side had responded. Computers on board a spacecraft moving with the Earth would have detected the assault quickly, but it might have taken the recruitment of larger, planet-bound machines, minutes away at light-speed, to repel it.

Until I'd encountered Campbell's theories, my working assumption had been that Sam's world was like a hidden message encoded in the Earth, with the different arithmetic giving different meanings to all the air, water and rock around us. But their matter was not bound to our matter; they didn't need our specks of dust or molecules of air to represent the dark integers. The two worlds split apart at a much lower level; vacuum could be rock, and rock, vacuum.

I said, 'So do you want the Nobel for physics, or peace?'

Campbell smiled modestly. 'Can I hold out for both?'

'That's the answer I was looking for.' I couldn't get the stupid

Cold War metaphors out of my brain: what would Sam's hot-headed colleagues think, if they knew that we were now flying spy planes over their territory? Saying 'screw them, they were doing it first!' might have been a fair response, but it was not a particularly helpful one.

I said, 'We're never going to match their Sputnik, unless you happen to know a trustworthy billionaire who wants to help us launch a space probe on a very strange trajectory. Everything we want to do has to work from Earth.'

'I'll tear up my letter to Richard Branson then, shall I?'

I stared at the map of the far-side solar system. 'There must be some relative motion between their star and ours. It can't have been this close for all that long.'

'I don't have enough accuracy in my measurements to make a meaningful estimate of the velocity,' Campbell said. 'But I've done some crude estimates of the distances between their stars, and it's much smaller than ours. So it's not all that unlikely to find *some* star this close to us, even if it's unlikely to be the same one that was close a thousand years ago. Then again, there might be a selection effect at work here: the whole reason Sam's civilisation managed to notice us at all was *because* we weren't shooting past them at a substantial fraction of light-speed.'

'Okay. So *maybe* this is their home system, but it could just as easily be an expeditionary base for a team that's been following our sun for thousands of years.'

'Yes.'

I said, 'Where do we go with this?'

'I can't increase the resolution much,' Campbell replied, 'without buying time on a lot more clusters.' It wasn't that he needed much processing power for the calculations, but there were minimum prices to be paid to do anything at all, and what would give us clearer pictures would be more computers, not more time on each one.

I said, 'We can't risk asking for volunteers, like the old days. We'd have to lie about what the download was for, and you can be certain that somebody would reverse-engineer it and catch us out.'

'Absolutely.'

I slept on the problem, then woke with an idea at four a.m. and went to my office, trying to flesh out the details before Campbell responded to my email. He was bleary-eyed when the messenger window opened; it was later in Wellington than in Sydney, but it looked as if he'd had as little sleep as I had.

I said, 'We use the internet.'

'I thought we decided that was too risky.'

'Not screensavers for volunteers; I'm talking about *the internet itself*. We work out a way to do the calculations using nothing but data packets and network routers. We bounce traffic all around the world, and we get the geographical resolution for free.'

'You've got to be joking, Bruno—'

'Why? *Any* computing circuit can be built by stringing together enough NAND gates; you think we can't leverage packet switching into a NAND gate? But that's just the proof that it's possible; I expect we can actually make it a thousand times tighter.'

Campbell said, 'I'm going to get some aspirin and come back.'

We roped in Alison to help, but it still took us six weeks to get a workable design, and another month to get it functioning. We ended up exploiting authentication and error-correction protocols built into the internet at several different layers; the heterogeneous approach not only helped us do all the calculations we needed, but made our gentle siphoning of computing power less likely to be detected and mistaken for anything malicious. In fact we were 'stealing' far less from the routers and servers of the net than if we'd sat down for a hardcore 3D multiplayer gaming session, but security systems had their own ideas about what constituted fair use and what was suspicious. The most important thing was not the size of the burden we imposed, but the signature of our behaviour.

Our new globe-spanning arithmetical telescope generated pictures far sharper than before, with kilometre-scale resolution out to a billion kilometres. This gave us crude relief-maps of the far-side planets, revealing mountains on four of them, and what might have been oceans on two of those four. If there were any artificial structures, they were either too small to see, or too subtle in their artificiality.

The relative motion of our sun and the star these planets orbited turned out to be about six kilometres per second. In the decade since Shanghai, the two solar systems had changed their relative location by about two billion kilometres. Wherever the computers were now that had fought with Luminous to control the border, they certainly hadn't been on any of these planets at the time. Perhaps there were two ships, with one following the Earth, and the other, heavier one saving fuel by merely following the sun.

Yuen had finally recovered his health, and the full cabal held an IM-conference to discuss these results.

'We should be showing these to geologists, xenobiologists . . . everyone,' Yuen lamented. He wasn't making a serious proposal, but I shared his sense of frustration.

Alison said, 'What I regret most is that we can't rub Sam's face in these pictures, just to show him that we're not as stupid as he thinks.'

'I imagine his own pictures are sharper,' Campbell replied.

'Which is as you'd expect,' Alison retorted, 'given a head start of a few centuries. If they're so brilliant on the far side, why do they need *us* to tell them what you did to jump the border?'

'They might have guessed precisely what I did,' he countered, 'but they could still be seeking confirmation. Perhaps what they really want is to rule out the possibility that we've discovered something different, something they've never even thought of.'

I gazed at the false colours of one contoured sphere, imagining grey-blue oceans, snow-topped mountains with alien forests, strange cities, wondrous machines. Even if that was pure fantasy and this temporary neighbour was barren, there had to be a living home world from which the ships that pursued us had been launched.

After Shanghai, Sam and his colleagues had chosen to keep us in the dark for ten years, but it had been our own decision to cement the mistrust by holding on to the secret of our accidental weapon. If they'd already guessed its nature, then they might already have found a defence against it, in which case our silence bought us no advantage at all to compensate for the suspicion it engendered.

If that assumption was wrong, though? Then handing over the details of Campbell's work could be just what the far-side hawks were waiting for, before raising their shields and crushing us.

I said, 'We need to make some plans. I want to stay hopeful, I want to keep looking for the best way forward, but we need to be prepared for the worst.'

Transforming that suggestion into something concrete required far more work than I'd imagined; it was three months before the pieces started coming together. When I finally shifted my gaze back to the everyday world, I decided that I'd earned a break. Kate had a free weekend approaching; I suggested a day in the Blue Mountains.

Her initial response was sarcastic, but when I persisted she softened a little, and finally agreed.

On the drive out of the city, the chill that had developed between us slowly began to thaw. We played JJJ on the car radio – laughing with disbelief as we realised that today's cutting-edge music consisted mostly of cover versions and re-samplings of songs that had been hits when we were in our twenties – and resurrected old running jokes from the time when we'd first met.

As we wound our way into the mountains, though, it proved impossible simply to turn back the clock. Kate said, 'Whoever you've been working for these last few months, can you put them on your blacklist?'

I laughed. 'That will scare them.' I switched to my best Brando voice. 'You're on Bruno Costanzo's blacklist. You'll never run distributed software efficiently in this town again.'

She said, 'I'm serious. I don't know what's so stressful about the work, or the people, but it's really screwing you up.'

I could have made her a promise, but it would have been hard enough to sound sincere as I spoke the words, let alone live up to them. I said, 'Beggars can't be choosers.'

She shook her head, her mouth tensed in frustration. 'If you really want a heart attack, fine. But don't pretend that it's all about money. We're never that broke, and we're never that rich. Unless it's all going into your account in Zürich.'

It took me a few seconds to convince myself that this was nothing more than a throw-away reference to Swiss banks. Kate knew about Alison, knew that we'd once been close, knew that we still kept in touch. She had plenty of male friends from her own past, and they all lived in Sydney; for more than five years, Alison and I hadn't even set foot on the same continent.

We parked the car, then walked along a scenic trail for an hour, mostly in silence. We found a spot by a stream, with tiered rocks smoothed by some ancient river, and ate the lunch I'd packed.

Looking out into the blue haze of the densely wooded valley below, I couldn't keep the image of the crowded skies of the far side from my mind. A dazzling richness surrounded us: alien worlds, alien life, alien culture. There had to be a way to end our mutual suspicion, and work towards a genuine exchange of knowledge.

As we started back towards the car, I turned to Kate. 'I know I've neglected you,' I said. 'I've been through a rough patch, but everything's going to change. I'm going to make things right.'

I was prepared for a withering rebuff, but for a long time she was silent. Then she nodded slightly and said, 'Okay.'

As she reached across and took my hand, my wrist began vibrating. I'd buckled to the pressure and bought a watch that shackled me to the net twenty-four hours a day.

I freed my hand from Kate's and lifted the watch to my face. The bandwidth reaching me out in the sticks wasn't enough for video, but a stored snapshot of Alison appeared on the screen.

'This is for *emergencies only*,' I snarled.

'Check out a newsfeed,' she replied. The acoustics were focused on my ears; Kate would get nothing but the bad-hearing-aid-at-a-party impression that made so many people want to punch their fellow commuters on trains.

'Why don't you just summarise whatever it is I'm meant to have noticed?'

Financial computing systems were going haywire, to an extent that was already being described as terrorism. Most trading was closed for the weekend, but some experts were predicting the crash of the century come Monday.

I wondered if the cabal itself was to blame; if we'd inadvertently corrupted the whole internet by coupling its behaviour to the defect. That was nonsense, though. Half the transactions being garbled were taking place on secure, interbank networks that shared no hardware with our global computer. This was coming from the far side.

'Have you contacted Sam?' I asked her.

'I can't raise him.'

'Where are you going?' Kate shouted angrily. I'd unconsciously broken into a jog; I wanted to get back to the car, back to the city, back to my office.

I stopped and turned to her. 'Run with me? Please? This is important.'

'You're joking! I've spent half a day hiking; I'm not running anywhere!'

I hesitated, fantasising for a moment that I could sit beneath a gum tree and orchestrate everything with my Dick Tracy watch before its battery went flat.

I said, 'You'd better call a taxi when you get to the road.'

'You're taking the car?' Kate stared at me, incredulous. 'You piece of shit!'

'I'm sorry.' I tossed my backpack on the ground and started sprinting.

'We need to deploy,' I told Alison.

'I know,' she said. 'We've already started.'

It was the right decision, but hearing it still loosened my bowels far more than the realisation that the far side were attacking us.

Whatever their motives, at least they were unlikely to do more harm than they intended. I was much less confident about our own abilities.

'Keep trying to reach Sam,' I insisted. 'This is a thousand times more useful if they know about it.'

Alison said, 'I guess this isn't the time for *Dr. Strangelove* jokes.'

Over the last three months we'd worked out a way to augment our internet 'telescope' software to launch a barrage of Campbell-style attacks on far-side propositions if it saw our own mathematics being encroached upon. The software couldn't protect the whole border, but there were millions of individual trigger points, forming a randomly shifting minefield. The plan had been to buy ourselves some security, without ever reaching the point of actual retaliation. We'd been waiting to complete a final round of tests before unleashing this version live on the net, but it would only take a matter of minutes to get it up and running.

'Anything being hit besides financials?' I asked.

'Not that I'm picking up.'

If the far side was deliberately targeting the markets, that was infinitely preferable to the alternative: that financial systems had simply been the most fragile objects in the path of a much broader assault. Most modern engineering and aeronautical systems were more interested in resorting to fall-backs than agonising over their failures. A bank's computer might declare itself irretrievably compromised and shut down completely, the instant certain totals failed to reconcile; those in a chemical plant or an airliner would be designed to fail more gracefully, trying simpler alternatives and bringing all available humans into the loop.

I said, 'Yuen and Tim—?'

'Both on board,' Alison confirmed. 'Monitoring the deployment, ready to tweak the software if necessary.'

'Good. You really won't need me at all, then, will you?'

Alison's reply dissolved into digital noise, and the connection cut out. I refused to read anything sinister into that; given my location, I was lucky to have any coverage at all. I ran faster, trying not to think about the time in Shanghai when Sam had taken a mathematical scalpel to all of our brains. Luminous had been screaming out our position like a beacon; we would not be so easy to locate this time. Still, with a cruder approach, the hawks could take a hatchet to everyone's head. *Would they go that far?* Only if this was meant as much more than a threat, much more than intimidation to make us hand over Campbell's algorithm. Only if this was the end game: no warning, no negotiations, just Sparseland wiped off the map for ever.

Fifteen minutes after Alison's call, I reached the car. Apart from the entertainment console it didn't contain a single microchip; I remembered the salesman laughing when I'd queried that twice. 'What are you afraid of? Y3K?' The engine started immediately.

I had an ancient secondhand laptop in the boot; I put it beside me on the passenger seat and started it booting up while I drove out on to the access road, heading for the highway. Alison and I had worked for a fortnight on a stripped-down operating system, as simple and robust as possible, to run on these old computers; if the far side kept reaching down from the arithmetic stratosphere, these would be like concrete bunkers compared to the glass skyscrapers of more modern machines. The four of us would also be running different versions of the OS, on CPUs with different instruction sets; our bunkers were scattered mathematically as well as geographically.

As I drove on to the highway, my watch stuttered back to life. Alison said, 'Bruno? Can you hear me?'

'Go ahead.'

'Three passenger jets have crashed,' she said. 'Poland, Indonesia, South Africa.'

I was dazed. Ten years before, when I'd tried to bulldoze his whole mathematical world into the sea, Sam had spared my life. Now the far side was slaughtering innocents.

'Is our minefield up?'

'It's been up for ten minutes, but nothing's tripped it yet.'

'You think they're steering through it?'

Alison hesitated. 'I don't see how. There's no way to predict a safe path.' We were using a quantum noise server to randomise the propositions we tested.

I said, 'We should trigger it manually. One counter-strike to start with, to give them something to think about.' I was still hoping that the downed jets were unintended, but we had no choice but to retaliate.

'Yeah.' Alison's image was live now; I saw her reach down for her mouse. She said, 'It's not responding. The net's too degraded.' All the fancy algorithms that the routers used, and that we'd leveraged so successfully for our imaging software, were turning them into paperweights. The internet was robust against high levels of transmission noise and the loss of thousands of connections, but not against the decay of arithmetic itself.

My watch went dead. I looked to the laptop; it was still working. I reached over and hit a single hotkey, launching a program that would try to reach Alison and the others the same way we'd talked to Sam: by modulating part of the border. In theory, the hawks might have moved the whole border – in which case we were screwed – but the border was vast, and it made more sense for them to target their computing resources on the specific needs of the assault itself.

A small icon appeared on the laptop's screen, a single letter A in reversed monochrome. I said, 'Is this working?'

'Yes,' Alison replied. The icon blinked out, then came back again. We were doing a Hedy Lamarr, hopping rapidly over a predetermined sequence of border points to minimise the chance of detection. Some of those points would be missing, but it looked as if enough of them remained intact.

The A was joined by a Y and a T. The whole cabal was online now, whatever that was worth. What we needed was S, but S was not answering.

Campbell said grimly, 'I heard about the planes. I've started an attack.' The tactic we had agreed upon was to take turns running different variants of Campbell's border-jumping algorithm from our scattered machines.

I said, 'The miracle is that they're not hitting us the same way we're hitting them. They're just pushing down part of the border with the old voting method, step by step. If we'd given them what they'd asked for, we'd all be dead by now.'

'Maybe not,' Yuen replied. 'I'm only halfway through a proof, but I'm ninety per cent sure that Tim's method is asymmetrical. It only works in one direction. Even if we'd told them about it, they couldn't have turned it against us.'

I opened my mouth to argue, but if Yuen was right that made perfect sense. The far side had probably been working on the same branch of mathematics for centuries; if there had been an equivalent weapon that could be used from their vantage point, they would have discovered it long ago.

My machine had synchronised with Campbell's, and it took over the assault automatically. We had no real idea what we were hitting, except that the propositions were further from the border, describing far simpler arithmetic on the dark integers than anything of ours that the far side had yet touched. *Were we crippling machines? Taking lives?* I was torn between a triumphant vision of retribution, and a sense of shame that we'd allowed it to come to this.

Every hundred metres or so, I passed another car sitting motionless by the side of the highway. I was far from the only person still driving, but I had a feeling Kate wouldn't have much luck getting a taxi. She had water in her backpack, and there was a small shelter at the spot where we'd parked. There was little to be gained by reaching my office now; the laptop could do everything that mattered, and I could run it from the car battery if necessary. If I turned around and went back for Kate, though, I'd have so much explaining to do that there'd be no time for anything else.

I switched on the car radio, but either its digital signal processor was too sophisticated for its own good, or all the local stations were out.

'Anyone still getting news?' I asked.

'I still have radio,' Campbell replied. 'No TV, no internet. Landlines and mobiles here are dead.' It was the same for Alison and Yuen. There'd been no more reports of disasters on the radio, but the stations were probably as isolated now as their listeners. Ham operators would still be calling each other, but journalists and newsrooms would not be in the loop. I didn't want to think about the contingency plans that might have been in place, given ten years' preparation and an informed population.

By the time I reached Penrith there were so many abandoned cars that the remaining traffic was almost gridlocked. I decided not to even try to reach home. I didn't know if Sam had literally scanned my brain in Shanghai and used that to target what he'd done to me then, and whether or not he could use the same neuroanatomical information against me now, wherever I was, but staying away from my usual haunts seemed like one more small advantage to cling to.

I found a petrol station, and it was giving priority to customers with functioning cars over hoarders who'd appeared on foot with empty cans. Their EFTPOS wasn't working, but I had enough cash for the petrol and some chocolate bars.

As dusk fell the streetlights came on; the traffic lights had never stopped working. All four laptops were holding up, hurling their grenades into the far side. The closer the attack front came to simple arithmetic, the more resistance it would face from natural processes voting at the border for near-side results. Our enemy had their supercomputers; we had every atom of the Earth, following its billion-year-old version of the truth.

We had modelled this scenario. The sheer arithmetical inertia of all that matter would buy us time, but in the long run a coherent, sustained, computational attack could still force its way through.

How would we die? Losing consciousness first, feeling no pain? Or was the brain more robust than that? Would all the cells of our bodies start committing apoptosis, once their biochemical errors mounted up beyond repair? Maybe it would be just like radiation sickness. We'd be burnt by decaying arithmetic, just as if it was nuclear fire.

My laptop beeped. I swerved off the road and parked on a

stretch of concrete beside a dark shopfront. A new icon had appeared on the screen: the letter S.

Sam said, 'Bruno, this was not my decision.'

'I believe you,' I said. 'But if you're just a messenger now, what's your message?'

'If you give us what we asked for, we'll stop the attack.'

'We're hurting you, aren't we?'

'We know we're hurting *you*,' Sam replied. Point taken: we were guessing, firing blind. He didn't have to ask about the damage we'd suffered.

I steeled myself, and followed the script the cabal had agreed upon. 'We'll give you the algorithm, but only if you retreat back to the old border, and then seal it.'

Sam was silent for four long heartbeats.

'Seal it?'

'I think you know what I mean.' In Shanghai, when we'd used Luminous to try to ensure that Industrial Algebra could not exploit the defect, we'd contemplated trying to seal the border rather than eliminating the defect altogether. The voting effect could only shift the border if it was crinkled in such a way that propositions on one side could be outnumbered by those on the other side. It was possible – given enough time and computing power – to smooth the border, to iron it flat. Once that was done, everywhere, the whole thing would become immovable. No force in the universe could shift it again.

Sam said, 'You want to leave us with no weapon against you, while you still have the power to harm us.'

'We won't have that power for long. Once you know exactly what we're using, you'll find a way to block it.'

There was a long pause. Then, 'Stop your attacks on us and we'll consider your proposal.'

'We'll stop our attacks when you pull the border back to the point where our lives are no longer at risk.'

'How would you even know that we've done that?' Sam replied. I wasn't sure if the condescension was in his tone or just his words, but either way I welcomed it. The lower the far side's opinion of our abilities, the more attractive the deal became for them.

I said, 'Then you'd better back up far enough for all our communications systems to recover. When I can get news reports and see that there are no more planes going down, no power plants exploding, then we'll start the ceasefire.'

Silence again, stretching out beyond mere hesitancy. His icon was still there, though, the S unblinking. I clutched at my shoulder, hoping that the burning pain was just tension in the muscle.

Finally: 'All right. We agree. We'll start shifting the border.'

I drove around looking for an all-night convenience store that might have had an old analogue TV sitting in a corner to keep the cashier awake – that seemed like a good bet to start working long before the wireless connection to my laptop – but Campbell beat me to it. New Zealand radio and TV were reporting that the 'digital blackout' appeared to be lifting, and ten minutes later Alison announced that she had internet access. A lot of the major servers were still down, or their sites weirdly garbled, but Reuters was starting to post updates on the crisis.

Sam had kept his word, so we halted the counter-strikes. Alison read from the Reuters site as the news came in. Seventeen planes had crashed, and four trains. There'd been fatalities at an oil refinery, and half a dozen manufacturing plants. One analyst put the global death toll at five thousand, and rising.

I muted the microphone on my laptop and spent thirty seconds shouting obscenities and punching the dashboard. Then I rejoined the cabal.

Yuen said, 'I've been reviewing my notes. If my instinct is worth anything, the theorem I mentioned before is correct: if the border is sealed, they'll have no way to touch us.'

'What about the upside for them?' Alison asked. 'Do you think they can protect themselves against Tim's algorithm, once they understand it?'

Yuen hesitated. 'Yes and no. Any cluster of near-side truth values it injects into the far side will have a non-smooth border, so they'll be able to remove it with sheer computing power. In that sense, they'll never be defenceless. But I don't see how there's anything they can do to prevent the attacks in the first place.'

'Short of wiping us out,' Campbell said.

I heard an infant sobbing. Alison said, 'That's Laura. I'm alone here. Give me five minutes.'

I buried my head in my arms. I still had no idea what the right course would have been. If we'd handed over Campbell's algorithm immediately, might the good will that bought us have averted the war? Or would the same attack merely have come sooner? What criminal vanity had ever made the three of us think we could shoulder this responsibility on our own? Five thousand people were dead. The hawks who had taken over on the far side would weigh up our offer and decide that they had no choice but to fight on.

And if the reluctant cabal had passed its burden to Canberra, to Zürich, to Beijing? Would there really have been peace? Or was I just wishing that there had been more hands steeped in the same blood, to share the guilt around?

The idea came from nowhere, sweeping away every other thought. I said, 'Is there any reason why the far side has to stay *connected*?'

'Connected to what?' Campbell asked.

'Connected to itself. Connected topologically. They should be able to send down a spike, then withdraw it, but leave behind a bubble of altered truth values: a kind of outpost, sitting within the near side, with a perfect, smooth border making it impregnable. Right?'

Yuen said, 'Perhaps. With both sides collaborating on the construction, that might be possible.'

'Then the question is, can we find a place where we can do that so that it kills off the chance to use Tim's method completely – without crippling any process that we need just to survive?'

'*Fuck you*, Bruno!' Campbell exclaimed happily. 'We give them one small Achilles tendon to slice . . . and then they've got nothing to fear from us!'

Yuen said, 'A watertight proof of something like that is going to take weeks, months.'

'Then we'd better start work. And we'd better feed Sam the first plausible conjecture we get, so they can use their own resources to help us with the proof.'

Alison came back online, and greeted the suggestion with cautious approval. I drove around until I found a quiet coffee shop. Electronic banking still wasn't working, and I had no cash left, but the waiter agreed to take my credit card number and a signed authority for a deduction of one hundred dollars; whatever I didn't eat and drink would be his tip.

I sat in the café, blanking out the world, steeping myself in the mathematics. Sometimes the four of us worked on separate tasks; sometimes we paired up, dragging each other out of dead ends and ruts. There were an infinite number of variations that could be made to Campbell's algorithm, but hour by hour we whittled away at the concept, finding the common ground that no version of the weapon could do without.

By four in the morning, we had a strong conjecture. I called Sam, and explained what we were hoping to achieve.

He said, 'This is a good idea. We'll consider it.'

The café closed. I sat in the car for a while, drained and numb, then I called Kate to find out where she was. A couple had given her a lift almost as far as Penrith, and when their car failed she'd walked the rest of the way home.

For close to four days, I spent most of my waking hours just sitting at my desk, watching as a wave of red inched its way across a map of the defect. The change of hue was not being rendered lightly; before each pixel turned red, twelve separate computers needed to confirm that the region of the border it represented was flat.

On the fifth day, Sam shut off his computers and allowed us to mount an attack from our side on the narrow corridor linking the bulk of the far side with the small enclave that now surrounded our Achilles heel. We wouldn't have suffered any real loss of essential arithmetic if this slender thread had remained, but keeping the corridor both small and impregnable had turned out to be impossible. The original plan was the only route to finality: to seal the border perfectly, the far side proper could not remain linked to its offshoot.

In the next stage, the two sides worked together to seal the enclave completely, polishing the scar where its umbilical had been sheared away. When that task was complete, the map showed it as a single burnished ruby. No known process could reshape it now. Campbell's method could have breached its border without touching it, reaching inside to reclaim it from within – but Campbell's method was exactly what this jewel ruled out.

At the other end of the vanished umbilical, Sam's machines set to work smoothing away the blemish. By early evening that, too, was done.

Only one tiny flaw in the border remained, now: the handful of propositions that enabled communication between the two sides. The cabal had debated the fate of this for hours. So long as this small wrinkle persisted, in principle it could be used to unravel everything, to mobilise the entire border again. It was true that, compared to the border as a whole, it would be relatively easy to monitor and defend such a small site, but a sustained burst of brute force computing from either side could still overpower any resistance and exploit it.

In the end, Sam's political masters had made the decision for us. What they had always aspired to was certainty, and even if their strength favoured them, this wasn't a gamble they were prepared to take.

I said, 'Good luck with the future.'

'Good luck to Sparseland,' Sam replied. I believed he'd tried to hold out against the hawks, but I'd never been certain of his friendship. When his icon faded from my screen, I felt more relief than regret.

I'd learnt the hard way not to assume that anything was permanent. Perhaps in a thousand years, someone would discover that Campbell's model was just an approximation to something deeper, and find a way to fracture these allegedly perfect walls. With any luck, by then both sides might also be better prepared to find a way to coexist.

I found Kate sitting in the kitchen. I said, 'I can answer your questions now, if that's what you want.' On the morning after the disaster, I'd promised her this time would come – within weeks, not months – and she'd agreed to stay with me until it did.

She thought for a while.

'Did you have something to do with what happened last week?'

'Yes.'

'Are you saying you unleashed the virus? You're the terrorist they're looking for?' To my great relief, she asked this in roughly the tone she might have used if I'd claimed to be Genghis Khan.

'No, I'm not the cause of what happened. It was my job to try and stop it, and I failed. But it wasn't any kind of computer virus.'

She searched my face. 'What was it, then? Can you explain that to me?'

'It's a long story.'

'I don't care. We've got all night.'

I said, 'It started in university. With an idea of Alison's. One brilliant, beautiful, crazy idea.'

Kate looked away, her face flushing, as if I'd said something deliberately humiliating. She knew I was not a mass-murderer. But there were other things about me of which she was less sure.

'The story starts with Alison,' I said. 'But it ends here, with you.'

CRYSTAL NIGHTS

1

'More caviar?' Daniel Cliff gestured at the serving dish and the cover irised from opaque to transparent. 'It's fresh, I promise you. My chef had it flown in from Iran this morning.'

'No thank you.' Julie Dehghani touched a napkin to her lips then laid it on her plate with a gesture of finality. The dining room overlooked the Golden Gate Bridge, and most people Daniel invited here were content to spend an hour or two simply enjoying the view, but he could see that she was growing impatient with his small talk.

Daniel said, 'I'd like to show you something.' He led her into the adjoining conference room. On the table was a wireless keyboard; the wall screen showed a Linux command line interface. 'Take a seat,' he suggested.

Julie complied. 'If this is some kind of audition, you might have warned me,' she said.

'Not at all,' Daniel replied. 'I'm not going to ask you to jump through any hoops. I'd just like you to tell me what you think of this machine's performance.'

She frowned slightly, but she was willing to play along. She ran some standard benchmarks. Daniel saw her squinting at the screen, one hand almost reaching up to where a desktop display would be so she could double-check the number of digits in the FLOPS rating by counting them off with one finger. There were a lot more than she'd been expecting, but she wasn't seeing double.

'That's extraordinary,' she said. 'Is this whole building packed with networked processors, with only the penthouse for humans?'

Daniel said, 'You tell me. Is it a cluster?'

'Hmm.' So much for not making her jump through hoops, but it wasn't really much of a challenge. She ran some different benchmarks, based on algorithms that were provably impossible to parallelise; however smart the compiler was, the steps these programs required would have to be carried out strictly in sequence.

The FLOPS rating was unchanged.

Julie said, 'All right, it's a single processor. Now you've got my attention. Where is it?'

'Turn the keyboard over.'

There was a charcoal-grey module, five centimetres square and five millimetres thick, plugged into an inset docking bay. Julie examined it, but it bore no manufacturer's logo or other identifying marks.

'This connects to the processor?' she asked.

'No. It *is* the processor.'

'You're joking.' She tugged it free of the dock, and the wall screen went blank. She held it up and turned it around, though Daniel wasn't sure what she was looking for. Somewhere to slip in a screwdriver and take the thing apart, probably. He said, 'If you break it, you own it, so I hope you've got a few hundred spare.'

'A few hundred grand? Hardly.'

'A few hundred million.'

Her face flushed. 'Of course. If it was a few hundred grand, everyone would have one.' She put it down on the table, then as an afterthought slid it a little further from the edge. 'As I said, you've got my attention.'

Daniel smiled. 'I'm sorry about the theatrics.'

'No, this deserved the build-up. What is it, exactly?'

'A single three-dimensional photonic crystal. No electronics to slow it down; every last component is optical. The architecture was nanofabricated with a method that I'd prefer not to describe in detail.'

'Fair enough.' She thought for a while. 'I take it you don't expect me to buy one. My research budget for the next thousand years would barely cover it.'

'In your present position. But you're not joined to the university at the hip.'

'So this is a job interview?'

Daniel nodded.

Julie couldn't help herself; she picked up the crystal and examined it again, as if there might yet be some feature that a human eye could discern. 'Can you give me a job description?'

'Midwife.'

She laughed. 'To what?'

'History,' Daniel said.

Her smile faded slowly.

'I believe you're the best AI researcher of your generation,' he said. 'I want you to work for me.' He reached over and took the crystal from her. 'With this as your platform, imagine what you could do.'

Julie said, 'What exactly would you want me to do?'

'For the last fifteen years,' Daniel said, 'you've stated that the ultimate goal of your research is to create conscious, human-level artificial intelligence.'

'That's right.'

'Then we want the same thing. What I want is for you to succeed.'

She ran a hand over her face; whatever else she was thinking, there was no denying that she was tempted. 'It's gratifying that you have so much confidence in my abilities,' she said. 'But we need to be clear about some things. This prototype is amazing, and if you ever get the production costs down I'm sure it will have some extraordinary applications. It would eat up climate forecasting, lattice QCD, astrophysical modelling, proteomics . . .'

'Of course.' Actually, Daniel had no intention of marketing the device. He'd bought out the inventor of the fabrication process with his own private funds; there were no other shareholders or directors to dictate his use of the technology.

'But AI,' Julie said, 'is different. We're in a maze, not a highway; there's nowhere that speed alone can take us. However many exaflops I have to play with, they won't spontaneously combust into consciousness. I'm not being held back by the university's computers; I have access to SHARCNET anytime I need it. I'm being held back by my own lack of insight into the problems I'm addressing.'

Daniel said, 'A maze is not a dead end. When I was twelve, I wrote a program for solving mazes.'

'And I'm sure it worked well,' Julie replied, 'for small, two-dimensional ones. But you know how those kind of algorithms scale. Put your old program on this crystal, and I could still design a maze in half a day that would bring it to its knees.'

'Of course,' Daniel conceded. 'Which is precisely why I'm interested in hiring you. You know a great deal more about the maze of AI than I do; any strategy you developed would be vastly superior to a blind search.'

'I'm not saying that I'm merely groping in the dark,' she said. 'If it was that bleak, I'd be working on a different problem entirely. But I don't see what difference this processor would make.'

'What created the only example of consciousness we know of?' Daniel asked.

'Evolution.'

'Exactly. But I don't want to wait three billion years, so I need to make the selection process a great deal more refined, and the sources of variation more targeted.'

Julie digested this. 'You want to try to *evolve* true AI? Conscious, human-level AI?'

'Yes.' Daniel saw her mouth tightening, saw her struggling to measure her words before speaking.

'With respect,' she said, 'I don't think you've thought that through.'

'On the contrary,' Daniel assured her. 'I've been planning this for twenty years.'

'Evolution,' she said, 'is about failure and death. Do you have any idea how many sentient creatures lived and died along the way to *Homo sapiens*? How much suffering was involved?'

'Part of your job would be to minimise the suffering.'

'*Minimise it?*' She seemed genuinely shocked, as if this proposal was even worse than blithely assuming that the process would raise no ethical concerns. 'What right do we have to inflict it at all?'

Daniel said, 'You're grateful to exist, aren't you? Notwithstanding the tribulations of your ancestors.'

'I'm grateful to exist,' she agreed, 'but in the human case the suffering wasn't deliberately inflicted by anyone, and nor was there any alternative way we could have come into existence. If there really *had* been a just creator, I don't doubt that he would have followed Genesis literally; he sure as hell would not have used evolution.'

'Just, *and omnipotent*,' Daniel suggested. 'Sadly, that second trait's even rarer than the first.'

'I don't think it's going to take omnipotence to create something in our own image,' she said. 'Just a little more patience and self-knowledge.'

'This won't be like natural selection,' Daniel insisted. 'Not that blind, not that cruel, not that wasteful. You'd be free to intervene as much as you'd wish, to take whatever palliative measures you felt appropriate.'

'*Palliative measures?*' Julie met his gaze, and he saw her expression flicker from disbelief to something darker. She stood up and glanced at her wristphone. 'I don't have any signal here. Would you mind calling me a taxi?'

Daniel said, 'Please, hear me out. Give me ten more minutes, then the helicopter will take you to the airport.'

'I'd prefer to make my own way home.' She gave Daniel a look that made it clear that this was not negotiable.

He called her a taxi, and they walked to the elevator.

'I know you find this morally challenging,' he said, 'and I respect that. I wouldn't dream of hiring someone who thought these were trivial issues. But if I don't do this, someone else will. Someone with far worse intentions than mine.'

'Really?' Her tone was openly sarcastic now. 'So how, exactly, does the mere existence of your project stop this hypothetical bin Laden of AI from carrying out his own?'

Daniel was disappointed; he'd expected her at least to understand what was at stake. He said, 'This is a race to decide between Godhood and enslavement. Whoever succeeds first will be unstoppable. I'm not going to be anyone's slave.'

Julie stepped into the elevator; he followed her.

She said, 'You know what they say the modern version of Pascal's Wager is? Sucking up to as many Transhumanists as possible, just in case one of them turns into God. Perhaps your motto should be "Treat every chatterbot kindly, it might turn out to be the deity's uncle."'

'We will be as kind as possible,' Daniel said. 'And don't forget, we can determine the nature of these beings. They will be happy to be alive, and grateful to their creator. We can select for those traits.'

Julie said, 'So you're aiming for *Übermenschen* that wag their tails when you scratch them behind the ears? You might find there's a bit of a trade-off there.'

The elevator reached the lobby. Daniel said, 'Think about this, don't rush to a decision. You can call me any time.' There was no commercial flight back to Toronto tonight; she'd be stuck in a hotel, paying money she could ill afford, thinking about the kind of salary she could demand from him now that she'd played hard to get. If she mentally recast all this obstinate moralising as a deliberate bargaining strategy, she'd have no trouble swallowing her pride.

Julie offered her hand, and he shook it. She said, 'Thank you for dinner.'

The taxi was waiting. He walked with her across the lobby. 'If you want to see AI in your lifetime,' he said, 'this is the only way it's going to happen.'

She turned to face him. 'Maybe that's true. We'll see. But better to spend a thousand years and get it right, than a decade and succeed by your methods.'

As Daniel watched the taxi drive away into the fog, he forced himself to accept the reality: she was never going to change her mind. Julie Dehghani had been his first choice, his ideal collaborator. He couldn't pretend that this wasn't a setback.

Still, no one was irreplaceable. However much it would have delighted him to have won her over, there were many more names on his list.

2

Daniel's wrist tingled as the message came through. He glanced down and saw the word PROGRESS! hovering in front of his watch face.

The board meeting was almost over; he disciplined himself and kept his attention focused for ten more minutes. WiddulHands.com had made him his first billion, and it was still the pre-eminent social networking site for the 0–3 age group. It had been fifteen years since he'd founded the company, and he had since diversified in many directions, but he had no intention of taking his hands off the levers.

When the meeting finished he blanked the wall screen and paced the empty conference room for half a minute, rolling his neck and stretching his shoulders. Then he said, 'Lucien.'

Lucien Crace appeared on the screen. 'Significant progress?' Daniel enquired.

'Absolutely.' Lucien was trying to maintain polite eye contact with Daniel, but something kept drawing his gaze away. Without waiting for an explanation, Daniel gestured at the screen and had it show him exactly what Lucien was seeing.

A barren, rocky landscape stretched to the horizon. Scattered across the rocks were dozens of crab-like creatures – some deep blue, some coral pink, though these weren't colours the locals would see, just species markers added to the view to make it easier to interpret. As Daniel watched, fat droplets of corrosive rain drizzled down from a passing cloud. This had to be the bleakest environment in all of Sapphire.

Lucien was still visible in an inset. 'See the blue ones over by the crater lake?' he said. He sketched a circle on the image to guide Daniel's attention.

'Yeah.' Five blues were clustered around a lone pink; Daniel gestured and the view zoomed in on them. The blues had opened up their prisoner's body, but it wasn't dead; Daniel was sure of that, because the pinks had recently acquired a trait that turned their bodies to mush the instant they expired.

'They've found a way to study it,' Lucien said. 'To keep it alive and study it.'

From the very start of the project, he and Daniel had decided to grant the Phites the power to observe and manipulate their own bodies as much as possible. In the DNA world, the inner workings of anatomy and heredity had only become accessible once highly sophisticated technology had been invented. In Sapphire, the barriers were designed to be far lower. The basic units of biology here were 'beads', small spheres that possessed a handful of simple properties but no complex internal biochemistry. Beads were larger than the cells of the DNA world, and Sapphire's diffractionless optics rendered them visible to the right kind of naked eye. Animals acquired beads from their diet, while in plants they replicated in the presence of sunlight, but unlike cells they did not themselves mutate. The beads in a Phite's body could be rearranged with a minimum of fuss, enabling a kind of self-modification that no human surgeon or prosthetics engineer could rival – and this skill was actually essential for at least one stage in every Phite's life: reproduction involved two Phites pooling their spare beads and then collaborating to 'sculpt' them into an infant, in part by directly copying each other's current body plans.

Of course these crabs knew nothing of the abstract principles of engineering and design, but the benefits of trial and error, of self-experimentation and cross-species plagiarism, had led them into an escalating war of innovation. The pinks had been the first to stop their corpses from being plundered for secrets, by stumbling on a way to make them literally fall apart *in extremis*; now it seemed the blues had found a way around that, and were indulging in a spot of vivisection-as-industrial-espionage.

Daniel felt a visceral twinge of sympathy for the struggling pink, but he brushed it aside. Not only did he doubt that the Phites were any more conscious than ordinary crabs, they certainly had a radically different relationship to bodily integrity. The pink was resisting because its dissectors were of a different species; if they had been its cousins it might not have put up any fight at all. When something happened in spite of your wishes, that was unpleasant by definition, but it would be absurd to imagine that the pink was in the kind of agony that an antelope being flayed by jackals would feel – let alone experiencing the existential terrors of a human trapped and mutilated by a hostile tribe.

'This is going to give them a tremendous advantage,' Lucien enthused.

'The blues?'

Lucien shook his head. 'Not blues over pinks; Phites over tradlife. Bacteria can swap genes, but this kind of active mimetics is unprecedented without cultural support. Da Vinci might have watched the birds in flight and sketched his gliders, but no lemur ever dissected the body of an eagle and then stole its tricks. They're going to have *innate* skills as powerful as whole strands of human technology. All this before they even have language.'

'Hmm.' Daniel wanted to be optimistic too, but he was growing wary of Lucien's hype. Lucien had a doctorate in genetic programming, but he'd made his name with FoodExcuses.com, a web service that trawled the medical literature to cobble together quasi-scientific justifications for indulging in your favourite culinary vice. He had the kind of technobabble that could bleed money out of venture capitalists down pat, and though Daniel admired that skill in its proper place, he expected a higher insight-to-bullshit ratio now that Lucien was on his payroll.

The blues were backing away from their captive. As Daniel watched, the pink sealed up its wounds and scuttled off towards a group of its own kind. The blues had now seen the detailed anatomy of the respiratory system that had been giving the pinks an advantage in the thin air of this high plateau. A few of the blues would try it out, and if it worked for them, the whole tribe would copy it.

'So what do you think?' Lucien asked.

'Select them,' Daniel said.

'Just the blues?'

'No, both of them.' The blues alone might have diverged into competing subspecies eventually, but bringing their old rivals along for the ride would help to keep them sharp.

'Done,' Lucien replied. In an instant, ten million Phites were erased, leaving the few thousand blues and pinks from these badlands to inherit the planet. Daniel felt no compunction; the extinction events he decreed were surely the most painless in history.

Now that the world no longer required human scrutiny, Lucien unthrottled the crystal and let the simulation race ahead; automated tools would let them know when the next interesting development arose. Daniel watched the population figures rising as his chosen species spread out and recolonised Sapphire.

Would their distant descendants rage against him, for this act of 'genocide' that had made room for them to flourish and prosper? That seemed unlikely. In any case, what choice did he have? He couldn't start manufacturing new crystals for every useless side-branch of the evolutionary tree. Nobody was wealthy enough to indulge in an exponentially growing number of virtual animal shelters at half a billion dollars apiece.

He was a just creator, but he was not omnipotent. His careful pruning was the only way.

3

In the months that followed, progress came in fits and starts. Several times, Daniel found himself rewinding history, reversing his decisions and trying a new path. Keeping every Phite variant alive was impractical, but he did retain enough information to resurrect lost species at will.

The maze of AI was still a maze, but the speed of the crystal served them well. Barely eighteen months after the start of Project Sapphire, the Phites were exhibiting a basic theory of mind: their actions showed that they could deduce what others knew about the world, as distinct from what they knew themselves. Other AI researchers had spliced this kind of thing into their programs by hand, but Daniel was convinced that his version was better integrated, more robust. Human-crafted software was brittle and inflexible; his Phites had been forged in the heat of change.

Daniel kept a close watch on his competitors, but nothing he saw gave him reason to doubt his approach. Sunil Gupta was raking in the cash from a search engine that could 'understand' all forms of text, audio and video, making use of fuzzy logic techniques that were at least forty years old. Daniel respected Gupta's business acumen, but in the unlikely event that his software ever became conscious, the sheer cruelty of having forced it to wade through the endless tides of blogorrhoea would surely see it turn on its creator and exact a revenge that made *The Terminator* look like a picnic. Angela Lindstrom was having some success with her cheesy AfterLife, in which dying clients gave heart-to-heart interviews to software that then constructed avatars able to converse with surviving relatives. And Julie Dehghani was still frittering away her talent, writing software for robots that played with coloured blocks side by side with human infants and learnt languages from adult volunteers by imitating the interactions of baby talk. Her prophecy of taking a thousand years to 'get it right' seemed to be on target.

As the second year of the project drew to a close, Lucien was contacting Daniel once or twice a month to announce a new breakthrough. By constructing environments that imposed suitable selection pressures, Lucien had generated a succession of new species that used simple tools, crafted crude shelters and even domesticated plants. They were still shaped more or less like crabs, but they were at least as intelligent as chimpanzees.

The Phites worked together by observation and imitation, guiding and reprimanding each other with a limited repertoire of gestures and cries, but as yet they lacked anything that could truly be called a language. Daniel grew impatient; to move beyond a handful of specialised skills, his creatures needed the power to map any object, any action, any prospect they might encounter in the world into their speech, and into their thoughts.

Daniel summoned Lucien and they sought a way forward. It was easy to tweak the Phites' anatomy to grant them the ability to generate more subtle vocalisations, but that alone was no more useful than handing a chimp a conductor's baton. What was needed was a way to make sophisticated planning and communications skills a matter of survival.

Eventually, he and Lucien settled on a series of environmental modifications, providing opportunities for the creatures to rise to the occasion. Most of these scenarios began with famine. Lucien blighted the main food crops, then offered a palpable reward for progress by dangling some tempting new fruit from a branch that was just out of reach. Sometimes that metaphor could almost be taken literally: he'd introduce a plant with a complex life cycle that required tricky processing to render it edible, or a new prey animal that was clever and vicious, but nutritionally well worth hunting in the end.

Time and again, the Phites failed the test, with localised species dwindling to extinction. Daniel watched in dismay; he had not grown sentimental, but he'd always boasted to himself that he'd set his standards higher than the extravagant cruelties of nature. He contemplated tweaking the creatures' physiology so that starvation brought a swifter, more merciful demise, but Lucien pointed out that he'd be slashing his chances of success if he curtailed this period of intense motivation. Each time a group died out, a fresh batch of mutated cousins rose from the dust to take their place; without that intervention, Sapphire would have been a wilderness within a few realtime days.

Daniel closed his eyes to the carnage and put his trust in sheer time, sheer numbers. In the end, that was what the crystal had bought him: when all else failed, he could give up any pretence of knowing how to achieve his aims and simply test one random mutation after another.

Months went by, sending hundreds of millions of tribes starving into their graves. But what choice did he have? If he fed these creatures milk and honey, they'd remain fat and stupid until the day he died. Their hunger agitated them, it drove them to search and strive, and while any human onlooker was tempted to colour such behaviour with their own emotional palette, Daniel told himself that the Phites' suffering was a shallow thing, little more than the instinct that jerked his own hand back from a flame before he'd even registered discomfort.

They were not the equal of humans. Not yet.

And if he lost his nerve, they never would be.

Daniel dreamt that he was inside Sapphire, but there were no Phites in sight. In front of him stood a sleek black monolith; a thin stream of pus wept from a crack in its smooth obsidian surface. Someone was holding him by the wrist, trying to force his hand into a reeking pit in the ground. The pit, he knew, was piled high with things he did not want to see, let alone touch.

He thrashed around until he woke, but the sense of pressure on his wrist remained. It was coming from his watch. As he focused on the one-word message he'd received, his stomach tightened. Lucien would not have dared to wake him at this hour for some run-of-the-mill result.

Daniel rose, dressed, then sat in his office sipping coffee. He did not know why he was so reluctant to make the call. He had been waiting for this moment for more than twenty years, but it would not be the pinnacle of his life. After this, there would be a thousand more peaks, each one twice as magnificent as the last.

He finished the coffee then sat a while longer, massaging his temples, making sure his head was clear. He would not greet this new era bleary-eyed, half-awake. He recorded all his calls, but this was one he would retain for posterity.

'Lucien,' he said. The man's image appeared, smiling. 'Success?'

'They're talking to each other,' Lucien replied.

'About what?'

'Food, weather, sex, death. The past, the future. You name it. They won't shut up.'

Lucien sent transcripts on the data channel and Daniel perused them. The linguistics software didn't just observe the Phites' behaviour and correlate it with the sounds they made; it peered right into their virtual brains and tracked the flow of information. Its task was far from trivial, and there was no guarantee that its translations were perfect, but Daniel did not believe it could hallucinate an entire language and fabricate these rich, detailed conversations out of thin air.

He flicked between statistical summaries, technical overviews of linguistic structure and snippets from the millions of conversations the software had logged. *Food, weather, sex, death.* As human dialogue the translations would have seemed utterly banal, but in context they were riveting. These were not chatterbots blindly following Markov chains, designed to impress the judges in a Turing test. The Phites were discussing matters by which they genuinely lived and died.

When Daniel brought up a page of conversational topics in alphabetical order, his eyes were caught by the single entry under the letter G. *Grief.* He tapped the link, and spent a few minutes reading through samples, illustrating the appearance of the concept following the death of a child, a parent, a friend.

He kneaded his eyelids. It was three in the morning; there was a sickening clarity to everything, the kind that only night could bring. He turned to Lucien.

'No more death.'

'Boss?' Lucien was startled.

'I want to make them immortal. Let them evolve culturally; let their ideas live and die. Let them modify their own brains, once they're smart enough; they can already tweak the rest of their anatomy.'

'Where will you put them all?' Lucien demanded.

'I can afford another crystal. Maybe two more.'

'That won't get you far. At the present birth rate—'

'We'll have to cut their fertility drastically, tapering it down to zero. After that, if they want to start reproducing again they'll really have to innovate.' They would need to learn about the outside world, and comprehend its alien physics well enough to design new hardware into which they could migrate.

Lucien scowled. 'How will we control them? How will we shape them? If we can't select the ones we want—'

Daniel said quietly, 'This is not up for discussion.' Whatever Julie Dehghani had thought of him, he was not a monster; if he believed that these creatures were as conscious as he was, he was not going to slaughter them like cattle – or stand by and let them die 'naturally', when the rules of this world were his to rewrite at will.

'We'll shape them through their memes,' he said. 'We'll kill off the bad memes, and help spread the ones we want to succeed.' He would need to keep an iron grip on the Phites and their culture, though, or he would never be able to trust them. If he wasn't going to literally *breed them* for loyalty and gratitude, he would have to do the same with their ideas.

Lucien said, 'We're not prepared for any of this. We're going to need new software, new analysis and intervention tools.'

Daniel understood. 'Freeze time in Sapphire. Then tell the team they've got eighteen months.'

4

Daniel sold his shares in WiddulHands, and had two more crystals built. One was to support a higher population in Sapphire, so there was as large a pool of diversity among the immortal Phites as possible; the other was to run the software – which Lucien had dubbed the Thought Police – needed to keep tabs on what they were doing. If human overseers had had to monitor and shape the evolving culture every step of the way, that would have slowed things down to a glacial pace. Still, automating the process completely was tricky, and Daniel preferred to err on the side of caution, with the Thought Police freezing Sapphire and notifying him whenever the situation became too delicate.

If the end of death was greeted by the Phites with a mixture of puzzlement and rejoicing, the end of birth was not so easy to accept. When all attempts by mating couples to sculpt their excess beads into offspring became as ineffectual as shaping dolls out of clay, it led to a mixture of persistence and distress that was painful to witness. Humans were accustomed to failing to conceive, but this was more like still-birth after still-birth. Even when Daniel intervened to modify the Phites' basic drives, some kind of cultural or emotional inertia kept many of them going through the motions. Though their new instincts urged them merely to pool their spare beads and then stop, sated, they would continue with the old version of the act regardless, forlorn and confused, trying to shape the useless puddle into something that lived and breathed.

Move on, Daniel thought. *Get over it.* There was only so much sympathy he could muster for immortal beings who would fill the galaxy with their children, if they ever got their act together.

The Phites didn't yet have writing, but they'd developed a strong oral tradition, and some put their mourning for the old ways into elegiac words. The Thought Police identified those memes, and ensured that they didn't spread far. Some Phites chose to kill themselves rather than live in the barren new world.

Daniel felt he had no right to stop them, but mysterious obstacles blocked the paths of anyone who tried, irresponsibly, to romanticise or encourage such acts.

The Phites could only die by their own volition, but those who retained the will to live were not free to doze the centuries away. Daniel decreed no more terrible famines, but he hadn't abolished hunger itself, and he kept enough pressure on the food supply and other resources to force the Phites to keep innovating, refining agriculture, developing trade.

The Thought Police identified and nurtured the seeds of writing, mathematics and natural science. The physics of Sapphire was a simplified, game-world model, not so arbitrary as to be incoherent, but not so deep and complex that you needed particle physics to get to the bottom of it. As crystal time sped forward and the immortals sought solace in understanding their world, Sapphire soon had its Euclid and Archimedes, its Galileo and its Newton; their ideas spread with supernatural efficiency, bringing forth a torrent of mathematicians and astronomers.

Sapphire's stars were just a planetarium-like backdrop, present only to help the Phites get their notions of heliocentricity and inertia right, but its moon was as real as the world itself. The technology needed to reach it was going to take a while, but that was all right; Daniel didn't want them getting ahead of themselves. There was a surprise waiting for them there, and his preference was for a flourishing of biotech and computing before they faced that revelation.

Between the absence of fossils, Sapphire's limited biodiversity and all the clunky external meddling that needed to be covered up, it was hard for the Phites to reach a grand Darwinian view of biology, but their innate skill with beads gave them a head start in the practical arts. With a little nudging, they began tinkering with their bodies, correcting some inconvenient anatomical quirks that they'd missed in their pre-conscious phase.

As they refined their knowledge and techniques, Daniel let them imagine that they were working towards restoring fertility; after all, that was perfectly true, even if their goal was a few conceptual revolutions further away than they realised. Humans had had their naïve notions of a Philosopher's Stone dashed, but they'd still achieved nuclear transmutation in the end.

The Phites, he hoped, would transmute *themselves*: inspect their own brains, make sense of them, and begin to improve them. It was a staggering task to expect of anyone; even Lucien and his team, with their God's-eye view of the creatures, couldn't come close. But when the crystal was running at full speed, the Phites could think millions of times faster than their creators. If Daniel could keep them from straying off course, everything that humanity might once have conceived of as the fruits of millennia of progress was now just a matter of months away.

5

Lucien said, 'We're losing track of the language.'

Daniel was in his Houston office; he'd come to Texas for a series of face-to-face meetings, to see if he could raise some much-needed cash by licensing the crystal fabrication process. He would have preferred to keep the technology to himself, but he was almost certain that he was too far ahead of his rivals now for any of them to stand a chance of catching up with him.

'What do you mean, losing track?' Daniel demanded. Lucien had briefed him just three hours before, and given no warning of an impending crisis.

The Thought Police, Lucien explained, had done their job well: they had pushed the neural self-modification meme for all it was worth, and now a successful form of 'brain boosting' was spreading across Sapphire. It required a detailed 'recipe' but no technological aids; the same innate skills for observing and manipulating beads that the Phites had used to copy themselves during reproduction were enough.

All of this was much as Daniel had hoped it would be, but there was an alarming downside. The boosted Phites were adopting a dense and complex new language, and the analysis software couldn't make sense of it.

'Slow them down further,' Daniel suggested. 'Give the linguistics more time to run.'

'I've already frozen Sapphire,' Lucien replied. 'The linguistics have been running for an hour, with the full resources of an entire crystal.'

Daniel said irritably, 'We can see exactly what they've done to their brains. How can we not understand the effects on the language?'

'In the general case,' Lucien said, 'deducing a language from nothing but neural anatomy is computationally intractable. With the old language, we were lucky; it had a simple structure, and it was highly correlated with obvious behavioural elements. The new language is much more abstract and conceptual. We might not even have our own correlates for half the concepts.'

Daniel had no intention of letting events in Sapphire slip out of his control. It was one thing to hope that the Phites would, eventually, be juggling real-world physics that was temporarily beyond his comprehension, but any bright ten-year-old could grasp the laws of their present universe, and their technology was still far from rocket science.

He said, 'Keep Sapphire frozen and study your records of the Phites who first performed this boost. If they understood what they were doing, we can work it out too.'

At the end of the week, Daniel signed the licensing deal and flew back to San Francisco. Lucien briefed him daily, and at Daniel's urging hired a dozen new computational linguists to help with the problem.

After six months, it was clear that they were getting nowhere. The Phites who'd invented the boost had had one big advantage as they'd tinkered with each other's brains: it had not been a purely theoretical exercise for them. They hadn't gazed at anatomical diagrams and then reasoned their way to a better design. They had *experienced* the effects of thousands of small experimental changes, and the results had shaped their intuition for the process. Very little of that intuition had been spoken aloud, let alone written down and formalised. And the process of decoding those insights from a purely structural view of their brains was every bit as difficult as decoding the language itself.

Daniel couldn't wait any longer. With the crystal heading for the market, and other comparable technologies approaching fruition, he couldn't allow his lead to melt away.

'We need the Phites themselves to act as translators,' he told Lucien. 'We need to contrive a situation where there's a large enough pool who choose not to be boosted that the old language continues to be used.'

'So we need maybe twenty-five per cent refusing the boost?' Lucien suggested. 'And we need the boosted Phites to want to keep them informed of what's happening, in terms that we can all understand.'

Daniel said, 'Exactly.'

'I think we can slow down the uptake of boosting,' Lucien mused, 'while we encourage a traditionalist meme that says it's better to span the two cultures and languages than replace the old entirely with the new.'

Lucien's team set to work, tweaking the Thought Police for the new task, then restarting Sapphire itself.

Their efforts seemed to yield the desired result: the Phites were corralled into valuing the notion of maintaining a link to their past, and while the boosted Phites surged ahead, they also worked hard to keep the unboosted in the loop.

It was a messy compromise, though, and Daniel wasn't happy with the prospect of making do with a watered-down, Sapphire-for-Dummies version of the Phites' intellectual achievements. What he really wanted was someone on the inside reporting to him directly, like a Phite version of Lucien.

It was time to start thinking about job interviews.

Lucien was running Sapphire more slowly than usual – to give the Thought Police a computational advantage now that they'd lost so much raw surveillance data – but even at the reduced rate, it took just six realtime days for the boosted Phites to invent computers, first as a mathematical formalism and, shortly afterwards, as a succession of practical machines.

Daniel had already asked Lucien to notify him if any Phite guessed the true nature of their world. In the past, a few had come up with vague metaphysical speculations that weren't too wide of the mark, but now that they had a firm grasp of the idea of universal computation, they were finally in a position to understand the crystal as more than an idle fantasy.

The message came just after midnight, as Daniel was preparing for bed. He went into his office and activated the intervention tool that Lucien had written for him, specifying a serial number for the Phite in question.

The tool prompted Daniel to provide a human-style name for his interlocutor, to facilitate communication. Daniel's mind went blank, but after waiting twenty seconds the software offered its own suggestion: Primo.

Primo was boosted, and he had recently built a computer of his own. Shortly afterwards, the Thought Police had heard him telling a couple of unboosted friends about an amusing possibility that had occurred to him.

Sapphire was slowed to a human pace, then Daniel took control of a Phite avatar and the tool contrived a meeting, arranging for the two of them to be alone in the shelter that Primo had built for himself. In accordance with the current architectural style the wooden building was actually still alive, self-repairing and anchored to the ground by roots.

Primo said, 'Good morning. I don't believe we've met.'

It was no great breach of protocol for a stranger to enter one's shelter uninvited, but Primo was understating his surprise; in this world of immortals, but no passenger jets, bumping into strangers anywhere was rare.

'I'm Daniel.' The tool would invent a Phite name for Primo to hear. 'I heard you talking to your friends last night about your new computer. Wondering what these machines might do in the future. Wondering if they could ever grow powerful enough to contain a whole world.'

'I didn't see you there,' Primo replied.

'I wasn't there,' Daniel explained. 'I live outside this world. I built the computer that contains this world.'

Primo made a gesture that the tool annotated as amusement, then he spoke a few words in the boosted language. *Insults? A jest? A test of Daniel's omniscience?* Daniel decided to bluff his way through, and act as if the words were irrelevant.

He said, 'Let the rain start.' Rain began pounding on the roof of the shelter. 'Let the rain stop.' Daniel gestured with one claw at a large cooking pot in a corner of the room. 'Sand. Flower. Fire. Water jug.' The pot obliged him, taking on each form in turn.

Primo said, 'Very well. I believe you, Daniel.' Daniel had had some experience reading the Phites' body language directly, and to him Primo seemed reasonably calm. Perhaps when you were as old as he was, and had witnessed so much change, such a revelation was far less of a shock than it would have been to a human at the dawn of the computer age.

'You created this world?' Primo asked him.

'Yes.'

'You shaped our history?'

'In part,' Daniel said. 'Many things have been down to chance, or to your own choices.'

'Did you stop us having children?' Primo demanded.

'Yes,' Daniel admitted.

'Why?'

'There is no room left in the computer. It was either that, or many more deaths.'

Primo pondered this. 'So you could have stopped the death of my parents, had you wished?'

'I could bring them back to life, if you want that.' This wasn't a lie; Daniel had stored detailed snapshots of all the last mortal Phites. 'But not yet; only when there's a bigger computer. When there's room for them.'

'Could you bring back *their* parents? And their parents' parents? Back to the beginning of time?'

'No. That information is lost.'

Primo said, 'What is this talk of waiting for a bigger computer? You could easily stop time from passing for us, and only start it again when your new computer is built.'

'No,' Daniel said, 'I can't. Because *I need you to build the computer*. I'm not like you: I'm not immortal, and my brain can't be boosted. I've done my best, now I need you to do better. The only way that can happen is if you learn the science of my world, and come up with a way to make this new machine.'

Primo walked over to the water jug that Daniel had magicked into being. 'It seems to me that you were ill-prepared for the task you set yourself. If you'd waited for the machine you really needed, our lives would not have been so hard. And if such a machine could not be built in your lifetime, what was to stop your grandchildren from taking on that task?'

'I had no choice,' Daniel insisted. 'I couldn't leave your creation to my descendants. There is a war coming between my people. I needed your help. I needed strong allies.'

'You have no friends in your own world?'

'Your time runs faster than mine. I needed the kind of allies that only your people can become, in time.'

Primo said, 'What exactly do you want of us?'

'To build the new computer you need,' Daniel replied. 'To grow in numbers, to grow in strength. Then to raise me up, to make me greater than I was, as I've done for you. When the war is won, there will be peace for ever. Side by side, we will rule a thousand worlds.'

'And what do you want of *me*?' Primo asked. 'Why are you speaking to me, and not to all of us?'

'Most people,' Daniel said, 'aren't ready to hear this. It's better that they don't learn the truth yet. But I need one person who can work for me directly. I can see and hear everything in your world, but I need you to make sense of it. I need you to understand things for me.'

Primo was silent.

Daniel said, 'I gave you life. How can you refuse me?'

6

Daniel pushed his way through the small crowd of protesters gathered at the entrance to his San Francisco tower. He could have come and gone by helicopter instead, but his security consultants had assessed these people as posing no significant threat. A small amount of bad PR didn't bother him; he was no longer selling anything that the public could boycott directly, and none of the businesses he dealt with seemed worried about being tainted by association. He'd broken no laws, and confirmed no rumours. A few feral cyberphiles waving placards reading 'Software Is Not Your Slave!' meant nothing.

Still, if he ever found out which one of his employees had leaked details of the project, he'd break their legs.

Daniel was in the elevator when Lucien messaged him: MOON VERY SOON! He halted the elevator's ascent and redirected it to the basement.

All three crystals were housed in the basement now, just centimetres away from the Play Pen: a vacuum chamber containing an atomic force microscope with fifty thousand independently movable tips, arrays of solid-state lasers and photo detectors, and thousands of micro-wells stocked with samples of all the stable chemical elements. The timelag between Sapphire and this machine had to be as short as possible, in order for the Phites to be able to conduct experiments in real-world physics while their own world was running at full speed.

Daniel pulled up a stool and sat beside the Play Pen. If he wasn't going to slow Sapphire down, it was pointless aspiring to watch developments as they unfolded. He'd probably view a replay of the lunar landing when he went up to his office, but by the time he screened it, it would be ancient history.

'One giant leap' would be an understatement; wherever the

Phites landed on the moon, they would find a strange black monolith waiting for them. Inside would be the means to operate the Play Pen; it would not take them long to learn the controls, or to understand what this signified. If they were really slow in grasping what they'd found, Daniel had instructed Primo to explain it to them.

The physics of the real world was far more complex than the kind the Phites were used to, but then, no human had ever been on intimate terms with quantum field theory either, and the Thought Police had already encouraged the Phites to develop most of the mathematics they'd need to get started. In any case, it didn't matter if the Phites took longer than humans to discover twentieth-century scientific principles and move beyond them. Seen from the outside, it would happen within hours, days, weeks at the most.

A row of indicator lights blinked on; the Play Pen was active. Daniel's throat went dry. The Phites were finally reaching out of their own world into his.

A panel above the machine displayed histograms classifying the experiments the Phites had performed so far. By the time Daniel was paying attention, they had already discovered the kinds of bonds that could be formed between various atoms, and constructed thousands of different small molecules. As he watched, they carried out spectroscopic analyses, built simple nano-machines, and manufactured devices that were, unmistakably, memory elements and logic gates.

The Phites wanted children, and they understood now that this was the only way. They would soon be building a world in which they were not just more numerous, but faster and smarter than they were inside the crystal. And that would be only the first of a thousand iterations. They were working their way towards Godhood, and they would lift up their own creator as they ascended.

Daniel left the basement and headed for his office. When he arrived, he called Lucien.

'They've built an atomic-scale computer,' Lucien announced. 'And they've fed some fairly complex software into it. It doesn't seem to be an upload, though. Certainly not a direct copy on the level of beads.' He sounded flustered; Daniel had forbidden him to risk screwing up the experiments by slowing down Sapphire, so even with Primo's briefings to help him it was difficult for him to keep abreast of everything.

'Can you model their computer, and then model what the software is doing?' Daniel suggested.

Lucien said, 'We only have six atomic physicists on the team; the Phites already outnumber us on that score by about a thousand to one. By the time we have any hope of making sense of this, they'll be doing something different.'

'What does Primo say?' The Thought Police hadn't been able to get Primo included in any of the lunar expeditions, but Lucien had given him the power to make himself invisible and teleport to any part of Sapphire or the lunar base. Wherever the action was, he was free to eavesdrop.

'Primo has trouble understanding a lot of what he hears; even the boosted aren't universal polymaths and instant experts in every kind of jargon. The gist of it is that the Lunar Project people have made a very fast computer in the Outer World, and it's going to help with the fertility problem . . . somehow.' Lucien laughed. 'Hey, maybe the Phites will do exactly what we did: see if they can evolve something smart enough to give them a hand. How cool would that be?'

Daniel was not amused. Somebody had to do some real work eventually; if the Phites just passed the buck, the whole enterprise would collapse like a pyramid scheme.

Daniel had some business meetings he couldn't put off. By the time he'd swept all the bullshit aside, it was early afternoon. The Phites had now built some kind of tiny solid-state accelerator, and were probing the internal structure of protons and neutrons by pounding them with high-speed electrons. An atomic computer wired up to various detectors was doing the data analysis, processing the results faster than any in-world computer could. The Phites had already figured out the standard quark model. Maybe they were going to skip uploading into nanocomputers and head straight for some kind of femtomachine?

Digests of Primo's briefings made no mention of using the strong force for computing, though. They were still just satisfying their curiosity about the fundamental laws. Daniel reminded himself of their history. They had burrowed down to what seemed like the foundations of physics before, only to discover that those simple rules were nothing to do with the ultimate reality. It made sense that they would try to dig as deeply as they could into the mysteries of the Outer World before daring to found a colony, let alone emigrate *en masse*.

By sunset the Phites were probing the surroundings of the Play Pen with various kinds of radiation. The levels were extremely low – certainly too low to risk damaging the crystals – so Daniel saw no need to intervene. The Play Pen itself did not have a massive power supply, it contained no radioisotopes, and the Thought Police would ring alarm bells and bring in human experts if some kind of tabletop fusion experiment got under way, so Daniel was reasonably confident that the Phites couldn't do anything stupid and blow the whole thing up.

Primo's briefings made it clear that they thought they were engaged in a kind of 'astronomy'. Daniel wondered if he should give them access to instruments for doing serious observations – the kind that would allow them to understand relativistic gravity and cosmology. Even if he bought time on a large telescope, though, just pointing it would take an eternity for the Phites. He wasn't going to slow Sapphire down and then grow old while they explored the sky; next thing they'd be launching space probes on thirty-year missions. Maybe it was time to ramp up the level of collaboration, and just hand them some astronomy texts and star maps? Human culture had its own hard-won achievements that the Phites couldn't easily match.

As the evening wore on, the Phites shifted their focus back to the subatomic world. A new kind of accelerator began smashing single gold ions together at extraordinary energies – though the total power being expended was still minuscule. Primo soon announced that they'd mapped all three generations of quarks and leptons. The Phites' knowledge of particle physics was drawing level with humanity's; Daniel couldn't follow the technical details any more, but the experts were giving it all the thumbs-up. Daniel felt a surge of pride; of course his children knew what they were doing, and if they'd reached the point where they could momentarily bamboozle him, soon he'd ask them to catch their breath and bring him up to speed. Before he permitted them to emigrate, he'd slow the crystals down and introduce himself to everyone. In fact, that might be the perfect time to set them their next task: to understand human biology, well enough to upload him. To make him immortal, to repay their debt.

He sat watching images of the Phites' latest computers, reconstructions based on data flowing to and from the AFM tips. Vast lattices of shimmering atoms stretched off into the distance, the electron clouds that joined them quivering like beads of mercury in some surreal liquid abacus. As he watched, an inset window told him that the ion accelerators had been redesigned and fired up again.

Daniel grew restless. He walked to the elevator. There was nothing he could see in the basement that he couldn't see from his office, but he wanted to stand beside the Play Pen, put his hand on the casing, press his nose against the glass. The era of Sapphire as a virtual world with no consequences in his own was coming to an end; he wanted to stand beside the thing itself and be reminded that it was as solid as he was.

The elevator descended, passing the tenth floor, the ninth, the eighth. Without warning, Lucien's voice burst from Daniel's watch, priority audio crashing through every barrier of privacy and protocol. 'Boss, there's radiation. Net power gain. Get to the helicopter, *now*.'

Daniel hesitated, contemplating an argument. If this was fusion, why hadn't it been detected and curtailed? He jabbed the stop button and felt the brakes engage. Then the world dissolved into brightness and pain.

7

When Daniel emerged from the opiate haze, a doctor informed him that he had burns to sixty per cent of his body. More from heat than from radiation. He was not going to die.

There was a net terminal by the bed. Daniel called Lucien and learnt what the physicists on the team had tentatively concluded, having studied the last of the Play Pen data that had made it off-site.

It seemed the Phites had discovered the Higgs field, and engineered a burst of something akin to cosmic inflation. What they'd done wasn't as simple as merely inflating a tiny patch of vacuum into a new universe, though. Not only had they managed to create a 'cool Big Bang', they had pulled a large chunk of ordinary matter into the pocket universe they'd made, after which the wormhole leading to it had shrunk to subatomic size and fallen through the Earth.

They had taken the crystals with them, of course. If they'd tried to upload themselves into the pocket universe through the lunar data link, the Thought Police would have stopped them. So they'd emigrated by another route entirely. They had snatched their whole substrate and run.

Opinions were divided over exactly what else the new universe would contain. The crystals and the Play Pen floating in a void, with no power source, would leave the Phites effectively dead, but some of the team believed there could be a thin plasma of protons and electrons too, created by a form of Higgs decay that bypassed the unendurable quark-gluon fireball of a hot Big Bang. If they'd built the right nanomachines, there was a chance that they could convert the Play Pen into a structure that would keep the crystals safe, while the Phites slept through the long wait for the first starlight.

The tiny skin samples the doctors had taken finally grew into sheets large enough to graft. Daniel bounced between dark waves of pain and medicated euphoria, but one idea stayed with him throughout the turbulent journey, like a guiding star: *Primo had betrayed him.* He had given the fucker life, entrusted him with power, granted him privileged knowledge, showered him with the favours of the Gods. And how had he been repaid? He was back to zero. He'd spoken to his lawyers; having heard rumours of an 'illegal radiation source', the insurance company was not going to pay out on the crystals without a fight.

Lucien came to the hospital, in person. Daniel was moved; they hadn't met face to face since the job interview. He shook the man's hand.

'You didn't betray me.'

Lucien looked embarrassed. 'I'm resigning, boss.'

Daniel was stung, but he forced himself to accept the news stoically. 'I understand; you have no choice. Gupta will have a crystal of his own by now. You have to be on the winning side, in the war of the Gods.'

Lucien put his resignation letter on the bedside table. 'What war? Are you still clinging to that fantasy where überdorks battle to turn the moon into computronium?'

Daniel blinked. 'Fantasy? If you didn't believe it, why were you working with me?'

'You paid me. Extremely well.'

'So how much will Gupta be paying you? I'll double it.'

Lucien shook his head, amused. 'I'm not going to work for Gupta. I'm moving into particle physics. The Phites weren't all that far ahead of us when they escaped; maybe forty or fifty years. Once we catch up, I guess a private universe will cost about as much as a private island; maybe less in the long run. But no one's going to be battling for control of this one, throwing grey goo around like monkeys flinging turds while they draw up their plans for Matrioshka brains.'

Daniel said, 'If you take any data from the Play Pen logs—'

'I'll honour all the confidentiality clauses in my contract.' Lucien smiled. 'But anyone can take an interest in the Higgs field; that's public domain.'

After he left, Daniel bribed the nurse to crank up his medication, until even the sting of betrayal and disappointment began to fade.

A universe, he thought happily. *Soon I'll have a universe of my own.*

But I'm going to need some workers in there, some allies, some companions. I can't do it all alone; someone has to carry the load.

STEVE FEVER

1

A few weeks after his fourteenth birthday, with the soya bean harvest fast approaching, Lincoln began having vivid dreams of leaving the farm and heading for the city. Night after night he pictured himself gathering supplies, trudging down to the highway and hitching his way to Atlanta.

There were problems with the way things got done in the dream, though, and each night in his sleep he struggled to resolve them. The larder would be locked, of course, so he dreamt up a side plot about collecting a stash of suitable tools for breaking in. There were sensors all along the farm's perimeter, so he dreamt about different ways of avoiding or disabling them.

Even when he had a scenario that seemed to make sense, daylight revealed further flaws. The grille that blocked the covered part of the irrigation ditch that ran beneath the fence was too strong to be snipped away with bolt-cutters, and the welding torch had a biometric lock.

When the harvest began, Lincoln contrived to get a large stone caught in the combine, and then volunteered to repair the damage. With his father looking on, he did a meticulous job, and when he received the expected praise he replied with what he hoped was a dignified mixture of pride and bemusement, 'I'm not a kid any more. I can handle the torch.'

'Yeah.' His father seemed embarrassed for a moment, then he

squatted down, put the torch into supervisor mode and added Lincoln's touch to the authorised list.

Lincoln waited for a moonless night. The dream kept repeating itself, thrashing impatiently against his skull, desperate to be made real.

When the night arrived and he left his room, barefoot in the darkness, he felt as if he was finally enacting some long-rehearsed performance: less a play than an elaborate dance that had seeped into every muscle in his body. First, he carried his boots to the back door and left them by the step. Then he took his backpack to the larder, the borrowed tools in different pockets so they wouldn't clank against each other. The larder door's hinges were attached on the inside, but he'd marked their positions with penknife scratches in the varnish that he'd practised finding by touch. His mother had secured the food store years before, after a midnight raid by Lincoln and his younger brother, Sam, but it was still just a larder, not a jewel-safe, and the awl bit through the wood easily enough, finally exposing the tip of one of the screws that held the hinges in place. The pliers he tried first couldn't grip the screw tightly enough to get it turning, but Lincoln had dreamt of an alternative. With the awl, he cleared away a little more wood, then he jammed a small hexagonal nut onto the screw's thread and used a T-handled socket wrench to turn them together. The screw couldn't move far, but this was enough to loosen it. He removed the nut and used the pliers, then with a few firm taps from a hammer, delivered via the socket wrench, the screw broke free of the wood.

He repeated the procedure five more times, freeing the hinges completely, then he strained against the door, keeping a firm grip on the handle, until the tongue of the lock slipped from its groove.

The larder was pitch-black, but he didn't risk using his flash-light; he found what he wanted by memory and touch, filling the backpack with enough provisions for a week. *After that?* He'd never wondered, in the dream. Maybe he'd find new friends in

Atlanta who'd help him. The idea struck a chord, as if it was a truth he was remembering, not a hopeful speculation.

The tool shed was locked securely, but Lincoln was still skinny enough to crawl through the hole in the back wall, hidden by junk for so long that it had fallen off the end of his father's repair list. This time he risked the flashlight and walked straight to the welding torch, rather than groping his way across the darkness. He manoeuvred it through the hole, and didn't bother rearranging the rotting timbers that had concealed the entrance. There was no point covering his tracks. He would be missed within minutes of his parents rising, no matter what, so the important thing now was speed.

He put on his boots and headed for the irrigation ditch. Their German shepherd, Melville, trotted up and started licking Lincoln's hand. Lincoln stopped and petted him for a few seconds, then firmly ordered him back towards the house. The dog made a soft wistful sound, but complied.

Twenty metres from the perimeter fence, Lincoln climbed into the ditch. The enclosed section was still a few metres away, but he crouched down immediately, practising the necessary constrained gait and shielding himself from the sensors' gaze. He clutched the torch under one arm, careful to keep it dry. The chill of the water didn't much bother him; his boots grew heavy, but he didn't know what the ditch concealed, and he'd rather have waterlogged boots than a rusty scrap of metal slicing his foot.

He entered the enclosed, concrete cylinder, then a few steps brought him to the metal grille. He switched on the torch and oriented himself by the light of its control panel. When he put on the goggles he was blind, but then he squeezed the trigger of the torch and the arc lit up the tunnel around him.

Each bar took just seconds to cut, but there were a lot of them. In the confined space the heat was oppressive; his T-shirt was soon soaked with sweat. Still, he had fresh clothes in his pack, and he could wash in the ditch once he was through. If he was still not respectable enough to get a ride, he'd walk to Atlanta.

'Young man, get out of there immediately.'

Lincoln shut off the arc. The voice, and those words, could only belong to his grandmother. For a few pounding heartbeats, he wondered if he'd imagined it, but then in the same unmistakable tone, ratcheted up a notch, she added, 'Don't play games with me, I don't have the patience for it.'

Lincoln slumped in the darkness, disbelieving. He'd dreamt his way through every detail, past every obstacle. How could she appear out of nowhere and ruin everything?

There wasn't room to turn around, so he crawled backwards to the mouth of the tunnel. His grandmother was standing on the bank of the ditch.

'What exactly do you think you're doing?' she demanded.

He said, 'I need to get to Atlanta.'

'Atlanta? All by yourself, in the middle of the night? What happened? You got a craving for some special kind of food we're not providing here?'

Lincoln scowled at her sarcasm, but knew better than to answer back. 'I've been dreaming about it,' he said, as if that explained everything. 'Night after night. Working out the best way to do it.'

His grandmother said nothing for a while, and when Lincoln realised that he'd shocked her into silence he felt a pang of fear himself.

She said, 'You have no earthly reason to run away. Is someone beating you? Is someone treating you badly?'

'No, ma'am.'

'So *why exactly is it* that you need to go?'

Lincoln felt his face grow hot with shame. How could he have missed it? How could he have fooled himself into believing that the obsession was his own? But even as he berated himself for his stupidity, his longing for the journey remained.

'You've got the fever, haven't you? You know where those kind of dreams come from: nanospam throwing a party in your brain. Ten billion idiot robots playing a game called *Steve At Home*.'

She reached down and helped him out of the ditch. The

113

thought crossed Lincoln's mind that he could probably over-power her, but then he recoiled from the idea in disgust. He sat down on the grass and put his head in his hands.

'Are you going to lock me up?' he asked.

'Nobody's turning anybody into a prisoner. Let's go talk to your parents. They're going to be thrilled.'

The four of them sat in the kitchen. Lincoln kept quiet and let the others argue, too ashamed to offer any opinions of his own. How could he have let himself sleepwalk like that? Plotting and scheming for weeks, growing ever prouder of his own ingenuity, but doing it all at the bidding of the world's stupidest, most despised dead man.

He still yearned to go to Atlanta. He itched to bolt from the room, scale the fence, and jog all the way to the highway. He could see the whole sequence in his mind's eye; he was already thinking through the flaws in the plan and hunting for ways to correct them.

He banged his head against the table. 'Make it stop! Get them out of me!'

His mother put an arm around his shoulders. 'You know we can't wave a magic wand and get rid of them. You've got the latest counterware. All we can do is send a sample to be analysed, do our bit to speed the process along.'

The cure could be months away, or years. Lincoln moaned pitifully. 'Then lock me up! Put me in the basement!'

His father wiped a glistening streak of sweat from his forehead. 'That's not going to happen. If I have to be beside you everywhere you go, we're still going to treat you like a human being.' His voice was strained, caught somewhere between fear and defiance.

Silence descended. Lincoln closed his eyes. Then his grand-mother spoke. 'Maybe the best way to deal with this is to let him scratch his damned itch.'

'What?' His father was incredulous.

'He wants to go to Atlanta. I can go with him.'

'*The Stevelets* want him in Atlanta,' his father replied.

'They're not going to harm him, they just want to borrow him.

And like it or not, they've already done that. Maybe the quickest way to get them to move on is to satisfy them.'

Lincoln's father said, 'You know they can't be satisfied.'

'Not completely. But every path they take has its dead end, and the sooner they find this one, the sooner they'll stop bothering him.'

His mother said, 'If we keep him here, that's a dead end for them too. If they want him in Atlanta, and he's not in Atlanta—'

'They won't give up that easily,' his grandmother replied. 'If we're not going to lock him up and throw away the key, they're not going to take a few setbacks and delays as some kind of proof that Atlanta's beyond all hope.'

Silence again. Lincoln opened his eyes. His father addressed Lincoln's grandmother. 'Are you sure you're not infected yourself?'

She rolled her eyes. 'Don't go all Body Snatchers on me, Carl. I know the two of you can't leave the farm right now. So if you want to let him go, I'll look after him.' She shrugged and turned her head away imperiously. 'I've said my piece. Now it's your decision.'

2

Lincoln drove the truck as far as the highway, then reluctantly let his grandmother take the wheel. He loved the old machine, which still had the engine his grandfather had installed, years before Lincoln was born, to run on their home-pressed soya bean oil.

'I plan to take the most direct route,' his grandmother announced. 'Through Macon. Assuming your friends have no objection.'

Lincoln squirmed. 'Don't call them that!'

'I'm sorry.' She glanced at him sideways. 'But I still need to know.'

Reluctantly, Lincoln forced himself to picture the drive ahead, and he felt a surge of *rightness* endorsing the plan. 'No problem with that,' he muttered. He was under no illusion that he could prevent the Stevelets from influencing his thoughts, but deliberately consulting them, as if there was a third person sitting in the cabin between them, made him feel much worse.

He turned to look out the window at the abandoned fields and silos passing by. He had been down this stretch of highway a hundred times, but each piece of blackened machinery now carried a disturbing new poignancy. The Crash had come thirty years ago, but it still wasn't truly over. The Stevelets aspired to do no harm – and supposedly they got better at that year by year – but they were still far too stupid and stubborn to be relied upon to get anything right. They had just robbed his parents of two skilled pairs of hands in the middle of the harvest; how could they imagine that that was harmless? Millions of people around the world had died in the Crash, and that couldn't all be blamed on panic and self-inflicted casualties. The government had been crazy, bombing half the farms in the south-east; everyone agreed now that it had only made things worse. But many other deaths could not have been avoided, except by the actions of the Stevelets themselves.

You couldn't reason with them, though. You couldn't shame them, or punish them. You just had to hope they got better at noticing when they were screwing things up, while they forged ahead with their impossible task.

'See that old factory?' Lincoln's grandmother gestured at a burnt-out metal frame drooping over slabs of cracked concrete, standing in a field of weeds. 'There was a conclave there, almost twenty years ago.'

Lincoln had been past the spot many times, and no one had ever mentioned this before. 'What happened? What did they try?'

'I heard it was meant to be a time machine. Some crackpot had put his plans on the net, and the Stevelets decided they had to check it out. About a hundred people were working there, and thousands of animals.'

Lincoln shivered. 'How long were they at it?'

'Three years.' She added quickly, 'But they've learnt to rotate the workers now. It's rare for them to hang on to any individual for more than a month or two.'

A month or two. A part of Lincoln recoiled, but another part thought: that wouldn't be so bad. A break from the farm, doing something different. Meeting new people, learning new skills, working with animals.

Rats, most likely.

Steve Hasluck had been part of a team of scientists developing a new kind of medical nanomachine, refining the tiny surgical instruments so they could make decisions of their own, on the spot. Steve's team had developed an efficient way of sharing computing power across a whole swarm, allowing them to run large, complex programs known as 'expert systems' that codified decades of biological and clinical knowledge into pragmatic lists of rules. The nanomachines didn't really 'know' anything, but they could churn through a very long list of 'if A and B, there's an eighty per cent chance of C' at blistering speed, and a good list gave them a good chance of cutting a lot of diseases off short.

Then Steve found out that he had cancer, and that his particular kind wasn't on anyone's list of rules.

He took a batch of the nanomachines and injected them into a room full of caged rats, along with samples of his tumour. The nanomachines could swarm all over the tumour cells, monitoring their actions constantly. The polymer radio antennas they built beneath the rats' skin let them share their observations and hunches from host to host, like their own high-speed wireless internet, as well as reporting their findings back to Steve himself. With that much information being gathered, how hard could it be to understand the problem, and fix it? But Steve and his colleagues couldn't make sense of the data. Steve got sicker, and all the gigabytes pouring out of the rats remained as useless as ever.

Steve tried putting new software into the swarms. If nobody knew how to cure his disease, why not let the swarms work it out? He gave them access to vast clinical databases and told them to extract their own rules. When the cure still failed to appear, he bolted on more software, including expert systems seeded with basic knowledge of chemistry and physics. From this starting point, the swarms worked out things about cell membranes and protein folding that no one had ever realised before, but none of it helped Steve.

Steve decided that the swarms still had too narrow a view. He gave them a general-purpose knowledge acquisition engine and let them drink at will from the entire web. To guide their browsing and their self-refinement, he gave them two clear goals. The first was to do no harm to their hosts. The second was to find a way to save his life, and failing that, to bring him back from the dead.

That last rider might not have been entirely crazy, because Steve had arranged to have his body preserved in liquid nitrogen. If that had happened, maybe the Stevelets would have spent the next thirty years ferrying memories out of his frozen brain. Unfortunately, Steve's car hit a tree at high speed just outside of Austin, Texas, and his brain ended up as flambé.

This made the news, and the Stevelets were watching. Between their lessons from the web and whatever instincts their creator had given them, they figured out that they were now likely to be incinerated themselves. That wouldn't have mattered to them, if not for the fact that they'd decided that the game wasn't over. There'd been nothing about resurrecting charred flesh in the online medical journals, but the web embraced a wider range of opinions. The swarms had read the sites of various groups who were convinced that self-modifying software could find ways to make itself smarter, and then smarter again, until nothing was beyond its reach. Resurrecting the dead was right there on every bullet-pointed menu of miracles.

The Stevelets knew that they couldn't achieve anything as a plume of smoke wafting out of a rat crematorium, so the first thing they engineered was a break-out. From the cages, from the building, from the city. The original nanomachines couldn't replicate themselves, and could be destroyed in an instant by a simple chemical trigger, but somewhere in the sewers or the fields or the silos, they had inspected and dissected each other to the point where they were able to reproduce. They took the opportunity to alter some old traits: the new generation of Stevelets lacked the suicide switch, and resisted external meddling with their software.

They might have vanished into the woods to build scarecrow Steves out of sticks and leaves, but their software roots gave their task rigour, of a kind. From the net, they had taken ten thousand crazy ideas about the world, and though they lacked the sense to see that they were crazy, they couldn't simply take anything on faith either. They had to test these claims, one by one, as they groped their way towards Stevescence. And while the web had suggested that with their power to self-modify they could achieve anything, they found that in reality there were countless crucial tasks which remained beyond their abilities. Even with the aid of dextrous mutant rats, Steveware Version 2 was never going to re-engineer the fabric of spacetime, or resurrect Steve in a virtual world.

Within months of their escape, it must have become clear to them that some hurdles could only be jumped with human assistance, because that was when they started borrowing people: doing them no physical harm, but infesting them with the kinds of ideas and compulsions that turned them into willing recruits.

The panic, the bombings, the Crash had followed. Lincoln hadn't witnessed the worst of it. He hadn't seen conclaves of harmless sleepwalkers burnt to death by mobs, or fields of grain napalmed by the government, lest they feed and shelter nests of rats.

Over the decades, the war had become more subtle. Counterware could keep the Stevelets at bay, for a while. The experts kept trying to subvert the Steveware, spreading modified Stevelets packed with propositions that aimed to cripple the swarms' ability to function, or, more ambitiously, make them believe that their job was done. In response, the Steveware had developed verification and encryption schemes that made it ever harder to corrupt or mislead. Some people still advocated cloning Steve from surviving pathology samples, but most experts doubted that the Steveware would be satisfied with that, or taken in by any misinformation that made the clone look like something more.

The Stevelets aspired to the impossible, and would accept no substitutes, while humanity longed to be left unmolested, to get on with more useful tasks. Lincoln had known no other world, but until now he'd viewed the struggle from the sidelines, save shooting the odd rat and queuing up for his counterware shots.

So what was his role now? Traitor? Double agent? Prisoner of war? People talked about sleepwalkers and zombies, but in truth there was still no right word for what he had become.

3

Late in the afternoon, as they approached Atlanta, Lincoln felt his sense of the city's geography warping, the significance of familiar landmarks shifting. *New information coming through.* He ran one hand over each of his forearms, where he'd heard the antennas often grew, but the polymer was probably too soft to feel beneath the skin. His parents could have wrapped his body in foil to mess with reception, and put him in a tent full of bottled air to keep out any of the slower, chemical signals that the Stevelets also used, but none of that would have rid him of the basic urge.

As they passed the airport, then the tangle of overpasses where the highway from Macon merged with the one from Alabama, Lincoln couldn't stop thinking about the baseball stadium up ahead. Had the Stevelets commandeered the home of the Braves? That would have made the news, surely, and ramped the war up a notch or two.

'Next exit,' he said. He gave directions that were half his own, half flowing from an eerie dream logic, until they turned a corner and the place where he knew he had to be came into view. It wasn't the stadium itself; that had merely been the closest landmark in his head, a beacon the Stevelets had used to help guide him. 'They booked a whole motel!' his grandmother exclaimed.

'Bought,' Lincoln guessed, judging from the amount of visible construction work. The Steveware controlled vast financial assets, some flat-out stolen from sleepwalkers, but much of it honestly acquired by trading the products of the rat factories: everything from high-grade pharmaceuticals to immaculately faked designer shoes.

The original parking lot was full, but there were signs showing the way to an overflow area near what had once been the pool. As they headed for reception, Lincoln's thoughts drifted weirdly to the time they'd come to Atlanta for one of Sam's spelling competitions.

There were three uniformed government Stevologists in the lobby, seated at a small table with some equipment. Lincoln went to the reception desk first, where a smiling young woman handed him two room keys before he'd had a chance to say a word. 'Enjoy the conclave,' she said. He didn't know if she was a zombie like him, or a former motel employee who'd been kept on, but she didn't need to ask him anything.

The government people took longer to deal with. His grandmother sighed as they worked their way through a questionnaire, then a woman called Dana took Lincoln's blood. 'They usually try to hide,' Dana said, 'but sometimes your counterware can bring us useful fragments, even when it can't stop the infection.'

As they ate their evening meal in the motel dining room, Lincoln tried meeting the eyes of the people around him. Some looked away nervously; others offered him encouraging smiles. He didn't feel as if he was being inducted into a cult, and that was not just from the lack of pamphlets or speeches. He hadn't been brainwashed into worshipping Steve; his opinion of the dead man was entirely unchanged. Like the desire to reach Atlanta in the first place, his task here would be far more focused and specific. To the Steveware he was a kind of machine, a machine it could instruct and tinker with the way Lincoln could control and customise his phone, but the Steveware no more expected him to share its final goal than he expected his own machines to enjoy his music, or respect his friends.

Lincoln knew that he dreamt that night, but when he woke he had trouble remembering the dream. He knocked on his grandmother's door; she'd been up for hours. 'I can't sleep in this place,' she complained. 'It's quieter than the farm.'

She was right, Lincoln realised. They were close to the highway, but traffic noise, music, sirens, all the usual city sounds, barely reached them.

They went down to breakfast. When they'd eaten, Lincoln was at a loss to know what to do. He went to the reception desk; the same woman was there.

He didn't need to speak. She said, 'They're not quite ready for you, sir. Feel free to watch TV, take a walk, use the gym. You'll know when you're needed.'

He turned to his grandmother. 'Let's take a walk.'

They left the motel and walked around the stadium, then headed east away from the highway, ending up in a leafy park a few blocks away. All the people around them were doing ordinary things: pushing their kids on swings, playing with their dogs. Lincoln's grandmother said, 'If you want to change your mind, we can always go home.'

As if his mind were his own to change. Still, at this moment the compulsion that had brought him here seemed to have waned. He didn't know if the Steveware had taken its eyes off him, or whether it was deliberately offering him a choice, a chance to back out.

He said, 'I'll stay.' He dreaded the idea of hitting the road only to find himself summoned back. Part of him was curious, too. He wanted to be brave enough to step inside the jaws of this whale, on the promise that he would be disgorged in the end.

They returned to the motel, ate lunch, watched TV, ate dinner. Lincoln checked his phone; his friends had been calling, wondering why he hadn't been in touch. He hadn't told anyone where he'd gone. He'd left it to his parents to explain everything to Sam.

He dreamt again, and woke clutching at fragments. Good times, an edge of danger, wide blue skies, the company of friends. It seemed more like a dream he could have had on his own than anything that might have come from the Steveware cramming his mind with equations so he could help test another crackpot idea that the swarms had collected thirty years ago by googling the physics of immortality.

Three more days passed, just as aimlessly. Lincoln began to wonder if he'd failed some test, or if there'd been a miscalculation leading to a glut of zombies.

Early in the morning of their fifth day in Atlanta, as Lincoln splashed water on his face in the bathroom, he felt the change. Shards of his recurrent dream glistened potently in the back of his mind, while a set of directions through the motel complex gelled in the foreground. He was being summoned. It was all he could do to bang on his grandmother's door and shout out a garbled explanation, before he set off down the corridor.

She caught up with him. 'Are you sleepwalking? Lincoln?'

'I'm still here, but they're taking me soon.'

She looked frightened. He grasped her hand and squeezed it. 'Don't worry,' he said. He'd always imagined that when the time came he'd be the one who was afraid, drawing his courage from her.

He turned a corner and saw the corridor leading into a large space that might once have been a room for conferences or weddings. Half a dozen people were standing around; Lincoln could tell that the three teenagers were fellow zombies, while the adults were just there to look out for them. The room had no furniture, but contained an odd collection of items, including four ladders and four bicycles. There was cladding on the walls, *soundproofing*, as if the whole building wasn't quiet enough already.

Out of the corner of his eye, Lincoln saw a dark mass of

quivering fur: a swarm of rats, huddled against the wall. For a moment his skin crawled, but then a heady sense of exhilaration swept his revulsion away. His own body held only the tiniest fragment of the Steveware; at last he could confront the thing itself.

He turned towards the rats and spread his arms. 'You called, and I came running. So what is it you want?' Disquietingly, memories of the Pied Piper story drifted into his head. Irresistible music lured the rats away. Then it lured away the children.

The rats gave him no answer, but the room vanished.

4

Ty hit a patch of dust on the edge of the road and it rose up around him. He whooped with joy and pedalled twice as hard, streaking ahead to leave his friends immersed in the cloud.

Errol caught up with him and reached across to punch him on the arm, as if he'd raised the dust on purpose. It was a light blow, not enough to be worth retribution; Ty just grinned at him.

It was a school day, but they'd all sneaked off together before lessons began. They couldn't do anything in town, there were too many people who'd know them, but then Dan had suggested heading for the water tower. His father had some spray-paint in the shed. They'd climb the tower and tag it.

There was a barbed-wire fence around the base of the tower, but Dan had already been out here at the weekend and started a tunnel, which didn't take them long to complete. When they were through, Ty looked up and felt his head swimming. Carlos said, 'We should have brought a rope.'

'We'll be okay.'

Chris said, 'I'll go first.'

'Why?' Dan demanded.

Chris took his fancy new phone from his pocket and waved it at them. 'Best camera angle. I don't want to be looking up your ass.'

Carlos said, 'Just promise you won't put it on the web. If my parents see this, I'm screwed.'

Chris laughed. 'Mine too. I'm not that stupid.'

'Yeah, well, you won't be on camera if you're holding the thing.'

Chris started up the ladder, then Dan went next, with one paint can in the back pocket of his jeans. Ty followed, then Errol and Carlos.

The air had been still down on the ground, but as they went higher a breeze came out of nowhere, cooling the sweat on Ty's back. The ladder started shuddering; he could see where it was bolted securely to the concrete of the tower, but in between it could still flex alarmingly. He'd treat it like a fairground ride, he decided: a little scary, but probably safe.

When Chris reached the top, Dan let go of the ladder with one hand, took the paint can, and reached out sideways into the expanse of white concrete. He quickly shaped a blue background, a distorted diamond, then called down to Errol, who was carrying the red.

When Ty had passed the can up he looked away, out across the expanse of brown dust. He could see the town in the distance. He glanced up and saw Chris leaning forward, gripping the ladder with one hand behind his back while he aimed the phone down at them.

Ty shouted up at him, 'Hey Scorsese! Make me famous!'

Dan spent five minutes adding finicky details in silver. Ty didn't mind; it was good just being here. He didn't need to mark the tower himself; whenever he saw Dan's tag he'd remember this feeling.

They clambered down, then sat at the base of the tower and passed the phone around, checking out Chris's movie.

5

Lincoln had three rest days before he was called again, this time for four days in succession. He fought hard to remember all the scenes he was sleepwalking through, but even with his grandmother adding her accounts of the 'play acting' she'd witnessed, he found it hard to hold on to the details.

Sometimes he hung out with the other actors, shooting pool in the motel's games room, but there seemed to be an unspoken taboo against discussing their roles. Lincoln doubted that the Steveware would punish them even if they managed to overcome the restraint, but it was clear that it didn't want them to piece too much together. It had even gone to the trouble of changing Steve's name – as Lincoln and the other actors heard it, though presumably not Steve himself – as if the anger they felt towards the man in their ordinary lives might have penetrated into their roles. Lincoln couldn't even remember his own mother's face when he was Ty; the farm, the Crash, the whole history of the last thirty years was gone from his thoughts entirely.

In any case, he had no wish to spoil the charade. Whatever the Steveware thought it was doing, Lincoln hoped it would believe it was working perfectly, all the way from Steve's small-town childhood to whatever age it needed to reach before it could write this creation into flesh and blood, congratulate itself on a job well done, and then finally, mercifully dissolve into rat piss and let the world move on.

A fortnight after they'd arrived, without warning, Lincoln was no longer needed. He knew it when he woke, and after breakfast the woman at reception asked him, politely, to pack his bags and hand back the keys. Lincoln didn't understand, but maybe Ty's family had moved out of Steve's home town, and the friends hadn't stayed in touch. Lincoln had played his part, now he was free.

When they returned to the lobby with their suitcases, Dana spotted them, and asked Lincoln if he was willing to be debriefed.

He turned to his grandmother. 'Are you worried about the traffic?' He'd already phoned his father and told him they'd be back by dinner time.

She said, 'You should do this. I'll wait in the truck.'

They sat at a table in the lobby. Dana asked his permission to record his words, and he told her everything he could remember.

When Lincoln had finished, he said, 'You're the Stevologist. You think they'll get there in the end?'

Dana gestured at her phone to stop recording. 'One estimate', she said, 'is that the Stevelets now comprise a hundred thousand times the computational resources of all the brains of all the human beings who've ever lived.'

Lincoln laughed. 'And they still need stage props and extras, to do a little VR?'

'They've studied the anatomy of ten million human brains, but I think they know that they still don't fully understand consciousness. They bring in real people for the bit parts, so they can concentrate on the star. If you gave them a particular human brain, I'm sure they could faithfully copy it into software, but anything more complicated starts to get murky. How do they know their Steve is conscious when they're not conscious themselves? He never gave them a reverse Turing test, a checklist they could apply. All they have is the judgement of people like you.'

Lincoln felt a surge of hope. 'He seemed real enough to me.' His memories were blurred – and he wasn't even absolutely certain which of Ty's four friends was Steve – but none of them had struck him as less than human.

Dana said, 'They have his genome. They have movies, they have blogs, they have emails: Steve's, and a lot of people who knew him. They have a thousand fragments of his life. Like the borders of a giant jigsaw puzzle.'

'So that's good, right? A lot of data is good?'

Dana hesitated. 'The scenes you described have been played out thousands of times before. They're trying to tweak their Steve to write the right emails, pull the right faces for the camera – by himself, without following a script like the extras. A lot of data sets the bar very high.'

As Lincoln walked out to the parking lot, he thought about the laughing, carefree boy he'd called Chris. Living for a few days, writing an email – then memory-wiped, reset, started again. Climbing a water tower, making a movie of his friends, but later turning the camera on himself, saying one wrong word – and wiped again.

A thousand times. A million times. The Steveware was infinitely patient, and infinitely stupid. Each time it failed it would change the actors, shuffle a few variables, then run the experiment over again. The possibilities were endless, but it would keep on trying until the sun burnt out.

Lincoln was tired. He climbed into the truck beside his grandmother, and they headed for home.

INDUCTION

1

Ikat spent three of the last four hours of 2099 out on the regolith, walking the length of her section of the launch gun, checking by eye for micrometeorite impacts or any other damage that the automatic systems might improbably have missed.

Four other junior engineers walked a few paces ahead of her, but Ikat had had enough of their company inside the base, and she kept her coms tuned to Earth, sampling the moods of the century's countdown.

The Pope had already issued a statement from Rio, imploring humanity to treat 'Christianity's twenty-first birthday' as an opportunity to embrace 'spiritual maturity'; the Council of Islamic Scholars in Brussels, surrendering to the ubiquity of the Gregorian calendar, had chimed in with a similar message of their own. In the pyrotechnic rivalry stakes, Sydney was planning to incinerate the decommissioned Harbour Bridge with artificial lightning, while Washington had arranged for no fewer than twenty-one ageing military satellites to plunge from the sky into the Potomac at the stroke of midnight.

There was no doubt, though, that Beijing had stolen the lion's share of global chatter with the imminent launch of the Orchid Seed. You could forget any purist's concept of lunar midnight; the clocks on Procellarum had been set to the easternmost of Earth's time zones ever since the construction of the base two decades before, so the official zeroing of the digits here would precede celebrations in all of the globe's major cities. The PR people really had planned that far ahead.

As she paced slowly along the regolith, Ikat kept her eyes diligently on the coolant pipes that weaved between the support struts to wrap the gun barrel, although she knew that this final check was mostly PR too. If the launch failed, it would be down to a flaw that no human eye could have detected. Six successful but unpublicised test firings made such a humiliation unlikely. Still, the gun's fixed bearing rendered a seventh, perfectly timed success indispensable. Only at 'midnight' would the device be aimed precisely at its target. If they had to wait a month for a relaunch, hundreds of upper-echelon bureaucrats back on Earth would probably be diving out of their penthouse windows before dawn. Ikat knew that she was far too low in the ranks to make a worthwhile scapegoat, but her career could still be blighted by the ignominy.

Her mother was calling from Bangkok. Ikat pondered her responsibilities, then decided to let the audio through. If she really couldn't walk, talk and spot a plume of leaking coolant at the same time, she should probably retire from her profession straight away.

'Just wishing you good luck, darling,' her mother said. 'And Happy New Year. Probably you'll be too busy celebrating to talk to me later.'

Ikat scowled. 'I was planning to call you when it reached midnight there. But Happy New Year anyway.'

'You'll call your father after the launch?'

'I expect so.' Her parents were divorced, but her mother still wanted harmony to flow in all directions, especially on such an occasion.

'Without him,' her mother said, 'you never would have had this chance.'

It was a strange way of putting it, but it was probably true. The Chinese space programme was cosmopolitan enough, but if her mother hadn't married a Chinese citizen and remained in the country for so long, Ikat doubted that she would have been plucked from provincial Bangkok and lofted all the way up to Procellarum. There were dozens of middle-ranking project engineers with highly specific skills who were not Chinese-born; they were quite likely the best people on the planet for their respective jobs. She was not in that league. Her academic results had secured her the placement, but they had not been so spectacular that she would have been headhunted across national borders.

'I'll call him,' she promised. 'After the launch.'

She cut the connection. She'd almost reached the end of Stage Nine, the ten-kilometre section of the barrel where the pellets would be accelerated from sixteen to eighteen per cent of lightspeed, before the final boost to twenty per cent. For the last three years, she had worked beneath various specialist managers, testing and retesting different subsystems: energy storage, electromagnets, cooling, data collection. It had been a once-in-a-lifetime education, arduous at times, but never boring. Still, she'd be glad to be going home. Maglev railways might seem anticlimactic after this, but she'd had enough of sharing a room with six other people, and the whole tiny complex with the same two hundred faces, year after year.

Back inside the base, Ikat felt restless. The last hour stretched out ahead of her, an impossible gulf. In the common room, Qing caught her eye, and she went to sit with him.

'Had any bites from your résumé?' he asked.

'I haven't published it yet. I want a long holiday first.'

He shook his head in dismay. 'How did you ever get here? You must be the least competitive person on Earth.'

Ikat laughed. 'At university I studied eighteen hours a day. I had no social life for six years.'

'So now you've got to put in some effort to get the pay-off.'

'This *is* the pay-off, you dope.'

'For a week or so after the launch,' Qing said, 'you could have the top engineering firms on the planet bidding for the prestige you'd bring them. That won't last for ever, though. People have a short attention span. This isn't the time to take a holiday.'

Ikat threw up her hands. 'What can I say? I'm a lost cause.'

Qing's expression softened; he was deadly serious about his own career, but when he lectured her it was just a kind of ritual, a role play that gave them something to talk about.

They passed the time with more riffs on the same theme, interleaved with gossip and bitching about their colleagues, but when the clock hit 11.50 it became impossible to remain blasé. Nobody could spend three years in a state of awe at the feat they were attempting, but ten minutes of sober contemplation suddenly seemed inadequate. Other probes had already been sent towards the stars, but the Orchid Seed would certainly outrace all those that had gone before it. It might yet be overtaken itself, but with no serious competitors even at the planning stage, there was a fair chance that the impending launch would come to be seen as the true genesis of interstellar travel.

As the conversation in the common room died away, someone turned up the main audio commentary that was going to the newsfeeds, and spread a dozen key image windows across the wall screens. The control room was too small to take everyone in the base; junior staff would watch the launch much as the public everywhere else did.

The schematics told Ikat a familiar story, but this was the moment to savour it anew. Three gigajoules of solar energy had already been packed into circulating currents in the superconducting batteries, ready to be tapped. That was not much, really; every significant payload launched from Earth had burnt up far more. One-third would be lost to heat and stray electromagnetic fields. The remainder would be fed into the motion of just one milligram of matter: the five hundred tiny pellets of the Orchid Seed that would race down the launch gun in three-thousandths of a second, propelled by a force that could have lofted a two-tonne weight back on Earth.

The pellets that comprised the seed were not physically connected, but they would move in synch in a rigid pattern, forming a kind of sparse crystal whose spacing allowed it to interact strongly with the microwave radiation in the gun. Out in deep space, in the decades spent in transit, the pattern would not be important, but the pellets would be kept close together by electrostatic trimming if and when they strayed, ready to take up perfect rank again when the time came to brake. First, in the coronal magnetic field of Prosperity B; again near its larger companion star, and finally in the ionosphere of Prosperity A's fourth planet, Duty, before falling into the atmosphere and spiralling to the ground.

One cycling image on the wall rehearsed the launch in slow motion, showing the crest of electromagnetic energy coursing down the barrel, field lines bunched tightly like a strange coiled spring. A changing electric field induced a magnetic field; a changing magnetic field induced an electric field. In free space such a change would spread at the speed of light – would *be* light, of some frequency or other – but the tailored geometry and currents of the barrel kept the wave reined in, always in step with the seed, devoted to the task of urging this precious cargo forward.

'If this screws up,' Qing observed forlornly, 'we'll be the laughing stock of the century.'

'You don't think Beijing's prepared for a cover-up?' Ikat joked.

'Some jealous fucker would catch us out,' Qing replied. 'I'll bet every dish on Earth is tuned to the seed's resonant frequency. If they get no echo, we'll all be building toilet blocks in Aksai Chin.'

It was 11.58 in Tonga, Tokelau and Procellarum. Ikat took Qing's hand and squeezed it. 'Relax,' she said. 'The worst you'll come to is building synchrotrons for eccentric billionaires in Kowloon.'

Qing said, 'You're cutting off my circulation.'

The room fell silent; a synthetic voice from the control room counted down the seconds. Ikat felt light-headed. The six test firings had worked, but who knew what damage they'd done, what stresses they'd caused, what structures they'd weakened? Lots of people, actually; the barrel was packed with instrumentation to measure exactly those things, and the answers were all very reassuring. Still—

'Minus three. Minus two. Minus one.'

A schematic of the launch gun flashed green, followed by a slow-motion reconstruction of the field patterns so flawless it was indistinguishable from the simulations. A new window opened, showing tracking echoes. The seed was moving away from the moon at sixty thousand kilometres per second, precisely along the expected trajectory. There was nothing more required of it: no second stage to fire, no course change, no reconfiguration. Now that it had been set in motion, all it had to do was coast on its momentum; it couldn't suddenly veer sideways, crashing and burning like some failed chemical rocket launched from the ground. Even if collisions or system failures over the coming decades wiped out some of the pellets, the seed as a whole could function with as little as a quarter of the original number. Unless the whole thing had been a fraud or a mass hallucination, there was now absolutely nothing that could pull the rug out from under this triumph; in three milliseconds, their success had become complete and irrevocable. At least for a century, until the seed reached its destination.

People were cheering; Ikat joined them, but her own cry came out as a tension-relieving sob. Qing put an arm around her shoulders. 'We did it,' he whispered. 'We've conquered the world.'

Not the stars? Not the galaxy? She laughed, but she didn't begrudge him this vanity. The fireworks to come in Sydney might be more spectacular, and the dying hawks burning up over Washington might bring their own sense of closure, but this felt like an opening out, an act of release, a joyful shout across the light-years.

Food and drink were wheeled out; the party began. In twenty minutes, the seed was further from the sun than Mars. In a day, it would be further than Pluto; in ten days, further than Pioneer 10. In six months, the Orchid Seed would have put more distance behind it than all of the targeted interstellar missions that had preceded it.

Ikat remembered to call her father once midnight came to Beijing.

'Happy New Year,' she greeted him.

'Congratulations,' he replied. 'Will you come and visit me once you get your Earth legs, or will you be too busy signing autographs?'

Fake biochemical signals kept the Procellarans' bones and muscles strong; it would only take a day or two to acclimatise her nervous system to the old dynamics again. 'Of course I'll visit you.'

'You did a good job,' he said. 'I'm proud of you.'

His praise made her uncomfortable. She wanted to express her gratitude to him – he'd done much more to help her than providing the accident of her birthplace – but she was afraid of sounding like a giddy movie star accepting an award.

As the party wound on and midnight skimmed the globe, the speechwriters of the world's leaders competed to heap praise upon Beijing's achievement. Ikat didn't care that it had all been done for the glory of a fading empire; it was more than a gesture of status and power.

Only one thing seemed bittersweet, as she contemplated the decades to come. She was twenty-eight years old, and there was every chance that these three years, these three milliseconds, would turn out to have been the pinnacle of her life.

2

The caller was persistent, Ikat gave him that. He refused to leave a message or engage with her assistant; he refused to explain his business to anyone but Ikat herself, in a realtime dialogue.

From her balcony she looked out across the treetops, listening to the birds and insects of the Mekong valley, and wondered if she wanted to be dragged back into the swirling currents of the world. The caller, whose name was Vikram Ali, had probably tracked her down in the hope of extracting a comment from her about the imminent arrival of signals from the Orchid Flower. That might have been an egotistical assumption, were it not for the fact that she'd heard of no other participant in the launch publishing anything on the matter, so it was clear that the barrel would have to be scraped. The project's most famous names were all dead or acorporeal – and the acorporeals were apparently Satisfied, rendering them even less interested in such worldly matters than an ageing flesh-bound recluse like Ikat.

She pondered her wishes and responsibilities. Most people now viewed the Orchid Seed as a curiosity, a sociological time capsule. Within decades of its launch, a new generation of telescopes had imaged and analysed its destination with such detail and clarity that the mission had come to seem redundant. All five planets in the Prosperity system appeared lifeless, and although there were astrophysical and geochemical subtleties that *in situ* measurements might yet reveal, with high-resolution maps of Duty splashed across the web, interest in the slightly better view that would arrive after a very long delay began to dwindle.

What was there for Ikat to say on the matter? Should she plead for the project to be taken seriously, as more than a quaint nationalist stunt from a bygone era? Maybe the top brass weren't Satisfied; maybe they were just embarrassed. The possibility annoyed her. No one who'd been sincere in their work on the Orchid Seed should be ashamed of what they'd done.

Ikat returned Vikram Ali's call. He responded immediately, and after the briefest of pleasantries came to the point.

'I represent Khamoush Holdings,' he said. 'Some time ago, we acquired various assets and obligations of the URC government, including a contractual relationship with you.'

'I see.' Ikat struggled to remember what she might have signed that could possibly be relevant a hundred and twenty years later. Had she promised to do media if asked? Her assistant had verified Khamoush Holding's bona fides, but all it knew about the Procellarum contract was that Ikat's copy had been lost in 2145, when an anarchist worm had scrambled three per cent of the planet's digital records.

'The opportunity has arisen for us to exploit one of our assets,' Ali continued, 'but we are contractually obliged to offer you the option of participating in the relevant activity.'

Ikat blinked. *Option?* Khamoush had bought some form of media rights, obviously, but would there be a clause saying they had to run down the ranks of the Orchid Seed team, offering each participant a chance to play spokesperson?

'Am I obliged to help you, or not?' she asked.

Now it was Ali's turn to be surprised. 'Obliged? Certainly not! We're not slave holders!' He looked downright offended.

Ikat said, 'Could we get the whole thing over in a day or two?'

Ali pondered this question deeply for a couple of seconds. 'You don't have the contract, do you?'

'I chose a bad archive,' Ikat confessed.

'So you have no idea what I'm talking about?'

'You want me to give interviews about the Orchid Seed, don't you?' Ikat said.

'Ultimately, yes,' Ali replied, 'but that's neither here nor there for now. I want to ask you if you're interested in travelling to Duty, taking a look around, and coming back.'

In the lobby of the hotel in Mumbai, Ikat learnt that someone else had accepted the offer from Khamoush Holdings.

'I thought you'd be rich and Satisfied by now,' she told Qing.

He smiled. 'Mildly rich. Never satisfied.'

They walked together to the office of Magic Beans Inc, Ikat holding her umbrella over both of them against the monsoon rain.

'My children think I'm insane,' Qing confessed.

'Mine too. But then, I told them that if they kept arguing, I'd make it a one-way journey.' Ikat laughed. 'Really, they ought to be grateful. No filial obligations for forty years straight. It's hard to imagine a greater gift.'

In the Magic Beans office, Ali showed them two robots, more or less identical to the ones the Orchid Flower, he hoped, would already have built on the surface of Duty. The original mission planners had never intended such a thing, but when Khamoush had acquired the assets they had begun the relevant R&D immediately. Forty years ago they had transmitted the blueprints for

137

these robots, in a message that would have arrived not long after the Orchid Seed touched down. Now that confirmation of the Flower's success in its basic mission had reached Earth, in a matter of months they would learn whether the nanomachines had also been able to scavenge the necessary materials to construct these welcoming receptacles.

'We're the only volunteers?' Qing asked, gazing at his prospective doppelgänger with uneasy fascination. 'I would have thought one of the acorporeals would have jumped at the chance.'

'Perhaps if we'd asked them early enough,' Ali replied. 'But once you're immersed in that culture, forty years must seem a very long time to be out of touch.'

Ikat was curious about the financial benefits Khamoush were hoping for; they turned out to revolve largely around a promotional deal with a manufacturer of prosthetic bodies. Although the designs the company sold were wildly different from these robots – even their Extreme Durability models were far more cosily organic – any link with the first interstellar explorers trudging across rugged landscapes on a distant, lifeless world carried enough resonance to be worth paying for.

Back in the hotel they sat in Qing's room, talking about the old times and speculating about the motives and fates of all their higher-ranked colleagues who'd turned down this opportunity. Perhaps, Ikat suggested, some of them simply had no wish to become acorporeal. Crossing over to software didn't preclude you from continuing to inhabit a prosthetic body back on Earth, but once you changed substrate the twin lures of virtual experience and self-modification were strong. 'That would be ironic,' she mused. 'To decline to engage with the physical universe in this way, for fear of ultimately losing touch with it.'

Qing said, 'I plan to keep my body frozen, and have my new self wired back into it when I return, synapse by synapse.'

Ikat smiled. 'I thought you said *mildly* rich.' That would be orders of magnitude more costly than her own plan: frozen body, prosthetic brain.

'They caught us at just the right stage in life,' Qing said. 'Still interested in reality, but not still doting on every new great-great-grandchild. Not yet acorporeal, but old enough that we already feel as if we've been on another planet for forty years.'

Ikat said, 'I'm amazed that they honoured our contracts, though. A good lawyer could have let them hand-pick their travellers.' The relevant clause had simply been a vague offer of preferential access to spin-off employment opportunities.

'Why shouldn't they want *us*?' Qing demanded, feigning indignation. 'We're seasoned astronauts, aren't we? We've already proved we could live together in Procellarum for three years, without driving each other crazy. Three months – with a whole planet to stretch our legs on – shouldn't be beyond us.'

Later that week, to Ikat's amazement, their psychological assessments proved Qing's point; their basic personality profiles really hadn't changed since the Procellarum days. Careers, marriages, children had left their marks, but if anything they were both more resilient.

They stayed in Mumbai, rehearsing in the robot bodies using telepresence links, and studying the data coming back from the Orchid Flower.

When confirmation arrived that the Flower really had built the robots Khamoush Holdings had requested, Ikat sent messages directly to her children and grandchildren, and then left it to them to pass the news further down the generations. Her parents were dead, and her children were tetchy centenarians; she loved them, but she did not feel like gathering them around her for a tearful *bon voyage*. The chances were they'd all still be here when she returned.

She and Qing spent a morning doing media, answering a minute but representative fraction of the questions submitted by interested news subscribers. Then Ikat's body was frozen, and her brain was removed, microtomed and scanned. At her request, her software was not formally woken on Earth prior to her departure; routine tests confirmed its functionality in a series of dreamlike scenarios which left no permanent memories.

Then the algorithm that described her was optimised,

compressed, encoded into a series of laser pulses, and beamed across twenty light-years, straight on to the petals of the Orchid Flower.

3

Ikat woke standing on a brown pebbled plain beneath a pale, salmon-coloured sky. Prosperity A had just risen; its companion, ten billion kilometres away, was visible but no competition, scarcely brighter than Venus from Earth.

Qing was beside her, and behind him was the Flower: the communications link and factory that the Orchid Seed had built. Products of the factory included hundreds of small rovers, which had dispersed to explore the planet's surface, and dozens of solar-powered gliders, which provided aerial views and aided with communications.

Qing said, 'Punch me, make it real.'

Ikat obliged with a gentle thump on his forearm. Their telepresence rehearsals had included virtual backdrops just like the Flower's actual surroundings, but they had not had full tactile feedback. The action punctured Ikat's own dreamy sense of déjà vu; they really had stepped out of the simulation into the thing itself.

They had the Flower brief them about its latest discoveries; they had been twenty years behind when they'd left Earth, and insentient beams of light for twenty more. The Flower had pieced together more details of Duty's geological history; with plate tectonics but no liquid water, the planet's surface was older than Earth's but not as ancient as the moon's.

Ikat felt a twinge of superfluousness; if the telescope images hadn't quite made the Orchid Flower redundant, there was precious little left for her and Qing. They were not here to play geologists, though; they were here to be here. Any science they did would be a kind of recreation, like an informed tourist's appreciation of some well-studied natural wonder back on Earth.

Qing started laughing. 'Twenty fucking *light-years*! Do you know how long that would take to walk? They should have tried harder to make us afraid.' Ikat reached out and put a hand on his shoulder. She felt a little existential vertigo herself, but she did not believe they faced any great risk. The forty lost years were a fait accompli, but she was reconciled to that.

'What's the worst that can happen?' she said. 'If something goes wrong, they'll just wake your body back on Earth, with no changes at all.'

Qing nodded slowly. 'But you had your brain diced, didn't you?'

'You know me, I'm a cheapskate.' Non-destructive scanning was more expensive, and Khamoush weren't paying for everything. 'But they can still load the back-up file into a prosthesis.'

'Assuming it's not eaten by an anarchist worm.'

'I arranged to have a physical copy put into a vault.'

'Ah, but what about the nihilist nanoware?'

'Then you and I will be the only survivors.'

Their bodies had no need for shelter from the elements, but the Flower had built them a simple hut for sanity's sake. As they inspected the spartan rooms together, Qing seemed to grow calm; as he'd said back on Earth, anything had to be easier than the conditions they'd faced on the moon. Food would have been too complex an indulgence, and Ikat had declined the software to grant her convincing hallucinations of five-course banquets every night.

Once they'd familiarised themselves with everything in the base camp, and done a few scripted Armstrong moments for the cameras to satisfy the promotional deal, they spent the morning hiking across the rock-strewn plain. There was a line of purplish mountains in the distance, almost lost in haze, but Ikat declined to ask the Flower for detailed aerial imagery. They could explore for themselves, find things for themselves. The longing to be some kind of irreplaceable pioneer, to be the first pair of eyes and hands, the first scrutinising intelligence, was impossible to extinguish completely, but they could find a way to satisfy it without self-delusion or charade.

Her fusion-powered body needed no rest, but at noon she stopped walking and sat cross-legged on the ground.

Qing joined her. She looked around at the barren rocks, the delicate sky, the far horizon. 'Twenty light-years?' she said. 'I'm glad I came.'

Their days were full of small challenges, and small discoveries. To cross a mountain range required skill and judgement as well as stamina; to understand the origins of each wind-blasted outcrop took careful observation and a strong visual imagination, as well as a grasp of the basic geological principles.

Still, even as they clambered down one treacherous, powdery cliff-face, Ikat wondered soberly if they'd reached the high-tide mark of human exploration. The Orchid Seed's modest speed and reach had never been exceeded; the giant telescopes had found no hints of life out to a hundred light-years, offering little motivation to launch a new probe. The shift to software was becoming cheaper every year, and if that made travel to the stars easier, there were a thousand more alluring destinations closer to home. When you could pack a lifetime of exotic experiences into a realtime hour, capped off with happiness by fiat, who would give up decades of contemporaneity to walk on a distant world? There were even VR games, based on telescope imagery, where people fought unlikely wars with implausible alien empires on the very ground she was treading.

'What are you planning to do when you get home?' she asked Qing that night. They had brought nothing with them from the base camp, so they simply slept on the ground beneath the stars.

'Back to work, I suppose.' He ran his own successful engineering consultancy, so successful that it didn't really need him. 'What else is there? I'm not interested in crawling up a computer's arse and pretending that I've gone to heaven. What about you?'

'I don't know. I was retired, happily enough. Waiting for death, I suppose.' It hadn't felt like that, though.

Qing said, 'These aren't the highest mountains on the planet, you know. The ones we've just crossed.'

'I know that.'

'There are some that reach into a pretty good vacuum.'

Duty's atmosphere was thin even on the ground; Ikat had no reason to doubt this assertion. 'What's your point?' she asked.

He turned to her and gave her his strangest robot smile. 'From a mountain like that, a coil gun could land a package of nano-machines on Patience.'

Patience was a third the mass of Duty, and had no atmosphere to speak of. 'To what end?'

Qing said, 'High vacuum, relativistic launch speeds. What we started doesn't have to stop here.'

She searched his face, unsure if he was serious. 'Do you think the Flower would give us what we needed? Who knows how Khamoush have programmed it?'

'I tested the nanoware, back on Procellarum. I know how to make it give us whatever we ask.'

Ikat thought it over. 'Do we know how to describe everything we'll need? To identify a new target? Plan a whole new mission?' The Orchard Seed had taken thousands of people decades to prepare.

Qing said, 'We'll need telescopes, computing resources. We can bootstrap our way up, step by step. Let's see how far we get in three months. And if we solve all the other problems, maybe we can go one step further: build a seed that will self-replicate when it reaches its destination, launching a couple of new seeds of its own.'

Ikat rose to her feet angrily. 'Not if you want my help! We have no right to spew mindless replicators in all directions. If someone from Earth wants to follow the seed we launch, and if they make their own decision when they get there to reach out further, then that's one thing, but I'm *not* starting any kind of self-sustaining chain reaction that colonises the galaxy while everyone sits at home playing VR games.'

Qing stood up and made a calming gesture, 'All right, all right! I was just thinking out loud. The truth is, we'll be struggling to launch *anything* before it's time to go home. But better to try than spend three months taking in the scenery.'

Ikat remained wary for a moment, then she laughed with relief. 'Absolutely. Let the real geologists back on Earth fret about these rocks; I've had enough of them already for a lifetime.'

They didn't wait for dawn; they headed back for the base camp immediately.

As they approached the mountains, Qing said, 'I thought it would give me some great sense of accomplishment, to come here and see with my own eyes that this thing I helped to start was finally complete. But if I could wish my descendants one blessing now, it would be never to see the end, never to find completion.'

Ikat stopped walking and mimed a toast. 'To the coming generations. May they always start something they can't finish.'

SINGLETON

2003

I was walking north along George Street towards Town Hall railway station, pondering the ways I might solve the tricky third question of my linear algebra assignment, when I encountered a small crowd blocking the footpath. I didn't give much thought to the reason they were standing there; I'd just passed a busy restaurant, and I often saw groups of people gathered outside. But once I'd started to make my way around them, moving into an alley rather than stepping out into the traffic, it became apparent that they were not just diners from a farewell lunch for a retiring colleague, putting off their return to the office for as long as possible. I could see for myself exactly what was holding their attention.

Twenty metres down the alley, a man was lying on his back on the ground, shielding his bloodied face with his hands, while two men stood over him, relentlessly swinging narrow sticks of some kind. At first I thought the sticks were pool cues, but then I noticed the metal hooks on the ends. I'd only ever seen these obscure weapons before in one other place: my primary school, where an appointed window monitor would use them at the start and end of each day. They were meant for opening and closing an old-fashioned kind of hinged pane when it was too high to reach with your hands.

I turned to the other spectators. 'Has anyone called the police?'

A woman nodded without looking at me and said, 'Someone used their mobile, a couple of minutes ago.'

The assailants must have realised that the police were on their way, but it seemed they were too committed to their task to abandon it until that was absolutely necessary. They were facing away from the crowd, so perhaps they weren't entirely reckless not to fear identification. The man on the ground was dressed like a kitchen hand. He was still moving, trying to protect himself, but he was making less noise than his attackers; the need, or the ability, to cry out in pain had been beaten right out of him.

As for calling for help, he could have saved his breath.

A chill passed through my body, a sick cold churning sensation that came a moment before the conscious realisation: *I'm going to watch someone be murdered, and I'm going to do nothing.* But this wasn't a drunken brawl, where a few bystanders could step in and separate the combatants; the two assailants had to be serious criminals, settling a score. Keeping your distance from something like that was just common sense. I'd go to court, I'd be a witness, but no one could expect anything more of me. Not when thirty other people had behaved in exactly the same way.

The men in the alley did not have guns. If they'd had guns, they would have used them by now. They weren't going to mow down anyone who got in their way. It was one thing not to make a martyr of yourself, but how many people could these two grunting slobs fend off with sticks?

I unstrapped my backpack and put it on the ground. Absurdly, that made me feel more vulnerable; I was always worried about losing my textbooks. *Think about this. You don't know what you're doing.* I hadn't been in so much as a fist-fight since I was thirteen. I glanced at the strangers around me, wondering if anyone would join in if I implored them to rush forward together. But that wasn't going to happen. I was a willowy, unimposing eighteen-year-old, wearing a T-shirt adorned with Maxwell's Equations. I had no presence, no authority. No one would follow me into the fray.

Alone, I'd be as helpless as the guy on the ground. These men would crack my skull open in an instant. There were half a dozen solid-looking office workers in their twenties in the crowd; if these weekend rugby players hadn't felt competent to intervene, what chance did I have?

I reached down for my backpack. If I wasn't going to help, there was no point being here at all. I'd find out what had happened on the evening news.

I started to retrace my steps, sick with self-loathing. This wasn't *Kristallnacht*. There'd be no embarrassing questions from my grandchildren. No one would ever reproach me.

As if that were the measure of everything.

'Fuck it.' I dropped my backpack and ran down the alley.

I was close enough to smell the three sweating bodies over the stench of rotting garbage before I was even noticed. The nearest of the attackers glanced over his shoulder, affronted, then amused. He didn't bother redeploying his weapon in mid-stroke; as I hooked an arm around his neck in the hope of overbalancing him, he thrust his elbow into my chest, winding me. I clung on desperately, maintaining the hold even though I couldn't tighten it. As he tried to prise himself loose, I managed to kick his feet out from under him. We both went down onto the asphalt; I ended up beneath him.

The man untangled himself and clambered to his feet. As I struggled to right myself, picturing a metal hook swinging into my face, someone whistled. I looked up to see the second man gesturing to his companion, and I followed his gaze. A dozen men and women were coming down the alley, advancing together at a brisk walk. It was not a particularly menacing sight – I'd seen angrier crowds with peace signs painted on their faces – but the sheer numbers were enough to guarantee some inconvenience. The first man hung back long enough to kick me in the ribs. Then the two of them fled.

I brought my knees up, then raised my head and got into a crouch. I was still winded, but for some reason it seemed vital not to remain flat on my back. One of the office workers grinned down at me. 'You fuckwit. You could have got killed.'

The kitchen hand shuddered, and snorted bloody mucus. His eyes were swollen shut, and when he laid his hands down beside him, I could see the bones of his knuckles through the torn skin. My own skin turned icy at this vision of the fate I'd courted for myself. But if it was a shock to realise how I might have ended up, it was just as sobering to think that I'd almost walked away and let them finish him off, when the intervention had actually cost me nothing.

I rose to my feet. People milled around the kitchen hand, asking each other about first aid. I remembered the basics from a course I'd done in high school, but the man was still breathing and he wasn't losing vast amounts of blood, so I couldn't think of anything helpful that an amateur could do in the circumstances. I squeezed my way out of the gathering and walked back to the street. My backpack was exactly where I'd left it; no one had stolen my books. I heard sirens approaching; the police and the ambulance would be there soon.

My ribs were tender, but I wasn't in agony. I'd cracked a rib falling off a trail-bike on the farm when I was twelve, and I was fairly sure that this was just bruising. For a while I walked bent over, but by the time I reached the station I found I could adopt a normal gait. I had some grazed skin on my arms, but I couldn't have appeared too battered, because no one on the train looked at me twice.

That night, I watched the news. The kitchen hand was described as being in a stable condition. I pictured him stepping out into the alley to empty a bucket of fish-heads into the garbage, to find the two of them waiting for him. I'd probably never learn what the attack had been about unless the case went to trial, and as yet the police hadn't even named any suspects. If the man had been in a fit state to talk in the alley, I might have asked him then, but any sense that I was entitled to an explanation was rapidly fading.

The reporter mentioned a student 'leading the charge of angry citizens' who'd rescued the kitchen hand, and then she spoke to an eyewitness, who described this young man as 'a New Ager, wearing some kind of astrological symbols on his shirt'. I snorted, then looked around nervously in case one of my housemates had made the improbable connection, but no one else was even in earshot.

Then the story was over.

I felt flat for a moment, cheated of the minor rush that fifteen seconds' fame might have delivered; it was like reaching into a biscuit tin when you thought there was one more chocolate chip left to find that there actually wasn't. I considered phoning my parents in Orange, just to talk to them from within the strange afterglow, but I'd established a routine and it was not the right day. If I called unexpectedly, they'd think something was wrong.

So, that was it. In a week's time, when the bruises had faded, I'd look back and doubt that the incident had ever happened.

I went upstairs to finish my assignment.

Francine said, 'There's a nicer way to think about this. If you do a change of variables, from x and y to z and z-conjugate, the Cauchy-Riemann equations correspond to the condition that the partial derivative of the function with respect to z-conjugate is equal to zero.'

We were sitting in the coffee shop, discussing the complex analysis lecture we'd had half an hour before. Half a dozen of us from the same course had got into the habit of meeting at this time every week, but today the others had failed to turn up. Maybe there was a movie being screened, or a speaker appearing on campus that I hadn't heard about.

I worked through the transformation she'd described. 'You're right,' I said. 'That's really elegant!'

Francine nodded slightly in assent, while retaining her characteristic jaded look. She had an undisguisable passion for mathematics, but she was probably bored out of her skull in class, waiting for the lecturers to catch up and teach her something she didn't already know.

I was nowhere near her level. In fact, I'd started the year poorly, distracted by my new surroundings: nothing so glamorous as the temptations of the night life, just the different sights and sounds and scale of the place, along with the bureaucratic demands of all the organisations that now impinged upon my life, from the university itself down to the shared house groceries sub-committee. In the last few weeks, though, I'd finally started hitting my stride. I'd got a part-time job, stacking shelves in a supermarket; the pay was lousy, but it was enough to take the edge off my financial anxieties, and the hours weren't so long that they left me with no time for anything but study.

I doodled harmonic contours on the notepaper in front of me. 'So what do you do for fun?' I said. 'Apart from complex analysis?'

Francine didn't reply immediately. This wasn't the first time we'd been alone together, but I'd never felt confident that I had the right words to make the most of the situation. At some point, though, I'd stopped fooling myself that there was ever going to be a perfect moment, with the perfect phrase falling from my lips: something subtle but intriguing slipped deftly into the conversation without disrupting the flow. So now I'd made my interest plain, with no attempt at artfulness or eloquence. She could judge me as she knew me from the last three months, and if she felt no desire to know me better, I would not be crushed.

'I write a lot of Perl scripts,' she said. 'Nothing complicated; just odds and ends that I give away as freeware. It's very relaxing.'

I nodded understandingly. I didn't think she was being deliberately discouraging; she just expected me to be slightly more direct.

'Do you like Deborah Conway?' I'd only heard a couple of her songs on the radio myself, but a few days before I'd seen a poster in the city announcing a tour.

'Yeah. She's great.'

I started thickening the conjugation bars over the variables I'd scrawled. 'She's playing at a club in Surry Hills,' I said. 'On Friday. Would you like to go?'

Francine smiled, making no effort now to appear world-weary. 'Sure. That would be nice.'

I smiled back. I wasn't giddy, I wasn't moonstruck, but I felt as if I were standing on the shore of an ocean, contemplating its breadth. I felt the way I felt when I opened a sophisticated monograph in the library, and was reduced to savouring the scent of the print and the crisp symmetry of the notation, understanding only a fraction of what I read: knowing there was something glorious ahead, but knowing too what a daunting task it would be to come to terms with it.

I said, 'I'll get the tickets on my way home.'

To celebrate the end of exams for the year, the household threw a party. It was a sultry November night, but the back yard wasn't much bigger than the largest room in the house, so we ended up opening all the doors and windows and distributing food and furniture throughout the ground floor and the exterior, front and back. Once the faint humid breeze off the river penetrated the depths of the house, it was equally sweltering and mosquito-ridden everywhere, indoors and out.

Francine and I stayed close for an hour or so, obeying the distinctive dynamics of a couple, until by some unspoken mutual understanding it became clear that we could wander apart for a while, and that neither of us was so insecure that we'd resent it.

I ended up in a corner of the crowded back yard, talking to Will, a biochemistry student who'd lived in the house for the last four years. On some level, he probably couldn't help feeling that his opinions about the way things were run should carry more weight than anyone else's, which had annoyed me greatly when I'd first moved in. We'd since become friends, though, and I was glad to have a chance to talk to him before he left to take up a scholarship in Germany.

In the middle of a conversation about the work he'd be doing, I caught sight of Francine, and he followed my gaze.

Will said, 'It took me a while to figure out what finally cured you of your homesickness.'

'I was never homesick.'

'Yeah, right.' He took a swig of his drink. 'She's changed you, though. You have to admit that.'

'I do. Happily. Everything's clicked since we got together.' Relationships were meant to screw up your studies, but my marks were soaring. Francine didn't tutor me; she just drew me into a state of mind where everything was clearer.

'The amazing thing is that you got together at all.' I scowled, and Will raised a hand placatingly. 'I just meant, when you first moved in, you were pretty reserved. And down on yourself. When we interviewed you for the room, you practically begged us to give it to someone more deserving.'

'Now you're taking the piss.'

He shook his head. 'Ask any of the others.'

I fell silent. The truth was, if I took a step back and contemplated my situation, I was as astonished as he was. By the time I'd left my home town, it had become clear to me that good fortune had nothing much to do with luck. Some people were born with wealth, or talent, or charisma. They started with an edge, and the benefits snowballed. I'd always believed that I had, at best, just enough intelligence and persistence to stay afloat in my chosen field; I'd topped every class in high school, but in a town the size of Orange that meant nothing, and I'd had no illusions about my fate in Sydney.

I owed it to Francine that my visions of mediocrity had not been fulfilled; being with her had transformed my life. But where had I found the nerve to imagine that I had anything to offer her in return?

'Something happened,' I admitted. 'Before I asked her out.'

'Yeah?'

I almost clammed up; I hadn't told anyone about the events in the alley, not even Francine. The incident had come to seem too personal, as if to recount it at all would be to lay my conscience bare. But Will was off to Munich in less than a week, and it was easier to confide in someone I didn't expect to see again.

When I finished, Will bore a satisfied grin, as if I'd explained everything. 'Pure karma,' he announced. 'I should have guessed.'

'Oh, very scientific.'

'I'm serious. Forget the Buddhist mystobabble; I'm talking

about the real thing. If you stick to your principles, of course things go better for you – assuming you don't get killed in the process. That's elementary psychology. People have a highly developed sense of reciprocity, of the appropriateness of the treatment they receive from each other. If things work out too well for them, they can't help asking, "What did I do to deserve this?" If you don't have a good answer, you'll sabotage yourself. Not all the time, but often enough. So if you do something that improves your self-esteem—'

'Self-esteem is for the weak,' I quipped. Will rolled his eyes. 'I don't think like that,' I protested.

'No? Why did you even bring it up, then?'

I shrugged. 'Maybe it just made me less pessimistic. I could have had the crap beaten out of me, but I didn't. That makes asking someone to a concert seem a lot less dangerous.' I was beginning to cringe at all this unwanted analysis, and I had nothing to counter Will's pop psychology except an equally folksy version of my own.

He could see I was embarrassed, so he let the matter drop. As I watched Francine moving through the crowd, though, I couldn't shake off an unsettling sense of the tenuousness of the circumstances that had brought us together. There was no denying that if I'd walked away from the alley, and the kitchen hand had died, I would have felt like shit for a long time afterwards. I would not have felt entitled to much out of my own life.

I hadn't walked away, though. And even if the decision had come down to the wire, why shouldn't I be proud that I'd made the right choice? That didn't mean everything that followed was tainted, like a reward from some sleazy, palm-greasing deity. I hadn't won Francine's affection in a mediaeval test of bravery; we'd chosen each other, and persisted with that choice, for a thousand complicated reasons.

We were together now; that was what mattered. I wasn't going to dwell on the path that had brought me to her, just to dredge up all the doubts and insecurities that had almost kept us apart.

2012

As we drove the last kilometre along the road south from Ar Rafidiyah, I could see the Wall of Foam glistening ahead of us in the morning sunlight. Insubstantial as a pile of soap bubbles, but still intact, after six weeks.

'I can't believe it's lasted this long,' I told Sadiq.

'You didn't trust the models?'

'Fuck, no. Every week, I thought we'd come over the hill and there'd be nothing but a shrivelled-up cobweb.'

Sadiq smiled. 'So you had no faith in my calculations?'

'Don't take it personally. There were a lot of things we could both have got wrong.'

Sadiq pulled off the road. His students, Hassan and Rashid, had climbed off the back of the truck and started towards the Wall before I'd even got my face mask on. Sadiq called them back and made them put on plastic boots and paper suits over their clothes, while the two of us did the same. We didn't usually bother with this much protection, but today was different.

Close up, the Wall almost vanished: all you noticed were isolated, rainbow-fringed reflections, drifting at a leisurely pace across the otherwise invisible film as water redistributed itself, following waves induced in the membrane by the interplay of air pressure, thermal gradients and surface tension. These images might easily have been separate objects, scraps of translucent plastic blowing around above the desert, held aloft by a breeze too faint to detect at ground level.

The further away you looked, though, the more crowded the hints of light became, and the less plausible any alternative hypothesis that denied the Wall its integrity. It stretched for a kilometre along the edge of the desert, and rose an uneven fifteen to twenty metres into the air. But it was merely the first, and smallest, of its kind, and the time had come to put it on the back of the truck and drive it all the way back to Basra.

Sadiq took a spray can of reagent from the cabin, and shook it as he walked down the embankment. I followed him, my heart in my mouth. The Wall had not dried out; it had not been torn apart or blown away, but there was still plenty of room for failure.

Sadiq reached up and sprayed what appeared from my vantage to be thin air, but I could see the fine mist of droplets strike the membrane. A breathy susurration rose up, like the sound from a steam iron, and I felt a faint warm dampness before the first silken threads appeared, crisscrossing the region where the polymer from which the Wall was built had begun to shift conformations. In one state, the polymer was soluble, exposing hydrophilic groups of atoms that bound water into narrow sheets of feather-light gel. Now, triggered by the reagent and powered by sunlight, it was tucking these groups into slick, oily cages, and expelling every molecule of water, transforming the gel into a desiccated web.

I just hoped it wasn't expelling anything else.

As the lacy net began to fall in folds at his feet, Hassan said something in Arabic, disgusted and amused. My grasp of the language remained patchy; Sadiq translated for me, his voice muffled by his face mask: 'He says probably most of the weight of the thing will be dead insects.' He shooed the youths back towards the truck before following himself, as the wind blew a glistening curtain over our heads. It descended far too slowly to trap us, but I hastened up the slope.

We watched from the truck as the Wall came down, the wave of dehydration propagating along its length. If the gel had been an elusive sight close up, the residue was entirely invisible in the distance; there was less substance to it than a very long pantyhose – albeit, pantyhose clogged with gnats.

The smart polymer was the invention of Sonja Helvig, a Norwegian chemist; I'd tweaked her original design for this application. Sadiq and his students were civil engineers, responsible for scaling everything up to the point where it could have a practical benefit. On those terms, this experiment was still nothing but a minor field trial.

I turned to Sadiq. 'You did some mine clearance once, didn't you?'

'Years ago.' Before I could say anything more, he'd caught my drift. 'You're thinking that might have been more satisfying? Bang, and it's gone, the proof is there in front of you?'

'One less mine, one less bomblet,' I said. 'However many thousands there were to deal with, at least you could tick each one off as a definite achievement.'

'That's true. It was a good feeling.' He shrugged. 'But what should we do? Give up on this, because it's harder?'

He took the truck down the slope, then supervised the students as they attached the wisps of polymer to the specialised winch they'd built. Hassan and Rashid were in their twenties, but they could easily have passed for adolescents. After the war, the dictator and his former backers in the west had found it mutually expedient to have a generation of Iraqi children grow up malnourished and without medical care, if they grew up at all. More than a million people had died under the sanctions. My own sick joke of a nation had sent part of its navy to join the blockade, while the rest stayed home to fend off boatloads of refugees from this, and other, atrocities. General Moustache was long dead, but his comrades-in-genocide with more salubrious addresses were all still at large: doing lecture tours, running think tanks, lobbying for the Nobel peace prize.

As the strands of polymer wound around a core inside the winch's protective barrel, the alpha count rose steadily. It was a good sign: the fine particles of uranium oxide trapped by the Wall had remained bound to the polymer during dehydration, and the reeling in of the net. The radiation from the few grams of U-238 we'd collected was far too low to be a hazard in itself; the thing to avoid was ingesting the dust, and even then the unpleasant effects were as much chemical as radiological. Hopefully, the polymer had also bound its other targets: the organic carcinogens that had been strewn across Kuwait and southern Iraq by the apocalyptic oil well fires. There was no way to determine that until we did a full chemical analysis.

We were all in high spirits on the ride back. What we'd plucked from the wind in the last six weeks wouldn't spare a single person from leukaemia, but it now seemed possible that over the years, over the decades, the technology would make a real difference.

I missed the connection in Singapore for a direct flight home to Sydney, so I had to go via Perth. There was a four-hour wait in Perth; I paced the transit lounge, restless and impatient. I hadn't set eyes on Francine since she'd left Basra three months earlier; she didn't approve of clogging up the limited bandwidth into Iraq with decadent video. When I'd called her from Singapore she'd been busy, and now I couldn't decide whether or not to try again.

Just when I'd resolved to call her, an email came through on my notepad, saying that she'd received my message and would meet me at the airport.

In Sydney, I stood by the baggage carousel, searching the crowd. When I finally saw Francine approaching, she was looking straight at me, smiling. I left the carousel and walked towards her; she stopped and let me close the gap, keeping her eyes fixed on mine. There was a mischievousness to her expression, as if she'd arranged some kind of prank, but I couldn't guess what it might be.

When I was almost in front of her, she turned slightly, and spread her arms. 'Ta-da!'

I froze, speechless. *Why hadn't she told me?*

I walked up to her and embraced her, but she'd read my expression. 'Don't be angry, Ben. I was afraid you'd come home early if you knew.'

'You're right, I would have.' My thoughts were piling up on top of each other; I had three months' worth of reactions to get through in fifteen seconds. *We hadn't planned this. We couldn't afford it. I wasn't ready.*

Suddenly I started weeping, too shocked to be selfconscious in the crowd. The knot of panic and confusion inside me dissolved. I held her more tightly, and felt the swelling in her body against my hip.

'Are you happy?' Francine asked.

I laughed and nodded, choking out the words: 'This is wonderful!'

I meant it. I was still afraid, but it was an exuberant fear. Another ocean had opened up before us. We would find our bearings. We would cross it together.

It took me several days to come down to Earth. We didn't have a real chance to talk until the weekend; Francine had a teaching position at UNSW, and though she could have set her own research aside for a couple of days, marking could wait for no one. There were a thousand things to plan; the six-month UNESCO fellowship that had paid for me to take part in the project in Basra had expired and I'd need to start earning money again soon, but the fact that I'd made no commitments yet gave me some welcome flexibility.

On Monday, alone in the flat again, I started catching up on all the journals I'd neglected. In Iraq I'd been obsessively single-minded, instructing my knowledge miner to keep me informed of work relevant to the Wall to the exclusion of everything else.

Skimming through a summary of six months' worth of papers, a report in *Science* caught my eye: *An Experimental Model for Decoherence in the Many-Worlds Cosmology*. A group at Delft University in the Netherlands had arranged for a simple quantum computer to carry out a sequence of arithmetic operations on a register which had been prepared to contain an equal superposition of binary representations of two different numbers. This in itself was nothing new; superpositions representing up to 128 numbers were now manipulated daily, albeit only under laboratory conditions, at close to absolute zero.

Unusually, though, at each stage of the calculation the qubits containing the numbers in question had been deliberately entangled with other, spare qubits in the computer. The effect of this was that the section performing the calculation had ceased to be in a pure quantum state: it behaved not as if it contained two numbers simultaneously, but as if there were merely an equal chance of it containing either one. This had undermined the quantum nature of the calculation, just as surely as if the whole machine had been imperfectly shielded and become entangled with objects in the environment.

There was one crucial difference, though: in this case, the experimenters had still had access to the spare qubits that had made the calculation behave classically. When they performed an appropriate measurement on the state of the computer *as a whole*, it was shown to have remained in a superposition all along. A single observation couldn't prove this, but the experiment had been repeated thousands of times, and within the margins of error, their prediction was confirmed: although the superposition had become undetectable when they ignored the spare qubits, it had never really gone away. *Both* classical calculations had always taken place simultaneously, even though they'd lost the ability to interact in a quantum-mechanical fashion.

I sat at my desk, pondering the result. On one level, it was just a scaling-up of the quantum eraser experiments of the '90s, but the image of a tiny computer program running through its paces, appearing 'to itself' to be unique and alone, while in fact a second, equally oblivious version had been executing beside it all along, carried a lot more resonance than an interference experiment with photons. I'd become used to the idea of quantum computers performing several calculations at once, but that conjuring trick had always seemed abstract and ethereal, precisely because the parts continued to act as a complicated whole right to the end. What struck home *here* was the stark demonstration of the way each calculation could come to appear as a distinct classical history, as solid and mundane as the shuffling of beads on an abacus.

When Francine arrived home I was cooking dinner, but I grabbed my notepad and showed her the paper.

'Yeah, I've seen it,' she said.

'What do you think?'

She raised her hands and recoiled in mock alarm.

'I'm serious.'

'What do you want me to say? Does this prove the Many Worlds interpretation? No. Does it make it easier to understand, to have a toy model like this? Yes.'

'But does it sway you at all?' I persisted. 'Do you believe the results would still hold, if they could be scaled up indefinitely?' From a toy universe, a handful of qubits, to the real one.

She shrugged. 'I don't really need to be swayed. I always thought the MWI was the most plausible interpretation anyway.'

I left it at that and went back to the kitchen while she pulled out a stack of assignments.

That night, as we lay in bed together, I couldn't get the Delft experiment out of my mind.

'Do you believe there are other versions of us?' I asked Francine.

'I suppose there must be.' She conceded the point as if it was something abstract and metaphysical, and I was being pedantic even to raise it. People who professed belief in the MWI never seemed to want to take it seriously, let alone personally.

'And that doesn't bother you?'

'No,' she said blithely. 'Since I'm powerless to change the situation, what's the use in being upset about it?'

'That's very pragmatic,' I said. Francine reached over and thumped me on the shoulder. 'That was a compliment!' I protested. 'I envy you for having come to terms with it so easily.'

'I haven't, really,' she admitted. 'I've just resolved not to let it worry me, which isn't quite the same thing.'

I turned to face her, though in the near-darkness we could barely see each other. I said, 'What gives you the most satisfaction in life?'

'I take it you're not in the mood to be fobbed off with a soppy romantic answer?' She sighed. 'I don't know. Solving problems. Getting things right.'

'What if for every problem you solve, there's someone just like you who fails, instead?'

'I cope with my failures,' she said. 'Let them cope with theirs.'

'You know it doesn't work like that. Some of them simply *don't* cope. Whatever you find the strength to do, there'll be someone else who won't.'

Francine had no reply.

I said, 'A couple of weeks ago, I asked Sadiq about the time he was doing mine clearance. He said it was more satisfying than mopping up DU; one little explosion, right before your eyes, and you know you've done something worthwhile. We all get moments in our lives like that, with that pure, unambiguous sense of achievement: whatever else we might screw up, at least there's one thing that we've done right.' I laughed uneasily. 'I think I'd go mad, if I couldn't rely on that.'

Francine said, 'You can. Nothing you've done will ever disappear from under your feet. No one's going to march up and take it away from you.'

'I know.' My skin crawled at the image of some less favoured alter ego turning up on our doorstep, demanding his dues. 'That seems so fucking selfish, though. I don't want everything that makes me happy to be at the expense of someone else. I don't want every choice to be like . . . fighting other versions of myself for the prize in some zero-sum game.'

'No.' Francine hesitated. 'But if the reality is like that, what can you do about it?'

Her words hung in the darkness. What could I do about it? Nothing. So did I really want to dwell on it, corroding the foundations of my own happiness, when there was absolutely nothing to be gained, for anyone?

'You're right. This is crazy.' I leant over and kissed her. 'I'd better let you get to sleep.'

'It's not crazy,' she said. 'But I don't have any answers.'

The next morning, after Francine had left for work, I picked up my notepad and saw that she'd mailed me an e-book: an anthology of cheesy 'alternate (sic) history' stories from the '90s, entitled *My God, It's Full of Tsars!* 'What if Gandhi had been a ruthless soldier of fortune? What if Theodore Roosevelt had faced a Martian invasion? What if the Nazis had had Janet Jackson's choreographer?'

I skimmed through the introduction, alternately cackling and groaning, then filed the book away and got down to work. I had a dozen minor administrative tasks to complete for UNESCO before I could start searching in earnest for my next position.

By mid-afternoon I was almost done, but the growing sense of achievement I felt at having buckled down and cleared away these tedious obligations brought with it the corollary: someone infinitesimally different from me – someone who had shared my entire history up until that morning – had procrastinated instead. The triviality of this observation only made it more unsettling; the Delft experiment was seeping into my daily life on the most mundane level.

I dug out the book Francine had sent and tried reading a few of the stories, but the authors' relentlessly camp take on the premise hardly amounted to a *reductio ad absurdum*, or even a comical existential balm. I didn't really care how hilarious it would have been if Marilyn Monroe had been involved in a bedroom farce with Richard Feynman and Richard Nixon. I just wanted to lose the suffocating conviction that everything I had become was a mirage; that my life had been nothing but a blinkered view of a kind of torture chamber, where every glorious reprieve I'd ever celebrated had in fact been an unwitting betrayal.

If fiction had no comfort to offer, what about fact? Even if the Many Worlds cosmology was correct, no one knew for certain what the consequences were. It was a fallacy that literally everything that was physically possible had to occur; most cosmologists I'd read believed that the universe as a whole possessed a single, definite quantum state, and while that state would appear from within as a multitude of distinct classical histories, there was no reason to assume that these histories amounted to some kind of exhaustive catalogue. The same thing held true on a smaller scale: every time two people sat down to a game of chess, there was no reason to believe that they played every possible game.

And if I'd stood in an alley, nine years before, struggling with my conscience? My subjective sense of indecision proved nothing, but even if I'd suffered no qualms and acted without hesitation, to find a human being in a quantum state of pure, unshakeable resolve would have been freakishly unlikely at best, and in fact was probably physically impossible.

'Fuck this.' I didn't know when I'd set myself up for this bout of paranoia, but I wasn't going to indulge it for another second. I banged my head against the desk a few times, then picked up my notepad and went straight to an employment site.

The thoughts didn't vanish entirely; it was too much like trying not to think of a pink elephant. Each time they recurred, though, I found I could shout them down with threats of taking myself straight to a psychiatrist. The prospect of having to explain such a bizarre mental problem was enough to give me access to hitherto untapped reserves of self-discipline.

By the time I started cooking dinner, I was feeling merely foolish. If Francine mentioned the subject again, I'd make a joke of it. I didn't need a psychiatrist. I was a little insecure about my good fortune, and still somewhat rattled by the news of impending fatherhood, but it would hardly have been healthier to take everything for granted.

My notepad chimed. Francine had blocked the video again, as if bandwidth, even here, was as precious as water.

'Hello.'

'Ben? I've had some bleeding. I'm in a taxi. Can you meet me at St Vincent's?'

Her voice was steady, but my own mouth went dry. 'Sure. I'll be there in fifteen minutes.' I couldn't add anything: *I love you, it will be all right, hold on.* She didn't need that, it would have jinxed everything.

Half an hour later, I was still caught in traffic, white-knuckled with rage and helplessness. I stared down at the dashboard, at the realtime map with every other gridlocked vehicle marked, and finally stopped deluding myself that at any moment I would turn into a magically deserted side street and weave my way across the city in just a few more minutes.

In the ward, behind the curtains drawn around her bed, Francine lay curled and rigid, her back turned, refusing to look at me. All I could do was stand beside her. The gynaecologist had yet to explain everything properly, but the miscarriage had been accompanied by complications, and she'd had to perform surgery.

Before I'd applied for the UNESCO fellowship, we'd discussed the risks. For two prudent, well-informed, shortterm visitors, the danger had seemed microscopic. Francine had never travelled out into the desert with me, and even for the locals in Basra the rates of birth defects and miscarriages had fallen a long way from their peaks. We were both taking contraceptives; condoms had seemed like overkill. *Had I brought it back to her from the desert? A speck of dust, trapped beneath my foreskin? Had I poisoned her while we were making love?*

Francine turned towards me. The skin around her eyes was grey and swollen, and I could see how much effort it took for her to meet my gaze. She drew her hands out from under the bedclothes and let me hold them; they were freezing.

After a while, she started sobbing, but she wouldn't release my hands. I stroked the back of her thumb with my own thumb, a tiny, gentle movement.

2020

'How do you feel now?' Olivia Maslin didn't quite make eye contact as she addressed me; the image of my brain activity painted on her retinas was clearly holding her attention.

'Fine,' I said. 'Exactly the same as I did before you started the infusion.'

I was reclining on something like a dentist's couch, halfway between sitting and lying, wearing a tight-fitting cap studded with magnetic sensors and inducers. It was impossible to ignore the slight coolness of the liquid flowing into the vein in my forearm, but that sensation was no different than it had been on the previous occasion, a fortnight before.

'Could you count to ten for me, please.'

I obliged.

'Now close your eyes and picture the same familiar face as the last time.'

She'd told me I could choose anyone; I'd picked Francine. I brought back the image, then suddenly recalled that, the first time, after contemplating the detailed picture in my head for a few seconds – as if I was preparing to give a description to the police – I'd started thinking about Francine herself. On cue, the same transition occurred again: the frozen, forensic likeness became flesh and blood.

I was led through the whole sequence of activities once more: reading the same short story ('Two Old-Timers' by F. Scott Fitzgerald), listening to the same piece of music (from Rossini's *The Thieving Magpie*), recounting the same childhood memory (my first day at school). At some point, I lost any trace of anxiety about repeating my earlier mental states with sufficient fidelity; after all, the experiment had been designed to cope with the inevitable variation between the two sessions. I was just one volunteer out of dozens, and half the subjects would be receiving nothing but saline on both occasions. For all I knew, I was one of them: a control, merely setting the baseline against which any real effect would be judged.

If I was receiving the coherence disruptors, though, then as far as I could tell they'd had no effect on me. My inner life hadn't evaporated as the molecules bound to the microtubules in my neurons, guaranteeing that any kind of quantum coherence those structures might otherwise have maintained would be lost to the environment in a fraction of a picosecond.

Personally, I'd never subscribed to Penrose's theory that quantum effects might play a role in consciousness; calculations dating back to a seminal paper by Max Tegmark, twenty years before, had already made sustained coherence in any neural structure extremely unlikely. Nevertheless, it had taken considerable ingenuity on the part of Olivia and her team to rule out the idea definitively, in a series of clear-cut experiments. Over the past two years, they'd chased the ghost away from each of the various structures that different factions of Penrose's disciples had anointed as the essential quantum components of the brain. The earliest proposal – the microtubules, huge polymeric molecules that formed a kind of skeleton inside every cell – had turned out to be the hardest to target for disruption. But now it was entirely possible that the cytoskeletons of my very own neurons were dotted with molecules that coupled them strongly to a noisy microwave field in which my skull was, definitely, bathed. In which case, my microtubules had about as much chance of exploiting quantum effects as I had of playing a game of squash with a version of myself from a parallel universe.

When the experiment was over, Olivia thanked me, then became even more distant as she reviewed the data. Raj, one of her graduate students, slid out the needle and stuck a plaster over the tiny puncture wound, then helped me out of the cap.

'I know you don't know yet if I was a control or not,' I said, 'but have you noticed significant differences, with anyone?' I was almost the last subject in the microtubule trials; any effect should have shown up by now.

Olivia smiled enigmatically. 'You'll just have to wait for publication.' Raj leant down and whispered, 'No, never.'

I climbed off the couch. 'The zombie walks!' Raj declaimed. I lunged hungrily for his brain; he ducked away, laughing, while Olivia watched us with an expression of pained indulgence. Die-hard members of the Penrose camp claimed that Olivia's experiments proved nothing, because even if people *behaved* identically while all quantum effects were ruled out, they could be doing this as mere automata, totally devoid of consciousness. When Olivia had offered to let her chief detractor experience coherence disruption for himself, he'd replied that this would be no more persuasive, because memories laid down while you were a zombie would be indistinguishable from ordinary memories, so that looking back on the experience, you'd notice nothing unusual.

This was sheer desperation; you might as well assert that everyone in the world but yourself was a zombie, and you were one, too, every second Tuesday. As the experiments were repeated by other groups around the world, those people who'd backed the Penrose theory as a scientific hypothesis, rather than adopting it as a kind of mystical dogma, would gradually accept that it had been refuted.

I left the neuroscience building and walked across the campus, back towards my office in the physics department. It was a mild, clear spring morning, with students out lying on the grass, dozing off with books balanced over their faces like tents. There were still some advantages to reading from old-fashioned sheaves of e-paper. I'd only had my own eyes chipped the year before, and though I'd adapted to the technology easily enough, I still found it disconcerting to wake on a Sunday morning to find Francine reading the *Herald* beside me with her eyes shut.

Olivia's results didn't surprise me, but it was satisfying to have the matter resolved once and for all: consciousness was a purely classical phenomenon. Among other things, this meant that there was no compelling reason to believe that software running on a classical computer could not be conscious. Of course, everything in the universe obeyed quantum mechanics at some level, but Paul Benioff, one of the pioneers of quantum computing, had shown back in the '80s that you could build a classical Turing machine from quantum mechanical parts, and over the last few years, in my spare time, I'd studied the branch of quantum computing theory that concerned itself with *avoiding* quantum effects.

Back in my office, I summoned up a schematic of the device I called the Qusp: the quantum singleton processor. The Qusp would employ all the techniques designed to shield the latest generation of quantum computers from entanglement with their environment, but it would use them to a very different end. A quantum computer was shielded so it could perform a multitude of parallel calculations, without each one spawning a separate history of its own, in which only one answer was accessible. The Qusp would perform just a single calculation at a time, but on its way to the unique result it would be able to pass safely through superpositions that included any number of alternatives, without those alternatives being made real. Cut off from the outside world during each computational step, it would keep its temporary quantum ambivalence as private and inconsequential as a daydream, never being forced to act out every possibility it dared to entertain.

The Qusp would still need to interact with its environment whenever it gathered data about the world, and that interaction would inevitably split it into different versions. If you attached a camera to the Qusp and pointed it at an ordinary object – a rock, a plant, a bird – that object could hardly be expected to possess a single classical history, and so neither would the combined system of Qusp plus rock, Qusp plus plant, Qusp plus bird.

The Qusp itself, though, would never initiate the split. In a given set of circumstances, it would only ever produce a single response. An AI running on the Qusp could make its decisions as whimsically, or with as much weighty deliberation, as it liked, but for each distinct scenario it confronted, in the end it would only make one choice, only follow one course of action.

I closed the file, and the image vanished from my retinas. For all the work I'd put into the design, I'd made no effort to build the thing. I'd been using it as little more than a talisman: whenever I found myself picturing my life as a tranquil dwelling built over a slaughterhouse, I'd summon up the Qusp as a symbol of hope. It was proof of a possibility, and a possibility was all it took. Nothing in the laws of physics could prevent a small portion of humanity's descendants from escaping their ancestors' dissipation.

Yet I'd shied away from any attempt to see that promise fulfilled, first-hand. In part, I'd been afraid of delving too deeply and uncovering a flaw in the Qusp's design, robbing myself of the one crutch that kept me standing when the horror swept over me. It had also been a matter of guilt: I'd been the one granted happiness, so many times, that it had seemed unconscionable to aspire to that state yet again. I'd knocked so many of my hapless cousins out of the ring, it was time I threw a fight and let the prize go to my opponent instead.

That last excuse was idiotic. The stronger my determination to build the Qusp, the more branches there would be in which it was real. Weakening my resolve was *not* an act of charity, surrendering the benefits to someone else; it merely impoverished every future version of me, and everyone they touched.

I did have a third excuse. It was time I dealt with that one too.

I called Francine.

'Are you free for lunch?' I asked. She hesitated; there was always work she could be doing. 'To discuss the Cauchy-Riemann equations?' I suggested.

She smiled. It was our code, when the request was a special one. 'All right. One o'clock?'

I nodded. 'I'll see you then.'

Francine was twenty minutes late, but that was less of a wait than I was used to. She'd been appointed deputy head of the mathematics department eighteen months before, and she still had some teaching duties as well as all the new administrative work. Over the last eight years, I'd had a dozen shortterm contracts with various bodies – government departments, corporations, NGOs – before finally ending up as a very lowly member of the physics department at our *alma mater*. I did envy her the prestige and security of her job, but I'd been happy with most of the work I'd done, even if it had been too scattered between disciplines to contribute to anything like a traditional career path.

I'd bought Francine a plate of cheese-and-salad sandwiches, and she attacked them hungrily as soon as she sat down. I said, 'I've got ten minutes at the most, haven't I?'

She covered her mouth with her hand and replied defensively, 'It could have waited until tonight, couldn't it?'

'Sometimes I can't put things off. I have to act while I still have the courage.'

At this ominous prelude she chewed more slowly. 'You did the second stage of Olivia's experiment this morning, didn't you?'

'Yeah.' I'd discussed the whole procedure with her before I volunteered.

'So I take it you didn't lose consciousness, when your neurons became marginally more classical than usual?' She sipped chocolate milk through a straw.

'No. Apparently no one ever loses anything. That's not official yet, but—'

Francine nodded, unsurprised. We shared the same position on the Penrose theory; there was no need to discuss it again now.

I said, 'I want to know if you're going to have the operation.'

She continued drinking for a few more seconds, then released the straw and wiped her upper lip with her thumb, unnecessarily. 'You want me to make up my mind about that, here and now?'

'No.' The damage to her uterus from the miscarriage could be repaired; we'd been discussing the possibility for almost five years. We'd both had comprehensive chelation therapy to remove any trace of U-238. We could have children in the usual way with a reasonable degree of safety, if that was what we wanted. 'But if you've already decided, I want you to tell me now.'

Francine looked wounded. 'That's unfair.'

'What is? Implying that you might not have told me, the instant you decided?'

'No. Implying that it's all in my hands.'

I said, 'I'm not washing my hands of the decision. You know how I feel. But you know I'd back you all the way, if you said you wanted to carry a child.' I believed I would have. Maybe it was a form of double-think, but I couldn't treat the birth of one more ordinary child as some kind of atrocity and refuse to be a part of it.

'Fine. But what will you do if I don't?' She examined my face calmly. I think she already knew, but she wanted me to spell it out.

'We could always adopt,' I observed casually.

'Yes, we could do that.' She smiled slightly; she knew that made me lose my ability to bluff, even faster than when she stared me down.

I stopped pretending that there was any mystery left; she'd seen right through me from the start. I said, 'I just don't want to do this, then discover that it makes you feel that you've been cheated out of what you really wanted.'

'It wouldn't,' she insisted. 'It wouldn't rule out anything. We could still have a natural child as well.'

'Not as easily.' This would not be like merely having work-aholic parents, or an ordinary brother or sister to compete with for attention.

'You only want to do this if I can promise you that it's the only child we'd ever have?' Francine shook her head. 'I'm not going to promise that. I don't intend having the operation any time soon, but I'm not going to swear that I won't change my mind. Nor am I going to swear that if we do this it will make no difference to what happens later. It will be a factor. How could it not be? But it won't be enough to rule anything in or out.'

I looked away, across the rows of tables, at all the students wrapped up in their own concerns. She was right; I was being unreasonable. I'd wanted this to be a choice with no possible downside, a way of making the best of our situation, but no one could guarantee that. It would be a gamble, like everything else.

I turned back to Francine.

'All right; I'll stop trying to pin you down. What I want to do right now is go ahead and build the Qusp. And when it's finished, if we're certain we can trust it . . . I want us to raise a child with it. I want us to raise an AI.'

2029

I met Francine at the airport, and we drove across São Paulo through curtains of wild, lashing rain. I was amazed that her plane hadn't been diverted; a tropical storm had just hit the coast, halfway between us and Rio.

'So much for giving you a tour of the city,' I lamented. Through the windscreen, our actual surroundings were all but invisible; the bright overlay we both perceived, surreally coloured and detailed, made the experience rather like perusing a 3D map while trapped in a car wash.

Francine was pensive, or tired from the flight. I found it hard to think of San Francisco as remote when the time difference was so small, and even when I'd made the journey north to visit her, it had been nothing compared to all the ocean-spanning marathons I'd sat through in the past.

We both had an early night. The next morning, Francine accompanied me to my cluttered workroom in the basement of the university's engineering department. I'd been chasing grants and collaborators around the world, like a child on a treasure hunt, slowly piecing together a device that few of my colleagues believed was worth creating for its own sake. Fortunately, I'd managed to find pretexts – or even genuine spin-offs – for almost every stage of the work. Quantum computing, per se, had become bogged down in recent years, stymied by both a shortage of practical algorithms and a limit to the complexity of super-positions that could be sustained. The Qusp had nudged the technological envelope in some promising directions, without making any truly exorbitant demands; the states it juggled were relatively simple, and they only needed to be kept isolated for milliseconds at a time.

I introduced Carlos, Maria and Jun, but then they made them-selves scarce as I showed Francine around. We still had a demon-stration of the 'balanced decoupling' principle set up on a bench, for the tour by one of our corporate donors the week before. What caused an imperfectly shielded quantum computer to decohere was the fact that each possible state of the device affected its environment slightly differently. The shielding itself could always be improved, but Carlos's group had perfected a way to buy a little more protection by sheer deviousness. In the demon-stration rig, the flow of energy through the device remained absolutely constant whatever state it was in, because any drop in power consumption by the main set of quantum gates was compensated for by a rise in a set of balancing gates, and vice versa. This gave the environment one less clue by which to discern internal differences in the processor, and to tear any superposition apart into mutually disconnected branches.

Francine knew all the theory backwards, but she'd never seen this hardware in action. When I invited her to twiddle the controls, she took to the rig like a child with a game console.

'You really should have joined the team,' I said.

'Maybe I did,' she countered. 'In another branch.'

She'd moved from UNSW to Berkeley two years before, not long after I'd moved from Delft to São Paulo; it was the closest suitable position she could find. At the time, I'd resented the fact that she'd refused to compromise and work remotely; with only five hours' difference, teaching at Berkeley from São Paulo would not have been impossible. In the end, though, I'd accepted the fact that she'd wanted to keep on testing me, testing both of us. If we weren't strong enough to stay together through the trials of a prolonged physical separation – or if I was not sufficiently committed to the project to endure whatever sacrifices it entailed – she did not want us proceeding to the next stage.

I led her to the corner bench, where a nondescript grey box half a metre across sat, apparently inert. I gestured to it and our retinal overlays transformed its appearance, 'revealing' a maze with a transparent lid embedded in the top of the device. In one chamber of the maze, a slightly cartoonish mouse sat motionless. Not quite dead, not quite sleeping.

'This is the famous Zelda?' Francine asked.

'Yes.' Zelda was a neural network, a stripped-down, stylised mouse brain. There were newer, fancier versions available, much closer to the real thing, but the ten-year-old public domain Zelda had been good enough for our purposes.

Three other chambers held cheese. 'Right now, she has no experience of the maze,' I explained. 'So let's start her up and watch her explore.' I gestured, and Zelda began scampering around, trying out different passages, deftly reversing each time she hit a cul-de-sac. 'Her brain is running on a Qusp, but the maze is implemented on an ordinary classical computer, so in terms of coherence issues, it's really no different from a physical maze.'

'Which means that each time she takes in information, she gets entangled with the outside world,' Francine suggested.

'Absolutely. But she always holds off doing that until the Qusp has completed its current computational step, and every qubit contains a definite zero or a definite one. She's never in two minds when she lets the world in, so the entanglement process doesn't split her into separate branches.'

Francine continued to watch, in silence. Zelda finally found one of the chambers containing a reward; when she'd eaten it, a hand scooped her up and returned her to her starting point, then replaced the cheese.

'Here are ten thousand previous trials, superimposed.' I replayed the data. It looked as if a single mouse was running through the maze, moving just as we'd seen her move when I'd begun the latest experiment. Restored each time to exactly the same starting condition, and confronted with exactly the same environment, Zelda – like any computer program with no truly random influences – had simply repeated herself. All ten thousand trials had yielded identical results.

To a casual observer, unaware of the context, this would have been a singularly unimpressive performance. Faced with exactly one situation, Zelda the virtual mouse did exactly one thing. So what? If you'd been able to wind back a flesh-and-blood mouse's memory with the same degree of precision, wouldn't it have repeated itself too?

Francine said, 'Can you cut off the shielding? And the balanced decoupling?'

'Yep.' I obliged her, and initiated a new trial.

Zelda took a different path this time, exploring the maze by a different route. Though the initial condition of the neural net was identical, the switching processes taking place within the Qusp were now opened up to the environment constantly, and super-positions of several different eigenstates – states in which the

Qusp's qubits possessed definite binary values, which in turn led to Zelda making definite choices – were becoming entangled with the outside world. According to the Copenhagen interpretation of quantum mechanics, this interaction was randomly 'collapsing' the superpositions into single eigenstates; Zelda was still doing just one thing at a time, but her behaviour had ceased to be deterministic. According to the MWI, the interaction was transforming the environment – Francine and me included – into a superposition with components that were coupled to each eigenstate; Zelda was actually running the maze in many different ways simultaneously, and other versions of us were seeing her take all those other routes.

Which scenario was correct?

I said, 'I'll reconfigure everything now, to wrap the whole set-up in a Delft cage.' A 'Delft cage' was jargon for the situation I'd first read about seventeen years before: instead of opening up the Qusp to the environment, I'd connect it to a second quantum computer and let *that* play the role of the outside world.

We could no longer watch Zelda moving about in real time, but after the trial was completed, it was possible to test the combined system of both computers against the hypothesis that it was in a pure quantum state in which Zelda had run the maze along hundreds of different routes, all at once. I displayed a representation of the conjectured state, built up by superimposing all the paths she'd taken in ten thousand unshielded trials.

The test result flashed up: CONSISTENT.

'One measurement proves nothing,' Francine pointed out.

'No.' I repeated the trial. Again, the hypothesis was not refuted. If Zelda had actually run the maze along just one path, the probability of the computers' joint state passing this imperfect test was about one per cent. For passing it twice, the odds were about one in ten thousand.

I repeated it a third time, then a fourth.

Francine said, 'That's enough.' She actually looked queasy. The image of the hundreds of blurred mouse trails on the display was not a literal photograph of anything, but if the old Delft experiment had been enough to give me a visceral sense of the reality of the multiverse, perhaps this demonstration had finally done the same for her.

'Can I show you one more thing?' I asked.

'Keep the Delft cage, but restore the Qusp's shielding?'

'Right.'

I did it. The Qusp was now fully protected once more whenever it was not in an eigenstate, but this time, it was the second quantum computer, not the outside world, to which it was intermittently exposed. If Zelda split into multiple branches again, then she'd only take that fake environment with her, and we'd still have our hands on all the evidence.

Tested against the hypothesis that no split had occurred, the verdict was: CONSISTENT. CONSISTENT. CONSISTENT.

We went out to dinner with the whole of the team, but Francine pleaded a headache and left early. She insisted that I stay and finish the meal, and I didn't argue; she was not the kind of person who expected you to assume that she was being politely selfless, while secretly hoping to be contradicted.

After Francine had left, Maria turned to me. 'So you two are really going ahead with the Frankenchild?' She'd been teasing me about this for as long as I'd known her, but apparently she hadn't been game to raise the subject in Francine's presence.

'We still have to talk about it.' I felt uncomfortable myself, now, discussing the topic the moment Francine was absent. Confessing my ambition when I applied to join the team was one thing; it would have been dishonest to keep my collaborators in the dark about my ultimate intentions. Now that the enabling technology was more or less completed, though, the issue seemed far more personal.

Carlos said breezily, 'Why not? There are so many others now. Sophie. Linus. Theo. Probably a hundred we don't even know about. It's not as if Ben's child won't have playmates.' Adai – Autonomously Developing Artificial Intelligences – had been appearing in a blaze of controversy every few months for the last four years. A Swiss researcher, Isabelle Schib, had taken the old models of morphogenesis that had led to software like Zelda, refined the technique by several orders of magnitude, and applied it to human genetic data. Wedded to sophisticated prosthetic bodies, Isabelle's creations inhabited the physical world and learnt from their experience, just like any other child.

Jun shook his head reprovingly. 'I wouldn't raise a child with no legal rights. What happens when you die? For all you know, it could end up as someone's property.'

I'd been over this with Francine. 'I can't believe that in ten or twenty years' time there won't be citizenship laws, somewhere in the world.'

Jun snorted. 'Twenty years! How long did it take the US to emancipate their slaves?'

Carlos interjected, 'Who's going to create an adai just to use it as a slave? If you want something biddable, write ordinary software. If you need consciousness, humans are cheaper.'

Maria said, 'It won't come down to economics. It's the nature of the things that will determine how they're treated.'

'You mean the xenophobia they'll face?' I suggested.

Maria shrugged. 'You make it sound like racism, but we aren't talking about human beings. Once you have software with goals of its own, free to do whatever it likes, where will it end? The first generation makes the next one better, faster, smarter; the second generation even more so. Before we know it, we're like ants to them.'

Carlos groaned. 'Not that hoary old fallacy! If you really believe that stating the analogy "ants are to humans, as humans are to x" is proof that it's possible to solve for x, then I'll meet you where the south pole is like the equator.'

I said, 'The Qusp runs no faster than an organic brain; we need to keep the switching rate low, because that makes the shielding requirements less stringent. It might be possible to nudge those parameters, eventually, but there's no reason in the world why an adai would be better equipped to do that than you or I would. As for making their own offspring smarter . . . even if Schib's group has been perfectly successful, they will have merely translated human neural development from one substrate to another. They won't have "improved" on the process at all – whatever that might mean. So if the adai have any advantage over us, it will be no more than the advantage shared by flesh-and-blood children: cultural transmission of one more generation's worth of experience.'

Maria frowned, but she had no immediate comeback.

Jun said dryly, 'Plus immortality.'

'Well, yes, there is that,' I conceded.

Francine was awake when I arrived home.

'Have you still got a headache?' I whispered.

'No.'

I undressed and climbed into bed beside her.

She said, 'You know what I miss the most? When we're fucking online?'

'This had better not be complicated; I'm out of practice.'

'Kissing.'

I kissed her, slowly and tenderly, and she melted beneath me. 'Three more months,' I promised, 'and I'll move up to Berkeley.'

'To be my kept man.'

'I prefer the term "unpaid but highly valued caregiver".' Francine stiffened. I said, 'We can talk about that later.' I started kissing her again, but she turned her face away.

'I'm afraid,' she said.

'So am I,' I assured her. 'That's a good sign. Everything worth doing is terrifying.'

'But not everything terrifying is good.'

I rolled over and lay beside her. She said, 'On one level, it's easy. What greater gift could you give a child than the power to make real decisions? What worse fate could you spare her from than being forced to act against her better judgement, over and over? When you put it like that, it's simple.

'But every fibre in my body still rebels against it. How will she feel, knowing what she is? How will she make friends? How will she belong? How will she not despise us for making her a freak? And what if we're robbing her of something she'd value: living a billion lives, never being forced to choose between them? What if she sees the gift as a kind of impoverishment?'

'She can always drop the shielding on the Qusp,' I said. 'Once she understands the issues, she can choose for herself.'

'That's true.' Francine did not sound mollified at all; she would have thought of that long before I'd mentioned it, but she wasn't looking for concrete answers. Every ordinary human instinct screamed at us that we were embarking on something *dangerous*, *unnatural*, *hubristic* – but those instincts were more about safe-guarding our own reputations than protecting our child-to-be. No parent, save the most wilfully negligent, would be pilloried if their flesh-and-blood child turned out to be ungrateful for life; if I'd railed against my own mother and father because I'd found fault in the existential conditions with which I'd been lumbered, it wasn't hard to guess which side would attract the most sym-pathy from the world at large. Anything that went wrong with *our* child would be grounds for lynching – however much love, sweat, and soul-searching had gone into her creation – because we'd had the temerity to be dissatisfied with the kind of fate that everyone else happily inflicted on their own.

I said, 'You saw Zelda today, spread across the branches. You know, deep down now, that the same thing happens to all of us.'

'Yes.' Something tore inside me as Francine uttered that admis-sion. I'd never really wanted her to feel it, the way I did.

I persisted. 'Would you willingly sentence your own child to that condition? And your grandchildren? And your great-grandchildren?'

'No,' Francine replied. A part of her hated me now; I could hear it in her voice. It was *my* curse, *my* obsession; before she met me, she'd managed to believe and not believe, taking her acceptance of the multiverse lightly.

I said, 'I can't do this without you.'

'You can, actually. More easily than any of the alternatives. You wouldn't even need a stranger to donate an egg.'

'I can't do it unless you're behind me. If you say the word, I'll stop here. We've built the Qusp. We've shown that it can work. Even if we don't do this last part ourselves, someone else will, in a decade or two.'

'If *we* don't do this,' Francine observed acerbically, 'we'll simply do it in another branch.'

I said, 'That's true, but it's no use thinking that way. In the end, I can't function unless I pretend that my choices are real. I doubt that anyone can.'

Francine was silent for a long time. I stared up into the darkness of the room, trying hard not to contemplate the near certainty that her decision would go both ways.

Finally, she spoke.

'Then let's make a child who doesn't need to pretend.'

2031

Isabelle Schib welcomed us into her office. In person, she was slightly less intimidating than she was online; it wasn't anything different in her appearance or manner, just the ordinariness of her surroundings. I'd envisaged her ensconced in some vast, pristine, high-tech building, not a couple of poky rooms on a back street in Basel.

Once the pleasantries were out of the way, Isabelle got straight to the point. 'You've been accepted,' she announced. 'I'll send you the contract later today.'

My throat constricted with panic; I should have been elated, but I just felt unprepared. Isabelle's group licensed only three new adai a year. The shortlist had come down to about a hundred couples, winnowed from tens of thousands of applicants. We'd travelled to Switzerland for the final selection process, carried out by an agency that ordinarily handled adoptions. Through all the interviews and questionnaires, all the personality tests and scenario challenges, I'd managed to half-convince myself that our dedication would win through in the end, but that had been nothing but a prop to keep my spirits up.

Francine said calmly, 'Thank you.'

I coughed. 'You're happy with everything we've proposed?' If there was going to be a proviso thrown in that rendered this miracle worthless, better to hear it now, before the shock had worn off and I'd started taking things for granted.

Isabelle nodded. 'I don't pretend to be an expert in the relevant fields, but I've had the Qusp's design assessed by several colleagues, and I see no reason why it wouldn't be an appropriate form of hardware for an adai. I'm entirely agnostic about the MWI, so I don't share your view that the Qusp is a necessity, but if you were worried that I might write you off as cranks because of it,' she smiled slightly, 'you should meet some of the other people I've had to deal with.

'I believe you have the adai's welfare at heart, and you're not suffering from any of the superstitions – technophobic *or* technophilic – that would distort the relationship. And as you'll recall, I'll be entitled to visits and inspections throughout your period of guardianship. If you're found to be violating any of the terms of the contract, your licence will be revoked, and I'll take charge of the adai.'

Francine said, 'What do you think the prospects are for a happier end to our guardianship?'

'I'm lobbying the European parliament, constantly,' Isabelle replied. 'Of course, in a few years' time several adai will reach the stage where their personal testimony begins contributing to the debate, but none of us should wait until then. The ground has to be prepared.'

We spoke for almost an hour, on this and other issues. Isabelle had become quite an expert at fending off the attentions of the media; she promised to send us a handbook on this, along with the contract.

'Did you want to meet Sophie?' Isabelle asked, almost as an afterthought.

Francine said, 'That would be wonderful.' Francine and I

had seen a video of Sophie at age four, undergoing a battery of psychological tests, but we'd never had a chance to converse with her, let alone meet her face to face.

The three of us left the office together, and Isabelle drove us to her home on the outskirts of the town.

In the car, the reality began sinking in anew. I felt the same mixture of exhilaration and claustrophobia that I'd experienced nineteen years before, when Francine had met me at the airport with news of her pregnancy. No digital conception had yet taken place, but if sex had ever felt half as loaded with risks and responsibilities as this, I would have remained celibate for life.

'No badgering, no interrogation,' Isabelle warned us as she pulled into the driveway.

I said, 'Of course not.'

Isabelle called out, 'Marco! Sophie!' as we followed her through the door. At the end of the hall, I heard childish giggling, and an adult male voice whispering in French. Then Isabelle's husband stepped out from behind the corner, a smiling, dark-haired young man, with Sophie riding on his shoulders. At first I couldn't look at her; I just smiled politely back at Marco, while noting glumly that he was at least fifteen years younger than I was. *How could I even think of doing this, at forty-six?* Then I glanced up and caught Sophie's eye. She gazed straight back at me for a moment, appearing curious and composed, but then a fit of shyness struck her and she buried her face in Marco's hair.

Isabelle introduced us, in English; Sophie was being raised to speak four languages, though in Switzerland that was hardly phenomenal. Sophie said, 'Hello' but kept her eyes lowered. Isabelle said, 'Come into the living room. Would you like something to drink?'

The five of us sipped lemonade, and the adults made polite, superficial conversation. Sophie sat on Marco's knees, squirming restlessly, sneaking glances at us. She looked exactly like an ordinary, slightly gawky, six-year-old girl. She had Isabelle's straw-coloured hair and Marco's brown eyes, whether by fiat or rigorous genetic simulation; she could have passed for their biological daughter. I'd read technical specifications describing her body, and seen an earlier version in action on the video, but the fact that it looked so plausible was the least of its designers' achievements. Watching her drinking, wriggling and fidgeting, I had no doubt that she felt herself inhabiting this skin, as much as I did my own. She was not a puppeteer posing as a child, pulling electronic strings from some dark cavern in her skull.

'Do you like lemonade?' I asked her.

She stared at me for a moment, as if wondering whether she should be affronted by the presumptuousness of this question, then replied, 'It tickles.'

In the taxi to the hotel, Francine held my hand tightly.

'Are you okay?' I asked.

'Yes, of course.'

In the elevator, she started crying. I wrapped my arms around her.

'She would have turned eighteen this year.'

'I know.'

'Do you think she's alive, somewhere?'

'I don't know. I don't know if that's a good way to think about it.'

Francine wiped her eyes. 'No. This will be her. That's the way to see it. This will be my girl. Just a few years late.'

Before flying home, we visited a small pathology lab, and left samples of our blood.

Our daughter's first five bodies reached us a month before her birth. I unpacked all five and laid them out in a row on the living room floor. With their muscles slack and their eyes rolled up, they looked more like tragic mummies than sleeping infants. I dismissed that grisly image; better to think of them as suits of clothes. The only difference was that we hadn't bought pyjamas quite so far ahead.

From wrinkled pink newborn to chubby eighteen-month-old, the progression made an eerie sight – even if an organic child's development, short of serious disease or malnourishment, would have been scarcely less predictable. A colleague of Francine's had lectured me a few weeks before about the terrible 'mechanical determinism' we'd be imposing on our child, and though his arguments had been philosophically naïve, this sequence of immutable snapshots from the future still gave me goosebumps.

The truth was, reality as a whole was deterministic, whether you had a Qusp for a brain or not; the quantum state of the multiverse at any moment determined the entire future. Personal experience – confined to one branch at a time – certainly *appeared* probabilistic, because there was no way to predict which local future you'd experience when a branch split, but the reason it was impossible to know that in advance was because the real answer was 'all of them'.

For a singleton, the only difference was that branches never split on the basis of your personal decisions. The world at large would continue to look probabilistic, but every choice you made was entirely determined by *who you were* and *the situation you faced*.

What more could anyone hope for? It was not as if *who you were* could be boiled down to some crude genetic or sociological profile; every shadow you'd seen on the ceiling at night, every cloud you'd watched drift across the sky, would have left some small imprint on the shape of your mind. Those events were fully determined too, when viewed across the multiverse – with different versions of you witnessing every possibility – but in practical terms, the bottom line was that no private investigator armed with your genome and a potted biography could plot your every move in advance.

Our daughter's choices – like everything else – had been written in stone at the birth of the universe, but that information could only be decoded by *becoming her* along the way. Her actions would flow from her temperament, her principles, her desires, and the fact that all of these qualities would themselves have prior causes did nothing to diminish their value. *Free will* was a slippery notion, but to me it simply meant that your choices were more or less consistent with your nature – which in turn was a provisional, constantly evolving consensus between a thousand different influences. Our daughter would not be robbed of the chance to act capriciously, or even perversely, but at least it would not be impossible for her ever to act wholly in accordance with her ideals.

I packed the bodies away before Francine got home. I wasn't sure if the sight would unsettle her, but I didn't want her measuring them up for more clothes.

The delivery began in the early hours of the morning of Sunday, 14 December, and was expected to last about four hours, depending on traffic. I sat in the nursery while Francine paced the hallway outside, both of us watching the data coming through over the fibre from Basel.

Isabelle had used our genetic information as the starting point for a simulation of the development *in utero* of a complete embryo, employing an 'adaptive hierarchy' model, with the highest resolution reserved for the central nervous system. The Qusp would take over this task, not only for the newborn child's brain, but also for the thousands of biochemical processes occurring outside the skull that the artificial bodies were not designed to perform. Apart from their sophisticated sensory and motor functions, the bodies could take in food and excrete wastes – for psychological and social reasons, as well as for the chemical energy this provided – and they breathed air, both in order to oxidise this fuel, and for vocalisation, but they had no blood, no endocrine system, no immune response.

The Qusp I'd built in Berkeley was smaller than the São Paulo version, but it was still six times as wide as an infant's skull. Until it was further miniaturised, our daughter's mind would sit in a box in a corner of the nursery, joined to the rest of her by a wireless data link. Bandwidth and timelag would not be an issue within the Bay Area, and if we needed to take her further afield before everything was combined, the Qusp wasn't too large or delicate to move.

As the progress bar I was overlaying on the side of the Qusp nudged 98 per cent, Francine came into the nursery looking agitated.

'We have to put it off, Ben. Just for a day. I need more time to prepare myself.'

I shook my head. 'You made me promise to say no if you asked me to do that.' She'd even refused to let me tell her how to halt the Qusp herself.

'Just a few hours,' she pleaded.

Francine seemed genuinely distressed, but I hardened my heart by telling myself that she was acting: testing me, seeing if I'd keep my word. 'No. No slowing down or speeding up, no pauses, no tinkering at all. This child has to hit us like a freight train, just like any other child would.'

'You want me to go into labour now?' she said sarcastically. When I'd raised the possibility, half-jokingly, of putting her on a course of hormones that would have mimicked some of the effects of pregnancy in order to make bonding with the child easier – for myself as well, indirectly – she'd almost bitten my head off. I hadn't been serious, because I knew it wasn't necessary. Adoption was the ultimate proof of that, but what we were doing was closer to claiming a child of our own from a surrogate.

'No. Just pick her up.'

Francine peered down at the inert form in the cot.

'I can't do it!' she wailed. 'When I hold her, she should feel as if she's the most precious thing in the world to me. How can I make her believe that, when I know I could bounce her off the walls without harming her?'

We had two minutes left. I felt my breathing grow ragged. I could send the Qusp a halt code, but what if that set the pattern? If one of us had had too little sleep, if Francine was late for work, if we talked ourselves into believing that our special child was so unique that we deserved a short holiday from her needs, what would stop us from doing the same thing again?

I opened my mouth to threaten her: *Either you pick her up, now, or I do it.* I stopped myself, and said, 'You know how much it would harm her psychologically if you dropped her. The very fact that you're afraid that you won't convey as much protectiveness as you need to will be just as strong a signal to her as anything else. *You care about her.* She'll sense that.'

Francine stared back at me dubiously.

I said, 'She'll know. I'm sure she will.'

Francine reached into the cot and lifted the slack body into her arms. Seeing her cradle the lifeless form, I felt an anxious twisting in my gut; I'd experienced nothing like this when I'd laid the five plastic shells out for inspection.

I banished the progress bar and let myself freefall through the final seconds: watching my daughter, willing her to move.

Her thumb twitched, then her legs scissored weakly. I couldn't see her face, so I watched Francine's expression. For an instant, I thought I could detect a horrified tightening at the corners of her mouth, as if she was about to recoil from this golem. Then the child began to bawl and kick, and Francine started weeping with undisguised joy.

As she raised the child to her face and planted a kiss on its wrinkled forehead, I suffered my own moment of disquiet. How easily that tender response had been summoned, when the body could as well have been brought to life by the kind of software used to animate the characters in games and films.

It hadn't, though. There'd been nothing false or easy about the road that had brought us to this moment – let alone the one that Isabelle had followed – and we hadn't even tried to fashion life from clay, from nothing. We'd merely diverted one small trickle from a river already four billion years old.

Francine held our daughter against her shoulder and rocked back and forth. 'Have you got the bottle? Ben?' I walked to the kitchen in a daze; the microwave had anticipated the happy event and the formula was ready.

I returned to the nursery and offered Francine the bottle. 'Can I hold her, before you start feeding?'

'Of course.' She leant forward to kiss me, then held out the child, and I took her the way I'd learnt to accept the babies of relatives and friends, cradling the back of her head beneath my hand. The distribution of weight, the heavy head, the play of the neck, felt the same as it did for any other infant. Her eyes were still screwed shut as she screamed and swung her arms.

'What's your name, my beautiful girl?' We'd narrowed the list down to about a dozen possibilities, but Francine had refused to settle on one until she'd seen her daughter take her first breath. 'Have you decided?'

'I want to call her Helen.'

Gazing down at her, that sounded too old to me. Old-fashioned, at least. Great-Aunt Helen. Helena Bonham-Carter. I laughed inanely, and she opened her eyes.

Hairs rose on my arms. The dark eyes couldn't quite search my face, but she was not oblivious to me. Love and fear coursed through my veins. *How could I hope to give her what she needed?* Even if my judgement had been faultless, my power to act upon it was crude beyond measure.

We were all she had, though. We would make mistakes, we would lose our way, but I had to believe that something would hold fast. Some portion of the overwhelming love and resolve that I felt right now would have to remain with every version of me who could trace his ancestry to this moment.

I said, 'I name you Helen.'

2041

'Sophie! *Sophie!*' Helen ran ahead of us towards the arrivals gate, where Isabelle and Sophie were emerging. Sophie, almost sixteen now, was much less demonstrative, but she smiled and waved.

Francine said, 'Do you ever think of moving?'

'Maybe if the laws change first in Europe,' I replied.

'I saw a job in Zürich I could apply for.'

'I don't think we should bend over backwards to bring them together. They probably get on better with just occasional visits, and the net. It's not as if they don't have other friends.'

Isabelle approached, and greeted us both with kisses on the

cheek. I'd dreaded her arrival the first few times, but by now she seemed more like a slightly overbearing cousin than a child protection officer whose very presence implied misdeeds.

Sophie and Helen caught up with us. Helen tugged at Francine's sleeve. 'Sophie's got a boyfriend! Daniel. She showed me his picture.' She swooned mockingly, one hand on her forehead.

I glanced at Isabelle, who said, 'He goes to her school. He's really very sweet.'

Sophie grimaced with embarrassment. 'Three-year-old *boys* are *sweet*.' She turned to me and said, 'Daniel is charming, and sophisticated, and *very* mature.'

I felt as if an anvil had been dropped on my chest. As we crossed the car park, Francine whispered, 'Don't have a heart attack yet. You've got a while to get used to the idea.'

The waters of the bay sparkled in the sunlight as we drove across the bridge to Oakland. Isabelle described the latest session of the European parliamentary committee into adai rights. A draft proposal granting personhood to any system containing and acting upon a significant amount of the information content of human DNA had been gaining support; it was a tricky concept to define rigorously, but most of the objections were Pythonesque rather than practical. 'Is the Human Proteomic Database a person? Is the Harvard Reference Physiological Simulation a person?' The HRPS modelled the brain solely in terms of what it removed from, and released into, the bloodstream; there was nobody home inside the simulation, quietly going mad.

Late in the evening, when the girls were upstairs, Isabelle began gently grilling us. I tried not to grit my teeth too much. I certainly didn't blame her for taking her responsibilities seriously; if, in spite of the selection process, we had turned out to be monsters, criminal law would have offered no remedies. Our obligations under the licensing contract were Helen's sole guarantee of humane treatment.

'She's getting good marks this year,' Isabelle noted. 'She must be settling in.'

'She is,' Francine replied. Helen was not entitled to a government-funded education, and most private schools had either been openly hostile, or had come up with such excuses as insurance policies that would have classified her as hazardous machinery. (Isabelle had reached a compromise with the airlines: Sophie had to be powered down, appearing to sleep during flights, but was not required to be shackled or stowed in the cargo hold.) The first community school we'd tried had not worked out, but we'd eventually found one close to the Berkeley campus where every parent involved was happy with the idea of Helen's presence. This had saved her from the prospect of joining a net-based school; they weren't so bad, but they were intended for children isolated by geography or illness, circumstances that could not be overcome by other means.

Isabelle bid us good night with no complaints or advice; Francine and I sat by the fire for a while, just smiling at each other. It was nice to have a blemish-free report for once.

The next morning, my alarm went off an hour early. I lay motionless for a while, waiting for my head to clear, before asking my knowledge miner why it had woken me.

It seemed Isabelle's visit had been beaten up into a major story in some east coast news bulletins. A number of vocal members of Congress had been following the debate in Europe, and they didn't like the way it was heading. Isabelle, they declared, had sneaked into the country as an agitator. In fact, she'd offered to testify to Congress any time they wanted to hear about her work, but they'd never taken her up on it.

It wasn't clear whether it was reporters or anti-adai activists who'd obtained her itinerary and done some digging, but all the details had now been splashed around the country, and protesters were already gathering outside Helen's school. We'd faced media packs, cranks and activists before, but the images the knowledge miner showed me were disturbing; it was five a.m. and the crowd had already encircled the school. I had a flashback to some news footage I'd seen in my teens, of young schoolgirls in Northern Ireland running the gauntlet of a protest by the opposing political faction; I could no longer remember who had been Catholic and who had been Protestant.

I woke Francine and explained the situation.

'We could just keep her home,' I suggested.

Francine looked torn, but she finally agreed. 'It will probably all blow over when Isabelle flies out on Sunday. One day off school isn't exactly capitulating to the mob.'

At breakfast, I broke the news to Helen.

'I'm not staying home,' she said.

'Why not? Don't you want to hang out with Sophie?'

Helen was amused. ' "Hang out"? Is that what the hippies used to say?' In her personal chronology of San Francisco, anything from before her birth belonged to the world portrayed in the tourist museums of Haight-Ashbury.

'Gossip. Listen to music. Interact socially in whatever manner you find agreeable.'

She contemplated this last, open-ended definition. 'Shop?'

'I don't see why not.' There was no crowd outside the house, and though we were probably being watched, the protest was too large to be a moveable feast. Perhaps all the other parents would keep their children home, leaving the various placard wavers to fight among themselves.

Helen reconsidered. 'No. We're doing that on Saturday. I want to go to school.'

I glanced at Francine. Helen added, 'It's not as if they can hurt me. I'm backed up.'

Francine said, 'It's not pleasant being shouted at. Insulted. Pushed around.'

'I don't think it's going to be *pleasant*,' Helen replied scornfully. 'But I'm not going to let them tell me what to do.'

To date, a handful of strangers had got close enough to yell abuse at her, and some of the children at her first school had been about as violent as (ordinary, drug-free, non-psychotic) nine-year-old bullies could be, but she'd never faced anything like this. I showed her the live newsfeed. She was not swayed. Francine and I retreated to the living room to confer.

I said, 'I don't think it's a good idea.' On top of everything else, I was beginning to suffer from a paranoid fear that Isabelle would blame us for the whole situation. Less fancifully, she could easily disapprove of us exposing Helen to the protesters. Even if that was not enough for her to terminate the licence immediately, eroding her confidence in us could lead to that fate, eventually.

Francine thought for a while. 'If we both go with her, both walk beside her, what are they going to do? If they lay a finger on us, it's assault. If they try to drag her away from us, it's theft.'

'Yes, but whatever they do, she gets to hear all the poison they spew out.'

'She watches the news, Ben. She's heard it all before.'

'Oh, shit.' Isabelle and Sophie had come down to breakfast; I could hear Helen calmly filling them in about her plans.

Francine said, 'Forget about pleasing Isabelle. If Helen wants to do this, knowing what it entails, and we can keep her safe, then we should respect her decision.'

I felt a sting of anger at the unspoken implication: having gone to such lengths to enable her to make meaningful choices, I'd be a hypocrite to stand in her way. *Knowing what it entails?* She was nine and a half years old.

I admired her courage, though, and I did believe that we could protect her.

I said, 'All right. You call the other parents. I'll inform the police.'

The moment we left the car, we were spotted. Shouts rang out, and a tide of angry people flowed towards us.

I glanced down at Helen and tightened my grip on her. 'Don't let go of our hands.'

She smiled at me indulgently, as if I was warning her about something trivial, like broken glass on the beach. 'I'll be all right, Dad.' She flinched as the crowd closed in, and then there were bodies pushing against us from every side, people jabbering in our faces, spittle flying. Francine and I turned to face each other, making something of a protective cage and a wedge through the adult legs. Frightening as it was to be submerged, I was glad my daughter wasn't at eye level with these people.

'Satan moves her! Satan is inside her! Out, Jezebel spirit!' A young woman in a high-collared lilac dress pressed her body against me and started praying in tongues.

'Gödel's theorem proves that the non-computable, non-linear world behind the quantum collapse is a manifest expression of Buddha-nature,' a neatly dressed youth intoned earnestly, establishing with admirable economy that he had no idea what any of these terms meant. 'Ergo, there can be no soul in the machine.'

'Cyber nano quantum. Cyber nano quantum. Cyber nano quantum.' That chant came from one of our would-be 'supporters', a middle-aged man in Lycra cycling shorts who was forcefully groping down between us, trying to lay his hand on Helen's head and leave a few flakes of dead skin behind; according to cult doctrine, this would enable her to resurrect him when she got around to establishing the Omega Point. I blocked his way as firmly as I could without actually assaulting him, and he wailed like a pilgrim denied admission to Lourdes.

'Think you're going to live for ever, Tinkerbell?' A leering old man with a matted beard poked his head out in front of us and spat straight into Helen's face.

'Arsehole!' Francine shouted. She pulled out a handkerchief and started mopping the phlegm away. I crouched down and stretched my free arm around them. Helen was grimacing with disgust as Francine dabbed at her, but she wasn't crying.

I said, 'Do you want to go back to the car?'

'*No.*'

'Are you sure?'

Helen screwed up her face in an expression of irritation. 'Why do you always ask me that? *Am I sure? Am I sure?* You're the one who sounds like a computer.'

'I'm sorry.' I squeezed her hand.

We ploughed on through the crowd. The core of the protesters turned out to be both saner and more civilised than the lunatics who'd got to us first; as we neared the school gates, people struggled to make room to let us through uninjured, at the same time as they shouted slogans for the cameras. 'Healthcare for all, not just the rich!' I couldn't argue with that sentiment, though adai were just one of a thousand ways the wealthy could spare their children from disease, and in fact they were among the cheapest: the total cost in prosthetic bodies up to adult size came to less than the median lifetime expenditure on healthcare in the US. Banning adai wouldn't end the disparity between rich and poor, but I could understand why some people considered it the ultimate act of selfishness to create a child who could live for ever. They probably never wondered about the fertility rates and resource use of their own descendants over the next few thousand years.

We passed through the gates, into a world of space and silence; any protester who trespassed here could be arrested immediately, and apparently none of them were sufficiently dedicated to Gandhian principles to seek out that fate.

Inside the entrance hall I squatted down and put my arms around Helen. 'Are you okay?'

'Yes.'

'I'm really proud of you.'

'You're shaking.' She was right; my whole body was trembling slightly. It was more than the crush and the confrontation, and the sense of relief that we'd come through unscathed. Relief was never absolute for me; I could never quite erase the images of other possibilities at the back of my mind.

One of the teachers, Carmela Peña, approached us, looking stoical; when they'd agreed to take Helen, all the staff and parents had known that a day like this would come.

Helen said, 'I'll be okay now.' She kissed me on the cheek, then did the same to Francine. 'I'm all right,' she insisted. 'You can go.'

Carmela said, 'We've got sixty per cent of the kids coming. Not bad, considering.'

Helen walked down the corridor, turning once to wave at us impatiently.

I said, 'No, not bad.'

A group of journalists cornered the five of us during the girls' shopping trip the next day, but media organisations had grown wary of lawsuits, and after Isabelle reminded them that she was presently enjoying 'the ordinary liberties of every private citizen' – a quote from a recent eight-figure judgement against *Celebrity Stalker* – they left us in peace.

The night after Isabelle and Sophie flew out, I went in to Helen's room to kiss her good night. As I turned to leave, she said, 'What's a Qusp?'

'It's a kind of computer. Where did you hear about that?'

'On the net. It said I had a Qusp, but Sophie didn't.'

Francine and I had made no firm decision as to what we'd tell her, and when. I said, 'That's right, but it's nothing to worry about. It just means you're a little bit different from her.'

Helen scowled. 'I don't want to be different from Sophie.'

'Everyone's different from everyone else,' I said glibly. 'Having a Qusp is just like . . . a car having a different kind of engine. It can still go to all the same places.' *Just not all of them at once.* 'You can both still do whatever you like. You can be as much like Sophie as you want.' That wasn't entirely dishonest; the crucial difference could always be erased simply by disabling the Qusp's shielding.

'I want to be the same,' Helen insisted. 'Next time I grow, why can't you give me what Sophie's got instead?'

'What you have is newer. It's better.'

'No one else has got it. Not just Sophie; none of the others.' Helen knew she'd nailed me: if it was newer and better, why didn't the younger adai have it too?

I said, 'It's complicated. You'd better go to sleep now; we'll talk about it later.' I fussed with the blankets and she stared at me resentfully.

I went downstairs and recounted the conversation to Francine. 'What do you think?' I asked her. 'Is it time?'

'Maybe it is,' she said.

'I wanted to wait until she was old enough to understand the MWI.'

Francine considered this. 'Understand it how well, though? She's not going to be juggling density matrices any time soon. And if we make it a big secret, she's just going to get half-baked versions from other sources.'

I flopped onto the couch. 'This is going to be hard.' I'd rehearsed the moment a thousand times, but in my imagination Helen had always been older, and there'd been hundreds of other adai with Qusps. In reality, no one had followed the trail we'd blazed. The evidence for the MWI had grown steadily stronger, but for most people it was still easy to ignore. Ever more sophisticated versions of rats running mazes just looked like elaborate computer games. You couldn't travel from branch to branch yourself, you couldn't spy on your parallel alter egos – and such feats would probably never be possible. 'How do you tell a nine-year-old girl that she's the only sentient being on the planet who can make a decision, and stick to it?'

Francine smiled. 'Not in those words, for a start.'

'No.' I put my arm around her. We were about to enter a minefield – and we couldn't help diffusing out across the perilous ground – but at least we had each other's judgement to keep us in check, to rein us in a little.

I said, 'We'll work it out. We'll find the right way.'

2050

Around four in the morning, I gave in to the cravings and lit my first cigarette in a month.

As I drew the warm smoke into my lungs, my teeth started chattering, as if the contrast had forced me to notice how cold the rest of my body had become. The red glow of the tip was the brightest thing in sight, but if there was a camera trained on me it would be infrared, so I'd been blazing away like a bonfire anyway. As the smoke came back up I spluttered like a cat choking on a fur ball; the first one was always like that. I'd taken up the habit at the surreal age of sixty, and even after five years on and off, my respiratory tract couldn't quite believe its bad luck.

For five hours, I'd been crouched in the mud at the edge of Lake Pontchartrain, a couple of kilometres west of the soggy ruins of New Orleans. Watching the barge, waiting for someone to come home. I'd been tempted to swim out and take a look around, but my aide sketched a bright red moat of domestic radar on the surface of the water, and offered no guarantee that I'd remain undetected even if I stayed outside the perimeter.

I'd called Francine the night before. It had been a short, tense conversation.

'I'm in Louisiana. I think I've got a lead.'

'Yeah?'

'I'll let you know how it turns out.'

'You do that.'

I hadn't seen her in the flesh for almost two years. After facing too many dead ends together, we'd split up to cover more ground: Francine had searched from New York to Seattle; I'd taken the south. As the months had slipped away, her determination to put every emotional reaction aside for the sake of the task had gradually eroded. One night, I was sure, grief had overtaken her, alone in some soulless motel room – and it made no difference that the same thing had happened to me, a month later or a week before. Because we had not experienced it together, it was not a shared pain, a burden made lighter. After forty-seven years, though we now had a single purpose as never before, we were starting to come adrift.

I'd learnt about Jake Holder in Baton Rouge, triangulating on rumours and fifth-hand reports of bar-room boasts. The boasts were usually empty; a prosthetic body equipped with software dumber than a microwave could make an infinitely pliable slave, but if the only way to salvage any trace of dignity when your buddies discovered that you owned the high-tech equivalent of a blow-up doll was to imply that there was somebody home inside, apparently a lot of men leapt at the chance.

Holder looked like something worse. I'd bought his lifetime purchasing records, and there'd been a steady stream of cyber-fetish porn over a period of two decades. Hardcore and pre-tentious; half the titles contained the word 'manifesto'. But the flow had stopped, about three months ago. The rumours were, he'd found something better.

I finished the cigarette, and slapped my arms to get the circula-tion going. *She would not be on the barge.* For all I knew, she'd heard the news from Brussels and was already halfway to Europe. That would be a difficult journey to make on her own, but there was no reason to believe that she didn't have loyal, trustworthy friends to assist her. I had too many out-of-date memories burnt into my skull: all the blazing, pointless rows, all the petty crimes, all the self-mutilation. Whatever had happened, whatever she'd been through, she was no longer the angry fifteen-year-old who'd left for school one Friday and never come back.

By the time she'd hit thirteen, we were arguing about every-thing. Her body had no need for the hormonal flood of puberty, but the software had ground on relentlessly, simulating all the neuroendocrine effects. Sometimes it had seemed like an act of torture to put her through that – instead of hunting for some magic shortcut to maturity – but the cardinal rule had been never to tinker, never to intervene, just to aim for the most faithful simulation possible of ordinary human development.

Whatever we'd fought about, she'd always known how to shut me up. 'I'm just a thing to you! An instrument! Daddy's little silver bullet!' I didn't care who she was, or what she wanted; I'd fashioned her solely to slay my own fears. (I'd lie awake after-wards, rehearsing lame counter-arguments. Other children were born for infinitely baser motives: to work the fields, to sit in boardrooms, to banish ennui, to save failing marriages.) In her eyes, the Qusp itself wasn't good or bad – and she turned down all my offers to disable the shielding; that would have let me off the hook too easily. But I'd made her a freak for my own selfish reasons; I'd set her apart even from the other adai, purely to grant myself a certain kind of comfort. 'You wanted to give birth to a singleton? Why didn't you just shoot yourself in the head every time you made a bad decision?'

When she went missing, we were afraid she'd been snatched from the street. But in her room, we'd found an envelope with the locator beacon she'd dug out of her body, and a note that read: *Don't look for me. I'm never coming back.*

I heard the tyres of a heavy vehicle squelching along the muddy track to my left. I hunkered lower, making sure I was hidden in the undergrowth. As the truck came to a halt with a faint metallic shudder, the barge disgorged an unmanned motorboat. My aide had captured the data streams exchanged, one specific challenge and response, but it had no clue how to crack the general case and mimic the barge's owner.

Two men climbed out of the truck. One was Jake Holder; I couldn't make out his face in the starlight, but I'd sat within a few metres of him in diners and bars in Baton Rouge, and my aide knew his somatic signature: the electromagnetic radiation from his nervous system and implants; his body's capacitative and inductive responses to small shifts in the ambient fields; the faint gamma-ray spectrum of his unavoidable, idiosyncratic load of radioisotopes, natural and Chernobylesque.

I did not know who his companion was, but I soon got the general idea.

'One thousand now,' Holder said. 'One thousand when you get back.' His silhouette gestured at the waiting motorboat.

The other man was suspicious. 'How do I know it will be what you say it is?'

'Don't call her "it",' Holder complained. 'She's not an object. She's my Lilith, my Lo-li-ta, my luscious clockwork succubus.' For one hopeful moment, I pictured the customer snickering at this overheated sales pitch and coming to his senses; brothels in Baton Rouge openly advertised machine sex, with skilled human puppeteers, for a fraction of the price. Whatever he imagined the special thrill of a genuine adai to be, he had no way of knowing that Holder didn't have an accomplice controlling the body on the barge in exactly the same fashion. He might even be paying two thousand dollars for a puppet job from Holder himself.

'Okay. But if she's not genuine . . .'

My aide overheard money changing hands, and it had modelled the situation well enough to know how I'd wish, always, to respond. 'Move now,' it whispered in my ear. I complied without hesitation; eighteen months before, I'd Pavloved myself into swift obedience, with all the pain and nausea modern chemistry could induce. The aide couldn't puppet my limbs – I couldn't afford the elaborate surgery – but it overlaid movement cues on my vision, a system I'd adapted from off-the-shelf choreography software, and I strode out of the bushes, right up to the motorboat.

The customer was outraged. 'What is this?'

I turned to Holder. 'You want to fuck him first, Jake? I'll hold him down.' There were things I didn't trust the aide to control; it set the boundaries, but it was better to let me improvise a little, and then treat my actions as one more part of the environment.

After a moment of stunned silence, Holder said icily, 'I've never seen this prick before in my life.' He'd been speechless for a little too long, though, to inspire any loyalty from a stranger; as he reached for his weapon, the customer backed away, then turned and fled.

Holder walked towards me slowly, gun outstretched. 'What's your game? Are you after her? Is that it?' His implants were mapping my body – actively, since there was no need for stealth – but I'd tailed him for hours in Baton Rouge, and my aide knew him like an architectural plan. Over the starlit grey of his form, it overlaid a schematic, flaying him down to brain, nerves and implants. A swarm of blue fireflies flickered into life in his motor cortex, prefiguring a peculiar shrug of the shoulders with no obvious connection to his trigger finger; before they'd reached the intensity that would signal his implants to radio the gun, my aide said, 'Duck.'

The shot was silent, but as I straightened up again I could smell the propellant. I gave up thinking and followed the dance steps. As Holder strode forward and swung the gun towards me, I turned sideways, grabbed his right hand, then punched him hard, repeatedly, in the implant on the side of his neck. He was a fetishist, so he'd chosen bulky packages, intentionally visible through the skin. They were not hard-edged, and they were not inflexible – he wasn't that masochistic – but once you sufficiently compressed even the softest biocompatible foam, it might as well have been a lump of wood. While I hammered the wood into the muscles of his neck, I twisted his forearm upwards. He dropped the gun; I put my foot on it and slid it back towards the bushes.

In ultrasound, I saw blood pooling around his implant. I paused while the pressure built up, then I hit him again and the swelling burst like a giant blister. He sagged to his knees, bellowing with pain. I took the knife from my back pocket and held it to his throat.

I made Holder take off his belt, and I used it to bind his hands behind his back. I led him to the motorboat, and when the two of us were on board, I suggested that he give it the necessary instructions. He was sullen but cooperative. I didn't feel anything; part of me still insisted that the transaction I'd caught him in was a hoax, and that there'd be nothing on the barge that couldn't be found in Baton Rouge.

The barge was old, wooden, smelling of preservatives and unvanquished rot. There were dirty plastic panes in the cabin windows, but all I could see in them was a reflected sheen. As we crossed the deck, I kept Holder intimately close, hoping that if there was an armed security system it wouldn't risk putting the bullet through both of us.

At the cabin door, he said resignedly, 'Don't treat her badly.' My blood went cold and I pressed my forearm to my mouth to stifle an involuntary sob.

I kicked open the door and saw nothing but shadows. I called out, 'Lights!' and two responded, in the ceiling and by the bed. Helen was naked, chained by the wrists and ankles. She looked up and saw me, then began to emit a horrified keening noise.

I pressed the blade against Holder's throat. 'Open those things!'
'The shackles?'

'Yes!'

'I can't. They're not smart; they're just welded shut.'

'Where are your tools?'

He hesitated. 'I've got some wrenches in the truck. All the rest are back in town.'

I looked around the cabin, then I led him into a corner and told him to stand there, facing the wall. I knelt by the bed.

'Ssshh. We'll get you out of here.' Helen fell silent. I touched her cheek with the back of my hand; she didn't flinch, but she stared back at me, disbelieving. 'We'll get you out.' The timber bedposts were thicker than my arms, the links of the chains wide as my thumb. I wasn't going to snap any part of this with my bare hands.

Helen's expression changed: I was real, she was not hallucinating. She said dully, 'I thought you'd given up on me. Woke one of the back-ups. Started again.'

I said, 'I'd never give up on you.'

'Are you sure?' She searched my face. 'Is this the edge of what's possible? Is this the worst it can get?'

I didn't have an answer to that.

I said, 'You remember how to go numb, for a shedding?'

She gave me a faint, triumphant smile. 'Absolutely.' She'd had to endure imprisonment and humiliation, but she'd always had the power to cut herself off from her body's senses.

'Do you want to do it now? Leave all this behind?'

'Yes.'

'You'll be safe soon. I promise you.'

'I believe you.' Her eyes rolled up.

I cut open her chest and took out the Qusp.

Francine and I had both carried spare bodies, and clothes, in the trunks of our cars. Adai were banned from domestic flights, so Helen and I drove along the interstate, up towards Washington DC, where Francine would meet us. We could claim asylum at the Swiss embassy; Isabelle had already set the machinery in motion.

Helen was quiet at first, almost shy with me, as if with a

stranger, but on the second day, as we crossed from Alabama into Georgia, she began to open up. She told me a little of how she'd hitchhiked from state to state, finding casual jobs that paid e-cash and needed no social security number, let alone biometric ID. 'Fruit picking was the best.'

She'd made friends along the way, and confided her nature to those she thought she could trust. She still wasn't sure whether or not she'd been betrayed. Holder had found her in a transients' camp under a bridge, and someone must have told him exactly where to look, but it was always possible that she'd been recognised by a casual acquaintance who'd seen her face in the media years before. Francine and I had never publicised her disappearance, never put up flyers or web pages, out of fear that it would only make the danger worse.

On the third day, as we crossed the Carolinas, we drove in near-silence again. The landscape was stunning, the fields strewn with flowers, and Helen seemed calm. Maybe this was what she needed the most: just safety, and peace.

As dusk approached, though, I felt I had to speak.

'There's something I've never told you,' I said. 'Something that happened to me when I was young.'

Helen smiled. 'Don't tell me you ran away from the farm? Got tired of milking and joined the circus?'

I shook my head. 'I was never adventurous. It was just a little thing.' I told her about the kitchen hand.

She pondered the story for a while. 'And that's why you built the Qusp? That's why you made me? In the end, it all comes down to that man in the alley?' She sounded more bewildered than angry.

I bowed my head. 'I'm sorry.'

'For what?' she demanded. 'Are you sorry that I was ever born?'

'No, but—'

'You didn't put me on that boat. Holder did that.'

I said, 'I brought you into a world with people like him. What I made you, made you a target.'

'And if I'd been flesh and blood?' she said. 'Do you think there aren't people like him, for flesh and blood? Or do you honestly believe that if you'd had an organic child, there would have been *no chance at all* that she'd have run away?'

I started weeping. 'I don't know. I'm just sorry I hurt you.'

Helen said, 'I don't blame you for what you did. And I understand it better now. You saw a spark of good in yourself, and you wanted to cup your hands around it, protect it, make it stronger. I understand that. I'm not that spark, but that doesn't matter. I know who I am, I know what my choices are, and I'm glad of that. I'm glad you gave me that.' She reached over and squeezed my hand. 'Do you think I'd feel *better*, here and now, just because some other version of me handled the same situations better?' She smiled. 'Knowing that other people are having a good time isn't much of a consolation to anyone.'

I composed myself. The car beeped to bring my attention to a booking it had made in a motel a few kilometres ahead.

Helen said, 'I've had time to think about a lot of things. Whatever the laws say, whatever the bigots say, all adai are part of the human race. And what *I* have is something almost every person who's ever lived thought they possessed. Human psychology, human culture, human morality, all evolved with the illusion that we lived in a single history. But we don't – so in the long run, something has to give. Call me old-fashioned, but I'd rather we tinker with our physical nature than abandon our whole identities.'

I was silent for a while. 'So what are your plans, now?'

'I need an education.'

'What do you want to study?'

'I'm not sure yet. A million different things. But in the long run, I know what I want to do.'

'Yeah?' The car turned off the highway, heading for the motel.

'You made a start,' she said, 'but it's not enough. There are people in billions of other branches where the Qusp hasn't been invented yet – and the way things stand, there'll always be branches without it. What's the point in us having this thing, if we don't share it? All those people deserve to have the power to make their own choices.'

'Travel between the branches isn't a simple problem,' I explained gently. 'That would be orders of magnitude harder than the Qusp.'

Helen smiled, conceding this, but the corners of her mouth took on the stubborn set I recognised as the precursor to a thousand smaller victories.

She said, 'Give me time, Dad. Give me time.'

ORACLE

1

On his eighteenth day in the tiger cage, Robert Stoney began to lose hope of emerging unscathed.

He'd woken a dozen times throughout the night with an overwhelming need to stretch his back and limbs, and none of the useful compromise positions he'd discovered in his first few days – the least-worst solutions to the geometrical problem of his confinement – had been able to dull his sense of panic. He'd been in far more pain in the second week, suffering cramps that felt as if the muscles of his legs were dying on the bone, but these new spasms had come from somewhere deeper, powered by a sense of urgency that revolved entirely around his own awareness of his situation.

That was what frightened him. Sometimes he could find ways to minimise his discomfort, sometimes he couldn't, but he'd been clinging to the thought that, in the end, all these fuckers could ever do was hurt him. That wasn't true, though. They could make him ache for freedom in the middle of the night, the way he might have ached with grief, or love. He'd always cherished the understanding that his self was a whole, his mind and body indivisible. But he'd failed to appreciate the corollary: through his body, they could touch every part of him. Change every part of him.

Morning brought a fresh torment: hay fever. The house was

somewhere deep in the countryside, with nothing to be heard in the middle of the day but birdsong. June had always been his worst month for hay fever, but in Manchester it had been tolerable. As he ate breakfast, mucus dripped from his face into the bowl of lukewarm oats they'd given him. He staunched the flow with the back of his hand, but suffered a moment of shuddering revulsion when he couldn't find a way to reposition himself to wipe his hand clean on his trousers. Soon he'd need to empty his bowels. They supplied him with a chamber pot whenever he asked, but they always waited two or three hours before removing it. The smell was bad enough, but the fact that it took up space in the cage was worse.

Towards the middle of the morning, Peter Quint came to see him. 'How are we today, Prof?' Robert didn't reply. Since the day Quint had responded with a puzzled frown to the suggestion that he had an appropriate name for a spook, Robert had tried to make at least one fresh joke at the man's expense every time they met, a petty but satisfying indulgence. But now his mind was blank, and in retrospect the whole exercise seemed like an insane distraction, as bizarre and futile as scoring philosophical points against some predatory animal while it gnawed on his leg.

'Many happy returns,' Quint said cheerfully.

Robert took care to betray no surprise. He'd never lost track of the days, but he'd stopped thinking in terms of the calendar date; it simply wasn't relevant. Back in the real world, to have forgotten his own birthday would have been considered a benign eccentricity. Here it would be taken as proof of his deterioration, and imminent surrender.

If he was cracking, he could at least choose the point of fissure. He spoke as calmly as he could, without looking up. 'You know I almost qualified for the Olympic marathon, back in forty-eight? If I hadn't done my hip in just before the trials, I might have competed.' He tried a self-deprecating laugh. 'I suppose I was never really much of an athlete. But I'm only forty-six. I'm not ready for a wheelchair yet.' The words did help: he could beg this way without breaking down completely, expressing an honest fear without revealing how much deeper the threat of damage went.

He continued, with a measured note of plaintiveness that he hoped sounded like an appeal to fairness, 'I just can't bear the thought of being crippled. All I'm asking is that you let me stand upright. Let me keep my health.'

Quint was silent for a moment, then he replied with a tone of thoughtful sympathy, 'It's unnatural, isn't it? Living like this: bent over, twisted, day after day. Living in an unnatural way is always going to harm you. I'm glad you can finally see that.'

Robert was tired; it took several seconds for the meaning to sink in. *It was that crude, that obvious?* They'd locked him in this cage, for all this time . . . as a kind of ham-fisted *metaphor* for his crimes?

He almost burst out laughing, but he contained himself. 'I don't suppose you know Franz Kafka?'

'Kafka?' Quint could never hide his voracity for names. 'One of your Commie chums, is he?'

'I very much doubt that he was ever a Marxist.'

Quint was disappointed, but prepared to make do with second-best. 'One of the other kind, then?'

Robert pretended to be pondering the question. 'On balance, I suspect that's not too likely either.'

'So why bring his name up?'

'I have a feeling he would have admired your methods, that's all. He was quite the connoisseur.'

'Hmm.' Quint sounded suspicious, but not entirely unflattered.

Robert had first set eyes on Quint in February of 1952. His house had been burgled the week before, and Arthur, a young man he'd been seeing since Christmas, had confessed to Robert that he'd given an acquaintance the address. Perhaps the two of them had planned to rob him, and Arthur had backed out at the last moment. In any case, Robert had gone to the police with an unlikely story about spotting the culprit in a pub, trying to sell an electric razor of the same make and model as the one taken from his house. No one could be charged on such flimsy evidence, so

Robert had had no qualms about the consequences if Arthur had turned out to be lying. He'd simply hoped to prompt an investigation that might turn up something more tangible.

The following day, the CID had paid Robert a visit. The man he'd accused was known to the police, and fingerprints taken on the day of the burglary matched the prints they had on file. However, at the time Robert claimed to have seen him in the pub, he'd been in custody already on an entirely different charge.

The detectives had wanted to know why he'd lied. To spare himself the embarrassment, Robert had explained, of spelling out the true source of his information. Why was that embarrassing?

'I'm involved with the informant.'

One detective, Mr Wills, had asked matter-of-factly, 'What exactly does that entail, sir?' And Robert – in a burst of frankness, as if honesty itself was sure to be rewarded – had told him every detail. He'd known it was still technically illegal, of course. But then, so was playing football on Easter Sunday. It could hardly be treated as a serious crime, like burglary.

The police had strung him along for hours, gathering as much information as they could before disabusing him of this misconception. They hadn't charged him immediately; they'd needed a statement from Arthur first. But then Quint had materialised the next morning, and spelt out the choices very starkly. Three years in prison, with hard labour. Or Robert could resume his war-time work – for just one day a week, as a handsomely paid consultant to Quint's branch of the secret service – and the charges would quietly vanish.

At first, he'd told Quint to let the courts do their worst. He'd been angry enough to want to take a stand against the preposterous law, and whatever his feelings for Arthur, Quint had suggested – gloatingly, as if it strengthened his case – that the younger, working-class man would be treated far more leniently than Robert, having been led astray by someone whose duty was to set an example for the lower orders. Three years in prison was an unsettling prospect, but it would not have been the end of the world; the Mark I had changed the way he worked, but he could still function with nothing but a pencil and paper, if necessary. Even if they'd had him breaking rocks from dawn to dusk he probably would have been able to daydream productively, and for all Quint's scaremongering he'd doubted it would come to that.

At some point, though, in the twenty-four hours Quint had given him to reach a decision, he'd lost his nerve. By granting the spooks their one day a week, he could avoid all the fuss and disruption of a trial. And though his work at the time – modelling embryological development – had been as challenging as anything he'd done in his life, he hadn't been immune to pangs of nostalgia for the old days, when the fate of whole fleets of battleships had rested on finding the most efficient way to extract logical contradictions from a bank of rotating wheels.

The trouble with giving in to extortion was, *it proved that you could be bought*. Never mind that the Russians could hardly have offered to intervene with the Manchester Constabulary next time he needed to be rescued. Never mind that he would scarcely have cared if an enemy agent had threatened to send such comprehensive evidence to the newspapers that there'd be no prospect of his patrons saving him again. He'd lost any chance to proclaim that what he did in bed with another willing partner was not an issue of national security; by saying yes to Quint, he'd made it one. By choosing to be corrupted once, he'd brought the whole torrent of clichés and paranoia down upon his head: he was vulnerable to blackmail, an easy target for entrapment, perfidious by nature. He might as well have posed *in flagrante delicto* with Guy Burgess on the steps of the Kremlin.

It wouldn't have mattered if Quint and his masters had merely decided that they couldn't trust him. The problem was – some six years after recruiting him, with no reason to believe that he had ever breached security in any way – they'd convinced themselves that they could neither continue to employ him, nor safely leave him in peace, until they'd rid him of the trait they'd used to control him in the first place.

Robert went through the painful, complicated process of rearranging his body so he could look Quint in the eye. 'You know, if it was legal there'd be nothing to worry about, would there? Why don't you devote some of your considerable Machiavellian talents to that end? Blackmail a few politicians. Set up a Royal Commission. It would only take you a couple of years. Then we could all get on with our real jobs.'

Quint blinked at him, more startled than outraged. 'You might as well say that we should legalise treason!'

Robert opened his mouth to reply, then decided not to waste his breath. Quint wasn't expressing a moral opinion. He simply meant that a world in which fewer people's lives were ruled by the constant fear of discovery was hardly one that a man in his profession would wish to hasten into existence.

When Robert was alone again, the time dragged. His hay fever worsened, until he was sneezing and gagging almost continuously; even with freedom of movement and an endless supply of the softest linen handkerchiefs, he would have been reduced to abject misery. Gradually, though, he grew more adept at dealing with the symptoms, delegating the task to some barely conscious part of himself. By the middle of the afternoon – covered in filth, eyes almost swollen shut – he finally managed to turn his mind back to his work.

For the past four years he'd been immersed in particle physics. He'd been following the field on and off since before the war, but the paper by Yang and Mills in '54, in which they'd generalised Maxwell's equations for electromagnetism to apply to the strong nuclear force, had jolted him into action.

After several false starts, he believed he'd discovered a useful way to cast gravity into the same form. In general relativity, if you carried a four-dimensional velocity vector around a loop that enclosed a curved region of spacetime, it came back rotated – a phenomenon highly reminiscent of the way more abstract vectors behaved in nuclear physics. In both cases, the rotations could be treated algebraically, and the traditional way to get a handle on this was to make use of a set of matrices of complex numbers whose relationships mimicked the algebra in question. Hermann

Weyl had catalogued most of the possibilities back in the '20s and '30s.

In spacetime, there were six distinct ways you could rotate an object: you could turn it around any of three perpendicular axes in space, or you could boost its velocity in any of the same three directions. These two kinds of rotation were complementary, or 'dual' to each other, with the ordinary rotations only affecting coordinates that were untouched by the corresponding boost, and vice versa. This meant that you could rotate something around, say, the x-axis, and speed it up in the same direction, without the two processes interfering.

When Robert had tried applying the Yang-Mills approach to gravity in the obvious way, he'd floundered. It was only when he'd shifted the algebra of rotations into a new, strangely skewed guise that the mathematics had begun to fall into place. Inspired by a trick that particle physicists used to construct fields with left- or right-handed spin, he'd combined every rotation with its own dual multiplied by i, the square root of minus one. The result was a set of rotations in four *complex* dimensions, rather than the four real ones of ordinary spacetime, but the relationships between them preserved the original algebra.

Demanding that these 'self-dual' rotations satisfy Einstein's equations turned out to be equivalent to ordinary general relativity, but the process leading to a quantum-mechanical version of the theory became dramatically simpler. Robert still had no idea how to interpret this, but as a purely formal trick it worked spectacularly well – and when the mathematics fell into place like that, it had to mean *something*.

He spent several hours pondering old results, turning them over in his mind's eye, rechecking and reimagining everything in the hope of forging some new connection, making no progress, but there'd always been days like that. It was a triumph merely to spend this much time doing what he would have done back in the real world – however mundane, or even frustrating, the same activity might have been in its original setting.

By evening, though, the victory began to seem hollow. He

hadn't lost his wits entirely, but he was frozen, stunted. He might as well have whiled away the hours reciting the base-32 multiplication table in Baudot code, just to prove that he still remembered it.

As the room filled with shadows, his powers of concentration deserted him completely. His hay fever had abated, but he was too tired to think, and in too much pain to sleep. This wasn't Russia, they couldn't hold him for ever; he simply had to wear them down with his patience. *But when, exactly, would they have to let him go?* And how much more patient could Quint be, with no pain, no terror, to erode his determination?

The moon rose, casting a patch of light on the far wall; hunched over, he couldn't see it directly, but it silvered the grey at his feet, and changed his whole sense of the space around him. The cavernous room mocking his confinement reminded him of nights he'd spent lying awake in the dormitory at Sherborne. A public school education did have one great advantage: however miserable you were afterwards, you could always take comfort in the knowledge that life would never be quite as bad again.

'This room smells of mathematics! Go out and fetch a disinfectant spray!' That had been his form-master's idea of showing what a civilised man he was: contempt for that loathsome subject, the stuff of engineering and other low trades. And as for Robert's chemistry experiments, like the beautiful colour-changing iodate reaction he'd learnt from Chris's brother—

Robert felt a familiar ache in the pit of his stomach. *Not now. I can't afford this now.* But the whole thing swept over him, unwanted, unbidden. He'd used to meet Chris in the library on Wednesdays; for months, that had been the only time they could spend together. Robert had been fifteen then, Chris a year older. If Chris had been plain, he still would have shone like a creature from another world. No one else in Sherborne had read Eddington on relativity, Hardy on mathematics. No one else's horizons stretched beyond rugby, sadism and the dimly satisfying prospect of reading classics at Oxford then vanishing into the maw of the civil service.

They had never touched, never kissed. While half the school had been indulging in passionless sodomy – as a rather literal-minded substitute for the much-too-difficult task of imagining women – Robert had been too shy even to declare his feelings. Too shy, and too afraid that they might not be reciprocated. It hadn't mattered. To have a friend like Chris had been enough.

In December of 1929, they'd both sat the exams for Trinity College, Cambridge. Chris had won a scholarship; Robert hadn't. He'd reconciled himself to their separation, and prepared for one more year at Sherborne without the one person who'd made it bearable. Chris would be following happily in the footsteps of Newton; just thinking of that would be some consolation.

Chris never made it to Cambridge. In February, after six days in agony, he'd died of bovine tuberculosis.

Robert wept silently, angry with himself because he knew that half his wretchedness was just self-pity, exploiting his grief as a disguise. He had to stay honest; once every source of unhappiness in his life melted together and became indistinguishable, he'd be like a cowed animal, with no sense of the past or the future. Ready to do anything to get out of the cage.

If he hadn't yet reached that point, he was close. It would only take a few more nights like the last one. Drifting off in the hope of a few minutes' blankness, to find that sleep itself shone a colder light on everything. Drifting off, then waking with a sense of loss so extreme it was like suffocation.

A woman's voice spoke from the darkness in front of him. 'Get off your knees!'

Robert wondered if he was hallucinating. He'd heard no one approach across the creaky floorboards.

The voice said nothing more. Robert rearranged his body so he could look up from the floor. There was a woman he'd never seen before, standing a few feet away.

She'd sounded angry, but as he studied her face in the moon-light through the slits of his swollen eyes, he realised that her anger was directed not at him, but at his condition. She gazed at him with an expression of horror and outrage, as if she'd chanced upon him being held like this in some respectable neighbour's basement, rather than an MI6 facility. Maybe she was one of the staff employed in the upkeep of the house, but had no idea what went on here? Surely those people were vetted and supervised, though, and threatened with life imprisonment if they ever set foot outside their prescribed domains.

For one surreal moment, Robert wondered if Quint had sent her to seduce him. It would not have been the strangest thing they'd tried. But she radiated such fierce self-assurance – such a sense of confidence that she could speak with the authority of her convictions, and expect to be heeded – that he knew she could never have been chosen for the role. No one in Her Majesty's government would consider self-assurance an attractive quality in a woman.

He said, 'Throw me the key, and I'll show you my Roger Bannister impression.'

She shook her head. 'You don't need a key. Those days are over.'

Robert started with fright. *There were no bars between them.* But the cage couldn't have vanished before his eyes; she must have removed it while he'd been lost in his reverie. He'd gone through the whole painful exercise of turning to face her as if he were still confined, without even noticing.

Removed it how?

He wiped his eyes, shivering at the dizzying prospect of freedom. 'Who are you?' An agent for the Russians, sent to liberate him from his own side? She'd have to be a zealot, then, or strangely naïve, to view his torture with such wide-eyed innocence.

She stepped forward, then reached down and took his hand. 'Do you think you can walk?' Her grip was firm, and her skin was cool and dry. She was completely unafraid; she might have been a good Samaritan in a public street helping an old man to his feet after a fall – not an intruder helping a threat to national security break out of therapeutic detention, at the risk of being shot on sight.

'I'm not even sure I can stand.' Robert steeled himself; maybe this woman was a trained assassin, but it would be too much to presume that if he cried out in pain and brought guards rushing in, she could still extricate him without raising a sweat. 'You haven't answered my question.'

'My name's Helen.' She smiled and hoisted him to his feet, looking at once like a compassionate child pulling open the jaws of a hunter's cruel trap, and a very powerful, very intelligent carnivore contemplating its own strength. 'I've come to change everything.'

Robert said, 'Oh, good.'

Robert found that he could hobble; it was painful and undignified, but at least he didn't have to be carried. Helen led him through the house; lights showed from some of the rooms, but there were no voices, no footsteps save their own, no signs of life at all. When they reached the tradesmen's entrance she unbolted the door, revealing a moonlit garden.

'Did you kill everyone?' he whispered. He'd made far too much noise to have come this far unmolested. Much as he had reason to despise his captors, mass murder on his behalf was a lot to take in.

Helen cringed. 'What a revolting idea! It's hard to believe sometimes how uncivilised you are.'

'You mean the British?'

'All of you!'

'I must say, your accent's rather good.'

'I watched a lot of cinema,' she explained. 'Mostly Ealing comedies. You never know how much that will help, though.'

'Quite.'

They crossed the garden, heading for a wooden gate in the hedge. Since murder was strictly for imperialists, Robert could only assume that she'd managed to drug everyone.

The gate was unlocked. Outside the grounds, a cobbled lane ran past the hedge, leading into forest. Robert was barefoot, but the stones weren't cold, and the slight unevenness of the path was welcome, restoring circulation to the soles of his feet.

As they walked, he took stock of his situation. He was out of captivity, thanks entirely to this woman. Sooner or later he was going to have to confront her agenda.

He said, 'I'm not leaving the country.'

Helen murmured assent, as if he'd passed a casual remark about the weather.

'And I'm not going to discuss my work with you.'

'Fine.'

Robert stopped and stared at her. She said, 'Put your arm across my shoulders.'

He complied; she was exactly the right height to support him comfortably. He said, 'You're not a Soviet agent, are you?'

Helen was amused. 'Is that really what you thought?'

'I'm not all that quick on my feet tonight.'

'No.' They began walking together. Helen said, 'There's a train station about three kilometres away. You can get cleaned up, rest there until morning, and decide where you want to go.'

'Won't the station be the first place they'll look?'

'They won't be looking anywhere for a while.'

The moon was high above the trees. The two of them could not have made a more conspicuous couple: a sensibly dressed, quite striking young woman, supporting a filthy, ragged tramp. If a villager cycled past, the best they could hope for was being mistaken for an alcoholic father and his martyred daughter.

Martyred all right: she moved so efficiently, despite the burden, that any onlooker would assume she'd been doing this for years. Robert tried altering his gait slightly, subtly changing the timing of his steps to see if he could make her falter, but Helen adapted instantly. If she knew she was being tested, though, she kept it to herself.

Finally he said, 'What did you do with the cage?'

'I time-reversed it.'

Hairs stood up on the back of his neck. Even assuming that she could do such a thing, it wasn't at all clear to him how that could have stopped the bars from scattering light and interacting with his body. It should merely have turned electrons into positrons, and killed them both in a shower of gamma-rays.

That conjuring trick wasn't his most pressing concern, though. 'I can think of only three places you might have come from,' he said.

Helen nodded, as if she'd put herself in his shoes and catalogued the possibilities. 'Rule out one; the other two are both right.'

She was not from an extrasolar planet. Even if her civilisation possessed some means of viewing Ealing comedies from a distance of light-years, she was far too sensitive to his specific human concerns.

She was from the future, but not his own.

She was from the future of another Everett branch.

He turned to her. 'No paradoxes.'

She smiled, deciphering his shorthand immediately. 'That's right. It's physically impossible to travel into your own past, unless you've made exacting preparations to ensure compatible boundary conditions. That *can* be achieved, in a controlled laboratory setting – but in the field it would be like trying to balance ten thousand elephants in an inverted pyramid, while the bottom one rode a unicycle: excruciatingly difficult, and entirely pointless.'

Robert was tongue-tied for several seconds, a horde of questions battling for access to his vocal chords. 'But how do you travel into the past at all?'

'It will take a while to bring you up to speed completely, but if you want the short answer: you've already stumbled on one of the clues. I read your paper in *Physical Review*, and it's correct as far as it goes. Quantum gravity involves four complex dimensions, but the only classical solutions – the only geometries that remain in phase under slight perturbations – have curvature that's either *self-dual*, or *anti-self-dual*. Those are the only stationary points of the action, for the complete Lagrangian. And both solutions appear, from the inside, to contain only four real dimensions.

'It's meaningless to ask which sector we're in, but we might as well call it self-dual. In that case, the anti-self-dual solutions have an arrow of time running backwards compared to ours.'

'Why?' As he blurted out the question, Robert wondered if he sounded like an impatient child to her. But if she suddenly vanished back into thin air, he'd have far fewer regrets for making a fool of himself this way than if he'd maintained a façade of sophisticated nonchalance.

Helen said, 'Ultimately, that's related to spin. And it's down to the mass of the neutrino that we can tunnel between sectors. But I'll need to draw you some diagrams and equations to explain it all properly.'

Robert didn't press her for more; he had no choice but to trust that she wouldn't desert him. He staggered on in silence, a wonderful ache of anticipation building in his chest. If someone had put this situation to him hypothetically, he would have piously insisted that he'd prefer to toil on at his own pace. But despite the satisfaction it had given him on the few occasions when he'd made genuine discoveries himself, what mattered in the end was understanding as much as you could, however you could. Better to ransack the past and the future than go through life in a state of wilful ignorance.

'You said you've come to change things?'

She nodded. 'I can't predict the future here, of course, but there are pitfalls in my own past that I can help you avoid. In my twentieth century, people discovered things too slowly. Everything changed much too slowly. Between us, I think we can speed things up.'

Robert was silent for a while, contemplating the magnitude of what she was proposing. Then he said, 'It's a pity you didn't come sooner. In this branch, about twenty years ago—'

Helen cut him off. 'I know. We had the same war. The same Holocaust, the same Soviet death toll. But we've yet to be able to avert that, anywhere. You can never do anything in just one history – even the most focused intervention happens across a broad "ribbon" of strands. When we try to reach back to the '30s and '40s, the ribbon overlaps with its own past to such a degree that all the worst horrors are *faits accomplis*. We can't shoot *any* version of Adolf Hitler, because we can't shrink the ribbon to the point where none of us would be shooting ourselves in the back. All we've ever managed are minor interventions, like sending projectiles back to the Blitz, saving a few lives by deflecting bombs.'

'What, knocking them into the Thames?'

'No, that would have been too risky. We did some modelling, and the safest thing turned out to be diverting them onto big, empty buildings: Westminster Abbey, Saint Paul's Cathedral.'

The station came into view ahead of them. Helen said, 'What do you think? Do you want to head back to Manchester?'

Robert hadn't given the question much thought. Quint could track him down anywhere, but the more people he had around him, the less vulnerable he'd be. In his house in Wilmslow he'd be there for the taking.

'I still have rooms at Cambridge,' he said tentatively.

'Good idea.'

'What are your own plans?'

Helen turned to him. 'I thought I'd stay with you.' She smiled at the expression on his face. 'Don't worry, I'll give you plenty of privacy. And if people want to make assumptions, let them. You already have a scandalous reputation; you might as well see it branch out in new directions.'

Robert said wryly, 'I'm afraid it doesn't quite work that way. They'd throw us out immediately.'

Helen snorted. 'They could try.'

'You may have defeated MI6, but you haven't dealt with Cambridge porters.' The reality of the situation washed over him anew at the thought of her in his study, writing out the equations for time travel on the blackboard. '*Why me?* I can appreciate that you'd want to make contact with someone who could understand how you came here – but why not Everett, or Yang, or Feynman? Compared to Feynman I'm a dilettante.'

Helen said, 'Maybe. But you have an equally practical bent, and you'll learn fast enough.'

There had to be more to it than that: thousands of people would have been capable of absorbing her lessons just as rapidly.

'The physics you've hinted at – in your past, did I discover all that?'

'No. Your *Physical Review* paper helped me track you down here, but in my own history that was never published.' There was a flicker of disquiet in her eyes, as if she had far greater disappointments in store on that subject.

Robert didn't care much either way; if anything, the less his alter ego had achieved, the less he'd be troubled by jealousy.

'Then what was it that made you choose me?'

'You really haven't guessed?' Helen took his free hand and held the fingers to her face; it was a tender gesture, but much more like a daughter's than a lover's. 'It's a warm night. No one's skin should be this cold.'

Robert gazed into her dark eyes, as playful as any human's, as serious, as proud. Given the chance, perhaps any decent person would have plucked him from Quint's grasp. But only one kind would feel a special obligation, as if they were repaying an ancient debt.

He said, 'You're a machine.'

2

John Hamilton, Professor of Mediaeval and Renaissance English at Magdalene College, Cambridge, read the last letter in the morning's pile of fan mail with a growing sense of satisfaction.

The letter was from a young American, a twelve-year-old girl in Boston. It opened in the usual way, declaring how much pleasure his books had given her, before going on to list her favourite scenes and characters. As ever, Jack was delighted that the stories had touched someone deeply enough to prompt them to respond this way. But it was the final paragraph that was by far the most gratifying:

However much other children might tease me, or grown-ups too when I'm older, I will NEVER, EVER stop believing in the

Kingdom of Nescia. Sarah stopped believing, and she was locked out of the Kingdom for ever. At first that made me cry, and I couldn't sleep all night because I was afraid I might stop believing myself one day. But I understand now that it's good to be afraid, because it will help me keep people from changing my mind. And if you're not willing to believe in magic lands, of course you can't enter them. There's nothing even Belvedere himself can do to save you, then.

Jack refilled and lit his pipe, then reread the letter. This was his vindication: the proof that through his books he could touch a young mind, and plant the seed of faith in fertile ground. It made all the scorn of his jealous, stuck-up colleagues fade into insignificance. Children understood the power of stories, the reality of myth, the need to believe in something beyond the dismal grey farce of the material world.

It wasn't a truth that could be revealed the 'adult' way: through scholarship, or reason. Least of all through philosophy, as Elizabeth Anscombe had shown him on that awful night at the Socratic Club. A devout Christian herself, Anscombe had nonetheless taken all the arguments against materialism from his popular book, *Signs and Wonders*, and trampled them into the ground. It had been an unfair match from the start: Anscombe was a professional philosopher, steeped in the work of everyone from Aquinas to Wittgenstein; Jack knew the history of ideas in mediaeval Europe intimately, but he'd lost interest in modern philosophy once it had been invaded by fashionable positivists. And *Signs and Wonders* had never been intended as a scholarly work; it had been good enough to pass muster with a sympathetic lay readership, but trying to defend his admittedly rough-and-ready mixture of common sense and useful shortcuts to faith against Anscombe's merciless analysis had made him feel like a country yokel stammering in front of a bishop.

Ten years later, he still burned with resentment at the humiliation she'd put him through, but he was grateful for the lesson she'd taught him. His earlier books, and his radio talks, had not been a complete waste of time – but the harpy's triumph had shown him just how pitiful human reason was when it came to the great questions. He'd begun working on the stories of Nescia years before, but it was only when the dust had settled on his most painful defeat that he'd finally recognised his true calling.

He removed his pipe, stood, and turned to face Oxford. 'Kiss my arse, Elizabeth!' he growled happily, waving the letter at her. This was a wonderful omen. It was going to be a very good day.

There was a knock at the door of his study.

'Come.'

It was his brother, William. Jack was puzzled – he hadn't even realised Willie was in town – but he nodded a greeting and motioned at the couch opposite his desk.

Willie sat, his face flushed from the stairs, frowning. After a moment he said, 'This chap Stoney.'

'Hmm?' Jack was only half listening as he sorted papers on his desk. He knew from long experience that Willie would take for ever to get to the point.

'Did some kind of hush-hush work during the war, apparently.'

'Who did?'

'Robert Stoney. Mathematician. Used to be up at Manchester, but he's a Fellow of Kings, and now he's back in Cambridge. Did some kind of secret war work. Same thing as Malcolm Mugger-idge, apparently. No one's allowed to say what.'

Jack looked up, amused. He'd heard rumours about Mugger-idge, but they all revolved around the business of analysing inter-cepted German radio messages. What conceivable use would a mathematician have been for that? Sharpening pencils for the intelligence analysts, presumably.

'What about him, Willie?' Jack asked patiently.

Willie continued reluctantly, as if he was confessing to some-thing mildly immoral, 'I paid him a visit yesterday. Place called the Cavendish. Old army friend of mine has a brother who works there. Got the whole tour.'

'I know the Cavendish. What's there to see?'

'He's doing things, Jack. *Impossible things.*'

223

'Impossible?'

'Looking inside people. Putting it on a screen, like a television.'

Jack sighed. 'Taking X-rays?'

Willie snapped back angrily, 'I'm not a fool; I know what an X-ray looks like. This is different. You can see the blood flow. You can watch your heart beating. You can follow a sensation through the nerves from . . . fingertip to brain. He says, soon he'll be able to watch a thought in motion.'

'Nonsense.' Jack scowled. 'So he's invented some gadget, some fancy kind of X-ray machine. What are you so agitated about?'

Willie shook his head gravely. 'There's more. That's just the tip of the iceberg. He's only been back in Cambridge a year, and already the place is overflowing with . . . wonders.' He used the word begrudgingly, as if he had no choice, but was afraid of conveying more approval than he intended.

Jack was beginning to feel a distinct sense of unease.

'What exactly is it you want me to do?' he asked.

Willie replied plainly, 'Go and see for yourself. Go and see what he's up to.'

The Cavendish Laboratory was a mid-Victorian building, designed to resemble something considerably older and grander. It housed the entire Department of Physics, complete with lecture theatres; the place was swarming with noisy undergraduates. Jack had had no trouble arranging a tour: he'd simply telephoned Stoney and expressed his curiosity, and no more substantial reason had been required.

Stoney had been allocated three adjoining rooms at the back of the building, and the 'spin resonance imager' occupied most of the first. Jack obligingly placed his arm between the coils, then almost jerked it out in fright when the strange, transected view of his muscles and veins appeared on the picture tube. He wondered if it could be some kind of hoax, but he clenched his fist slowly and watched the image do the same, then made several unpredictable movements which it mimicked equally well.

'I can show you individual blood cells, if you like,' Stoney offered cheerfully.

Jack shook his head; his current, unmagnified flaying was quite enough to take in.

Stoney hesitated, then added awkwardly, 'You might want to talk to your doctor at some point. It's just that, your bone density's rather—' He pointed to a chart on the screen beside the image. 'Well, it's quite a bit below the normal range.'

Jack withdrew his arm. He'd already been diagnosed with osteoporosis, and he'd welcomed the news: it meant that he'd taken a small part of Joyce's illness – the weakness in her bones – into his own body. God was allowing him to suffer a little in her stead.

If Joyce were to step between these coils, what might that reveal? But there'd be nothing to add to her diagnosis. Besides, if he kept up his prayers, and kept up both their spirits, in time her remission would blossom from an uncertain reprieve into a fully-fledged cure.

He said, 'How does this work?'

'In a strong magnetic field, some of the atomic nuclei and electrons in your body are free to align themselves in various ways with the field.' Stoney must have seen Jack's eyes beginning to glaze over; he quickly changed tack. 'Think of it as being like setting a whole lot of spinning tops whirling, as vigorously as possible, then listening carefully as they slow down and tip over. For the atoms in your body, that's enough to give some clues as to what kind of molecule, and what kind of tissue, they're in. The machine listens to atoms in different places by changing the way it combines all the signals from billions of tiny antennae. It's like a whispering gallery where we can play with the time that signals take to travel from different places, moving the focus back and forth through any part of your body, thousands of times a second.'

Jack pondered this explanation. Though it sounded complicated, in principle it wasn't that much stranger than X-rays.

'The physics itself is old hat,' Stoney continued, 'but for

imaging, you need a very strong magnetic field, and you need to make sense of all the data you've gathered. Nevill Mott made the superconducting alloys for the magnets. And I managed to persuade Rosalind Franklin from Birkbeck to collaborate with us, to help perfect the fabrication process for the computing circuits. We cross-link lots of little Y-shaped DNA fragments, then selectively coat them with metal; Rosalind worked out a way to use X-ray crystallography for quality control. We paid her back with a purpose-built computer that will let her solve hydrated protein structures in real time, once she gets her hands on a bright enough X-ray source.' He held up a small, unprepossessing object, rimmed with protruding gold wires. 'Each logic gate is roughly a hundred Ångstroms cubed, and we grow them in three-dimensional arrays. That's a million, million, million switches in the palm of my hand.'

Jack didn't know how to respond to this claim. Even when he couldn't quite follow the man there was something mesmerising about his ramblings, like a cross between William Blake and nursery talk.

'If computers don't excite you, we're doing all kinds of other things with DNA.' Stoney ushered him into the next room, which was full of glassware, and seedlings in pots beneath strip lights. Two assistants seated at a bench were toiling over microscopes; another was dispensing fluids into test tubes with a device that looked like an overgrown eye-dropper.

'There are a dozen new species of rice, corn and wheat here. They all have at least double the protein and mineral content of existing crops, and each one uses a different biochemical repertoire to protect itself against insects and fungi. Farmers have to get away from monocultures; it leaves them too vulnerable to disease, and too dependent on chemical pesticides.'

Jack said, 'You've bred these? All these new varieties, in a matter of months?'

'No, no! Instead of hunting down the heritable traits we needed in the wild, and struggling for years to produce cross-breeds bearing all of them, we designed every trait from scratch. Then we manufactured DNA that would make the tools the plants need, and inserted it into their germ cells.'

Jack demanded angrily, 'Who are you to say what a plant needs?'

Stoney shook his head innocently. 'I took my advice from agricultural scientists, who took their advice from farmers. They know what pests and blights they're up against. Food crops are as artificial as Pekinese. Nature didn't hand them to us on a plate, and if they're not working as well as we need them to, nature isn't going to fix them for us.'

Jack glowered at him, but said nothing. He was beginning to understand why Willie had sent him here. The man came across as an enthusiastic tinkerer, but there was a breathtaking arrogance lurking behind the boyish exterior.

Stoney explained a collaboration he'd brokered between scientists in Cairo, Bogotá, London and Calcutta, to develop vaccines for polio, smallpox, malaria, typhoid, yellow fever, tuberculosis, influenza and leprosy. Some were the first of their kind; others were intended as replacements for existing vaccines. 'It's important that we create antigens without culturing the pathogens in animal cells that might themselves harbour viruses. The teams are all looking at variants on a simple, cheap technique that involves putting antigen genes into harmless bacteria that will double as delivery vehicles and adjuvants, then freeze-drying them into spores that can survive tropical heat without refrigeration.'

Jack was slightly mollified; this all sounded highly admirable. What business Stoney had instructing doctors on vaccines was another question. Presumably his jargon made sense to them, but when exactly had this mathematician acquired the training to make even the most modest suggestions on the topic?

'You're having a remarkably productive year,' he observed.

Stoney smiled. 'The muse comes and goes for all of us. But I'm really just the catalyst in most of this. I've been lucky enough to find some people – here in Cambridge, and further afield – who've been willing to chance their arm on some wild ideas. They've done the real work.' He gestured towards the next room. 'My own pet projects are through here.'

The third room was full of electronic gadgets, wired up to picture tubes displaying both phosphorescent words and images resembling engineering blueprints come to life. In the middle of one bench, incongruously, sat a large cage containing several hamsters.

Stoney fiddled with one of the gadgets, and a face like a stylised drawing of a mask appeared on an adjacent screen. The mask looked around the room, then said, 'Good morning, Robert. Good morning, Professor Hamilton.'

Jack said, 'You had someone record those words?'

The mask replied, 'No, Robert showed me photographs of all the teaching staff at Cambridge. If I see anyone I know from the photographs, I greet them.' The face was crudely rendered, but the hollow eyes seemed to meet Jack's. Stoney explained, 'It has no idea what it's saying, of course. It's just an exercise in face and voice recognition.'

Jack responded stiffly, 'Of course.'

Stoney motioned to Jack to approach and examine the hamster cage. He obliged him. There were two adult animals, presumably a breeding pair. Two pink young were suckling from the mother, who reclined in a bed of straw.

'Look closely,' Stoney urged him. Jack peered into the nest, then cried out an obscenity and backed away.

One of the young was exactly what it seemed. The other was a machine, wrapped in ersatz skin, with a nozzle clamped to the warm teat.

'That's the most monstrous thing I've ever seen!' Jack's whole body was trembling. 'What possible reason could you have to do that?'

Stoney laughed and made a reassuring gesture, as if his guest was a nervous child recoiling from a harmless toy. 'It's not hurting her! And the point is to discover what it takes for the mother to accept it. To "reproduce one's kind" means having some set of parameters as to what that is. Scent, and some aspects of appearance, are important cues in this case, but through trial and error I've also pinned down a set of behaviours that lets the simulacrum pass through every stage of the life cycle. An acceptable child, an acceptable sibling, an acceptable mate.'

Jack stared at him, nauseated. 'These animals fuck your machines?'

Stoney was apologetic. 'Yes, but hamsters will fuck anything. I'll really have to shift to a more discerning species, in order to test that properly.'

Jack struggled to regain his composure. 'What on Earth possessed you to do this?'

'In the long run,' Stoney said mildly, 'I believe this is something we're going to need to understand far better than we do at present. Now that we can map the structures of the brain in fine detail, and match its raw complexity with our computers, it's only a matter of a decade or so before we build machines that think.

'That in itself will be a vast endeavour, but I want to ensure that it's not stillborn from the start. There's not much point creating the most marvellous children in history, only to find that some awful mammalian instinct drives us to strangle them at birth.'

Jack sat in his study drinking whisky. He'd telephoned Joyce after dinner, and they'd chatted for a while, but it wasn't the same as being with her. The weekends never came soon enough, and by Tuesday or Wednesday any sense of reassurance he'd gained from seeing her had slipped away entirely.

It was almost midnight now. After speaking to Joyce, he'd spent three more hours on the telephone, finding out what he could about Stoney, milking his connections, such as they were; Jack had only been at Cambridge for five years, so he was still very much an outsider. Not that he'd ever been admitted into any inner circles back at Oxford: he'd always belonged to a small, quiet group of dissenters against the tide of fashion. Whatever else might be said about the Tiddlywinks, they'd never had their hands on the levers of academic power.

A year ago, while on sabbatical in Germany, Stoney had resigned suddenly from a position he'd held at Manchester for a decade. He'd returned to Cambridge, despite having no official posting to take up. He'd started collaborating informally with various people at the Cavendish, until the head of the place, Mott, had invented a job description for him, and given him a modest salary, the three rooms Jack had seen, and some students to assist him.

Stoney's colleagues were uniformly amazed by his spate of successful inventions. Though none of his gadgets were based on entirely new science, his skill at seeing straight to the heart of existing theories and plucking some practical consequence from them was unprecedented. Jack had expected some jealous back-stabbing, but no one seemed to have a bad word to say about Stoney. He was willing to turn his scientific Midas touch to the service of anyone who approached him, and it sounded to Jack as if every would-be sceptic or enemy had been bought off with some rewarding insight into their own field.

Stoney's personal life was rather murkier. Half of Jack's informants were convinced that the man was a confirmed pansy, but others spoke of a beautiful, mysterious woman named Helen, with whom he was plainly on intimate terms.

Jack emptied his glass and stared out across the courtyard. *Was it pride to wonder if he might have received some kind of prophetic vision?* Fifteen years earlier, when he'd written *The Broken Planet*, he'd imagined that he'd merely been satirising the hubris of modern science. His portrait of the evil forces behind the sardonically named Laboratory Overseeing Various Experiments had been intended as a deadly serious metaphor, but he'd never expected to find himself wondering if real fallen angels were whispering secrets in the ears of a Cambridge don.

How many times, though, had he told his readers that the devil's greatest victory had been convincing the world that he did not exist? The devil was *not* a metaphor, a mere symbol of human weakness: he was a real, scheming presence, acting in time, acting in the world, as much as God Himself.

And hadn't Faustus' damnation been sealed by the most beautiful woman of all time: Helen of Troy?

Jack's skin crawled. He'd once written a humorous newspaper column called 'Letters from a Demon', in which a Senior Tempter offered advice to a less experienced colleague on the best means to lead the faithful astray. Even that had been an exhausting, almost corrupting experience; adopting the necessary point of view, however whimsically, had made him feel that he was withering inside. The thought that a cross between the *Faustbuch* and *The Broken Planet* might be coming to life around him was too terrifying to contemplate. He was no hero out of his own fiction – not even a mild-mannered Cedric Duffy, let alone a modern Pendragon. And he did not believe that Merlin would rise from the woods to bring chaos to that hubristic Tower of Babel, the Cavendish Laboratory.

Nevertheless, if he was the only person in England who suspected Stoney's true source of inspiration, who else would act?

Jack poured himself another glass. There was nothing to be gained by procrastinating. He would not be able to rest until he knew what he was facing: a vain, foolish overgrown boy who was having a run of good luck – or a vain, foolish overgrown boy who had sold his soul and imperilled all humanity.

'A *Satanist*? You're accusing me of being a Satanist?'

Stoney tugged angrily at his dressing gown; he'd been in bed when Jack had pounded on the door. Given the hour, it had been remarkably civil of him to accept a visitor at all, and he appeared so genuinely affronted now that Jack was almost prepared to apologise and slink away. He said, 'I had to ask you—'

'You have to be doubly foolish to be a Satanist,' Stoney muttered.

'Doubly?'

'Not only do you need to believe all the nonsense of Christian theology, you then have to turn around and back the pre-ordained, guaranteed-to-fail, absolutely futile *losing side*.' He held up his hand, as if he believed he'd anticipated the only possible objection to this remark, and wished to spare Jack the trouble of wasting his breath by uttering it. 'I *know*, some people claim it's all really about some pre-Christian deity: Mercury, or Pan – guff like that. But assuming that we're not talking about some complicated mislabelling of objects of worship, I really can't think of anything more insulting. You're comparing me to someone like . . . *Huysmans*, who was basically just a very dim Catholic.'

Stoney folded his arms and settled back on the couch, waiting for Jack's response.

Jack's head was thick from the whisky; he wasn't at all sure how to take this. It was the kind of smart-arsed undergraduate drivel he might have expected from any smug atheist – but then, short of a confession, exactly what kind of reply would have constituted evidence of guilt? *If you'd sold your soul to the devil, what lie would you tell in place of the truth?* Had he seriously believed that Stoney would claim to be a devout churchgoer, as if that were the best possible answer to put Jack off the scent?

He had to concentrate on things he'd seen with his own eyes, facts that could not be denied.

'You're plotting to overthrow nature, bending the world to the will of man.'

Stoney sighed. 'Not at all. More refined technology will help us tread more lightly. We have to cut back on pollution and pesticides as rapidly as possible. Or do you want to live in a world where all the animals are born as hermaphrodites, and half the Pacific islands disappear in storms?'

'Don't try telling me that you're some kind of guardian of the animal kingdom. You want to replace us all with machines!'

'Does every Zulu or Tibetan who gives birth to a child, and wants the best for it, threaten you in the same way?'

Jack bristled. 'I'm not a racist. A Zulu or Tibetan has a *soul*.'

Stoney groaned and put his head in his hands. 'It's half past one in the morning! Can't we have this debate some other time?'

Someone banged on the door. Stoney looked up, disbelieving. 'What is this? Grand Central Station?'

He crossed to the door and opened it. A dishevelled, unshaven man pushed his way into the room. 'Quint? What a pleasant—'

The intruder grabbed Stoney and slammed him against the wall. Jack exhaled with surprise. Quint turned bloodshot eyes on him.

'Who the fuck are you?'

'John Hamilton. Who the fuck are you?'

'Never you mind. Just stay put.' He jerked Stoney's arm up behind his back with one hand, while grinding his face into the wall with the other. 'You're mine now, you piece of shit. No one's going to protect you this time.'

Stoney addressed Jack through a mouth squashed against the masonry. 'Dith ith Pether Quinth, my own perthonal thpook. I did make a Fauthtian bargain. But with thtrictly temporal—'

'Shut up!' Quint pulled a gun from his jacket and held it to Stoney's head.

Jack said, 'Steady on.'

'Just how far do your connections go?' Quint screamed. 'I've had memos disappear, sources clam up – and now my superiors are treating *me* like some kind of traitor! Well, don't worry: when I'm through with you, I'll have the names of the entire network.' He turned to address Jack again. 'And don't *you* think you're going anywhere.'

Stoney said, 'Leave him out of dith. He'th at Magdalene. You mutht know by now: all the thpieth are at Thrinity.'

Jack was shaken by the sight of Quint waving his gun around, but the implications of this drama came as something of a relief. Stoney's ideas must have had their genesis in some secret war-time research project. He hadn't made a deal with the devil after all, but he'd broken the Official Secrets Act, and now he was paying the price.

Stoney flexed his body and knocked Quint backwards. Quint staggered, but didn't fall; he raised his arm menacingly, but there was no gun in his hand. Jack looked around to see where it had fallen, but he couldn't spot it anywhere. Stoney landed a kick squarely in Quint's testicles, barefoot, but Quint wailed with pain. A second kick sent him sprawling.

Stoney called out, 'Luke? *Luke!* Would you come and give me a hand?'

A solidly built man with tattooed forearms emerged from Stoney's bedroom, yawning and tugging his braces into place. At the sight of Quint, he groaned. 'Not again!'

Stoney said, 'I'm sorry.'

Luke shrugged stoically. The two of them managed to grab hold of Quint, then they dragged him struggling out the door. Jack waited a few seconds, then searched the floor for the gun. But it wasn't anywhere in sight, and it hadn't slid under the furniture; none of the crevices where it might have ended up were so dark that it would have been lost in shadow. It was not in the room at all.

Jack went to the window and watched the three men cross the courtyard, half expecting to witness an assassination. But Stoney and his lover merely lifted Quint into the air between them, and tossed him into a shallow, rather slimy-looking pond.

Jack spent the ensuing days in a state of turmoil. He wasn't ready to confide in anyone until he could frame his suspicions clearly, and the events in Stoney's rooms were difficult to interpret unambiguously. He couldn't state with absolute certainty that Quint's gun had vanished before his eyes. But surely the fact that Stoney was walking free proved that he was receiving supernatural protection? And Quint himself, confused and demoralised, had certainly had the appearance of a man who'd been demonically confounded at every turn.

If this was true, though, Stoney must have bought more with his soul than immunity from worldly authority. *The knowledge itself* had to be Satanic in origin, as the legend of Faustus described it. Tollers had been right, in his great essay 'Mythopoesis': myths were remnants of man's pre-lapsarian capacity to apprehend, directly, the great truths of the world. Why else would they resonate in the imagination, and survive from generation to generation?

By Friday, a sense of urgency gripped him. He couldn't take his confusion back to Potter's Barn, back to Joyce and the boys. This had to be resolved, if only in his own mind, before he returned to his family.

With Wagner on the gramophone, he sat and meditated on the challenge he was facing. Stoney had to be thwarted, but how? Jack had always said that the Church of England – apparently so quaint and harmless, a Church of cake stalls and kindly spinsters – was like a fearsome army in the eyes of Satan. But even if his master was quaking in Hell, it would take more than a few stern words from a bicycling vicar to force Stoney to abandon his obscene plans.

But Stoney's intentions, in themselves, didn't matter. He'd been granted the power to dazzle and seduce, but not to force his will upon the populace. What mattered was how his plans were viewed by others. And the way to stop him was to open people's eyes to the true emptiness of his apparent cornucopia.

The more he thought and prayed about it, the more certain Jack became that he'd discerned the task required of him. No denunciation from the pulpits would suffice; people wouldn't turn down the fruits of Stoney's damnation on the mere say-so of the Church. Why would anyone reject such lustrous gifts, without a carefully reasoned argument?

Jack had been humiliated once, defeated once, trying to expose the barrenness of materialism. But might that not have been a form of preparation? He'd been badly mauled by Anscombe, but she'd made an infinitely gentler enemy than the one he now confronted. He had suffered from her taunts – but what was *suffering*, if not the chisel God used to shape his children into their true selves?

His role was clear, now. He would find Stoney's intellectual Achilles heel, and expose it to the world.

He would debate him.

3

Robert gazed at the blackboard for a full minute, then started laughing with delight. 'That's so beautiful!'

'Isn't it?' Helen put down the chalk and joined him on the couch. 'Any more symmetry, and nothing would happen: the universe would be full of crystalline blankness. Any less, and it would all be uncorrelated noise.'

Over the months, in a series of tutorials, Helen had led him through a small part of the century of physics that had separated them at their first meeting, down to the purely algebraic structures that lay beneath spacetime and matter. Mathematics catalogued everything that was not self-contradictory; within that vast inventory, physics was an island of structures rich enough to contain their own beholders.

Robert sat and mentally reviewed everything he'd learnt, trying to apprehend as much as he could in a single image. As he did, a part of him waited fearfully for a sense of disappointment, a sense of anticlimax. *He might never see more deeply into the nature of the world. In this direction, at least, there was nothing more to be discovered.*

But anticlimax was impossible. To become jaded with *this* was impossible. However familiar he became with the algebra of the universe, it would never grow less marvellous.

Finally he asked, 'Are there other islands?' Not merely other histories, sharing the same underlying basis, but other realities entirely.

'I suspect so,' Helen replied. 'People have mapped some possibilities. I don't know how that could ever be confirmed, though.'

Robert shook his head, sated. 'I won't even think about that. I need to come down to Earth for a while.' He stretched his arms and leant back, still grinning.

Helen said, 'Where's Luke today? He usually shows up by now, to drag you out into the sunshine.'

The question wiped the smile from Robert's face. 'Apparently I make poor company. Being insufficiently fanatical about darts and football.'

'He's left you?' Helen reached over and squeezed his hand sympathetically. A little mockingly, too.

Robert was annoyed; she never said anything, but he always felt that she was judging him. 'You think I should grow up, don't you? Find someone more like myself. Some kind of *soulmate*.' He'd meant the word to sound sardonic, but it emerged rather differently.

'It's your life,' she said.

A year before, that would have been a laughable claim, but it was almost the truth now. There was a *de facto* moratorium on prosecutions, while the recently acquired genetic and neurological evidence was being assessed by a parliamentary subcommittee. Robert had helped plant the seeds of the campaign, but he'd played no real part in it; other people had taken up the cause. In a matter of months, it was possible that Quint's cage would be smashed, at least for everyone in Britain.

The prospect filled him with a kind of vertigo. He might have broken the laws at every opportunity, but they had still moulded him. The cage might not have left him crippled, but he'd be lying to himself if he denied that he'd been stunted.

He said, 'Is that what happened, in your past? I ended up in some . . . lifelong partnership?' As he spoke the words, his mouth went dry, and he was suddenly afraid that the answer would be yes. *With Chris. The life he'd missed out on was a life of happiness with Chris.*

'No.'

'Then . . . what?' he pleaded. 'What did I do? How did I live?' He caught himself, suddenly selfconscious, but added, 'You can't blame me for being curious.'

Helen said gently, 'You don't want to know what you can't change. All of that is part of your own causal past now, as much as it is of mine.'

'If it's part of my own history,' Robert countered, 'don't I deserve to know it? This man wasn't me, but he brought you to me.'

Helen considered this. 'You accept that he was someone else? Not someone whose actions you're responsible for?'

'Of course.'

She said, 'There was a trial, in 1952. For "Gross Indecency contrary to Section 11 of the Criminal Amendment Act of 1885". He wasn't imprisoned, but the court ordered hormone treatments.'

'*Hormone treatments?*' Robert laughed. 'What – testosterone, to make him more of a man?'

'No, oestrogen. Which in men reduces the sex drive. There are side-effects, of course. Gynaecomorphism, among other things.'

Robert felt physically sick. *They'd chemically castrated him, with drugs that had made him sprout breasts.* Of all the bizarre abuse to which he'd been subjected, nothing had been as horrifying as that.

Helen continued, 'The treatment lasted six months, and the effects were all temporary. But two years later, he took his own life. It was never clear exactly why.'

Robert absorbed this in silence. He didn't want to know anything more.

After a while, he said, 'How do you bear it? Knowing that in some branch or other, every possible form of humiliation is being inflicted on someone?'

Helen said, 'I don't *bear it*. I change it. That's why I'm here.'

Robert bowed his head. 'I know. And I'm grateful that our histories collided. But . . . how many histories don't?' He struggled to find an example, though it was almost too painful to contemplate; since their first conversation, it was a topic he'd deliberately pushed to the back of his mind. 'There's not just an unchangeable Auschwitz in each of our pasts, there are an astronomical number of others – along with an astronomical number of things that are even worse.'

Helen said bluntly, 'That's not true.'

'What?' Robert looked up at her, startled.

She walked to the blackboard and erased it. 'Auschwitz has happened, for both of us, and no one I'm aware of has ever prevented it – but that doesn't mean that *nobody* stops it, anywhere.' She began sketching a network of fine lines on the blackboard. 'You and I are having this conversation in countless microhistories – sequences of events where various different things happen with subatomic particles throughout the universe – but that's irrelevant to us, we can't tell those strands apart, so we might as well treat them all as one history.' She pressed the chalk down hard to make a thick streak that covered everything she'd drawn. 'The quantum decoherence people call this "coarse graining". Summing over all these indistinguishable details is what gives rise to classical physics in the first place.

'Now, "the two of us" would have first met in many perceivably different coarse-grained histories – and furthermore, you've since diverged by making different choices, and experiencing different external possibilities, after those events.' She sketched two intersecting ribbons of coarse-grained histories, and then showed each history diverging further.

'World War II and the Holocaust certainly happened in both of *our* pasts – but that's no proof that the total is so vast that it might as well be infinite. Remember, what stops us successfully intervening is the fact that we're reaching back to a point where some of the parallel interventions start to bite their own tail. So when we fail, it can't be counted twice: it's just confirming what we already know.'

Robert protested, 'But what about all the versions of '30s Europe that don't happen to lie in either your past or mine? Just because we have no direct evidence for a Holocaust in those branches, that hardly makes it unlikely.'

Helen said, 'Not unlikely *per se*, without intervention. But not fixed in stone either. We'll keep trying, refining the technology, until we can reach branches where there's no overlap with our own past in the '30s. And there must be other, separate ribbons of intervention that happen in histories we can never even know about.'

239

Robert was elated. He'd imagined himself clinging to a rock of improbable good fortune in an infinite sea of suffering – struggling to pretend, for the sake of his own sanity, that the rock was all there was. But what lay around him was not inevitably worse; it was merely unknown. In time, he might even play a part in ensuring that every last tragedy was *not* repeated across billions of worlds.

He re-examined the diagram. 'Hang on. Intervention doesn't end divergence, though, does it? You reached *us*, a year ago, but in at least some of the histories spreading out from that moment, won't we still have suffered all kinds of disasters, and reacted in all kinds of self-defeating ways?'

'Yes,' Helen conceded, 'but fewer than you might think. If you merely listed every sequence of events that superficially appeared to have a non-zero probability, you'd end up with a staggering catalogue of absurdist tragedies. But when you calculate everything more carefully, and take account of Planck-scale effects, it turns out to be nowhere near as bad. There are *no* coarse-grained histories where boulders assemble themselves out of dust and rain from the sky, or everyone in London or Madras goes mad and slaughters their children. Most macroscopic systems end up being quite robust – people included. Across histories, the range of natural disasters, human stupidity and sheer bad luck isn't overwhelmingly greater than the range you're aware of from this history alone.'

Robert laughed. 'And that's not bad enough?'

'Oh, it is. But that's the best thing about the form I've taken.'

'I'm sorry?'

Helen tipped her head and regarded him with an expression of disappointment. 'You know, you're still not as quick on your feet as I'd expected.'

Robert's face burnt, but then he realised what he'd missed and his resentment vanished.

'*You don't diverge?* Your hardware is designed to end the process? Your environment, your surroundings, will still split you into different histories – but on a coarse-grained level, you don't contribute to the process yourself?'

'That's right.'

Robert was speechless. Even after a year, she could still toss him a hand grenade like this.

Helen said, 'I can't help living in many worlds; that's beyond my control. But I do know that I'm one person. Faced with a choice that puts me on a knife edge, I know I won't split and take every path.'

Robert hugged himself, suddenly cold. 'Like I do. Like I have. Like all of us poor creatures of flesh.'

Helen came and sat beside him. 'Even that's not irrevocable. Once you've taken this form – if that's what you choose – you can meet your other selves, reverse some of the scatter. Give some a chance to undo what they've done.'

This time, Robert grasped her meaning at once. 'Gather myself together? Make myself whole?'

Helen shrugged. 'If it's what you want. If you see it that way.'

He stared back at her, disoriented. Touching the bedrock of physics was one thing, but this possibility was too much to take in.

Someone knocked on the study door. The two of them exchanged wary glances, but it wasn't Quint, back for more punishment. It was a porter bearing a telegram.

When the man had left, Robert opened the envelope.

'Bad news?' Helen asked.

He shook his head. 'Not a death in the family, if that's what you meant. It's from John Hamilton. He's challenging me to a debate. On the topic "Can a Machine Think?"'

'What, at some university function?'

'No. On the BBC. Four weeks from tomorrow.' He looked up. 'Do you think I should do it?'

'Radio or television?'

Robert reread the message. 'Television.'

Helen smiled. 'Definitely. I'll give you some tips.'

'On the subject?'

'No! That would be cheating.' She eyed him appraisingly. 'You can start by throwing out your electric razor. Get rid of the permanent five o'clock shadow.'

Robert was hurt. 'Some people find that quite attractive.'

Helen replied firmly, 'Trust me on this.'

The BBC sent a car to take Robert down to London. Helen sat beside him in the back seat.

'Are you nervous?' she asked.

'Nothing that an hour of throwing up won't cure.'

Hamilton had suggested a live broadcast, 'to keep things interesting', and the producer had agreed. Robert had never been on television; he'd taken part in a couple of radio discussions on the future of computing, back when the Mark I had first come into use, but even those had been taped.

Hamilton's choice of topic had surprised him at first, but in retrospect it seemed quite shrewd. A debate on the proposition that 'Modern Science is the Devil's Work' would have brought howls of laughter from all but the most pious viewers, whereas the purely metaphorical claim that 'Modern Science is a Faustian Pact' would have had the entire audience nodding sagely in agreement, while carrying no implications whatsoever. If you weren't going to take the whole dire fairy tale literally, everything was 'a Faustian Pact' in some sufficiently watered-down sense: everything had a potential downside, and this was as pointless to assert as it was easy to demonstrate.

Robert had met considerable incredulity, though, when he'd explained to journalists where his own research was leading. To date, the press had treated him as a kind of eccentric British Edison, churning out inventions of indisputable utility, and no one seemed to find it at all surprising or alarming that he was also, frankly, a bit of a loon. But Hamilton would have a chance to exploit, and reshape, that perception. If Robert insisted on defending his goal of creating machine intelligence, not as an amusing hobby that might have been chosen by a public relations firm to make him appear endearingly daft, but as both the

ultimate vindication of materialist science and the logical end-
point of most of his life's work, Hamilton could use a victory
tonight to cast doubt on everything Robert had done, and everything he symbolised. By asking, not at all rhetorically, 'Where will
this all end?', he was inviting Robert to step forward and hang
himself with the answer.

The traffic was heavy for a Sunday evening, and they arrived at
the Shepherd's Bush studios with only fifteen minutes until the
broadcast. Hamilton had been collected by a separate car, from
his family home near Oxford. As they crossed the studio Robert
spotted him, conversing intensely with a dark-haired young man.

He whispered to Helen, 'Do you know who that is with
Hamilton?'

She followed his gaze, then smiled cryptically. Robert said,
'What? Do you recognise him from somewhere?'

'Yes, but I'll tell you later.'

As the make-up woman applied powder, Helen ran through her
long list of rules again. 'Don't stare into the camera, or you'll look
like you're peddling soap powder. But don't avert your eyes. You
don't want to look shifty.'

The make-up woman whispered to Robert, 'Everyone's an
expert.'

'Annoying, isn't it?' he confided.

Michael Polanyi, an academic philosopher who was well
known to the public after presenting a series of radio talks, had
agreed to moderate the debate. Polanyi popped into the make-up
room, accompanied by the producer; they chatted with Robert for
a couple of minutes, setting him at ease and reminding him of the
procedure they'd be following.

They'd only just left him when the floor manager appeared.
'We need you in the studio now, please, Professor.' Robert followed her, and Helen pursued him part of the way. 'Breathe
slowly and deeply,' she urged him.

'As if you'd know,' he snapped.

Robert shook hands with Hamilton then took his seat on one
side of the podium. Hamilton's young adviser had retreated into

the shadows; Robert glanced back to see Helen watching from a similar position. It was like a duel: they both had seconds. The floor manager pointed out the studio monitor, and as Robert watched it was switched between the feeds from two cameras: a wide shot of the whole set, and a closer view of the podium, including the small blackboard on a stand beside it. He'd once asked Helen whether television had progressed to far greater levels of sophistication in her branch of the future, once the pioneering days were left behind, but the question had left her uncharacteristically tongue-tied.

The floor manager retreated behind the cameras, called for silence, then counted down from ten, mouthing the final numbers.

The broadcast began with an introduction from Polanyi: concise, witty, and non-partisan. Then Hamilton stepped up to the podium. Robert watched him directly while the wide-angle view was being transmitted, so as not to appear rude or distracted. He only turned to the monitor when he was no longer visible himself.

'Can a machine think?' Hamilton began. 'My intuition tells me: *no*. My heart tells me: *no*. I'm sure that most of you feel the same way. But that's not enough, is it? In this day and age, we aren't allowed to rely on our hearts for anything. We need something scientific. We need some kind of proof.

'Some years ago, I took part in a debate at Oxford University. The issue then was not whether machines might behave like people, but whether people themselves might *be* mere machines. Materialists, you see, claim that we are all just a collection of purposeless atoms, colliding at random. Everything we do, everything we feel, everything we say, comes down to some sequence of events that might as well be the spinning of cogs, or the opening and closing of electrical relays.

'To me, this was self-evidently false. What point could there be, I argued, in even conversing with a materialist? By his own admission, the words that came out of his mouth would be the result of nothing but a mindless, mechanical process! By his own theory, he could have no reason to think that those words would be the truth! Only believers in a transcendent human soul could claim any interest in the truth.'

Hamilton nodded slowly, a penitent's gesture. 'I was wrong, and I was put in my place. This might be self-evident to *me*, and it might be self-evident to *you*, but it's certainly not what philosophers call an "analytical truth": it's not actually a nonsense, a contradiction in terms, to believe that we are mere machines. There might, there just *might*, be some reason why the words that emerge from a materialist's mouth are truthful, despite their origins lying entirely in unthinking matter.

'There might.' Hamilton smiled wistfully. 'I had to concede that possibility, because I only had my instinct, my gut feeling, to tell me otherwise.

'But the reason I only had my instinct to guide me was because I'd failed to learn of an event that had taken place many years before. A discovery made in 1930, by an Austrian mathematician named Kurt Gödel.'

Robert felt a shiver of excitement run down his spine. He'd been afraid that the whole contest would degenerate into theology, with Hamilton invoking Aquinas all night – or Aristotle, at best. But it looked as if his mysterious adviser had dragged him into the twentieth century, and they were going to have a chance to debate the real issues after all.

'What is it that we *know* Professor Stoney's computers can do, and do well?' Hamilton continued. 'Arithmetic! In a fraction of a second, they can add up a million numbers. Once we've told them, very precisely, what calculations to perform, they'll complete them in the blink of an eye – even if those calculations would take you or me a lifetime.

'But do these machines *understand* what it is they're doing? Professor Stoney says, "Not yet. Not right now. Give them time. Rome wasn't built in a day."' Hamilton nodded thoughtfully. 'Perhaps that's fair. His computers are only a few years old. They're just babies. Why should they understand anything, so soon?

'But let's stop and think about this a bit more carefully. A computer, as it stands today, is simply a machine that does arithmetic, and Professor Stoney isn't proposing that they're going to sprout new kinds of brains all on their own. Nor is he proposing *giving* them anything really new. He can already let them look at the world with television cameras, turning the pictures into a stream of numbers describing the brightness of different points on the screen . . . on which the computer can then perform *arithmetic*. He can already let them speak to us with a special kind of loudspeaker, to which the computer feeds a stream of numbers to describe how loud the sound should be . . . a stream of numbers produced by more *arithmetic*.

'So the world can come into the computer, as numbers, and words can emerge, as numbers too. All Professor Stoney hopes to add to his computers is a "cleverer" way to do the arithmetic that takes the first set of numbers and churns out the second. It's that "clever arithmetic", he tells us, that will make these machines think.'

Hamilton folded his arms and paused for a moment. 'What are we to make of this? Can *doing arithmetic*, and nothing more, be enough to let a machine *understand* anything? My instinct certainly tells me no, but who am I that you should trust my instinct?

'So, let's narrow down the question of understanding, and to be scrupulously fair, let's put it in the most favourable light possible for Professor Stoney. If there's one thing a computer *ought* to be able to understand – as well as us, if not better – it's arithmetic itself. If a computer could think at all, it would surely be able to grasp the nature of its own best talent.

'The question, then, comes down to this: can you *describe* all of arithmetic, *using* nothing but arithmetic? Thirty years ago – long before Professor Stoney and his computers came along – Professor Gödel asked himself exactly that question.

'Now, you might be wondering how anyone could even *begin* to describe the rules of arithmetic, using nothing but arithmetic itself.' Hamilton turned to the blackboard, picked up the chalk, and wrote two lines:

$$\text{If } x+z = y+z$$
$$\text{then } x = y$$

'This is an important rule, but it's written in symbols, not numbers, because it has to be true for *every* number, every x, y and z. But Professor Gödel had a clever idea: why not use a code, like spies use, where every symbol is assigned a number?' Hamilton wrote:

The code for 'a' is 1.
The code for 'b' is 2.

'And so on. You can have a code for every letter of the alphabet, and for all the other symbols needed for arithmetic: plus signs, equals signs, that kind of thing. Telegrams are sent this way every day, with a code called the Baudot code, so there's really nothing strange or sinister about it.

'All the rules of arithmetic that we learnt at school can be written with a carefully chosen set of symbols, which can then be translated into numbers. Every question as to what does or does not *follow from* those rules can then be seen anew, as a question about numbers. If *this* line follows from *this* one,' Hamilton indicated the two lines of the cancellation rule, 'we can see it in the relationship between their code numbers. We can judge each inference, and declare it valid or not, purely by doing arithmetic.

'So, given *any* proposition at all about arithmetic – such as the claim that "there are infinitely many prime numbers" – we can restate the notion that we have a proof for that claim in terms of code numbers. If the code number for our claim is x, we can say "There is a number p, ending with the code number x, that passes our test for being the code number of a valid proof." '

Hamilton took a visible breath.

'In 1930, Professor Gödel used this scheme to do something rather ingenious.' He wrote on the blackboard:

There DOES NOT EXIST a number p meeting the following condition: p is the code number of a valid proof of this claim.

'Here is a claim about arithmetic, about numbers. It has to be either true or false. So let's start by supposing that it happens to be true. Then there *is no* number p that is the code number for a proof of this claim. So this is a true statement about arithmetic, but it can't be proved merely by *doing* arithmetic!'

Hamilton smiled. 'If you don't catch on immediately, don't worry; when I first heard this argument from a young friend of mine, it took a while for the meaning to sink in. But remember: the only hope a computer has for understanding *anything* is by doing arithmetic, and we've just found a statement that *cannot* be proved with mere arithmetic.

'Is this statement really true, though? We mustn't jump to conclusions, we mustn't damn the machines too hastily. Suppose this claim is false! Since it claims there is no number p that is the code number of its own proof, to be false there would have to be such a number, after all. And that number would encode the "proof" of an acknowledged falsehood!'

Hamilton spread his arms triumphantly. 'You and I, like every schoolboy, know that you can't prove a falsehood from sound premises – and if the premises of arithmetic aren't sound, what is? So *we* know, as a matter of certainty, that this statement is true.

'Professor Gödel was the first to see this, but with a little help and perseverance, any educated person can follow in his footsteps. *A machine could never do that.* We might divulge to a machine our own knowledge of this fact, offering it as something to be taken on trust, but the machine could neither stumble on this truth for itself, nor truly comprehend it when we offered it as a gift.

'You and I *understand* arithmetic, in a way that no electronic calculator ever will. What hope has a machine, then, of moving beyond its own most favourable milieu and comprehending any wider truth?

'None at all, ladies and gentlemen. Though this detour into mathematics might have seemed arcane to you, it has served a very down-to-Earth purpose. It has proved – beyond refutation by even the most ardent materialist or the most pedantic philosopher

– what we common folk knew all along: no machine will ever think.'

Hamilton took his seat. For a moment, Robert was simply exhilarated; coached or not, Hamilton had grasped the essential features of the incompleteness proof, and presented them to a lay audience. What might have been a night of shadow-boxing – with no blows connecting, and nothing for the audience to judge but two solo performances in separate arenas – had turned into a genuine clash of ideas.

As Polanyi introduced him and he walked to the podium, Robert realised that his usual shyness and selfconsciousness had evaporated. He was filled with an altogether different kind of tension: he sensed more acutely than ever what was at stake.

When he reached the podium, he adopted the posture of someone about to begin a prepared speech, but then he caught himself, as if he'd forgotten something. 'Bear with me for a moment.' He walked around to the far side of the blackboard and quickly wrote a few words on it, upside down. Then he resumed his place.

'Can a machine think? Professor Hamilton would like us to believe that he's settled the issue once and for all, by coming up with a statement that *we* know is true, but a particular machine – programmed to explore the theorems of arithmetic in a certain rigid way – would never be able to produce. Well . . . we all have our limitations.' He flipped the blackboard over to reveal what he'd written on the opposite side:

If Robert Stoney speaks these words, he will NOT be telling the truth.

He waited a few beats, then continued, 'What I'd like to explore, though, is not so much a question of limitations, as of opportunities. How exactly is it that we've all ended up with this mysterious ability to know that Gödel's statement is true? Where does this advantage, this great insight, come from? From our souls? From some immaterial entity that no machine could ever possess? Is that the only possible source, the only conceivable explanation? Or might it come from something a little less ethereal?

'As Professor Hamilton explained, we believe Gödel's statement is true because we trust the rules of arithmetic not to lead us into contradictions and falsehoods. But where does that trust come from? How does it arise?'

Robert turned the blackboard back to Hamilton's side, and pointed to the cancellation rule. 'If x plus z equals y plus z, then x equals y. Why is this so *reasonable*? We might not learn to put it quite like this until we're in our teens, but if you showed a young child two boxes – without revealing their contents – added an equal number of shells, or stones, or pieces of fruit to both, and then let the child look inside to see that each box now contained the same number of items, it wouldn't take any formal education for the child to understand that the two boxes must have held the same number of things to begin with.

'The child knows, we all know, how a certain kind of object behaves. Our lives are steeped in direct experience of whole numbers: whole numbers of coins, stamps, pebbles, birds, cats, sheep, buses. If I tried to persuade a six-year-old that I could put three stones in a box, remove one of them, and be left with four . . . he'd simply laugh at me. Why? It's not merely that he's sure to have taken one thing away from three to get two, on many prior occasions. Even a child understands that some things that appear reliable will eventually fail: a toy that works perfectly, day after day, for a month or a year, can still break. But not arithmetic, not taking one from three. He can't even picture *that* failing. Once you've lived in the world, once you've seen how it works, the failure of arithmetic becomes unimaginable.

'Professor Hamilton suggests that this is down to our souls. But what would he say about a child reared in a world of water and mist, never in the company of more than one person at a time, never taught to count on his fingers and toes. I doubt that such a child would possess the same certainty that you and I have, as to the impossibility of arithmetic ever leading him astray. To banish whole numbers entirely from his world would require very strange surroundings, and a level of deprivation amounting to cruelty, but would that be enough to rob a child of his *soul*?

'A computer, programmed to pursue arithmetic as Professor Hamilton has described, is subject to far more deprivation than that child. If I'd been raised with my hands and feet tied, my head in a sack, and someone shouting orders at me, I doubt that I'd have much grasp of reality – and I'd still be better prepared for the task than such a computer. It's a great mercy that a machine treated that way wouldn't be able to think: if it could, the shackles we'd placed upon it would be criminally oppressive.

'But that's hardly the fault of the computer, or a revelation of some irreparable flaw in its nature. If we want to judge the potential of our machines with any degree of honesty, we have to play fair with them, not saddle them with restrictions that we'd never dream of imposing on ourselves. There really is no point comparing an eagle with a spanner, or a gazelle with a washing machine: it's our jets that fly and our cars that run, albeit in quite different ways from any animal.

'*Thought* is sure to be far harder to achieve than those other skills, and to do so we might need to mimic the natural world far more closely. But I believe that once a machine is endowed with facilities resembling the inborn tools for learning that we all have as our birthright, and is set free to learn the way a child learns, through experience, observation, trial and error, hunches and failures – instead of being handed a list of instructions that it has no choice but to obey – we will finally be in a position to compare like with like.

'When that happens, and we can meet and talk and argue with these machines – about arithmetic, or any other topic – there'll be no need to take the word of Professor Gödel, or Professor Hamilton, or myself, for anything. We'll invite them down to the local pub, and interrogate them in person. And if we play fair with them, we'll use the same experience and judgement we use with any friend, or guest, or stranger, to decide for ourselves whether or not they can think.'

The BBC put on a lavish assortment of wine and cheese in a small room off the studio. Robert ended up in a heated argument with

Polanyi, who revealed himself to be firmly on the negative side, while Helen flirted shamelessly with Hamilton's young friend, who turned out to have a PhD in algebraic geometry from Cambridge; he must have completed the degree just before Robert had come back from Manchester. After exchanging some polite formalities with Hamilton, Robert kept his distance, sensing that any further contact would not be welcome.

An hour later, though, after getting lost in the maze of corridors on his way back from the toilets, Robert came across Hamilton sitting alone in the studio, weeping.

He almost backed away in silence, but Hamilton looked up and saw him. With their eyes locked, it was impossible to retreat.

Robert said, 'It's your wife?' He'd heard that she'd been seriously ill, but the gossip had included a miraculous recovery. Some friend of the family had laid hands on her a year ago, and she'd gone into remission.

Hamilton said, 'She's dying.'

Robert approached and sat beside him. 'From what?'

'Breast cancer. It's spread throughout her body. Into her bones, into her lungs, into her liver.' He sobbed again, a helpless spasm, then caught himself angrily. '*Suffering is the chisel God uses to shape us.* What kind of idiot comes up with a line like that?'

Robert said, 'I'll talk to a friend of mine, an oncologist at Guy's Hospital. He's doing a trial of a new genetic treatment.'

Hamilton stared at him. 'One of your *miracle cures*?'

'No, no. I mean, only very indirectly.'

Hamilton said angrily, 'She won't take your poison.'

Robert almost snapped back: *She won't? Or you won't let her?* But it was an unfair question. In some marriages, the lines blurred. It was not for him to judge the way the two of them faced this together.

'They go away in order to be with us in a new way, even closer than before.' Hamilton spoke the words like a defiant incantation, a declaration of faith that would ward off temptation, whether or not he entirely believed it.

Robert was silent for a while, then he said, 'I lost someone close to me, when I was a boy. And I thought the same thing. I thought he was still with me, for a long time afterwards. Guiding me. Encouraging me.' It was hard to get the words out; he hadn't spoken about this to anyone for almost thirty years. 'I dreamt up a whole theory to explain it, in which "souls" used quantum uncertainty to control the body during life, and communicate with the living after death, without breaking any laws of physics. The kind of thing every science-minded seventeen-year-old probably stumbles on, and takes seriously for a couple of weeks, before realising how nonsensical it is. But I had a good reason not to see the flaws, so I clung to it for almost two years. Because I missed him so much, it took me that long to understand what I was doing, how I was deceiving myself.'

Hamilton said pointedly, 'If you'd not tried to explain it, you might never have lost him. He might still be with you now.'

Robert thought about this. 'I'm glad he's not, though. It wouldn't be fair on either of us.'

Hamilton shuddered. 'Then you can't have loved him very much, can you?' He put his head in his arms. 'Just fuck off, now, will you.'

Robert said, 'What exactly would it take, to prove to you that I'm not in league with the devil?'

Hamilton turned red eyes on him and announced triumphantly, 'Nothing will do that! I saw what happened to Quint's gun!'

Robert sighed. 'That was a conjuring trick. Stage magic, not black magic.'

'Oh yes? Show me how it's done, then. Teach me how to do it, so I can impress my friends.'

'It's rather technical. It would take all night.'

Hamilton laughed humourlessly. 'You can't deceive me. I saw through you from the start.'

'Do you think X-rays are Satanic? Penicillin?'

'Don't treat me like a fool. There's no comparison.'

'*Why not?* Everything I've helped develop is part of the same continuum. I've read some of your writing on mediaeval culture, and you're always berating modern commentators for presenting it as unsophisticated. No one really thought the Earth was flat. No one really treated every novelty as witchcraft. So why view any of my work any differently than a fourteenth-century man would view twentieth-century medicine?'

Hamilton replied, 'If a fourteenth-century man was suddenly faced with twentieth-century medicine, don't you think he'd be entitled to wonder how it had been revealed to his con-temporaries?'

Robert shifted uneasily on his chair. Helen hadn't sworn him to secrecy, but he'd agreed with her view: it was better to wait, to spread the knowledge that would ground an understanding of what had happened, before revealing any details of the contact between branches.

But this man's wife was dying, needlessly. And Robert was tired of keeping secrets. Some wars required it, but others were better won with honesty.

He said, 'I know you hate H.G. Wells. But what if he was right about one little thing?'

Robert told him everything, glossing over the technicalities but leaving out nothing substantial. Hamilton listened without inter-rupting, gripped by a kind of unwilling fascination. His expres-sion shifted from hostile to incredulous, but there were also hints of begrudging amazement, as if he could at least appreciate some of the beauty and complexity of the picture Robert was painting.

But when Robert had finished, Hamilton said merely, 'You're a grand liar, Stoney. But what else should I expect, from the King of Lies?'

Robert was in a sombre mood on the drive back to Cambridge. The encounter with Hamilton had depressed him, and the ques-tion of who'd swayed the nation in the debate seemed remote and abstract in comparison.

Helen had taken a house in the suburbs, rather than inviting scandal by cohabiting with him, though her frequent visits to his rooms seemed to have had almost the same effect. Robert walked her to the door.

'I think it went well, don't you?' she said.

'I suppose so.'

'I'm leaving tonight,' she added casually. 'This is goodbye.'

'What?' Robert was staggered. 'Everything's still up in the air! I still need you!'

She shook her head. 'You have all the tools you need, all the clues. And plenty of local allies. There's nothing truly urgent I could tell you, now, that you couldn't find out just as quickly on your own.'

Robert pleaded with her, but her mind was made up. The driver beeped the horn; Robert gestured to him impatiently.

'You know, my breath's frosting visibly,' he said, 'and you're producing nothing. You really ought to be more careful.'

She laughed. 'It's a bit late to worry about that.'

'Where will you go? Back home? Or off to twist another branch?'

'Another branch. But there's something I'm planning to do on the way.'

'What's that?'

'Do you remember once, you wrote about an Oracle? A machine that could solve the halting problem?'

'Of course.' Given a device that could tell you in advance whether a given computer program would halt, or go on running for ever, you'd be able to prove or disprove any theorem whatsoever about the integers: the Goldbach conjecture, Fermat's Last Theorem, anything. You'd simply show this 'Oracle' a program that would loop through all the integers, testing every possible set of values and only halting if it came to a set that violated the conjecture. You'd never need to run the program itself; the Oracle's verdict on whether or not it halted would be enough.

Such a device might or might not be possible, but Robert had proved more than twenty years before that no ordinary computer, however ingeniously programmed, would suffice. If program H could always tell you in a finite time whether or not program X would halt, you could tack on a small addition to H to create program Z, which perversely and deliberately went into an infinite loop whenever it examined a program that halted. If Z examined itself, it would either halt eventually, or run for ever. But either possibility contradicted the alleged powers of program H: if Z actually ran for ever, it would be because H had claimed that it wouldn't, and vice versa. Program H could not exist.

'Time travel,' Helen said, 'gives me a chance to become an Oracle. There's a way to exploit the inability to change your own past, a way to squeeze an infinite number of timelike paths – none of them closed, but some of them arbitrarily near to it – into a finite physical system. Once you do that, you can solve the halting problem.'

'How?' Robert's mind was racing. 'And once you've done that . . . what about higher cardinalities? An Oracle for Oracles, able to test conjectures about the real numbers?'

Helen smiled enigmatically. 'The first problem should only take you forty or fifty years to solve. As for the rest,' she pulled away from him, moving into the darkness of the hallway, 'what makes you think I know the answer myself?' She blew him a kiss, then vanished from sight.

Robert took a step towards her, but the hallway was empty.

He walked back to the car, sad and exalted, his heart pounding.

The driver asked wearily, 'Where to now, sir?'

Robert said, 'Further up, and further in.'

4

The night after the funeral, Jack paced the house until three a.m. When would it be bearable? *When?* She'd shown more strength and courage, dying, than he felt within himself right now. But she'd share it with him, in the weeks to come. She'd share it with them all.

In bed, in the darkness, he tried to sense her presence around him. But it was forced, it was premature. It was one thing to have faith that she was watching over him, but quite another to expect to be spared every trace of grief, every trace of pain.

He waited for sleep. He needed to get some rest before dawn, or how would he face her children in the morning?

Gradually, he became aware of someone standing in the darkness at the foot of the bed. As he examined and re-examined the shadows, he formed a clear image of the apparition's face.

It was his own. Younger, happier, surer of himself.

Jack sat up. 'What do you want?'

'I want you to come with me.' The figure approached; Jack recoiled, and it halted.

'Come with you, where?' Jack demanded.

'To a place where she's waiting.'

Jack shook his head. 'No. I don't believe you. She said she'd come for me herself, when it was time. She said she'd guide me.'

'She didn't understand, then,' the apparition insisted gently. 'She didn't know I could fetch you myself. Do you think I'd send her in my place? Do you think I'd shirk the task?'

Jack searched the smiling, supplicatory face. 'Who are you?' *His own soul, in Heaven, remade?* Was this a gift God offered everyone? To meet, before death, the very thing you would become – if you so chose? So that even this would be an act of free will?

The apparition said, 'Stoney persuaded me to let his friend treat Joyce. We lived on, together. More than a century has passed. And now we want you to join us.'

Jack choked with horror. 'No! This is a trick! *You're the Devil!*'

The thing replied mildly, 'There is no Devil. And no God, either. Just people. But I promise you: people with the powers of gods are kinder than any god we ever imagined.'

Jack covered his face. 'Leave me be.' He whispered fervent prayers, and waited. It was a test, a moment of vulnerability, but God wouldn't leave him naked like this, face to face with the Enemy, for longer than he could endure.

He uncovered his face. The thing was still with him.

It said, 'Do you remember, when your faith came to you? The

257

sense of a shield around you melting away, like armour you'd worn to keep God at bay?'

'Yes.' Jack acknowledged the truth defiantly; he wasn't frightened that this abomination could see into his past, into his heart.

'That took strength: to admit that you needed God. But it takes the same kind of strength, again, to understand that *some needs can never be met.* I can't promise you Heaven. We have no disease, we have no war, we have no poverty. But we have to find our own love, our own goodness. There is no final word of comfort. We only have each other.'

Jack didn't reply; this blasphemous fantasy wasn't even worth challenging. He said, 'I know you're lying. Do you really imagine that I'd leave the boys alone here?'

'They'd go back to America, back to their father. How many years do you think you'd have with them, if you stay? They've already lost their mother. It would be easier for them now, a single clean break.'

Jack shouted angrily, 'Get out of my house!'

The thing came closer, and sat on the bed. It put a hand on his shoulder. Jack sobbed, 'Help me!' But he didn't know whose aid he was invoking any more.

'Do you remember the scene in *The Seat of Oak*? When the Harpy traps everyone in her cave underground, and tries to convince them that there is no Nescia? Only this drab underworld is real, she tells them. Everything else they think they've seen was just make-believe.' Jack's own young face smiled nostalgically. 'And we had dear old Shrugweight reply: he didn't think much of this so-called "real world" of hers. And even if she was right, since four little children could make up a better world, he'd rather go on pretending that their imaginary one was real.

'But we had it all upside down! The real world is richer, and stranger, and more beautiful than anything ever imagined. Milton, Dante, John the Divine are the ones who trapped you in a drab, grey underworld. That's where you are now. But if you give me your hand, I can pull you out.'

Jack's chest was bursting. *He couldn't lose his faith. He'd kept it through worse than this. He'd kept it through every torture and in-dignity God had inflicted on his wife's frail body. No one could take it from him now.* He crooned to himself, 'In my time of trouble, He will find me.'

The cool hand tightened its grip on his shoulder. 'You can be with her, now. Just say the word, and you will become a part of me. I will take you inside me, and you will see through my eyes, and we will travel back to the world where she still lives.'

Jack wept openly. 'Leave me in peace! Just leave me to mourn her!'

The thing nodded sadly. 'If that's what you want.'

'I do! *Go!*'

'When I'm sure.'

Suddenly Jack thought back to the long rant Stoney had deliv-ered in the studio. Every choice went every way, Stoney had claimed. No decision could ever be final.

'Now I know you're lying!' he shouted triumphantly. 'If you believed everything Stoney told you, how could my choice ever mean a thing? I would always say yes to you, and I would always say no! It would all be the same!'

The apparition replied solemnly, 'While I'm here with you, touching you, *you can't be divided.* Your choice will count.'

Jack wiped his eyes and gazed into its face. It seemed to believe every word it was speaking. What if this truly was his metaphys-ical twin, speaking as honestly as he could, and not merely the Devil in a mask? Perhaps there was a grain of truth in Stoney's awful vision; perhaps this was another version of himself, a living person who honestly believed that the two of them shared a history.

Then it was a visitor sent by God, to humble him. To teach him compassion towards Stoney. To show Jack that he too, with a little less faith, and a little more pride, might have been damned for ever.

Jack stretched out a hand and touched the face of this poor lost soul. *There, but for the grace of God, go I.*

He said, 'I've made my choice. Now leave me.'

Author's note: where the lives of the fictional characters of this story parallel those of real historical figures, I've drawn on biographies by Andrew Hodges and A.N. Wilson. The self-dual formulation of general relativity was discovered by Abhay Ashtekar in 1986, and has since led to ground-breaking developments in quantum gravity, but the implications drawn from it here are fanciful.

BORDER GUARDS

In the early afternoon of his fourth day out of sadness, Jamil was wandering home from the gardens at the centre of Noether when he heard shouts from the playing field behind the library. On the spur of the moment, without even asking the city what game was in progress, he decided to join in.

As he rounded the corner and the field came into view, it was clear from the movements of the players that they were in the middle of a quantum soccer match. At Jamil's request, the city painted the wave function of the hypothetical ball across his vision, and tweaked him to recognise the players as the members of two teams without changing their appearance at all. Maria had once told him that she always chose a literal perception of colour-coded clothing instead; she had no desire to use pathways that had evolved for the sake of sorting people into those you defended and those you slaughtered. But almost everything that had been bequeathed to them was stained with blood, and to Jamil it seemed a far sweeter victory to adapt the worst relics to his own ends than to discard them as irretrievably tainted.

The wave function appeared as a vivid auroral light, a quick-silver plasma bright enough to be distinct in the afternoon sun-light, yet unable to dazzle the eye or conceal the players running through it. Bands of colour representing the complex phase of the wave swept across the field, parting to wash over separate rising lobes of probability before hitting the boundary and boun-cing back again, inverted. The match was being played by the oldest, simplest rules: semi-classical, non-relativistic. The ball was confined to the field by an infinitely high barrier, so there was no question of it tunnelling out, leaking away as the match progressed. The players were treated classically: their movements pumped energy into the wave, enabling transitions from the game's opening state – with the ball spread thinly across the entire field – into the range of higher-energy modes needed to localise it. But localisation was fleeting; there was no point forming a nice sharp wave packet in the middle of the field in the hope of kicking it around like a classical object. You had to shape the wave in such a way that all of its modes – cycling at different frequencies, travelling with different velocities – would come into phase with each other, for a fraction of a second, within the goal itself. Achieving that was a matter of energy levels, and timing.

Jamil had noticed that one team was under-strength. The umpire would be skewing the field's potential to keep the match fair, but a new participant would be especially welcome for the sake of restoring symmetry. He watched the faces of the players, most of them old friends. They were frowning with con-centration, but breaking now and then into smiles of delight at their small successes, or their opponents' ingenuity.

He was badly out of practice, but if he turned out to be dead weight he could always withdraw. And if he misjudged his skills, and lost the match with his incompetence? No one would care. The score was nil-all; he could wait for a goal, but that might be an hour or more in coming. Jamil communed with the umpire, and discovered that the players had decided in advance to allow new entries at any time.

Before he could change his mind, he announced himself. The wave froze, and he ran on to the field. People nodded greetings, mostly making no fuss, though Ezequiel shouted, 'Welcome back!' Jamil suddenly felt fragile again; though he'd ended his long seclusion four days before, it was well within his power, still, to be dismayed by everything the game would involve. His recovery felt like a finely balanced optical illusion, a figure and ground that could change roles in an instant, a solid cube that could evert into a hollow.

The umpire guided him to his allotted starting position, opposite a woman he hadn't seen before. He offered her a formal bow, and she returned the gesture. This was no time for introductions, but he asked the city if she'd published a name. She had: Margit.

The umpire counted down in their heads. Jamil tensed, regretting his impulsiveness. For seven years he'd been dead to the world. After four days back, what was he good for? His muscles were incapable of atrophy, his reflexes could never be dulled, but he'd chosen to live with an unconstrained will, and at any moment his wavering resolve could desert him.

The umpire said, 'Play.' The frozen light around Jamil came to life, and he sprang into motion.

Each player was responsible for a set of modes, particular harmonics of the wave that were theirs to fill, guard, or deplete as necessary. Jamil's twelve modes cycled at between 1,000 and 1,250 millihertz. The rules of the game endowed his body with a small, fixed potential energy, which repelled the ball slightly and allowed different modes to push and pull on each other through him, but if he stayed in one spot as the modes cycled, every influence he exerted would eventually be replaced by its opposite, and the effect would simply cancel itself out.

To drive the wave from one mode to another, you needed to move, and to drive it efficiently you needed to exploit the way the modes fell in and out of phase with each other: to take from a 1,000 millihertz mode and give to a 1,250, you had to act in synch with the quarter-hertz beat between them. It was like pushing a child's swing at its natural frequency, but rather than setting a single child in motion, you were standing between two swings and acting more as an intermediary: trying to time your interventions in such a way as to speed up one child at the other's expense. The way you pushed on the wave at a given time and place was out of your hands completely, but by changing location in just the right way you could gain control over the interaction. Every pair of modes had a spatial beat between them – like the moiré pattern formed by two sheets of woven fabric held up to the light together, shifting from transparent to opaque as the gaps between the threads fell in and out of alignment. Slicing through this cyclic landscape offered the perfect means to match the accompanying chronological beat.

Jamil sprinted across the field at a speed and angle calculated to drive two favourable transitions at once. He'd gauged the current spectrum of the wave instinctively, watching from the sidelines, and he knew which of the modes in his charge would contribute to a goal and which would detract from the probability. As he cut through the shimmering bands of colour, the umpire gave him tactile feedback to supplement his visual estimates and calculations, allowing him to sense the difference between a cyclic tug, a to and fro that came to nothing, and the gentle but persistent force that meant he was successfully riding the beat.

Chusok called out to him urgently, 'Take, take! Two-ten!' Everyone's spectral territory overlapped with someone else's, and you needed to pass amplitude from player to player as well as trying to manage it within your own range. *Two-ten* – a harmonic with two peaks across the width of the field and ten along its length, cycling at 1,160 millihertz – was filling up as Chusok drove unwanted amplitude from various lower-energy modes into it. It was Jamil's role to empty it, putting the amplitude somewhere useful. Any mode with an even number of peaks across the field was unfavourable for scoring, because it had a node – a zero point between the peaks – smack in the middle of both goals.

Jamil acknowledged the request with a hand signal and shifted his trajectory. It was almost a decade since he'd last played the game, but he still knew the intricate web of possibilities by heart: he could drain the two-ten harmonic into the three-ten, five-two and five-six modes – all with 'good parity', peaks along the centre-line – in a single action.

As he pounded across the grass, carefully judging the correct angle by sight, increasing his speed until he felt the destructive beats give way to a steady force like a constant breeze, he suddenly recalled a time – centuries before, in another city – when he'd played with one team, week after week, for forty years. Faces and voices swam in his head. Hashim, Jamil's ninety-eighth child, and Hashim's granddaughter Laila had played beside him. But he'd burnt his house and moved on, and when that era touched him at all now it was like an unexpected gift. The scent of the grass, the shouts of the players, the soles of his feet striking the ground, resonated with every other moment he'd spent the same way, bridging the centuries, binding his life together. He never truly felt the scale of it when he sought it out deliberately; it was always small things, tightly focused moments like this, that burst the horizon of his everyday concerns and confronted him with the astonishing vista.

The two-ten mode was draining faster than he'd expected; the see-sawing centre-line dip in the wave was vanishing before his eyes. He looked around, and saw Margit performing an elaborate Lissajous manoeuvre, smoothly orchestrating a dozen transitions at once. Jamil froze and watched her, admiring her virtuosity while he tried to decide what to do next; there was no point competing with her when she was doing such a good job of completing the task Chusok had set him.

Margit was his opponent, but they were both aiming for exactly the same kind of spectrum. The symmetry of the field meant that any scoring wave would work equally well for either side – but only one team could be the first to reap the benefit, the first to have more than half the wave's probability packed into their goal. So the two teams were obliged to cooperate at first, and it was only as the wave took shape from their combined efforts that it gradually became apparent which side would gain by sculpting it to perfection as rapidly as possible, and which would gain by spoiling it for the first chance, then honing it for the rebound.

Penina chided him over her shoulder as she jogged past, 'You want to leave her to clean up four-six, as well?' She was smiling, but Jamil was stung; he'd been motionless for ten or fifteen seconds. It was not forbidden to drag your feet and rely on your opponents to do all the work, but it was regarded as a shamefully impoverished strategy. It was also very risky, handing them the opportunity to set up a wave that was almost impossible to exploit yourself.

He reassessed the spectrum and quickly sorted through the alternatives. Whatever he did would have unwanted side-effects; there was no magic way to avoid influencing modes in other players' territory, and any action that would drive the transitions he needed would also trigger a multitude of others, up and down the spectrum. Finally, he made a choice that would weaken the offending mode while causing as little disruption as possible.

Jamil immersed himself in the game, planning each transition two steps in advance, switching strategy halfway through a run if he had to, but staying in motion until the sweat dripped from his body, until his calves burnt, until his blood sang. He wasn't blinded to the raw pleasures of the moment, or to memories of games past, but he let them wash over him, like the breeze that rose up and cooled his skin with no need for acknowledgement. Familiar voices shouted terse commands at him; as the wave came closer to a scoring spectrum every trace of superfluous conversation vanished, every idle glance gave way to frantic, purposeful gestures. To a bystander, this might have seemed like the height of dehumanisation: twenty-two people reduced to grunting cogs in a pointless machine. Jamil smiled at the thought but refused to be distracted into a complicated imaginary rebuttal. Every step he took was the answer to that, every hoarse plea to Yann or Joracy, Chusok or Maria, Eudore or Halide. These were his friends, and he was back among them. Back in the world.

The first chance of a goal was thirty seconds away, and the opportunity would fall to Jamil's team; a few tiny shifts in amplitude would clinch it. Margit kept her distance, but Jamil could sense her eyes on him constantly – and literally feel her at work through his skin as she slackened his contact with the wave. In theory, by mirroring your opponent's movements at the correct position on the field you could undermine everything they did, though in practice not even the most skilful team could keep the spectrum completely frozen. Going further and spoiling was a tug-of-war you didn't want to win too well: if you degraded the wave too much, your opponent's task – spoiling your own subsequent chance at a goal – became far easier.

Jamil still had two bad-parity modes that he was hoping to weaken, but every time he changed velocity to try a new transition, Margit responded in an instant, blocking him. He gestured to Chusok for help; Chusok had his own problems with Ezequiel, but he could still make trouble for Margit by choosing where he placed unwanted amplitude. Jamil shook sweat out of his eyes; he could see the characteristic 'stepping stone' pattern of lobes forming, a sign that the wave would soon converge on the goal, but from the middle of the field it was impossible to judge their shape accurately enough to know what, if anything, remained to be done.

Suddenly, Jamil felt the wave push against him. He didn't waste time looking around for Margit; Chusok must have succeeded in distracting her. He was almost at the boundary line, but he managed to reverse smoothly, continuing to drive both the transitions he'd been aiming for.

Two long lobes of probability, each modulated by a series of oscillating mounds, raced along the sides of the field. A third, shorter lobe running along the centre-line melted away, reappeared, then merged with the others as they touched the end of the field, forming an almost rectangular plateau encompassing the goal.

The plateau became a pillar of light, growing narrower and higher as dozens of modes, all finally in phase, crashed together against the impenetrable barrier of the field's boundary. A shallow residue was still spread across the entire field, and a diminishing sequence of elliptical lobes trailed away from the goal like a staircase, but most of the wave that had started out lapping around their waists was now concentrated in a single peak that towered above their heads, nine or ten metres tall.

For an instant, it was motionless.

Then it began to fall.

The umpire said, 'Forty-nine point eight.'

The wave packet had not been tight enough.

Jamil struggled to shrug off his disappointment and throw his instincts into reverse. The other team had fifty seconds now, to fine-tune the spectrum and ensure that the reflected packet was just a fraction narrower when it reformed, at the opposite end of the field.

As the pillar collapsed, replaying its synthesis in reverse, Jamil caught sight of Margit. She smiled at him calmly, and it suddenly struck him: *She'd known they couldn't make the goal. That was why she'd stopped opposing him.* She'd let him work towards sharpening the wave for a few seconds, knowing that it was already too late for him, knowing that her own team would gain from the slight improvement.

Jamil was impressed; it took an extraordinary level of skill and confidence to do what she'd just done. For all the time he'd spent away, he knew exactly what to expect from the rest of the players, and in Margit's absence he would probably have been wishing out loud for a talented newcomer to make the game interesting again. Still, it was hard not to feel a slight sting of resentment. Someone should have warned him just how good she was.

With the modes slipping out of phase, the wave undulated all over the field again, but its reconvergence was inevitable: unlike a wave of water or sound, it possessed no hidden degrees of freedom to grind its precision into entropy. Jamil decided to ignore Margit; there were cruder strategies than mirror-blocking that worked almost as well. Chusok was filling the two-ten mode now; Jamil chose the four-six as his spoiler. All they had to do was keep the wave from growing much sharper, and it didn't matter whether they achieved this by preserving the status quo, or by nudging it from one kind of bluntness to another.

The steady resistance he felt as he ran told Jamil that he was driving the transition, unblocked, but he searched in vain for some visible sign of success. When he reached a vantage point where he could take in enough of the field in one glance to judge the spectrum properly, he noticed a rapidly vibrating shimmer across the width of the wave. He counted nine peaks: good parity. Margit had pulled most of the amplitude straight out of his spoiler mode and fed it into *this*. It was a mad waste of energy to aim for such an elevated harmonic, but no one had been looking there, no one had stopped her.

The scoring pattern was forming again, he only had nine or ten seconds left to make up for all the time he'd wasted. Jamil chose the strongest good-parity mode in his territory, and the emptiest bad one, computed the velocity that would link them, and ran.

He didn't dare turn to watch the opposition goal; he didn't want to break his concentration. The wave retreated around his feet, less like an Earthly ebb tide than an ocean drawn into the sky by a passing black hole. The city diligently portrayed the shadow that his body would have cast, shrinking in front of him as the tower of light rose.

The verdict was announced. 'Fifty point one.'

The air was filled with shouts of triumph – Ezequiel's the loudest, as always. Jamil sagged to his knees, laughing. It was a curious feeling, familiar as it was: he cared, and he didn't. If he'd been wholly indifferent to the outcome of the game there would have been no pleasure in it, but obsessing over every defeat – or every victory – could ruin it just as thoroughly. He could almost see himself walking the line, orchestrating his response as carefully as any action in the game itself.

He lay down on the grass to catch his breath before play resumed. The outer face of the microsun that orbited Laplace was shielded with rock, but light reflected skywards from the land beneath it crossed the 100,000-kilometre width of the 3-toroidal universe to give a faint glow to the planet's nightside. Though only a sliver was lit directly, Jamil could discern the full disk of the opposite hemisphere in the primary image at the zenith: continents and oceans that lay, by a shorter route, 12,000 or so kilometres beneath him. Other views in the lattice of images spread across the sky were from different angles, and showed substantial crescents of the dayside itself. The one thing you couldn't find in any of these images, even with a telescope, was your own city. The topology of this universe let you see the back of your head, but never your reflection.

Jamil's team lost, three-nil. He staggered over to the fountains at the edge of the field and slaked his thirst, shocked by the pleasure of the simple act. Just to be alive was glorious now, but once he felt this way, anything seemed possible. He was back in synch, back in phase, and he was going to make the most of it, for however long it lasted.

He caught up with the others, who'd headed down towards the river. Ezequiel hooked an arm around his neck, laughing. 'Bad luck, Sleeping Beauty! You picked the wrong time to wake. With Margit, we're invincible.'

Jamil ducked free of him. 'I won't argue with that.' He looked around. 'Speaking of whom—'

Penina said, 'Gone home. She plays, that's all. No frivolous socialising after the match.'

Chusok added, 'Or any other time.' Penina shot Jamil a glance that meant: not for want of trying on Chusok's part.

Jamil pondered this, wondering why it annoyed him so much. On the field, she hadn't come across as aloof and superior. Just unashamedly good.

He queried the city, but she'd published nothing besides her name. Nobody expected – or wished – to hear more than the tiniest fraction of another person's history, but it was rare for anyone to start a new life without carrying through something from the old as a kind of calling card, some incident or achievement from which your new neighbours could form an impression of you.

They'd reached the riverbank. Jamil pulled his shirt over his head. 'So what's her story? She must have told you something.'

Ezequiel said, 'Only that she learnt to play a long time ago; she won't say where or when. She arrived in Noether at the end of last year, and grew a house on the southern outskirts. No one sees her around much. No one even knows what she studies.'

Jamil shrugged, and waded in. 'Ah well. It's a challenge to rise to.' Penina laughed and splashed him teasingly. He protested, 'I *meant*, beating her at the game.'

Chusok said wryly, 'When you turned up, I thought you'd be our secret weapon. The one player she didn't know inside out already.'

'I'm glad you didn't tell me that. I would have turned around and fled straight back into hibernation.'

'I know. That's why we all kept quiet.' Chusok smiled. 'Welcome back.'

Penina said, 'Yeah, welcome back, Jamil.'

Sunlight shone on the surface of the river. Jamil ached all over, but the cool water was the perfect place to be. If he wished, he could build a partition in his mind at the point where he stood right now, and never fall beneath it. Other people lived that way, and it seemed to cost them nothing. Contrast was overrated; no sane person spent half their time driving spikes into their flesh for the sake of feeling better when they stopped. Ezequiel lived every day with the happy boisterousness of a five-year-old; Jamil sometimes found this annoying, but then any kind of disposition would irritate someone. His own stretches of meaningless sombreness weren't exactly a boon to his friends.

Chusok said, 'I've invited everyone to a meal at my house tonight. Will you come?'

Jamil thought it over, then shook his head. He still wasn't ready. He couldn't force-feed himself with normality; it didn't speed his recovery, it just drove him backwards.

Chusok looked disappointed, but there was nothing to be done about that. Jamil promised him, 'Next time. Okay?'

Ezequiel sighed. 'What are we going to do with you? You're worse than Margit!' Jamil started backing away, but it was too late. Ezequiel reached him in two casual strides, bent down and grabbed him around the waist, hoisted him effortlessly onto one shoulder, then flung him through the air into the depths of the river.

Jamil was woken by the scent of woodsmoke. His room was still filled with the night's grey shadows, but when he propped himself up on one elbow and the window obliged him with transparency, the city was etched clearly in the predawn light.

He dressed and left the house, surprised at the coolness of the dew on his feet. No one else in his street seemed to be up; had they failed to notice the smell, or did they already know to expect it? He turned a corner and saw the rising column of smoke, faintly lit with red from below. The flames and the ruins were still hidden from him, but he knew whose house it was.

When he reached the dying blaze, he crouched in the heat-withered garden, cursing himself. Chusok had offered him the chance to join him for his last meal in Noether. Whatever hints you dropped, it was customary to tell no one that you were moving on. If you still had a lover, if you still had young children, you never deserted them. But friends, you warned in subtle ways. Before vanishing.

Jamil covered his head with his arms. He'd lived through this countless times before, but it never became easier. If anything it grew worse, as every departure was weighted with the memories of others. His brothers and sisters had scattered across the branches of the New Territories. He'd walked away from his father and mother when he was too young and confident to realise how much it would hurt him, decades later. His own children had all abandoned him eventually, far more often than he'd left them. It was easier to leave an ex-lover than a grown child: something burnt itself out in a couple, almost naturally, as if ancestral biology had prepared them for at least that one rift.

Jamil stopped fighting the tears. But as he brushed them away, he caught sight of someone standing beside him. He looked up. It was Margit.

He felt a need to explain. He rose to his feet and addressed her. 'This was Chusok's house. We were good friends. I'd known him for ninety-six years.'

Margit gazed back at him neutrally. 'Boo hoo. Poor baby. You'll never see your friend again.'

Jamil almost laughed, her rudeness was so surreal. He pushed on, as if the only conceivable, polite response was to pretend that he hadn't heard her. 'No one is the kindest, the most generous, the most loyal. It doesn't matter. That's not the point. Everyone's unique. Chusok was Chusok.' He banged a fist against his chest, utterly heedless now of her contemptuous words. 'There's a hole in me, and it will never be filled.' That was the truth, even though he'd grow around it. *He should have gone to the meal, it would have cost him nothing.*

'You must be a real emotional Swiss cheese,' observed Margit tartly.

Jamil came to his senses. 'Why don't you fuck off to some other universe? No one wants you in Noether.'

Margit was amused. 'You *are* a bad loser.'

Jamil gazed at her, honestly confused for a moment; the game had slipped his mind completely. He gestured at the embers. 'What are you doing here? Why did you follow the smoke, if it wasn't regret at not saying goodbye to him when you had the chance?' He wasn't sure how seriously to take Penina's light-hearted insinuation, but if Chusok had fallen for Margit, and it had not been reciprocated, that might even have been the reason he'd left.

She shook her head calmly. 'He was nothing to me. I barely spoke to him.'

'Well, that's your loss.'

'From the look of things, I'd say the loss was all yours.'

He had no reply. Margit turned and walked away.

Jamil crouched on the ground again, rocking back and forth, waiting for the pain to subside.

Jamil spent the next week preparing to resume his studies. The library had near-instantaneous contact with every artificial universe in the New Territories, and the additional light-speed lag between Earth and the point in space from which the whole tree-structure blossomed was only a few hours. Jamil had been to Earth, but only as a tourist; land was scarce, they accepted no migrants. There were remote planets you could live on, in the home universe, but you had to be a certain kind of masochistic purist to want that. The precise reasons why his ancestors had entered the New Territories had been forgotten generations before – and it would have been presumptuous to track them down and ask them in person – but given a choice between the then even-more-crowded Earth, the horrifying reality of interstellar distances, and an endlessly extensible branching chain of worlds which could be traversed within a matter of weeks, the decision wasn't exactly baffling.

Jamil had devoted most of his time in Noether to studying the category of representations of Lie groups on complex vector spaces – a fitting choice, since Emmy Noether had been a pioneer of group theory, and if she'd lived to see this field blossom she would probably have been in the thick of it herself. Representations of Lie groups lay behind most of physics: each kind of subatomic particle was really nothing but a particular way of representing the universal symmetry group as a set of rotations of complex vectors. Organising this kind of structure with category theory was ancient knowledge, but Jamil didn't care; he'd long ago reconciled himself to being a student, not a discoverer. The greatest gift of consciousness was the ability to take the patterns of the world inside you, and for all that he would have relished the thrill of being the first at anything, with ten-to-the-sixteenth people alive that was a futile ambition for most.

In the library, he spoke with fellow students of his chosen field on other worlds, or read their latest works. Though they were not researchers, they could still put a new pedagogical spin on old material, enriching the connections with other fields, finding ways to make the complex, subtle truth easier to assimilate without sacrificing the depth and detail that made it worth knowing in the first place. They would not advance the frontiers of knowledge. They would not discover new principles of nature, or invent new technologies. But to Jamil, understanding was an end in itself.

He rarely thought about the prospect of playing another match, and when he did the idea was not appealing. With Chusok gone, the same group could play ten-to-a-side without Jamil to skew the numbers. Margit might even choose to swap teams, if only for the sake of proving that her current team's monotonous string of victories really had been entirely down to her.

When the day arrived, though, he found himself unable to stay away. He turned up intending to remain a spectator, but Ryuichi had deserted Ezequiel's team, and everyone begged Jamil to join in.

As he took his place opposite Margit, there was nothing in her demeanour to acknowledge their previous encounter: no lingering contempt, but no hint of shame either. Jamil resolved to put it out of his mind; he owed it to his fellow players to concentrate on the game.

They lost, five-nil.

Jamil forced himself to follow everyone to Eudore's house, to celebrate, commiserate, or, as it turned out, to forget the whole thing. After they'd eaten, Jamil wandered from room to room, enjoying Eudore's choice of music but unable to settle into any conversation. No one mentioned Chusok in his hearing.

He left just after midnight. Laplace's near-full primary image and its eight brightest gibbous companions lit the streets so well that there was no need for anything more. Jamil thought: Chusok might have merely travelled to another city, one beneath his gaze right now. And wherever he'd gone, he might yet choose to stay in touch with his friends from Noether.

And his friends from the next town, and the next?

Century after century?

Margit was sitting on Jamil's doorstep, holding a bunch of white flowers in one hand.

Jamil was irritated. 'What are you doing here?'

'I came to apologise.'

He shrugged. 'There's no need. We feel differently about certain things. That's fine. I can still face you on the playing field.'

'I'm not apologising for a difference of opinion. I wasn't honest with you. I was cruel.' She shaded her eyes against the glare of the planet and looked up at him. 'You were right: it was my loss. I wish I'd known your friend.'

He laughed curtly. 'Well, it's too late for that.'

She said simply, 'I know.'

Jamil relented. 'Do you want to come in?' Margit nodded, and he instructed the door to open for her. As he followed her inside, he said, 'How long have you been here? Have you eaten?'

'No.'

'I'll cook something for you.'

'You don't have to do that.'

He called out to her from the kitchen, 'Think of it as a peace offering. I don't have any flowers.'

Margit replied, 'They're not for you. They're for Chusok's house.'

Jamil stopped rummaging through his vegetable bins, and walked back into the living room. 'People don't usually do that in Noether.'

Margit was sitting on the couch, staring at the floor. She said, 'I'm so lonely here. I can't bear it any more.'

He sat beside her. 'Then why did you rebuff him? You could at least have been friends.'

She shook her head. 'Don't ask me to explain.'

Jamil took her hand. She turned and embraced him, trembling miserably. He stroked her hair. 'Ssshh.'

She said, 'Just sex. I don't want anything more.'

He groaned softly. 'There's no such thing as that.'

'I just need someone to touch me again.'

'I understand.' He confessed, 'So do I. But that won't be all. So don't ask me to promise there'll be nothing more.'

Margit took his face in her hands and kissed him. Her mouth tasted of woodsmoke.

Jamil said, 'I don't even know you.'

'No one knows anyone any more.'

'That's not true.'

'No, it's not,' she conceded gloomily. She ran a hand lightly along his arm. Jamil wanted badly to see her smile, so he made each dark hair thicken and blossom into a violet flower as it passed beneath her fingers.

She did smile, but she said, 'I've seen that trick before.'

Jamil was annoyed. 'I'm sure to be a disappointment all round, then. I expect you'd be happier with some kind of novelty. A unicorn, or an amoeba.'

She laughed. 'I don't think so.' She took his hand and placed it against her breast. 'Do you ever get tired of sex?'

'Do you ever get tired of breathing?'

'I can go for a long time without thinking about it.'

He nodded. 'But then one day you stop and fill your lungs with air, and it's still as sweet as ever.'

Jamil didn't know what he was feeling any more. Lust. Compassion. Spite. She'd come to him hurting, and he wanted to help her, but he wasn't sure that either of them really believed this would work.

Margit inhaled the scent of the flowers on his arm. 'Are they the same colour? Everywhere else?'

He said, 'There's only one way to find out.'

Jamil woke in the early hours of the morning, alone. He'd half expected Margit to flee like this, but she could have waited till dawn. He would have obligingly feigned sleep while she dressed and tip-toed out.

Then he heard her. It was not a sound he would normally have associated with a human being, but it could not have been anything else.

He found her in the kitchen, curled around a table leg, wailing rhythmically. He stood back and watched her, afraid that anything he did would only make things worse. She met his gaze in the half-light, but kept up the mechanical whimper. Her eyes weren't blank; she was not delirious, or hallucinating. She knew exactly who, and where, she was.

Finally, Jamil knelt in the doorway. He said, 'Whatever it is, you can tell me. And we'll fix it. We'll find a way.'

She bared her teeth. 'You can't *fix it*, you stupid child.' She resumed the awful noise.

'Then just tell me. Please?' He stretched out a hand towards her.

He hadn't felt quite so helpless since his very first daughter, Aminata, had come to him as an inconsolable six-year-old, rejected by the boy to whom she'd declared her undying love. He'd been twenty-four years old; a child himself. More than a thousand years ago. *Where are you now, Nata?*

Margit said, 'I promised I'd never tell.'

'Promised who?'

'Myself.'

'Good. They're the easiest kind to break.'

She started weeping. It was a more ordinary sound, but it was even more chilling. She was not a wounded animal now, an alien being suffering some incomprehensible pain. Jamil approached her cautiously; she let him wrap his arms around her shoulders.

He whispered, 'Come to bed. The warmth will help. Just being held will help.'

She spat at him derisively, 'It won't bring her back.'

'Who?'

Margit stared at him in silence, as if he'd said something shocking.

Jamil insisted gently, 'Who won't it bring back?' She'd lost a friend, badly, the way he'd lost Chusok. That was why she'd sought him out. He could help her through it. They could help each other through it.

She said, 'It won't bring back the dead.'

Margit was seven thousand five hundred and ninety-four years old. Jamil persuaded her to sit at the kitchen table. He wrapped her in blankets, then fed her tomatoes and rice as she told him how she'd witnessed the birth of his world.

The promise had shimmered just beyond reach for decades. Almost none of her contemporaries had believed it would happen, though the truth should have been plain for centuries: *the human body was a material thing*. In time, with enough knowledge and effort, it would become possible to safeguard it from any kind of deterioration, any kind of harm. Stellar evolution and cosmic entropy might or might not prove insurmountable, but there'd be aeons to confront those challenges. In the middle of the twenty-first century, the hurdles were ageing, disease, violence, and an overcrowded planet.

'Grace was my best friend. We were students.' Margit smiled. 'Before everyone was a student. We'd talk about it, but we didn't believe we'd see it happen. It would come in another century. It would come for our great-great-grandchildren. We'd hold infants on our knees in our twilight years and tell ourselves: *this one will never die.*

'When we were both twenty-two, something happened. To both of us.' She lowered her eyes. 'We were kidnapped. We were raped. We were tortured.'

Jamil didn't know how to respond. These were just words to him: he knew their meaning, he knew these acts would have hurt her, but she might as well have been describing a mathematical theorem. He stretched a hand across the table, but Margit ignored it. He said awkwardly, 'This was . . . the Holocaust?'

She looked up at him, shaking her head, almost laughing at his naïveté. 'Not even one of them. Not a war, not a pogrom. Just one psychopathic man. He locked us in his basement, for six months. He'd killed seven women.' Tears began spilling down her cheeks. 'He showed us the bodies. They were buried right where we slept. He showed us how we'd end up, when he was through with us.'

Jamil was numb. He'd known all his adult life what had once been possible – what had once happened, to real people – but it had all been consigned to history long before his birth. In retrospect it seemed almost inconceivably stupid, but he'd always imagined that the changes had come in such a way that no one still living had experienced these horrors. There'd been no escaping the bare minimum, the logical necessity: his oldest living ancestors must have watched their parents fall peacefully into eternal sleep. But not this. Not a flesh-and-blood woman, sitting in front of him, who'd been forced to sleep in a killer's graveyard.

He put his hand over hers, and choked out the words. 'This man . . . *killed* Grace? He killed your friend?'

Margit began sobbing, but she shook her head. 'No, no. We got out!' She twisted her mouth into a smile. 'Someone stabbed the stupid fucker in a bar-room brawl. We dug our way out while he was in hospital.' She put her face down on the table and wept, but she held Jamil's hand against her cheek. He couldn't understand what she'd lived through, but that didn't mean he couldn't console her. Hadn't he touched his mother's face the same way, when she was sad beyond his childish comprehension?

She composed herself, and continued, 'We made a resolution, while we were in there. If we survived, there'd be no more empty promises. No more daydreams. What he'd done to those seven women – and what he'd done to us – would become impossible.'

And it had. Whatever harm befell your body, you had the power to shut off your senses and decline to experience it. If the flesh was damaged, it could always be repaired or replaced. In the unlikely event that your jewel itself was destroyed, everyone had back-ups, scattered across universes. No human being could inflict physical pain on another. In theory, you could still be killed, but it would take the same kind of resources as destroying a galaxy. The only people who seriously contemplated either were the villains in very bad operas.

Jamil's eyes narrowed in wonder. She'd spoken those last words with such fierce pride that there was no question of her having failed.

'*You* are Ndoli? You invented the jewel?' As a child, he'd been told that the machine in his skull had been designed by a man who'd died long ago.

Margit stroked his hand, amused. 'In those days, very few Hungarian women could be mistaken for Nigerian men. I've never changed my body that much, Jamil. I've always looked much as you see me.'

Jamil was relieved; if she'd been Ndoli himself, he might have succumbed to sheer awe and started babbling idolatrous nonsense. 'But you worked with Ndoli? You and Grace?'

She shook her head. 'We made the resolution, and then we floundered. We were mathematicians, not neurologists. There were a thousand things going on at once: tissue engineering, brain imaging, molecular computers. We had no real idea where to put our efforts, which problems we should bring our strengths to bear upon. Ndoli's work didn't come out of the blue for us, but we played no part in it.

'For a while, almost everyone was nervous about switching from the brain to the jewel. In the early days, the jewel was a separate device that learnt its task by mimicking the brain, and it had to be handed control of the body at one chosen moment. It took another fifty years before it could be engineered to replace the brain incrementally, neuron by neuron, in a seamless transition throughout adolescence.'

So Grace had lived to see the jewel invented, but held back, and died before she could use it? Jamil kept himself from blurting out this conclusion; all his guesses had proved wrong so far.

Margit continued. 'Some people weren't just nervous, though. You'd be amazed how vehemently Ndoli was denounced in certain quarters. And I don't just mean the fanatics who churned out paranoid tracts about "the machines" taking over, with their evil inhuman agendas. Some people's antagonism had nothing to do with the specifics of the technology. They were opposed to immortality in principle.'

Jamil laughed. '*Why?*'

'Ten thousand years' worth of sophistry doesn't vanish overnight,' Margit observed dryly. 'Every human culture had expended vast amounts of intellectual effort on the problem of coming to terms with death. Most religions had constructed elaborate lies about it, making it out to be something other than it was – though a few were dishonest about life, instead. But even most secular philosophies were warped by the need to pretend that *death was for the best*.

'It was the naturalistic fallacy at its most extreme – and its most transparent, but that didn't stop anyone. Since any child could tell you that death was meaningless, contingent, unjust and abhorrent beyond words, it was a hallmark of sophistication to believe otherwise. Writers had consoled themselves for centuries with smug puritanical fables about immortals who'd long for

281

death – who'd *beg* for death. It would have been too much to expect all those who were suddenly faced with the reality of its banishment to confess that they'd been whistling in the dark. And would-be moral philosophers – mostly those who'd experienced no greater inconvenience in their lives than a late train or a surly waiter – began wailing about the destruction of the human spirit by this hideous blight. We needed death and suffering, to put steel into our souls! Not horrible, horrible *freedom and safety*!'

Jamil smiled. 'So there were buffoons. But in the end, surely they swallowed their pride? If we're walking in a desert and I tell you that the lake you see ahead is a mirage, I might cling stubbornly to my own belief, to save myself from disappointment. But when we arrive, and I'm proven wrong, I *will* drink from the lake.'

Margit nodded. 'Most of the loudest of these people went quiet in the end. But there were subtler arguments, too. Like it or not, all our biology and all of our culture *had* evolved in the presence of death. And almost every righteous struggle in history, every worthwhile sacrifice, had been against suffering, against violence, against death. Now, that struggle would become impossible.'

'Yes.' Jamil was mystified. 'But only because it had triumphed.'

Margit said gently, 'I know. There was no sense to it. And it was always my belief that anything worth fighting for – over centuries, over millennia – was worth attaining. It *can't* be noble to toil for a cause, and even to die for it, unless it's also noble to succeed. To claim otherwise isn't sophistication, it's just a kind of hypocrisy. If it's better to travel than arrive, you shouldn't start the voyage in the first place.

'I told Grace as much, and she agreed. We laughed together at what we called the *tragedians*: the people who denounced the coming age as the age without martyrs, the age without saints, the age without revolutionaries. There would never be another Gandhi, another Mandela, another Aung San Suu Kyi – and yes, that *was* a kind of loss, but would any great leader have sentenced humanity to eternal misery, for the sake of providing a suitable backdrop for eternal heroism? Well, some of them would have. But the downtrodden themselves had better things to do.'

Margit fell silent. Jamil cleared her plate away, then sat opposite her again. It was almost dawn.

'Of course, the jewel was not enough,' Margit continued. 'With care, Earth could support forty billion people, but where would the rest go? The jewel made virtual reality the easiest escape route: for a fraction of the space, a fraction of the energy, it could survive without a body attached. Grace and I weren't horrified by that prospect, the way some people were. But it was not the best outcome, it was not what most people wanted, the way they wanted freedom from death.

'So we studied gravity, we studied the vacuum.'

Jamil feared making a fool of himself again, but from the expression on her face he knew he wasn't wrong this time. *M. Osvát and G. Füst.* Co-authors of the seminal paper, but no more was known about them than those abbreviated names. 'You gave us the New Territories?'

Margit nodded slightly. 'Grace and I.'

Jamil was overwhelmed with love for her. He went to her and knelt down to put his arms around her waist. Margit touched his shoulder. 'Come on, get up. Don't treat me like a god, it just makes me feel old.'

He stood, smiling abashedly. Anyone in pain deserved his help – but if he was not in her debt, the word had no meaning.

'And Grace?' he asked.

Margit looked away. 'Grace completed her work, and then decided that she was a tragedian, after all. Rape was impossible. Torture was impossible. Poverty was vanishing. Death was receding into cosmology, into metaphysics. It was everything she'd hoped would come to pass. And for her, suddenly faced with that fulfilment, everything that remained seemed trivial.

'One night, she climbed into the furnace in the basement of her building. Her jewel survived the flames, but she'd erased it from within.'

*

It was morning now. Jamil was beginning to feel disoriented; Margit should have vanished in daylight, an apparition unable to persist in the mundane world.

'I'd lost other people who were close to me,' she said. 'My parents. My brother. Friends. And so had everyone around me, then. I wasn't special: grief was still commonplace. But decade by decade, century by century, we shrank into insignificance, those of us who knew what it meant to lose someone for ever. We're less than one in a million, now.

'For a long time, I clung to my own generation. There were enclaves, there were ghettos, where everyone understood the old days. I spent two hundred years married to a man who wrote a play called *We Who Have Known the Dead* – which was every bit as pretentious and self-pitying as you'd guess from the title.' She smiled at the memory. 'It was a horrible, self-devouring world. If I'd stayed in it much longer, I would have followed Grace. I would have begged for death.'

She looked up at Jamil. 'It's people like you I want to be with: *people who don't understand.* Your lives aren't trivial, any more than the best parts of our own were: all the tranquillity, all the beauty, all the happiness that made the sacrifices and the life-and-death struggles worthwhile.

'The tragedians were wrong. They had everything upside down. Death never gave meaning to life: it was always the other way round. All of its gravitas, all of its significance, was stolen from the things it ended. But the value of life always lay entirely in itself – not in its loss, not in its fragility.

'Grace should have lived to see that. She should have lived long enough to understand that the world hadn't turned to ash.'

Jamil sat in silence, turning the whole confession over in his mind, trying to absorb it well enough not to add to her distress with a misjudged question. Finally, he ventured, 'Why do you hold back from friendship with us, though? Because we're just children to you? Children who can't understand what you've lost?'

Margit shook her head vehemently. 'I don't *want you* to

understand! People like me are the only blight on this world, the only poison.' She smiled at Jamil's expression of anguish, and rushed to silence him before he could swear that she was nothing of the kind. 'Not in everything we do and say, or everyone we touch: I'm not claiming that we're tainted, in some fatuous mythological sense. But when I left the ghettos, I promised myself that I wouldn't bring the past with me. Sometimes that's an easy vow to keep. Sometimes it's not.'

'You've broken it tonight,' Jamil said plainly. 'And neither of us have been struck down by lightning.'

'I know.' She took his hand. 'But I was wrong to tell you what I have, and I'll fight to regain the strength to stay silent. I stand at the border between two worlds, Jamil. I remember death, and I always will. But my job now is to guard that border. To keep that knowledge from invading your world.'

'We're not as fragile as you think,' he protested. 'We all know something about loss.'

Margit nodded soberly. 'Your friend Chusok has vanished into the crowd. That's how things work now: how you keep yourselves from suffocating in a jungle of endlessly growing connections, or fragmenting into isolated troupes of repertory players, endlessly churning out the same lines.

'You have your little deaths – and I don't call them that to deride you. But I've seen both. And I promise you, they're not the same.'

In the weeks that followed, Jamil resumed in full the life he'd made for himself in Noether. Five days in seven were for the difficult beauty of mathematics. The rest were for his friends.

He kept playing matches, and Margit's team kept winning. In the sixth game, though, Jamil's team finally scored against her. Their defeat was only three to one.

Each night, Jamil struggled with the question. What exactly did he owe her? Eternal loyalty, eternal silence, eternal obedience? She hadn't sworn him to secrecy; she'd extracted no promises at all. But he knew she was trusting him to comply with her wishes, so what right did he have to do otherwise?

Eight weeks after the night he'd spent with Margit, Jamil found himself alone with Penina in a room in Joracy's house. They'd been talking about the old days. Talking about Chusok.

Jamil said, 'Margit lost someone, very close to her.'

Penina nodded matter-of-factly, but curled into a comfortable position on the couch and prepared to take in every word.

'Not in the way we've lost Chusok. Not in the way you think at all.'

Jamil approached the others, one by one. His confidence ebbed and flowed. He'd glimpsed the old world, but he couldn't pretend to have fathomed its inhabitants. What if Margit saw this as worse than betrayal – as a further torture, a further rape?

But he couldn't stand by and leave her to the torture she'd inflicted on herself.

Ezequiel was the hardest to face. Jamil spent a sick and sleepless night beforehand, wondering if this would make him a monster, a corrupter of children, the epitome of everything Margit believed she was fighting.

Ezequiel wept freely, but he was not a child. He was older than Jamil, and he had more steel in his soul than any of them.

He said, 'I guessed it might be that. I guessed she might have seen the bad times. But I never found a way to ask her.'

The three lobes of probability converged, melted into a plateau, rose into a pillar of light.

The umpire said, 'Fifty-five point nine.' It was Margit's most impressive goal yet.

Ezequiel whooped joyfully and ran towards her. When he scooped her up in his arms and threw her across his shoulders, she laughed and indulged him. When Jamil stood beside him and they made a joint throne for her with their arms, she frowned down at him and said, 'You shouldn't be doing this. You're on the losing side.'

The rest of the players converged on them, cheering, and they started down towards the river. Margit looked around nervously. 'What is this? We haven't finished playing.'

Penina said, 'The game's over early, just this once. Think of this as an invitation. We want you to swim with us. We want you to talk to us. We want to hear everything about your life.'

Margit's composure began to crack. She squeezed Jamil's shoulder. He whispered, 'Say the word, and we'll put you down.'

Margit didn't whisper back; she shouted miserably, 'What do you want from me, you parasites? I've won your fucking game for you! What more do you want?'

Jamil was mortified. He stopped and prepared to lower her, prepared to retreat, but Ezequiel caught his arm.

Ezequiel said, 'We want to be your border guards. We want to stand beside you.'

Christa added, 'We can't face what you've faced, but we want to understand. As much as we can.'

Joracy spoke, then Yann, Narcyza, Maria, Halide. Margit looked down on them, weeping, confused.

Jamil burnt with shame. He'd hijacked her, humiliated her. He'd made everything worse. She'd flee Noether, flee into a new exile, more alone than ever.

When everyone had spoken, silence descended. Margit trembled on her throne.

Jamil faced the ground. He couldn't undo what he'd done. He said quietly, 'Now you know our wishes. Will you tell us yours?'

'Put me down.'

Jamil and Ezequiel complied.

Margit looked around at her teammates and opponents, her children, her creation, her would-be friends.

She said, 'I want to go to the river with you. I'm seven thousand years old, and I want to learn to swim.'

Author's note: Readers can find an interactive illustration of quantum soccer at *www.gregegan.net/BORDER/Soccer/Soccer.html*

RIDING THE CROCODILE

1

In their ten thousand three hundred and ninth year of marriage, Leila and Jasim began contemplating death. They had known love, raised children, and witnessed the flourishing generations of their offspring. They had travelled to a dozen worlds and lived among a thousand cultures. They had educated themselves many times over, proved theorems, and acquired and abandoned artistic sensibilities and skills. They had not lived in every conceivable manner, far from it, but what room would there be for the multitude if each individual tried to exhaust the permutations of existence? There were some experiences, they agreed, that everyone should try, and others that only a handful of people in all of time need bother with. They had no wish to give up their idiosyncrasies, no wish to uproot their personalities from the niches they had settled in long ago, let alone start cranking mechanically through some tedious enumeration of all the other people they might have been. They had been themselves, and for that they had done, more or less, enough.

Before dying, though, they wanted to attempt something grand and audacious. It was not that their lives were incomplete, in need of some final flourish of affirmation. If some unlikely calamity had robbed them of the chance to orchestrate this finalé, the closest of their friends would never have remarked upon, let alone mourned, its absence. There was no aesthetic compulsion to be satisfied, no aching existential void to be filled. Nevertheless, it was what they both wanted, and once they had acknowledged this to each other their hearts were set on it.

Choosing the project was not a great burden; that task required nothing but patience. They knew they'd recognise it when it came to them. Every night before sleeping, Jasim would ask Leila, 'Did you see it yet?'

'No. Did you?'

'Not yet.'

Sometimes Leila would dream that she'd found it in her dreams, but the transcripts proved otherwise. Sometimes Jasim felt sure that it was lurking just below the surface of his thoughts, but when he dived down to check it was nothing but a trick of the light.

Years passed. They occupied themselves with simple pleasures: gardening, swimming in the surf, talking with their friends, catching up with their descendants. They had grown skilled at finding pastimes that could bear repetition. Still, were it not for the nameless adventure that awaited them they would have thrown a pair of dice each evening and agreed that two sixes would end it all.

One night, Leila stood alone in the garden, watching the sky. From their home world, Najib, they had travelled only to the nearest stars with inhabited worlds, each time losing just a few decades to the journey. They had chosen those limits so as not to alienate themselves from friends and family, and it had never felt like much of a constraint. True, the civilisation of the Amalgam wrapped the galaxy, and a committed traveller could spend two hundred thousand years circling back home, but what was to be gained by such an overblown odyssey? The dozen worlds of their neighbourhood held enough variety for any traveller, and whether more distant realms were filled with fresh novelties or endless repetition hardly seemed to matter. To have a goal, a destination, would be one thing, but to drown in the sheer plenitude of worlds for its own sake seemed utterly pointless.

A destination? Leila overlaid the sky with information, most of it by necessity millennia out of date. There were worlds with spectacular views of nebulas and star clusters, views that could be guaranteed still to be in existence if they travelled to see them, but would taking in such sights first-hand be so much better than immersion in the flawless images already available in Najib's library? To blink away ten thousand years just to wake beneath a cloud of green and violet gas, however lovely, seemed like a terrible anticlimax.

The stars tingled with self-aggrandisement, plaintively tugging at her attention. The architecture here, the rivers, the festivals! Even if these tourist attractions could survive the millennia, even if some were literally unique, there was nothing that struck her as a fitting prelude to death. If she and Jasim had formed some whimsical attachment, centuries before, to a world on the other side of the galaxy rumoured to hold great beauty or interest, and if they had talked long enough about chasing it down when they had nothing better to do, then keeping that promise might have been worth it, even if the journey led them to a world in ruins. They had no such cherished destination, though, and it was too late to cultivate one now.

Leila's gaze followed a thinning in the advertising, taking her to the bulge of stars surrounding the galaxy's centre. The disk of the Milky Way belonged to the Amalgam, whose various ancestral species had effectively merged into a single civilisation, but the central bulge was inhabited by beings who had declined to do so much as communicate with those around them. All attempts to send probes into the bulge – let alone the kind of engineering spores needed to create the infrastructure for travel – had been gently but firmly rebuffed, with the intruders swatted straight back out again. The Aloof had maintained their silence and isolation since before the Amalgam itself had even existed.

The latest news on this subject was twenty thousand years old, but the status quo had held for close to a million years. If she and Jasim travelled to the innermost edge of the Amalgam's domain, the chances were exceptionally good that the Aloof would not have changed their ways in the meantime. In fact, it would be no disappointment at all if the Aloof had suddenly thrown open their borders: that unheralded thaw would itself be an extraordinary thing to witness. If the challenge remained, though, all the better.

She called Jasim to the garden and pointed out the richness of stars, unadorned with potted histories.

'We go where?' he asked.

'As close to the Aloof as we're able.'

'And do what?'

'Try to observe them,' she said. 'Try to learn something about them. Try to make contact, in whatever way we can.'

'You don't think that's been tried before?'

'A million times. Not so much lately, though. Maybe while the interest on our side has ebbed, they've been changing, growing more receptive.'

'Or maybe not.' Jasim smiled. He had appeared a little stunned by her proposal at first, but the idea seemed to be growing on him. 'It's a hard, hard problem to throw ourselves against. But it's not futile. Not quite.' He wrapped her hands in his. 'Let's see how we feel in the morning.'

In the morning, they were both convinced. They would camp at the gates of these elusive strangers and try to rouse them from their indifference.

They summoned the family from every corner of Najib. There were some grandchildren and more distant descendants who had settled in other star systems, decades away at light-speed, but they chose not to wait to call them home for this final farewell.

Two hundred people crowded the physical house and garden, while two hundred more confined themselves to the virtual wing. There was talk and food and music, like any other celebration, and Leila tried to undercut any edge of solemnity that she felt creeping in. As the night wore on, though, each time she kissed a child or grandchild, each time she embraced an old friend, she thought: this could be the last time, ever. There had to be a last time, she couldn't face ten thousand more years, but a part of her spat and struggled like a cornered animal at the thought of each warm touch fading to nothing.

As dawn approached, the party shifted entirely into the acorporeal. People took on fancy dress from myth or xenology, or just joked and played with their illusory bodies. It was all very calm and gentle, nothing like the surreal excesses she remembered from her youth, but Leila still felt a tinge of vertigo. When her son Khalid made his ears grow and spin, this amiable silliness carried a hard message: the machinery of the house had ripped her mind from her body, as seamlessly as ever, but this time she would never be returning to the same flesh.

Sunrise brought the first of the goodbyes. Leila forced herself to release each proffered hand, to unwrap her arms from around each nonexistent body. She whispered to Jasim, 'Are you going mad too?'

'Of course.'

Gradually the crowd thinned out. The wing grew quiet. Leila found herself pacing from room to room, as if she might yet chance upon someone who'd stayed behind, then she remembered urging the last of them to go, her children and friends tearfully retreating down the hall. She skirted inconsolable sadness, then lifted herself above it and went looking for Jasim.

He was waiting for her outside their room.

'Are you ready to sleep?' he asked her gently.

She said, 'For an aeon.'

2

Leila woke in the same bed as she'd lain down in. Jasim was still sleeping beside her. The window showed dawn, but it was not the usual view of the cliffs and the ocean.

Leila had the house brief her. After twenty thousand years – travelling more or less at light-speed, pausing only for a microsecond or two at various way-stations to be cleaned up and amplified – the package of information bearing the two of them had arrived safely at Nazdeek-be-Beegane. This world was not crowded, and it had been tweaked to render it compatible with a range of metabolic styles. The house had negotiated a site where they could live embodied in comfort if they wished.

Jasim stirred and opened his eyes. 'Good morning. How are you feeling?'

'Older.'

'Really?'

Leila paused to consider this seriously. 'No. Not even slightly. How about you?'

'I'm fine. I'm just wondering what's out there.' He raised himself up to peer through the window. The house had been instantiated on a wide, empty plain, covered with low stalks of green and yellow vegetation. They could eat these plants, and the house had already started a spice garden while they slept. He stretched his shoulders. 'Let's go and make breakfast.'

They went downstairs, stepping into freshly minted bodies, then out into the garden. The air was still, the sun already warm. The house had tools prepared to help them with the harvest. It was the nature of travel that they had come empty-handed, and they had no relatives here, no fifteenth cousins, no friends of friends. It was the nature of the Amalgam that they were welcome nonetheless, and the machines that supervised this world on behalf of its inhabitants had done their best to provide for them.

'So this is the afterlife,' Jasim mused, scything the yellow stalks. 'Very rustic.'

'Speak for yourself,' Leila retorted. 'I'm not dead yet.' She put down her own scythe and bent to pluck one of the plants out by its roots.

The meal they made was filling but bland. Leila resisted the urge to tweak her perceptions of it; she preferred to face the challenge of working out decent recipes, which would make a useful counterpoint to the more daunting task they'd come here to attempt.

They spent the rest of the day just tramping around, exploring their immediate surroundings. The house had tapped into a nearby stream for water, and sunlight, stored, would provide all the power they needed. From some hills about an hour's walk away they could see into a field with another building, but they decided to wait a little longer before introducing themselves to their neighbours. The air had a slightly odd smell, due to the range of components needed to support other metabolic styles, but it wasn't too intrusive.

The onset of night took them by surprise. Even before the sun had set a smattering of stars began appearing in the east, and for a moment Leila thought that these white specks against the fading blue were some kind of exotic atmospheric phenomenon, perhaps small clouds forming in the stratosphere as the temperature dropped. When it became clear what was happening, she beckoned to Jasim to sit beside her on the bank of the stream and watch the stars of the bulge come out.

They'd come at a time when Nazdeek lay between its sun and the galactic centre. At dusk one half of the Aloof's dazzling territory stretched from the eastern horizon to the zenith, with the stars' slow march westward against a darkening sky only revealing more of their splendour.

'You think that was to die for?' Jasim joked as they walked back to the house.

'We could end this now, if you're feeling unambitious.'

He squeezed her hand. 'If this takes ten thousand years, I'm ready.'

It was a mild night, they could have slept outdoors, but the spectacle was too distracting. They stayed downstairs, in the physical wing. Leila watched the strange thicket of shadows cast by the furniture sliding across the walls. These neighbours never sleep, she thought. When we come knocking, they'll ask what took us so long.

3

Hundreds of observatories circled Nazdeek, built then abandoned by others who'd come on the same quest. When Leila saw the band of pristine space junk mapped out before her – orbits scrupulously maintained and swept clean by robot sentinels for aeons – she felt as if she'd found the graves of their predecessors, stretching out in the field behind the house as far as the eye could see.

Nazdeek was prepared to offer them the resources to loft another package of instruments into the vacuum if they wished, but many of the abandoned observatories were perfectly functional, and most had been left in a compliant state, willing to take instructions from anyone.

Leila and Jasim sat in their living room and woke machine after machine from millennia of hibernation. Some, it turned out, had not been sleeping at all, but had been carrying on systematic observations, accumulating data long after their owners had lost interest.

In the crowded stellar precincts of the bulge, disruptive gravitational effects made planet formation rarer than it was in the disk, and orbits less stable. Nevertheless, planets had been found. A few thousand could be tracked from Nazdeek, and one observatory had been monitoring their atmospheric spectra for the last twelve millennia. In all of those worlds for all of those years, there were no signs of atmospheric composition departing from plausible, purely geochemical models. That meant no wild life, and no crude industries. It didn't prove that these worlds were uninhabited, but it suggested either that the Aloof went to great lengths to avoid leaving chemical fingerprints, or they lived in an entirely different fashion from any of the civilisations that had formed the Amalgam.

Of the eleven forms of biochemistry that had been found scattered around the galactic disk, all had given rise eventually to hundreds of species with general intelligence. Of the multitude of civilisations that had emerged from those roots, all contained cultures that had granted themselves the flexibility of living as software, but they also all contained cultures that persisted with corporeal existence. Leila herself would never have willingly given up either mode, but while it was easy to imagine a sub-culture doing so, for a whole species it seemed extraordinary. In a sense, the intertwined civilisation of the Amalgam owed its exist-ence to the fact that there was as much cultural variation within every species as there was between one species and another. In that explosion of diversity, overlapping interests were inevitable.

If the Aloof were the exception, and their material culture had shrunk to nothing but a few discreet processors – each with the energy needs of a gnat, scattered throughout a trillion cubic light-years of dust and blazing stars – then finding them would be impossible.

Of course, that worst-case scenario couldn't quite be true. The sole reason the Aloof were assumed to exist at all was the fact that some component of their material culture was tossing back every probe that was sent into the bulge. However discreet that machin-ery was, it certainly couldn't be sparse: given that it had managed to track, intercept and reverse the trajectories of billions of indi-vidual probes that had been sent in along thousands of different routes, relativistic constraints on the information flow implied that the Aloof had some kind of presence at more or less every star at the edge of the bulge.

Leila and Jasim had Nazdeek brief them on the most recent attempts to enter the bulge, but even after forty thousand years the basic facts hadn't changed. There was no crisply delineated barrier marking the Aloof's territory, but at some point within a border region about fifty light-years wide, every single probe that was sent in ceased to function. The signals from those carrying in-flight beacons or transmitters went dead without warning. A century or so later, they would appear again at almost the same point, travelling in the opposite direction: back to where they'd come from. Those that were retrieved and examined were found to be unharmed, but their data logs contained nothing from the missing decades.

Jasim said, 'The Aloof could be dead and gone. They built the perfect fence, but now it's outlasted them. It's just guarding their ruins.'

Leila rejected this emphatically. 'No civilisation that's spread to more than one star system has ever vanished completely. Sometimes they've changed beyond recognition, but not one has ever died without descendants.'

'That's a fact of history, but it's not a universal law,' Jasim persisted. 'If we're going to argue from the Amalgam all the time, we'll get nowhere. If the Aloof weren't exceptional, we wouldn't be here.'

'That's true. But I won't accept that they're dead until I see some evidence.'

'What would count as evidence? Apart from a million years of silence?'

Leila said, 'Silence could mean anything. If they're really dead, we'll find something more, something definite.'

'Such as?'

'If we see it, we'll know.'

They began the project in earnest, reviewing data from the ancient observatories, stopping only to gather food, eat and sleep. They had resisted making detailed plans back on Najib, reasoning that any approach they mapped out in advance was likely to be rendered obsolete once they learnt about the latest investigations. Now that they'd arrived and found the state of play utterly unchanged, Leila wished that they'd come armed with some clear options for dealing with the one situation they could have prepared for before they'd left.

In fact, though they might have felt like out-of-touch amateurs back on Najib, now that the Aloof had become their entire *raison d'être* it was far harder to relax and indulge in the kind of speculation that might actually bear fruit, given that every systematic approach had failed. Having come twenty thousand light-years for this, they couldn't spend their time daydreaming, turning the problem over in the backs of their minds while they surrendered to the rhythms of Nazdeek's rural idyll. So they studied everything that had been tried before, searching methodically for a new approach, hoping to see the old ideas with fresh eyes, hoping that – by chance if for no other reason – they might lack some crucial blind spot that had afflicted all of their predecessors.

After seven months without results or inspiration, it was Jasim who finally dragged them out of the rut. 'We're getting nowhere,' he said. 'It's time to accept that, put all this aside and go visit the neighbours.'

Leila stared at him as if he'd lost his mind. 'Go visit them? How? What makes you think that they're suddenly going to let us in?'

He said, 'The neighbours. Remember? Over the hill. The ones who might actually want to talk to us.'

4

Their neighbours had published a précis stating that they welcomed social contact in principle, but might take a while to respond. Jasim sent them an invitation, asking if they'd like to join them in their house, and waited.

After just three days, a reply came back. The neighbours did not want to put them to the trouble of altering their own house physically, and preferred not to become acorporeal at present. Given the less stringent requirements of Leila and Jasim's own species when embodied, might they wish to come instead to the neighbours' house?

Leila said, 'Why not?' They set a date and time.

The neighbours' précis included all the biological and sociological details needed to prepare for the encounter. Their biochemistry was carbon-based and oxygen-breathing, but employed a different replicator to Leila and Jasim's DNA. Their ancestral phenotype resembled a large furred snake, and when embodied they generally lived in nests of a hundred or so. The minds of the individuals were perfectly autonomous, but solitude was an alien and unsettling concept for them.

Leila and Jasim set out late in the morning, in order to arrive early in the afternoon. There were some low, heavy clouds in the sky, but it was not completely overcast, and Leila noticed that when the sun passed behind the clouds, she could discern some of the brightest stars from the edge of the bulge.

Jasim admonished her sternly, 'Stop looking. This is our day off.'

The Snakes' building was a large squat cylinder resembling a water tank, which turned out to be packed with something mossy and pungent. When they arrived at the entrance, three of their hosts were waiting to greet them, coiled on the ground near the mouth of a large tunnel emerging from the moss. Their bodies were almost as wide as their guests', and some eight or ten metres long. Their heads bore two front-facing eyes, but their other sense organs were not prominent. Leila could make out their mouths, and knew from the briefing how many rows of teeth lay behind them, but the wide pink gashes stayed closed, almost lost in the grey fur.

The Snakes communicated with a low-frequency thumping, and their system of nomenclature was complex, so Leila just mentally tagged the three of them with randomly chosen, slightly exotic names – Tim, John and Sarah – and tweaked her translator so she'd recognise intuitively who was who, who was addressing her, and the significance of their gestures.

'Welcome to our home,' said Tim enthusiastically.

'Thank you for inviting us,' Jasim replied.

'We've had no visitors for quite some time,' explained Sarah. 'So we really are delighted to meet you.'

'How long has it been?' Leila asked.

'Twenty years,' said Sarah.

'But we came here for the quiet life,' John added. 'So we expected it would be a while.'

Leila pondered the idea of a clan of a hundred ever finding a quiet life, but then, perhaps unwelcome intrusions from outsiders were of a different nature to family dramas.

'Will you come into the nest?' Tim asked. 'If you don't wish to enter we won't take offence, but everyone would like to see you, and some of us aren't comfortable coming out into the open.'

Leila glanced at Jasim. He said privately, 'We can push our vision to IR. And tweak ourselves to tolerate the smell.'

Leila agreed.

'Okay,' Jasim told Tim.

Tim slithered into the tunnel and vanished in a quick, elegant motion, then John motioned with his head for the guests to follow. Leila went first, propelling herself up the gentle slope with her knees and elbows. The plant the Snakes cultivated for the nest formed a cool, dry, resilient surface. She could see Tim ten metres or so ahead, like a giant glow-worm shining with body heat, slowing down now to let her catch up. She glanced back at Jasim, who looked even weirder than the Snakes now, his face and arms blotched with strange bands of radiance from the exertion.

After a few minutes, they came to a large chamber. The air was humid, but after the confines of the tunnel it felt cool and fresh. Tim led them towards the centre, where about a dozen other Snakes were already waiting to greet them. They circled the guests excitedly, thumping out a delighted welcome. Leila felt a surge of adrenalin; she knew that she and Jasim were in no danger, but the sheer size and energy of the creatures was overwhelming.

'Can you tell us why you've come to Nazdeek?' asked Sarah.

'Of course.' For a second or two Leila tried to maintain eye contact with her, but like all the other Snakes she kept moving restlessly, a gesture that Leila's translator imbued with a sense of warmth and enthusiasm. As for lack of eye contact, the Snakes' own translators would understand perfectly that some aspects of ordinary, polite human behaviour became impractical under the circumstances, and would not mislabel her actions. 'We're here to learn about the Aloof,' she said.

'The Aloof?' At first Sarah just seemed perplexed, then Leila's translator hinted at a touch of irony. 'But they offer us nothing.'

Leila was tongue-tied for a moment. The implication was subtle but unmistakable. Citizens of the Amalgam had a protocol for dealing with each other's curiosity: they published a précis, which spelled out clearly any information that they wished people in general to know about them, and also specified what, if any, further enquiries would be welcome. However, a citizen was perfectly entitled to publish no précis at all and have that decision respected. When no information was published, and no invitation offered, you simply had no choice but to mind your own business.

'They offer us nothing as far as we can tell,' she said, 'but that might be a misunderstanding, a failure to communicate.'

'They send back all the probes,' Tim replied. 'Do you really think we've misunderstood what that means?'

Jasim said, 'It means that they don't want us physically intruding on their territory, putting our machines right next to their homes, but I'm not convinced that it proves that they have no desire to communicate whatsoever.'

'We should leave them in peace,' Tim insisted. 'They've seen the probes, so they know we're here. If they want to make contact, they'll do it in their own time.'

'Leave them in peace,' echoed another Snake. A chorus of affirmation followed from others in the chamber.

Leila stood her ground. 'We have no idea how many different species and cultures might be living in the bulge. *One of them* sends back the probes, but for all we know there could be a thousand others who don't yet even know that the Amalgam has tried to make contact.'

This suggestion set off a series of arguments, some between guests and hosts, some between the Snakes themselves. All the while, the Snakes kept circling excitedly, while new ones entered the chamber to witness the novel sight of these strangers.

When the clamour about the Aloof had quietened down enough for her to change the subject, Leila asked Sarah, 'Why have you come to Nazdeek yourself?'

'It's out of the way, off the main routes. We can think things over here, undisturbed.'

'But you could have the same amount of privacy anywhere. It's all a matter of what you put in your précis.'

Sarah's response was imbued with a tinge of amusement. 'For us, it would be unimaginably rude to cut off all contact explicitly, by decree. Especially with others from our own ancestral species. To live a quiet life, we had to reduce the likelihood of encountering anyone who would seek us out. We had to make the effort of rendering ourselves physically remote, in order to reap the benefits.'

'Yet you've made Jasim and myself very welcome.'

'Of course. But that will be enough for the next twenty years.'

So much for resurrecting their social life. 'What exactly is it that you're pondering in this state of solitude?'

'The nature of reality. The uses of existence. The reasons to live, and the reasons not to.'

Leila felt the skin on her forearms tingle. She'd almost forgotten that she'd made an appointment with death, however uncertain the timing.

She explained how she and Jasim had made their decision to embark on a grand project before dying.

'That's an interesting approach,' Sarah said. 'I'll have to give it some thought.' She paused, then added, 'Though I'm not sure that you've solved the problem.'

'What do you mean?'

'Will it really be easier now to choose the right moment to give up your life? Haven't you merely replaced one delicate judgement with an even more difficult one: deciding when you've exhausted the possibilities for contacting the Aloof?'

'You make it sound as if we have no chance of succeeding.' Leila was not afraid of the prospect of failure, but the suggestion that it was inevitable was something else entirely.

Sarah said, 'We've been here on Nazdeek for fifteen thousand years. We don't pay much attention to the world outside the nest, but even from this cloistered state we've seen many people break their backs against this rock.'

'So when will you accept that your own project is finished?' Leila countered. 'If you still don't have what you're looking for after fifteen thousand years, when will you admit defeat?'

'I have no idea,' Sarah confessed. 'I have no idea, any more than you do.'

5

When the way forward first appeared, there was nothing to set it apart from a thousand false alarms that had come before it.

It was their seventeenth year on Nazdeek. They had launched their own observatory – armed with the latest refinements culled from around the galaxy – fifteen years before, and it had been confirming the null results of its predecessors ever since.

They had settled into an unhurried routine, systematically exploring the possibilities that observation hadn't yet ruled out. Between the scenarios that were obviously stone cold dead – the presence of an energy-rich, risk-taking, extroverted civilisation in the bulge actively seeking contact by every means at its disposal – and the infinite number of possibilities that could never be distinguished at this distance from the absence of all life, and the absence of all machinery save one dumb but efficient gatekeeper, tantalising clues would bubble up out of the data now and then, only to fade into statistical insignificance in the face of continued scrutiny.

Tens of billions of stars lying within the Aloof's territory could be discerned from Nazdeek, some of them evolving or violently interacting on a timescale of years or months. Black holes were flaying and swallowing their companions. Neutron stars and white dwarfs were stealing fresh fuel and flaring into novas. Star clusters were colliding and tearing each other apart. If you gathered data on this whole menagerie for long enough, you could expect to see almost anything. Leila would not have been surprised to wander into the garden at night and find a great welcome sign spelled out in the sky, before the fortuitous pattern of novas faded and the message dissolved into randomness again.

When their gamma-ray telescope caught a glimmer of something odd – the nuclei of a certain isotope of fluorine decaying from an excited state, when there was no nearby source of the kind of radiation that could have put the nuclei into that state in the first place – it might have been just another random, unexplained fact to add to a vast pile. When the same glimmer was seen again, not far away, Leila reasoned that if a gas cloud enriched with fluorine could be affected at one location by an unseen radiation source, it should not be surprising if the same thing happened elsewhere in the same cloud.

It happened again. The three events lined up in space and time in a manner suggesting a short pulse of gamma-rays in the form of a tightly focused beam, striking three different points in the gas cloud. Still, in the mountains of data they had acquired from their predecessors, coincidences far more compelling than this had occurred hundreds of thousands of times.

With the fourth flash, the balance of the numbers began to tip. The secondary gamma-rays reaching Nazdeek gave only a weak and distorted impression of the original radiation, but all four flashes were consistent with a single, narrow beam. There were thousands of known gamma-ray sources in the bulge, but the frequency of the radiation, the direction of the beam, and the time profile of the pulse did not fit with any of them.

The archives revealed a few dozen occasions when the same kind of emissions had been seen from fluorine nuclei under similar conditions. There had never been more than three connected events before, but one sequence had occurred along a path not far from the present one.

Leila sat by the stream and modelled the possibilities. If the beam was linking two objects in powered flight, prediction was impossible. If receiver and transmitter were mostly in freefall, though, and only made corrections occasionally, the past and present data combined gave her a plausible forecast for the beam's future orientation.

Jasim looked into her simulation, a thought-bubble of stars and equations hovering above the water. 'The whole path will lie out of bounds,' he said.

'No kidding.' The Aloof's territory was more or less spherical, which made it a convex set: you couldn't get between any two points that lay inside it without entering the territory itself. 'But look how much the beam spreads out. From the fluorine data, I'd say it could be tens of kilometres wide by the time it reaches the receiver.'

'So they might not catch it all? They might let some of the beam escape into the disk?' He sounded unpersuaded.

Leila said, 'Look, if they really were doing everything possible to hide this, we would never have seen these blips in the first place.'

'Gas clouds with this much fluorine are extremely rare. They obviously picked a frequency that wouldn't be scattered under ordinary circumstances.'

'Yes, but that's just a matter of getting the signal through the local environment. We choose frequencies ourselves that won't interact with any substance that's likely to be present along the route, but no choice is perfect, and we just live with that. It seems to me that they've done the same thing. If they were fanatical purists, they'd communicate by completely different methods.'

'All right.' Jasim reached into the model. 'So where can we go that's in the line of sight?'

The short answer was: nowhere. If the beam was not blocked completely by its intended target it would spread out considerably as it made its way through the galactic disk, but it would not grow so wide that it would sweep across a single point where the Amalgam had any kind of outpost.

Leila said, 'This is too good to miss. We need to get a decent observatory into its path.'

Jasim agreed. 'And we need to do it before these nodes decide they've drifted too close to something dangerous, and switch on their engines for a course correction.'

They crunched through the possibilities. Wherever the Amalgam had an established presence, the infrastructure already on the ground could convert data into any kind of material object. Transmitting yourself to such a place, along with whatever you needed, was simplicity itself: light-speed was the only real constraint. Excessive demands on the local resources might be denied, but modest requests were rarely rejected.

Far more difficult was building something new at a site with raw materials but no existing receiver; in that case, instead of pure data, you needed to send an engineering spore of some kind. If you were in a hurry, not only did you need to spend energy boosting the spore to relativistic velocities – a cost that snowballed due to the mass of protective shielding – you then had to waste much of the time you gained on a lengthy braking phase, or the spore would hit its target with enough energy to turn it into plasma. Interactions with the interstellar medium could be used to slow down the spore, avoiding the need to carry yet more mass to act as a propellant for braking, but the whole business was disgustingly inefficient.

Harder still was getting anything substantial to a given point in the vast empty space between the stars. With no raw materials to hand at the destination, everything had to be moved from somewhere else. The best starting point was usually to send an engineering spore into a cometary cloud, loosely bound gravitationally to its associated star, but not every such cloud was open to plunder, and everything took time, and obscene amounts of energy.

To arrange for an observatory to be delivered to the most accessible point along the beam's line of sight, travelling at the correct velocity, would take about fifteen thousand years all told. That assumed that the local cultures who owned the nearest facilities, and who had a right to veto the use of the raw materials, acceded immediately to their request.

'How long between course corrections?' Leila wondered. If the builders of this hypothetical network were efficient, the nodes could drift for a while in interstellar space without any problems, but in the bulge everything happened faster than in the disk, and the need to counter gravitational effects would come much sooner. There was no way to make a firm prediction, but they could easily have as little as eight or ten thousand years.

Leila struggled to reconcile herself to the reality. 'We'll try at this location, and if we're lucky we might still catch something. If not, we'll try again after the beam shifts.' Sending the first observatory chasing after the beam would be futile; even with the present freefall motion of the nodes, the observation point would be moving at a substantial fraction of light-speed relative to the local stars. Magnified by the enormous distances involved, a small change in direction down in the bulge could see the beam lurch thousands of light-years sideways by the time it reached the disk.

Jasim said, 'Wait.' He magnified the region around the projected path of the beam.

'What are you looking for?'

He asked the map, 'Are there two outposts of the Amalgam lying on a straight line that intersects the beam?'

The map replied in a tone of mild incredulity. 'No.'

'That was too much to hope for. Are there three lying on a plane that intersects the beam?'

The map said, 'There are about ten-to-the-eighteen triples that meet that condition.'

Leila suddenly realised what it was he had in mind. She laughed and squeezed his arm. 'You are completely insane!'

Jasim said, 'Let me get the numbers right first, then you can mock me.' He rephrased his question to the map. 'For how many of those triples would the beam pass between them, intersecting the triangle whose vertices they lie on?'

'About ten-to-the-sixth.'

'How close to us is the closest point of intersection of the beam with any of those triangles – if the distance in each case is measured via the worst of the three outposts, the one that makes the total path longest.'

307

'Seven thousand four hundred and twenty-six light-years.'

Leila said, 'Collision braking. With three components?'

'Do you have a better idea?'

Better than twice as fast as the fastest conventional method? 'Nothing comes to mind. Let me think about it.'

Braking against the flimsy interstellar medium was a slow process. If you wanted to deliver a payload rapidly to a point that fortuitously lay somewhere on a straight line between two existing outposts, you could fire two separate packages from the two locations and let them 'collide' when they met – or rather, let them brake against each other magnetically. If you arranged for the packages to have equal and opposite momenta, they would come to a halt without any need to throw away reaction mass or clutch at passing molecules, and some of their kinetic energy could be recovered as electricity and stored for later use.

The aim and the timing had to be perfect. Relativistic packages did not make in-flight course corrections, and the data available at each launch site about the other's precise location was always a potentially imperfect prediction, not a rock-solid statement of fact. Even with the Amalgam's prodigious astrometric and computing resources, achieving millimetre alignments at thousand-light-year distances could not be guaranteed.

Now Jasim wanted to make three of these bullets meet, perform an elaborate electromagnetic dance and end up with just the right velocity needed to keep tracking the moving target of the beam.

In the evening, back in the house, they sat together working through simulations. It was easy to find designs that would work if everything went perfectly, but they kept hunting for the most robust variation, the one that was most tolerant of small misalignments. With standard two-body collision braking, the usual solution was to have the first package, shaped like a cylinder, pass right through a hole in the second package. As it emerged from the other side and the two moved apart again, the magnetic fields were switched from repulsive to attractive. Several 'bounces' followed, and in the process as much of the kinetic energy as possible was gradually converted into superconducting currents for storage, while the rest was dissipated as electromagnetic radiation. Having three objects meeting at an angle would not only make the timing and positioning more critical, it would destroy the simple, axial symmetry and introduce a greater risk of instability.

It was dawn before they settled on the optimal design, which effectively split the problem in two. First, package one, a sphere, would meet package two, a torus, threading the gap in the middle, then bouncing back and forth through it seventeen times. The plane of the torus would lie at an angle to its direction of flight, allowing the sphere to approach it head-on. When the two finally came to rest with respect to each other, they would still have a component of their velocity carrying them straight towards package three, a cylinder with an axial borehole.

Because the electromagnetic interactions were the same as the two-body case – self-centring, intrinsically stable – a small amount of misalignment at each of these encounters would not be fatal. The usual two-body case, though, didn't require the combined package, after all the bouncing and energy dissipation was completed, to be moving on a path so precisely determined that it could pass through yet another narrow hoop.

There were no guarantees, and in the end the result would be in other people's hands. They could send requests to the three outposts, asking for these objects to be launched at the necessary times on the necessary trajectories. The energy needs hovered on the edge of politeness, though, and it was possible that one or more of the requests would simply be refused.

Jasim waved the models away and they stretched out on the carpet, side by side.

He said, 'I never thought we'd get this far. Even if this is only a mirage, I never thought we'd find one worth chasing.'

Leila said, 'I don't know what I expected. Some kind of great folly: some long, exhausting, exhilarating struggle that felt like wandering through a jungle for years and ending up utterly lost.'

'And then what?'

'Surrender.'

Jasim was silent for a while. Leila could sense that he was brooding over something, but she didn't press him.

He said, 'Should we travel to this observatory ourselves, or wait here for the results?'

'We should go. Definitely! I don't want to hang around here for fifteen thousand years, waiting. We can leave the Nazdeek observatories hunting for more beam fluorescence and broadcasting the results, so we'll hear about them wherever we end up.'

'That makes sense.' Jasim hesitated, then added, 'When we go, I don't want to leave a back-up.'

'Ah.' They'd travelled from Najib leaving nothing of themselves behind: if their transmission had somehow failed to make it to Nazdeek, no stored copy of the data would ever have woken to resume their truncated lives. Travel within the Amalgam's established network carried negligible risks, though. If they flung themselves towards the hypothetical location of this yet-to-be-assembled station in the middle of nowhere, it was entirely possible that they'd sail off to infinity without ever being instantiated again.

Leila said, 'Are you tired of what we're doing? Of what we've become?'

'It's not that.'

'This one chance isn't the be-all and end-all. Now that we know how to hunt for the beams, I'm sure we'll find this one again after its shifts. We could find a thousand others, if we're persistent.'

'I know that,' he said. 'I don't want to stop, I don't want to end this. But I want to *risk* ending it. Just once. While that still means something.'

Leila sat up and rested her head on her knees. She could understand what he was feeling, but it still disturbed her.

Jasim said, 'We've already achieved something extraordinary. No one's found a clue like this in a million years. If we leave that to posterity, it will be pursued to the end, we can be sure of that. But I desperately want to pursue it myself. With you.'

'And because you want that so badly, you need to face the chance of losing it?'

'Yes.'

It was one thing they had never tried. In their youth, they would never have knowingly risked death. They'd been too much in love, too eager for the life they'd yet to live; the stakes would have been unbearably high. In the twilight years, back on Najib, it would have been an easy thing to do, but an utterly insipid pleasure.

Jasim sat up and took her hand. 'Have I hurt you with this?'

'No, no.' She shook her head pensively, trying to gather her thoughts. She didn't want to hide her feelings, but she wanted to express them precisely, not blurt them out in a confusing rush. 'I always thought we'd reach the end together, though. We'd come to some point in the jungle, look around, exchange a glance, and know that we'd arrived. Without even needing to say it aloud.'

Jasim drew her to him and held her. 'All right, I'm sorry. Forget everything I said.'

Leila pushed him away, annoyed. 'This isn't something you can take back. If it's the truth, it's the truth. Just give me some time to decide what I want.'

They put it aside and buried themselves in work: polishing the design for the new observatory, preparing the requests to send to the three outposts. One of the planets they would be petitioning belonged to the Snakes, so Leila and Jasim went to visit the nest for a second time, to seek advice on the best way to beg for this favour. Their neighbours seemed more excited just to see them again than they were at the news that a tiny rent had appeared in the Aloof's million-year-old cloak of discretion. When Leila gently pushed her on this point, Sarah said, 'You're here, here and now, our guests in flesh and blood. I'm sure I'll be dead long before the Aloof are willing to do the same.'

Leila thought: What kind of strange greed is it that I'm suffering from? I can be fêted by creatures who rose up from the dust through a completely different molecule from my own ancestors. I can sit among them and discuss the philosophy of life and death. The Amalgam has already joined every willing participant in the galaxy into one vast conversation. And I want to go and eavesdrop on the Aloof? Just because they've played hard to get for a million years?

They dispatched requests for the three modules to be built and launched by their three as-yet unwitting collaborators, specifying the final countdown to the nanosecond but providing a ten-year period for the project to be debated. Leila felt optimistic; however blasé the Nazdeek nest had been, she suspected that no spacefaring culture really could resist the chance to peek behind the veil.

They had thirty-six years to wait before they followed in the wake of their petitions; on top of the ten-year delay, the new observatory's modules would be travelling at a fraction of a per cent below light-speed, so they needed a head start.

No more tell-tale gamma-ray flashes appeared from the bulge, but Leila hadn't expected any so soon. They had sent the news of their discovery to other worlds close to the Aloof's territory, so eventually a thousand other groups with different vantage points would be searching for the same kind of evidence and finding their own ways to interpret and exploit it. It hurt a little, scattering their hard-won revelation to the wind for anyone to use – perhaps even to beat them to some far greater prize – but they'd relied on the generosity of their predecessors from the moment they'd arrived on Nazdeek, and the sheer scale of the overall problem made it utterly perverse to cling selfishly to their own small triumph.

As the day of their departure finally arrived, Leila came to a decision. She understood Jasim's need to put everything at risk, and in a sense she shared it. If she had always imagined the two of them ending this together – struggling on, side by side, until the way forward was lost and the undergrowth closed in on them – then *that* was what she'd risk. She would take the flip side to his own wager.

When the house took their minds apart and sent them off to chase the beam, Leila left a copy of herself frozen on Nazdeek. If no word of their safe arrival reached it by the expected time, it would wake and carry on the search.

Alone.

6

'Welcome to Trident. We're honoured by the presence of our most distinguished guest.'

Jasim stood beside the bed, waving a triangular flag. Red, green and blue in the corners merged to white in the centre.

'How long have you been up?'

'About an hour,' he said. Leila frowned, and he added apologetically, 'You were sleeping very deeply, I didn't want to disturb you.'

'I should be the one giving the welcome,' she said. 'You're the one who might never have woken.'

The bedroom window looked out into a dazzling field of stars. It was not a view facing the bulge – by now Leila could recognise the distinctive spectra of the region's stars with ease – but even these disk stars were so crisp and bright that this was like no sky she had ever seen.

'Have you been downstairs?' she said.

'Not yet. I wanted us to decide on that together.' The house had no physical wing here; the tiny observatory had no spare mass for such frivolities as embodying them, let alone constructing architectural follies in the middle of interstellar space. 'Downstairs' would be nothing but a scape that they were free to design at will.

'Everything worked,' she said, not quite believing it.

Jasim spread his arms. 'We're here, aren't we?'

They watched a reconstruction of the first two modules coming together. The timing and the trajectories were as near to perfect as they could have hoped for, and the superconducting magnets had been constructed to a standard of purity and homogeneity that made the magnetic embrace look like an idealised simulation. By the time the two had locked together, the third module was just minutes away. Some untraceable discrepancy between reality and prediction in the transfer of momentum to radiation had the composite moving at a tiny angle away from its expected course, but when it met the third module the magnetic fields still meshed in a stable configuration, and there was energy to spare to nudge the final assembly precisely into step with the predicted swinging of the Aloof's beam.

The Amalgam had lived up to its promise: three worlds full of beings they had never met, who owed them nothing, who did not even share their molecular ancestry, had each diverted enough energy to light up all their cities for a decade, and followed the instructions of strangers down to the atom, down to the nano-second, in order to make this work.

What happened now was entirely in the hands of the Aloof.

Trident had been functioning for about a month before its designers had arrived to take up occupancy. So far, it had not yet observed any gamma-ray signals spilling out of the bulge. The particular pulse that Leila and Jasim had seen triggering fluores-cence would be long gone, of course, but the usefulness of their present location was predicated on three assumptions: the Aloof would use the same route for many other bursts of data; some of the radiation carrying that data would slip past the intended receiver; and the two nodes of the network would have continued in freefall long enough for the spilt data to be arriving here still, along the same predictable path.

Without those three extra components, delivered by their least reliable partners, Trident would be worthless.

'Downstairs,' Leila said. 'Maybe a kind of porch with glass walls?'

'Sounds fine to me.'

She conjured up a plan of the house and sketched some ideas, then they went down to try them out at full scale.

They had been into orbit around Najib, and they had travelled embodied to its three beautiful, barren sibling worlds, but they had never been in interstellar space before. Or at least, they had never been conscious of it.

They were still not truly embodied, but you didn't need flesh and blood to feel the vacuum around you; to be awake and plugged in to an honest depiction of your surroundings was enough. The nearest of Trident's contributor worlds was six hundred light-years away. The distance to Najib was unthinkable. Leila paced around the porch, looking out at the stars, vertiginous in her virtual body, unsteady in the phoney gravity.

It had been twenty-eight thousand years since they'd left Najib. All her children and grandchildren had almost certainly chosen death, long ago. No messages had been sent after them to Nazdeek; Leila had asked for that silence, fearing that it would be unbearably painful to hear news, day after day, to which she could give no meaningful reply, about events in which she could never participate. Now she regretted that. She wanted to read the lives of her grandchildren, as she might the biography of an ancestor. She wanted to know how things had ended up, like the time traveller she was.

A second month of observation passed, with nothing. A data feed reaching them from Nazdeek was equally silent. For any new hint of the beam's location to reach Nazdeek, and then the report of that to reach Trident, would take thousands of years longer than the direct passage of the beam itself, so if Nazdeek saw evidence that the beam was 'still' on course, that would be old news about a pulse they had not been here to intercept. However, if Nazdeek reported that the beam had shifted, at least that would put them out of their misery immediately, and tell them that Trident had been built too late.

Jasim made a vegetable garden on the porch and grew exotic food in the starlight. Leila played along and ate beside him; it was a harmless game. They could have painted anything at all around the house: any planet they'd visited, drawn from their memories, any imaginary world. If this small pretence was enough to keep them sane and anchored to reality, so be it.

Now and then, Leila felt the strangest of the many pangs of isolation Trident induced: here, the knowledge of the galaxy was no longer at her fingertips. Their descriptions as travellers had encoded their vast personal memories, declarative and episodic, and their luggage had included prodigious libraries, but she was used to having so much more. Every civilised planet held a storehouse of information that was simply too bulky to fit into Trident, along with a constant feed of exabytes of news flooding in from other worlds. Wherever you were in the galaxy, some news was old news, some cherished theories long discredited, some facts hopelessly out of date. Here, though, Leila knew, there were billions of rigorously established truths – the results of hundreds of millennia of thought, experiment and observation – that had slipped out of her reach. Questions that any other child of the Amalgam could expect to have answered instantly would take twelve hundred years to receive a reply.

No such questions actually came into her mind, but there were still moments when the mere fact of it was enough to make her feel unbearably rootless, cut adrift not only from her past and her people, but from civilisation itself.

Trident shouted: 'Data!'

Leila was halfway through recording a postcard to the Nazdeek Snakes. Jasim was on the porch watering his plants. Leila turned to see him walking through the wall, commanding the bricks to part like a gauze curtain.

They stood side by side, watching the analysis emerge.

A pulse of gamma-rays of the expected frequency, from precisely the right location, had just washed over Trident. The beam was greatly attenuated by distance, not to mention having had most of its energy intercepted by its rightful owner, but more than enough had slipped past and reached them for Trident to make sense of the nature of the pulse.

It was, unmistakably, modulated with information. There were precisely repeated phase shifts in the radiation that were unimaginable in any natural gamma-ray source, and which would have been pointless in any artificial beam produced for any purpose besides communication.

The pulse had been three seconds long, carrying about ten-to-the-twenty-fourth bits of data. The bulk of this appeared to be random, but that did not rule out meaningful content, it simply implied efficient encryption. The Amalgam's network sent encrypted data via robust classical channels like this, while sending the keys needed to decode it by a second, quantum channel. Leila had never expected to get hold of unencrypted data, laying bare the secrets of the Aloof in an instant. To have clear evidence that someone in the bulge was talking to someone else, and to have pinned down part of the pathway connecting them, was vindication enough.

There was more, though. Between the messages themselves, Trident had identified brief, orderly, unencrypted sequences. Everything was guesswork to a degree, but with such a huge slab of data statistical measures were powerful indicators. Part of the data looked like routing information, addresses for the messages as they were carried through the network. Another part looked like information about the nodes' current and future trajectories. If Trident really had cracked that, they could work out where to position its successor. In fact, if they placed the successor close enough to the bulge, they could probably keep that one observatory constantly inside the spill from the beam.

Jasim couldn't resist playing devil's advocate. 'You know, this could just be one part of whatever throws the probes back in our faces talking to another part. The Aloof themselves could still be dead, while their security system keeps humming with paranoid gossip.'

Leila said blithely, 'Hypothesise away. I'm not taking the bait.'

She turned to embrace him, and they kissed. She said, 'I've forgotten how to celebrate. What happens now?'

He moved his fingertips gently along her arm. Leila opened up the scape, creating a fourth spatial dimension. She took his hand, kissed it, and placed it against her beating heart. Their bodies reconfigured, nerve-endings crowding every surface, inside and out.

Jasim climbed inside her, and she inside him, the topology of the scape changing to wrap them together in a mutual embrace. Everything vanished from their lives but pleasure, triumph and each other's presence, as close as it could ever be.

7

'Are you here for the Listening Party?'

The chitinous heptapod, who'd been wandering the crowded street with a food-cart dispensing largesse at random, offered Leila a plate of snacks tailored to her and Jasim's preferences. She accepted it, then paused to let Tassef, the planet they'd just set foot on, brief her as to the meaning of this phrase. People, Tassef explained, had travelled to this world from throughout the region in order to witness a special event. Some fifteen thousand years before, a burst of data from the Aloof's network had been picked up by a nearby observatory. In isolation, these bursts meant very little; however, the locals were hopeful that at least one of several proposed observatories near Massa, on the opposite side of the bulge, would have seen spillage including many of the same data packets, forty thousand years before. If any such observations had in fact taken place, news of their precise contents should now, finally, be about to reach Tassef by the longer, disk-based routes of the Amalgam's own network. Once the two observations could be compared, it would become clear which messages from the earlier Eavesdropping session had made their way to the part of the Aloof's network that could be sampled from Tassef. The comparison would advance the project of mapping all the symbolic addresses seen in the data onto actual physical locations.

Leila said, 'That's not why we came, but now we know, we're even more pleased to be here.'

The heptapod emitted a chirp that Leila understood as a gracious welcome, then pushed its way back into the throng.

Jasim said, 'Remember when you told me that everyone would get bored with the Aloof while we were still in transit?'

'I said that would happen eventually. If not this trip, the next one.'

'Yes, but you said it five journeys ago.'

Leila scowled, preparing to correct him, but then she checked and he was right.

They hadn't expected Tassef to be so crowded when they'd chosen it as their destination, some ten thousand years before. The planet had given them a small room in this city, Shalouf, and imposed a thousand-year limit on their presence if they wished to remain embodied without adopting local citizenship. More than a billion visitors had arrived over the last fifty years, anticipating the news of the observations from Massa, but unable to predict the precise time it would reach Tassef because the details of the observatories' trajectories had still been in transit.

She confessed, 'I never thought a billion people would arrange their travel plans around this jigsaw puzzle.'

'Travel plans?' Jasim laughed. 'We chose to have our own deaths revolve around the very same thing.'

'Yes, but we're just weird.'

Jasim gestured at the crowded street. 'I don't think we can compete on that score.'

They wandered through the city, drinking in the decades-long carnival atmosphere. There were people of every phenotype Leila had encountered before, and more: bipeds, quadrupeds, hexapods, heptapods, walking, shuffling, crawling, scuttling, or soaring high above the street on feathered, scaled or membranous wings. Some were encased in their preferred atmospheres; others, like Leila and Jasim, had chosen instead to be embodied in ersatz flesh that didn't follow every ancestral chemical dictate. Physics and geometry tied evolution's hands, and many attempts to solve the same problems had converged on similar answers, but the galaxy's different replicators still managed their idiosyncratic twists. When Leila let her translator sample the cacophony of voices and signals at random, she felt as if the whole disk, the whole Amalgam, had converged on this tiny metropolis.

In fact, most of the travellers had come just a few hundred light-years to be here. She and Jasim had chosen to keep their role in the history of Eavesdropping out of their précis, and Leila caught herself with a rather smug sense of walking among the crowd like some unacknowledged sage, bemused by the late-blooming, and no doubt superficial, interest of the masses. On reflection, though, any sense of superior knowledge was hard to justify, when most of these people would have grown up steeped in developments that she was only belatedly catching up with. A new generation of observatories had been designed while she and Jasim were in transit, based on 'strong bullets': specially designed femtomachines, clusters of protons and neutrons stable only for trillionths of a second, launched at ultra-relativistic speeds so great that time dilation enabled them to survive long enough to collide with other components and merge into tiny, short-lived gamma-ray observatories. The basic trick that had built Trident had gone from a one-off gamble into a miniaturised, mass-produced phenomenon, with literally billions of strong bullets being fired continuously from thousands of planets around the inner disk.

Femtomachines themselves were old hat, but it had taken the technical challenges of Eavesdropping to motivate someone into squeezing a few more tricks out of them. Historians had always understood that in the long run, technological progress was a horizontal asymptote: once people had more or less everything they wanted that was physically possible, every incremental change would take exponentially longer to achieve, with diminishing returns and ever less reason to bother. The Amalgam would probably spend an aeon inching its way closer to the flat-line, but this was proof that shifts of circumstance alone could still trigger a modest renaissance or two, without the need for any radical scientific discovery or even a genuinely new technology.

They stopped to rest in a square, beside a small fountain gushing aromatic hydrocarbons. The Tassef locals, quadrupeds with slick, rubbery hides, played in the sticky black spray then licked each other clean.

Jasim shaded his eyes from the sun. He said, 'We've had our autumn child, and we've seen its grandchildren prosper. I'm not sure what's left.'

'No.' Leila was in no rush to die, but they'd sampled fifty thousand years of their discovery's consequences. They'd followed in the wake of the news of the gamma-ray signals as it circled the inner disk, spending less than a century conscious as they sped from world to world. At first they'd been hunting for some vital new role to play, but they'd slowly come to accept that the avalanche they'd triggered had out-raced them. Physical and logical maps of the Aloof's network were being constructed, as fast as the laws of physics allowed. Billions of people on thousands of planets, scattered around the inner rim of the Amalgam's territory, were sharing their observations to help piece together the living skeleton of their elusive neighbours. When that project was complete it would not be the end of anything, but it could mark the start of a long hiatus. The encrypted classical data would never yield anything more than traffic routes; no amount of ingenuity could extract its content. The quantum keys that could unlock it, assuming the Aloof even used such things, would be absolutely immune to theft, duplication, or surreptitious sampling. One day, there would be another breakthrough, and everything would change again, but did they want to wait a hundred thousand years, a million, just to see what came next?

The solicitous heptapods – not locals, but visitors from a world thirty light-years away who had nonetheless taken on some kind of innate duty of hospitality – seemed to show up whenever anyone was hungry. Leila tried to draw this second one into conversation, but it politely excused itself to rush off and feed someone else.

Leila said, 'Maybe this is it. We'll wait for the news from Massa, then celebrate for a while, then finish it.'

Jasim took her hand. 'That feels right to me. I'm not certain, but I don't think I'll ever be.'

'Are you tired?' she said. 'Bored?'

'Not at all,' he replied. 'I feel *satisfied*. With what we've done, what we've seen. And I don't want to dilute that. I don't want to hang around for ever, watching it fade, until we start to feel the way we did on Najib all over again.'

'No.'

They sat in the square until dusk, and watched the stars of the bulge come out. They'd seen this dazzling jewelled hub from every possible angle now, but Leila never grew tired of the sight.

Jasim gave an amused, exasperated sigh. 'That beautiful, maddening, unreachable place. I think the whole Amalgam will be dead and gone without anyone setting foot inside it.'

Leila felt a sudden surge of irritation, which deepened into a sense of revulsion. 'It's a place, like any other place! Stars, gas, dust, planets. It's not some metaphysical realm. It's not even far away. Our own home world is twenty times more distant.'

'Our own home world doesn't have an impregnable fence around it. If we really wanted to, we could go back there.'

Leila was defiant. 'If we really wanted to, we could enter the bulge.'

Jasim laughed. 'Have you read something in those messages that you didn't tell me about? How to say "open sesame" to the gatekeepers?'

Leila stood, and summoned a map of the Aloof's network to superimpose across their vision, criss-crossing the sky with slender cones of violet light. One cone appeared head-on, as a tiny circle: the beam whose spillage came close to Tassef. She put her hand on Jasim's shoulder and zoomed in on that circle. It opened up before them like a beckoning tunnel.

She said, 'We know where this beam is coming from. We don't know for certain that the traffic between these particular nodes runs in both directions, but we've found plenty of examples where it does. If we aim a signal from here, back along the path of the spillage, and we make it wide enough, then we won't just hit the sending node. We'll hit the receiver as well.'

Jasim was silent.

'We know the data format,' she continued. 'We know the routing information. We can address the data packets to a node on the other side of the bulge, one where the spillage comes out at Massa.'

Jasim said, 'What makes you think they'll accept the packets?'

'There's nothing in the format we don't understand, nothing we can't write for ourselves.'

'Nothing in the unencrypted part. If there's an authorisation, even a checksum, in the encrypted part, then any packet without that will be tossed away as noise.'

'That's true,' she conceded.

'Do you really want to do this?' he said. Her hand was still on his shoulder, she could feel his body growing tense.

'Absolutely.'

'We mail ourselves from here to Massa, as unencrypted, classical data that anyone can read, anyone can copy, anyone can alter or corrupt?'

'A moment ago you said they'd throw us away as noise.'

'That's the least of our worries.'

'Maybe.'

Jasim shuddered, his body almost convulsing. He let out a string of obscenities, then made a choking sound. 'What's wrong with you? Is this some kind of test? If I call your bluff, will you admit that you're joking?'

Leila shook her head. 'And no, it's not revenge for what you did on the way to Trident. This is our chance. *This* is what we were waiting to do – not the Eavesdropping, that's nothing! The bulge is right here in front of us. The Aloof are in there, somewhere. We can't force them to engage with us, but we can get closer to them than anyone has ever been before.'

'If we go in this way, they could do anything to us.'

'They're not barbarians. They haven't made war on us. Even the engineering spores come back unharmed.'

'If we infest their network, that's worse than an engineering spore.'

'"Infest"! None of these routes are crowded. A few exabytes passing through is nothing.'

'You have no idea how they'll react.'

'No,' she confessed. 'I don't. But I'm ready to find out.'

Jasim stood. 'We could send a test message first. Then go to Massa and see if it arrived safely.'

'We could do that,' Leila conceded. 'That would be a sensible plan.'

'So you agree?' Jasim gave her a wary, frozen smile. 'We'll send a test message. Send an encyclopaedia. Send greetings in some universal language.'

'Fine. We'll send all of those things first. But I'm not waiting more than one day after that. I'm not going to Massa the long way. I'm taking the shortcut, I'm going through the bulge.'

8

The Amalgam had been so generous to Leila, and local interest in the Aloof so intense, that she had almost forgotten that she was not, in fact, entitled to a limitless and unconditional flow of resources, to be employed to any end that involved her obsession.

When she asked Tassef for the means to build a high-powered gamma-ray transmitter to aim into the bulge, it interrogated her for an hour, then replied that the matter would require a prolonged and extensive consultation. It was, she realised, no use protesting that compared to hosting a billion guests for a couple of centuries, the cost of this was nothing. The sticking point was not the energy use, or any other equally microscopic consequence for the comfort and amenity of the Tassef locals. The issue was whether her proposed actions might be seen as unwelcome and offensive by the Aloof, and whether that affront might in turn provoke some kind of retribution.

Countless probes and spores had been gently and patiently returned from the bulge unharmed, but they'd come blundering in at less than light-speed. A flash of gamma-rays could not be intercepted and returned before it struck its chosen target. Though it seemed to Leila that it would be a trivial matter for the network to choose to reject the data, it was not unreasonable to suppose that the Aloof's sensibilities might differ on this point from her own.

Jasim had left Shalouf for a city on the other side of the planet. Leila's feelings about this were mixed; it was always painful when they separated, but the reminder that they were not irrevocably welded together also brought an undeniable sense of space and freedom. She loved him beyond measure, but that was not the final word on every question. She was not certain that she would not relent in the end, and die quietly beside him when the news came through from Massa; there were moments when it seemed utterly perverse, masochistic and self-aggrandising to flee from that calm, dignified end for the sake of trying to cap their modest revolution with a new and spectacularly dangerous folly. Nor though, was she certain that Jasim would not change his own mind, and take her hand while they plunged off this cliff together.

When the months dragged on with no decision on her request, no news from Massa and no overtures from her husband, Leila became an orator, travelling from city to city promoting her scheme to blaze a trail through the heart of the bulge. Her words and image were conveyed into virtual fora, but her physical presence was a way to draw attention to her cause, and Listening Party pilgrims and Tassefi alike packed the meeting places when she came. She mastered the locals' language and style, but left it inflected with some suitably alien mannerisms. The fact that a rumour had arisen that she was one of the First Eavesdroppers did no harm to her attendance figures.

When she reached the city of Jasim's self-imposed exile, she searched the audience for him in vain. As she walked out into the night a sense of panic gripped her. She felt no fear for herself, but the thought of him dying here alone was unbearable.

She sat in the street, weeping. How had it come to this? They had been prepared for a glorious failure, prepared to be broken by the Aloof's unyielding silence, and instead the fruits of their labour had swept through the disk, reinvigorating a thousand cultures. How could the taste of success be so bitter?

Leila imagined calling out to Jasim, finding him, holding him again, repairing their wounds.

A splinter of steel remained inside her, though. She looked up into the blazing sky. The Aloof were there, waiting, daring her to stand before them. To come this far, then step back from the edge for the comfort of a familiar embrace, would diminish her. She would not retreat.

The news arrived from Massa: forty thousand years before, the spillage from the far side of the bulge had been caught in time. Vast swathes of the data matched the observations that Tassef had been holding in anticipation of this moment, for the last fifteen thousand years.

There was more: reports of other correlations from other observatories followed within minutes. As the message from Massa had been relayed around the inner disk, a cascade of similar matches with other stores of data had been found.

By seeing where packets dropped out of the stream, their abstract addresses became concrete, physical locations within the bulge. As Leila stood in Shalouf's main square in the dusk, absorbing the reports, the Aloof's network was growing more solid, less ethereal, by the minute.

The streets around her were erupting with signs of elation: polyglot shouts, chirps and buzzes, celebratory scents and vivid pigmentation changes. Bursts of luminescence spread across the square. Even the relentlessly sober heptapods had abandoned their food-carts to lie on their backs, spinning with delight. Leila wheeled around, drinking it in, commanding her translator to punch the meaning of every disparate gesture and sound deep into her brain, unifying the kaleidoscope into a single emotional charge.

As the stars of the bulge came out, Tassef offered an overlay for everyone to share, with the newly mapped routes shining like golden highways. From all around her, Leila picked up the signals of those who were joining the view: people of every civilisation, every species, every replicator were seeing the Aloof's secret roads painted across the sky.

Leila walked through the streets of Shalouf, feeling Jasim's absence sharply, but too familiar with that pain to be overcome by it. If the joy of this moment was muted, every celebration would be blighted in the same way, now. She could not expect anything else. She would grow inured to it.

Tassef spoke to her.

'The citizens have reached a decision. They will grant your request.'

'I'm grateful.'

'There is a condition. The transmitter must be built at least twenty light-years away, either in interstellar space, or in the circumstellar region of an uninhabited system.'

'I understand.' This way, in the event that the Aloof felt threatened to the point of provoking destructive retribution, Tassef would survive an act of violence, at least on a stellar scale, directed against the transmitter itself.

'We advise you to prepare your final plans for the hardware, and submit them when you're sure they will fulfil your purpose.'

'Of course.'

Leila went back to her room, and reviewed the plans she had already drafted. She had anticipated the Tassefi wanting a considerable safety margin, so she had worked out the energy budgets for detailed scenarios involving engineering spores and forty-seven different cometary clouds that fell within Tassef's jurisdiction. It took just seconds to identify the best one that met the required conditions, and she lodged it without hesitation.

Out on the streets, the Listening Party continued. For the billion pilgrims, this was enough: they would go home, return to their grandchildren, and die happy in the knowledge that they had finally seen something new in the world. Leila envied them; there'd been a time when that would have been enough for her, too.

She left her room and rejoined the celebration, talking, laughing, dancing with strangers, letting herself grow giddy with the moment. When the sun came up, she made her way home, stepping lightly over the sleeping bodies that filled the street.

The engineering spores were the latest generation: strong bullets launched at close to light-speed that shed their momentum by diving through the heart of a star, and then rebuilding themselves at atomic density as they decayed in the stellar atmosphere. In effect, the dying femtomachines constructed nanomachines bearing the same blueprints as they'd carried within themselves at nuclear densities, and which then continued out to the cometary cloud to replicate and commence the real work of mining raw materials and building the gamma-ray transmitter.

Leila contemplated following in their wake, sending herself as a signal to be picked up by the as-yet-unbuilt transmitter. It would not have been as big a gamble as Jasim's with Trident; the strong bullets had already been used successfully this way in hundreds of similar stars.

In the end, she chose to wait on Tassef for a signal that the transmitter had been successfully constructed, and had tested, aligned and calibrated itself. If she was going to march blindly into the bulge, it would be absurd to stumble and fall prematurely, before she even reached the precipice.

When the day came, some ten thousand people gathered in the centre of Shalouf to bid the traveller a safe journey. Leila would have preferred to slip away quietly, but after all her lobbying she had surrendered her privacy, and the Tassefi seemed to feel that she owed them this last splash of colour and ceremony.

Forty-six years after the Listening Party, most of the pilgrims had returned to their homes, but of the few hundred who had lingered in Shalouf nearly all had showed up for this curious footnote to the main event. Leila wasn't sure that anyone here believed the Aloof's network would do more than bounce her straight back into the disk, but the affection these well-wishers expressed seemed genuine. Someone had even gone to the trouble of digging up a phrase in the oldest known surviving language of her ancestral species: *safar bekheyr*, may your journey be blessed. They had written it across the sky in an ancient script that she'd last seen eighty thousand years before, and it had been spread among the crowd phonetically so that everyone she met could offer her this hopeful farewell as she passed.

Tassef, the insentient delegate of all the planet's citizens, addressed the crowd with some sombre ceremonial blather. Leila's mind wandered, settling on the observation that she was probably partaking in a public execution. No matter. She had said goodbye to her friends and family long ago. When she stepped through the ceremonial gate, which had been smeared with a tarry mess that the Tassefi considered the height of beauty, she would close her eyes and recall her last night on Najib, letting the intervening millennia collapse into a dream. Everyone chose death in the end, and no one's exit was perfect. Better to rely on your own flawed judgements, better to make your own ungainly mess of it, than live in the days when nature would simply take you at random.

As Tassef fell silent, a familiar voice rose up from the crowd.

'Are you still resolved to do this foolish thing?'

Leila glared down at her husband. 'Yes, I am.'

'You won't reconsider?'

'NO.'

'Then I'm coming with you.'

Jasim pushed his way through the startled audience, and climbed onto the stage.

Leila spoke to him privately. 'You're embarrassing us both.'

He replied the same way. 'Don't be petty. I know I've hurt you, but the blame lies with both of us.'

'Why are you doing this? You've made your own wishes very plain.'

'Do you think I can watch you walk into danger and not walk beside you?'

'You were ready to die if Trident failed. You were ready to leave me behind then.'

'Once I spoke my mind on that you gave me no choice. You insisted.' He took her hand. 'You know I only stayed away from you all this time because I hoped it would dissuade you. I failed. So now I'm here.'

Leila's heart softened. 'You're serious? You'll come with me?'

Jasim said, 'Whatever they do to you, let them do it to us both.'

Leila had no argument to make against this, no residue of

anger, no false solicitousness. She had always wanted him beside her at the end, and she would not refuse him now.

She spoke to Tassef. 'One more passenger. Is that acceptable?' The energy budget allowed for a thousand years of test transmissions to follow in her wake; Jasim would just be a minor blip of extra data.

'It's acceptable.' Tassef proceeded to explain the change to the assembled crowd, and to the onlookers scattered across the planet.

Jasim said, 'We'll interweave the data from both of us into a single packet. I don't want to end up at Massa and find they've sent you to Jahnom by mistake.'

'All right.' Leila arranged the necessary changes. None of the Eavesdroppers yet knew that they were coming, and no message sent the long way could warn them in time, but the data they sent into the bulge would be prefaced by instructions that anyone in the Amalgam would find clear and unambiguous, asking that their descriptions only be embodied if they were picked up at Massa. If they were found in other spillage along the way, they didn't want to be embodied multiple times. And if they did not emerge at Massa at all, so be it.

Tassef's second speech came to an end. Leila looked down at the crowd one last time, and let her irritation with the whole bombastic ceremony dissipate into amusement. If she had been among the sane, she might easily have turned up herself to watch a couple of ancient fools try to step onto the imaginary road in the sky and wish them *safar bekheyr*.

She squeezed Jasim's hand, and they walked towards the gate.

9

Leila's fingers came together, her hand empty. She felt as if she was falling, but nothing in sight appeared to be moving. Then again, all she could see was a distant backdrop, its scale and proximity impossible to judge: thousands of fierce blue stars against the blackness of space.

She looked around for Jasim, but she was utterly alone. She could see no vehicle or other machine that might have disgorged her into this emptiness. There was not even a planet below her, or a single brightest star to which she might be bound. Absurdly, she was breathing. Every other cue told her that she was drifting through vacuum, probably through interstellar space. Her lungs kept filling and emptying, though. The air, and her skin, felt neither hot nor cold.

Someone or something had embodied her, or was running her as software. She was not on Massa, she was sure of that; she had never visited that world, but nowhere in the Amalgam would a guest be treated like this. Not even one who arrived unannounced in data spilling out from the bulge.

Leila said, 'Are you listening to me? Do you understand me?' She could hear her own voice, flat and without resonance. The acoustics made perfect sense in a vast, empty, windless place, if not an airless one.

Anywhere in the Amalgam, you *knew* whether you were embodied or not; it was the nature of all bodies, real or virtual, that declarative knowledge of every detail was there for the asking. Here, when Leila tried to summon the same information, her mind remained blank. It was like the strange absence she'd felt on Trident, when she'd been cut off from the repositories of civilisation, but here the amputation had reached all the way inside her.

She inhaled deeply, but there was no noticeable scent at all, not even the whiff of her own body odour that she would have expected, whether she was wearing her ancestral phenotype or any of the forms of ersatz flesh that she adopted when the environment demanded it. She pinched the skin of her forearm; it felt more like her original skin than any of the substitutes she'd ever worn. They might have fashioned this body out of something both remarkably lifelike and chemically inert, and placed her in a vast, transparent container of air, but she was beginning to pick up a strong stench of ersatz physics. Air and skin alike, she suspected, were made of bits, not atoms.

So where was Jasim? Were they running him too, in a separate scape? She called out his name, trying not to make the exploratory cry sound plaintive. She understood all too well now why he'd tried so hard to keep her from this place, and why he'd been unable to face staying behind: the thought that the Aloof might be doing something unspeakable to his defenceless consciousness, in some place she couldn't hope to reach or see, was like a white-hot blade pressed to her heart. All she could do was try to shut off the panic and talk down the possibility. *All right, he's alone here, but so am I, and it's not that bad.* She would put her faith in symmetry; if they had not abused her, why would they have harmed Jasim?

She forced herself to be calm. The Aloof had taken the trouble to grant her consciousness, but she couldn't expect the level of amenity she was accustomed to. For a start, it would be perfectly reasonable if her hosts were unable or unwilling to plug her into any data source equivalent to the Amalgam's libraries, and perhaps the absence of somatic knowledge was not much different. Rather than deliberately fooling her about her body, maybe they had looked at the relevant data channels and decided that *anything* they fed into them would be misleading. Understanding her transmitted description well enough to bring her to consciousness was one thing, but it didn't guarantee that they knew how to translate the technical details of their instantiation of her into her own language.

And if this ignorance-plus-honesty excuse was too sanguine to swallow, it wasn't hard to think of the Aloof as being pathologically secretive without actually being malicious. If they wanted to keep quiet about the way they'd brought her to life lest it reveal something about themselves, that too was understandable. They need not be doing it for the sake of tormenting her.

Leila surveyed the sky around her, and felt a jolt of recognition. She'd memorised the positions of the nearest stars to the target node where her transmission would first be sent, and now a matching pattern stood out against the background in a collection of distinctive constellations. She was being shown the sky from that node. This didn't prove anything about her actual location, but the simplest explanation was that the Aloof had instantiated her here, rather than sending her on through the network. The stars were in the positions she'd predicted for her time of arrival, so if this was the reality, there had been little delay in choosing how to deal with the intruder. No thousand-year-long deliberations, no passing of the news to a distant decision-maker. Either the Aloof themselves were present here, or the machinery of the node was so sophisticated that they might as well have been. She could not have been woken by accident; it had to have been a deliberate act. It made her wonder if the Aloof had been expecting something like this for millennia.

'What now?' she asked. Her hosts remained silent. 'Toss me back to Tassef?' The probes with their reversed trajectories bore no record of their experience; perhaps the Aloof wouldn't incorporate these new memories into her description before returning her. She spread her arms imploringly. 'If you're going to erase this memory, why not speak to me first? I'm in your hands completely, you can send me to the grave with your secrets. Why wake me at all if you don't want to talk?'

In the silence that followed, Leila had no trouble imagining one answer: to study her. It was a mathematical certainty that some questions about her behaviour could never be answered simply by examining her static description; the only reliable way to predict what she'd do in any given scenario was to wake her and confront her with it. They might, of course, have chosen to wake her any number of times before, without granting her memories of the previous instantiations. She experienced a moment of sheer existential vertigo: this could be the thousandth, the billionth, in a vast series of experiments, as her captors permuted dozens of variables to catalogue her responses.

The vertigo passed. Anything was possible, but she preferred to entertain more pleasant hypotheses.

'I came here to talk,' she said. 'I understand that you don't want us sending in machinery, but there must be something we can discuss, something we can learn from each other. In the disk, every time two spacefaring civilisations met, they found they had something in common. Some mutual interests, some mutual benefits.'

At the sound of her own earnest speech dissipating into the virtual air around her, Leila started laughing. The arguments she'd been putting for centuries to Jasim, to her friends on Najib, to the Snakes on Nazdeek, seemed ridiculous now, embarrassing. How could she face the Aloof and claim that she had anything to offer them that they had not considered, and rejected, hundreds of thousands of years before? The Amalgam had never tried to keep its nature hidden. The Aloof would have watched them, studied them from afar, and consciously chosen isolation. To come here and list the advantages of contact as if they'd never crossed her hosts' minds was simply insulting.

Leila fell silent. If she had lost faith in her role as cultural envoy, at least she'd proved to her own satisfaction that there was something in here smarter than the slingshot fence the probes had encountered. The Aloof had not embraced her, but the whole endeavour had not been in vain. To wake in the bulge, even to silence, was far more than she'd ever had the right to hope for.

She said, 'Please, just bring me my husband now, then we'll leave you in peace.'

This entreaty was met in the same way as all the others. Leila resisted speculating again about experimental variables. She did not believe that a million-year-old civilisation was interested in testing her tolerance to isolation, robbing her of her companion and seeing how long she took to attempt suicide. The Aloof did not take orders from her; fine. If she was neither an experimental subject to be robbed of her sanity, nor a valued guest whose every wish was granted, there had to be some other relationship between them that she had yet to fathom. She had to be conscious for a reason.

She searched the sky for a hint of the node itself, or any other feature she might have missed, but she might as well have been living inside a star map, albeit one shorn of the usual annotations. The Milky Way, the plane of stars that bisected the sky, was hidden by the thicker clouds of gas and dust here, but Leila had her bearings; she knew which way led deeper into the bulge, and which way led back out to the disk.

She contemplated Tassef's distant sun with mixed emotions, as a sailor might look back on the last sight of land. As the yearning for that familiar place welled up, a cylinder of violet light appeared around her, encircling the direction of her gaze. For the first time, Leila felt her weightlessness interrupted: a gentle acceleration was carrying her forward along the imaginary beam.

'No! Wait!' She closed her eyes and curled into a ball. The acceleration halted, and when she opened her eyes the tunnel of light was gone.

She let herself float limply, paying no attention to anything in the sky, waiting to see what happened if she kept her mind free of any desire for travel.

After an hour like this, the phenomenon had not recurred. Leila turned her gaze in the opposite direction, into the bulge. She cleared her mind of all timidity and nostalgia and imagined the thrill of rushing deeper into this violent, spectacular, alien territory. At first there was no response from the scape, but then she focused her attention sharply in the direction of a second node, the one she'd hoped her transmission would be forwarded to from the first, on its way through the galactic core.

The same violet light, the same motion. This time, Leila waited a few heartbeats longer before she broke the spell.

Unless this was some pointlessly sadistic game, the Aloof were offering her a clear choice. She could return to Tassef, return to the Amalgam. She could announce that she'd put a toe in these mysterious waters, and lived to tell the tale. Or she could dive into the bulge, as deep as she'd ever imagined, and see where the network took her.

'No promises?' she asked. 'No guarantee I'll come out the other side? No intimations of contact, to tempt me further?' She was thinking aloud, she did not expect answers. Her hosts, she was beginning to conclude, viewed strangers through the prism of a strong, but very sharply delineated, sense of obligation. They sent back the insentient probes to their owners, scrupulously intact. They had woken this intruder to give her the choice: did she really want to go where her transmission suggested, or had she wandered in here like a lost child who just needed to find the way home? They would do her no harm, and send her on no journey without her consent, but those were the limits of their duty of care. They did not owe her any account of themselves. She would get no greeting, no hospitality, no conversation.

'What about Jasim? Will you give me a chance to consult with him?' She waited, picturing his face, willing his presence, hoping they might read her mind if her words were beyond them. If they could decode a yearning towards a point in the sky, surely this wish for companionship was not too difficult to comprehend? She tried variations, dwelling on the abstract structure of their intertwined data in the transmission, hoping this might clarify the object of her desire if his physical appearance meant nothing to them.

She remained alone.

The stars that surrounded her spelled out the only choices on offer. If she wanted to be with Jasim once more before she died, she had to make the same decision as he did.

Symmetry demanded that he faced the same dilemma.

How would he be thinking? He might be tempted to retreat to the safety of Tassef, but he'd reconciled with her in Shalouf for the sole purpose of following her into danger. He would understand that she'd want to go deeper, would want to push all the way through to Massa, opening up the shortcut through the core, proving it safe for future travellers.

Would he understand, too, that she'd feel a pang of guilt at this presumptuous line of thought, and that she'd contemplate making a sacrifice of her own? He had braved the unknown for her, and they had reaped the reward already: they had come closer to the Aloof than anyone in history. Why couldn't that be enough?

For all Leila knew, her hosts might not even wake her again before Massa. What would she be giving up if she turned back now?

More to the point, what would Jasim expect of her? That she'd march on relentlessly, following her obsession to the end, or that she'd put her love for him first?

The possibilities multiplied in an infinite regress. They knew each other as well as two people could, but they didn't carry each other's minds inside them.

Leila drifted through the limbo of stars, wondering if Jasim had already made his decision. Having seen that the Aloof were not the torturers he'd feared, had he already set out for Tassef, satisfied that she faced no real peril at their hands? Or had he reasoned that their experience at this single node meant nothing? This was not the Amalgam, the culture could be a thousand times more fractured.

This cycle of guesses and doubts led nowhere. If she tried to pursue it to the end she'd be paralysed. There were no guarantees; she could only choose the least worst case. If she returned to Tassef, only to find that Jasim had gone on alone through the bulge, it would be unbearable: she would have lost him for nothing. If that happened, she could try to follow him, returning to the bulge immediately, but she would already be centuries behind him.

If she went on to Massa, and it was Jasim who retreated, at least she'd know that he'd ended up in safety. She'd know, too, that he had not been desperately afraid for her, that the Aloof's benign indifference at this first node had been enough to persuade him that they'd do her no harm.

That was her answer: she had to continue, all the way to Massa. With the hope, but no promise, that Jasim would have thought the same way.

The decision made, she lingered in the scape, not from any second thoughts, but from a reluctance to give up lightly the opportunity she'd fought so hard to attain. She didn't know if any member of the Aloof was watching and listening to her, reading her thoughts, examining her desires. Perhaps they were so indifferent and incurious that they'd delegated everything to insentient software, and merely instructed their machines to babysit her while she made up her mind where she wanted to go. She still had to make one last attempt to reach them, or she would never die in peace.

'Maybe you're right,' she said. 'Maybe you've watched us for the last million years, and seen that we have nothing to offer you. Maybe our technology is backwards, our philosophy naïve, our customs bizarre, our manners appalling. If that's true, though, if we're so far beneath you, you could at least point us in the right direction. Offer us some kind of argument as to why we should change.'

Silence.

Leila said, 'All right. Forgive my impertinence. I have to tell you honestly, though, that we won't be the last to bother you. The Amalgam is full of people who will keep trying to find ways to reach you. This is going to go on for another million years, until we believe that we understand you. If that offends you, don't judge us too harshly. We can't help it. It's who we are.'

She closed her eyes, trying to assure herself that there was nothing she'd regret having left unsaid.

'Thank you for granting us safe passage,' she added, 'if that's what you're offering. I hope my people can return the favour one day, if there's anywhere you want to go.'

She opened her eyes and sought out her destination: deeper into the network, on towards the core.

10

The mountains outside the town of Astraahat started with a gentle slope that promised an easy journey, but gradually grew steeper. Similarly, the vegetation was low and sparse in the foothills, but became steadily thicker and taller the higher up the slope you went.

Jasim said, 'Enough.' He stopped and leant on his climbing stick.

'One more hour?' Leila pleaded.

He considered this. 'Half an hour resting, then half an hour walking?'

'One hour resting, then one hour walking.'

He laughed wearily. 'All right. One of each.'

The two of them hacked away at the undergrowth until there was a place to sit.

Jasim poured water from the canteen into her hands and she splashed her face clean.

They sat in silence for a while, listening to the sounds of the unfamiliar wildlife. Under the forest canopy it was almost twilight, and when Leila looked up into the small patch of sky above them she could see the stars of the bulge, like tiny, pale, translucent beads.

At times it felt like a dream, but the experience never really left her. The Aloof had woken her at every node, shown her the view, given her a choice. She had seen a thousand spectacles, from one side of the core to the other: cannibalistic novas, dazzling clusters of newborn stars, twin white dwarfs on the verge of collision. She had seen the black hole at the galaxy's centre, its accretion disk glowing with X-rays, slowly tearing stars apart.

It might have been an elaborate lie, a plausible simulation, but every detail accessible from disk-based observatories confirmed what she had witnessed. If anything had been changed, or hidden from her, it must have been small. Perhaps the artefacts of the Aloof themselves had been painted out of the view, though Leila thought it was just as likely that the marks they'd left on their territory were so subtle, anyway, that there'd been nothing to conceal.

Jasim said sharply, 'Where are you?'

She lowered her gaze and replied mildly, 'I'm here, with you. I'm just remembering.'

When they'd woken on Massa, surrounded by delirious, cheering Eavesdroppers, they'd been asked: *What happened in there?*

What did you see? Leila didn't know why she'd kept her mouth shut and turned to her husband before replying, instead of letting every detail come tumbling out immediately. Perhaps she just hadn't known where to begin.

For whatever reason, it was Jasim who had answered first. 'Nothing. We stepped through the gate on Tassef, and now here we are. On the other side of the bulge.'

For almost a month, she'd flatly refused to believe him. *Nothing? You saw nothing?* It had to be a lie, a joke. It had to be some kind of revenge.

That was not in his nature, and she knew it. Still, she'd clung to that explanation for as long as she could, until it became impossible to believe any longer, and she'd asked for his forgiveness.

Six months later, another traveller had spilled out of the bulge. One of the die-hard Listening Party pilgrims had followed in their wake and taken the shortcut. Like Jasim, this heptapod had seen nothing, experienced nothing.

Leila had struggled to imagine why she might have been singled out. So much for her theory that the Aloof felt morally obliged to check that each passenger on their network knew what they were doing, unless they'd decided that her actions were enough to demonstrate that intruders from the disk, considered generically, were making an informed choice. Could just one sample of a working, conscious version of their neighbours really be enough for them to conclude that they understood everything they needed to know? Could this capriciousness, instead, have been part of a strategy to lure in more visitors, with the enticing possibility that each one might, with luck, witness something far beyond all those who'd preceded them? Or had it been part of a scheme to discourage intruders by clouding the experience with uncertainty? The simplest act of discouragement would have been to discard all unwelcome transmissions, and the most effective incentive would have been to offer a few plain words of welcome, but then the Aloof would not have been the Aloof if they'd followed such reasonable dictates.

Jasim said, 'You know what I think. You wanted to wake so

badly, they couldn't refuse you. They could tell I didn't care as much. It was as simple as that.'

'What about the heptapod? It went in alone. It wasn't just tagging along to watch over someone else.'

He shrugged. 'Maybe it acted on the spur of the moment. They all seem unhealthily keen to me, whatever they're doing. Maybe the Aloof could discern its mood more clearly.'

Leila said, 'I don't believe a word of that.'

Jasim spread his hands in a gesture of acceptance. 'I'm sure you could change my mind in five minutes, if I let you. But if we walked back down this hill and waited for the next traveller from the bulge, and the next, until the reason some of them received the grand tour and some didn't finally became plain, there would still be another question, and another. Even if I wanted to live for ten thousand years more, I'd rather move on to something else. And in this last hour . . .' He trailed off.

Leila said, 'I know. You're right.'

She sat, listening to the strange chirps and buzzes emitted by creatures she knew nothing about. She could have absorbed every recorded fact about them in an instant, but she didn't care, she didn't need to know.

Someone else would come after them, to understand the Aloof, or advance that great, unruly, frustrating endeavour by the next increment. She and Jasim had made a start, that was enough. What they'd done was more than she could ever have imagined, back on Najib. Now, though, was the time to stop, while they were still themselves: enlarged by the experience, but not disfigured beyond recognition.

They finished their water, drinking the last drops. They left the canteen behind. Jasim took her hand and they climbed together, struggling up the slope side by side.

GLORY

1

An ingot of metallic hydrogen gleamed in the starlight, a narrow cylinder half a metre long with a mass of about a kilogram. To the naked eye it was a dense, solid object, but its lattice of tiny nuclei immersed in an insubstantial fog of electrons was one part matter to two hundred trillion parts empty space. A short distance away was a second ingot, apparently identical to the first, but composed of antihydrogen.

A sequence of finely tuned gamma-rays flooded into both cylinders. The protons that absorbed them in the first ingot spat out positrons and were transformed into neutrons, breaking their bonds to the electron cloud that glued them in place. In the second ingot, antiprotons became antineutrons.

A further sequence of pulses herded the neutrons together and forged them into clusters; the antineutrons were similarly rearranged. Both kinds of cluster were unstable, but in order to fall apart they first had to pass through a quantum state that would have strongly absorbed a component of the gamma-rays constantly raining down on them. Left to themselves, the probability of them being in this state would have increased rapidly, but each time they measurably failed to absorb the gamma-rays, the probability fell back to zero. The quantum Zeno effect endlessly reset the clock, holding the decay in check.

The next series of pulses began shifting the clusters into the space that had separated the original ingots. First neutrons, then antineutrons, were sculpted together in alternating layers. Though the clusters were ultimately unstable, while they persisted they were inert, sequestering their constituents and preventing them from annihilating their counterparts. The end point of this process of nuclear sculpting was a sliver of compressed matter and antimatter, sandwiched together into a needle one micron wide.

The gamma-ray lasers shut down, the Zeno effect withdrew its prohibitions. For the time it took a beam of light to cross a neutron, the needle sat motionless in space. Then it began to burn, and it began to move.

The needle was structured like a meticulously crafted firework, and its outer layers ignited first. No external casing could have channelled this blast, but the pattern of tensions woven into the needle's construction favoured one direction for the debris to be expelled. Particles streamed backwards; the needle moved forwards. The shock of acceleration could not have been borne by anything built from atomic-scale matter, but the pressure bearing down on the core of the needle prolonged its life, delaying the inevitable.

Layer after layer burnt itself away, blasting the dwindling remnant forward ever faster. By the time the needle had shrunk to a tenth of its original size it was moving at ninety-eight per cent of light-speed; to a bystander this could scarcely have been improved upon, but from the needle's perspective there was still room to slash its journey's duration by orders of magnitude.

When just one-thousandth of the needle remained, its time, compared to the neighbouring stars, was passing five hundred times more slowly. Still the layers kept burning, the protective clusters unravelling as the pressure on them was released. The needle could only reach close enough to light-speed to slow down time as much as it required if it could sacrifice a large enough proportion of its remaining mass. The core of the needle could only survive for a few trillionths of a second, while its journey would take two hundred million seconds as judged by the stars. The proportions had been carefully matched, though: out of the two kilograms of matter and antimatter that had been woven together at the launch, only a few million neutrons were needed as the final payload.

By one measure, seven years passed. For the needle, its last trillionths of a second unwound, its final layers of fuel blew away and at the moment its core was ready to explode it reached its destination, plunging from the near-vacuum of space straight into the heart of a star.

Even here, the density of matter was insufficient to stabilise the core, yet far too high to allow it to pass unhindered. The core was torn apart. But it did not go quietly, and the shockwaves it carved through the fusing plasma endured for a million kilometres: all the way through to the cooler outer layers on the opposite side of the star. These shockwaves were shaped by the payload that had formed them, and though the initial pattern imprinted on them by the disintegrating cluster of neutrons was enlarged and blurred by its journey, on an atomic scale it remained sharply defined. Like a mould stamped into the seething plasma it encouraged ionised molecular fragments to slip into the troughs and furrows that matched their shape, and then brought them together to react in ways that the plasma's random collisions would never have allowed. In effect, the shockwaves formed a web of catalysts, carefully laid out in both time and space, briefly transforming a small corner of the star into a chemical factory operating on a nanometre scale.

The products of this factory sprayed out of the star, riding the last traces of the shockwave's momentum: a few nanograms of elaborate, carbon-rich molecules, sheathed in a protective fullerene weave. Travelling at seven hundred kilometres per second, a fraction below the velocity needed to escape from the star completely, they climbed out of its gravity well, slowing as they ascended.

Four years passed, but the molecules were stable against the ravages of space. By the time they'd travelled a billion kilometres they had almost come to a halt, and they would have fallen back to die in the fires of the star that had forged them if their journey had not been timed so that the star's third planet, a gas giant, was waiting to urge them forward. As they fell towards it, the giant's third moon moved across their path. Eleven years after the needle's launch, its molecular offspring rained down on to the methane snow.

The tiny heat of their impact was not enough to damage them, but it melted a microscopic puddle in the snow. Surrounded by food, the molecular seeds began to grow. Within hours, the area was teeming with nanomachines, some mining the snow and the minerals beneath it, others assembling the bounty into an intricate structure, a rectangular panel a couple of metres wide.

From across the light-years, an elaborate sequence of gamma-ray pulses fell upon the panel. These pulses were the needle's true payload, the passengers for whom it had merely prepared the way, transmitted in its wake four years after its launch. The panel decoded and stored the data, and the army of nanomachines set to work again, this time following a far more elaborate blueprint. The miners were forced to look further afield to find all the elements that were needed, while the assemblers laboured to reach their goal through a sequence of intermediate stages, carefully designed to protect the final product from the vagaries of the local chemistry and climate.

After three months' work, two small fusion-powered spacecraft sat in the snow. Each one held a single occupant, waking for the first time in their freshly minted bodies, yet endowed with memories of an earlier life.

Joan switched on her communications console. Anne appeared on the screen, three short pairs of arms folded across her thorax in a posture of calm repose. They had both worn virtual bodies with the same anatomy before, but this was the first time they had become Noudah in the flesh.

'We're here. Everything worked,' Joan marvelled. The language she spoke was not her own, but the structure of her new brain and body made it second nature.

Anne said, 'Now comes the hard part.'

'Yes.' Joan looked out from the spacecraft's cockpit. In the distance, a fissured blue-grey plateau of water ice rose above the snow. Nearby, the nanomachines were busy disassembling the gamma-ray receiver. When they had erased all traces of their handiwork they would wander off into the snow and catalyse their own destruction.

Joan had visited dozens of planet-bound cultures in the past, taking on different bodies and languages as necessary, but those cultures had all been plugged in to the Amalgam, the meta-civilisation that spanned the galactic disk. However far from home she'd been, the means to return to familiar places had always been close at hand. The Noudah had only just mastered interplanetary flight, and they had no idea that the Amalgam existed. The closest node in the Amalgam's network was seven light-years away, and even that was out of bounds to her and Anne now: they had agreed not to risk disclosing its location to the Noudah, so any transmission they sent could only be directed to a decoy node that they'd set up more than twenty light-years away.

'It will be worth it,' Joan said.

Anne's Noudah face was immobile, but chromatophores sent a wave of violet and gold sweeping across her skin in an expression of cautious optimism. 'We'll see.' She tipped her head to the left, a gesture preceding a friendly departure.

Joan tipped her own head in response, as if she'd been doing so all her life. 'Be careful, my friend,' she said.

'You too.'

Anne's ship ascended so high on its chemical thrusters that it shrank to a speck before igniting its fusion engine and streaking away in a blaze of light. Joan felt a pang of loneliness; there was no predicting when they would be reunited.

Her ship's software was primitive; the whole machine had been scrupulously matched to the Noudah's level of technology. Joan knew how to fly it herself if necessary, and on a whim she switched off the autopilot and manually activated the ascent thrusters. The control panel was crowded, but having six hands helped.

2

The world the Noudah called home was the closest of the system's five planets to their sun. The average temperature was one hundred and twenty degrees Celsius, but the high atmospheric pressure allowed liquid water to exist across the entire surface. The chemistry and dynamics of the planet's crust had led to a relatively flat terrain, with a patchwork of dozens of disconnected seas but no globe-spanning ocean. From space, these seas appeared as silvery mirrors, bordered by a violet and brown tarnish of vegetation.

The Noudah were already leaving their most electromagnetically promiscuous phase of communications behind, but the short-lived oasis of Amalgam-level technology on Baneth, the gas giant's moon, had had no trouble eavesdropping on their chatter and preparing an updated cultural briefing which had been spliced into Joan's brain.

The planet was still divided into the same eleven political units as it had been fourteen years before, the time of the last broadcasts that had reached the node before Joan's departure. Tira and Ghahar, the two dominant nations in terms of territory, economic activity and military power, also occupied the vast majority of significant Niah archaeological sites.

Joan had expected that they'd be noticed as soon as they left Baneth – the exhaust from their fusion engines glowed like the sun – but their departure had triggered no obvious response, and now that they were coasting they'd be far harder to spot. As Anne drew closer to the home world, she sent a message to Tira's traffic control centre. Joan tuned in to the exchange.

'I come in peace from another star,' Anne said. 'I seek permission to land.'

There was a delay of several seconds more than the light-speed lag, then a terse response. 'Please identify yourself and state your location.'

Anne transmitted her coordinates and flight plan.

'We confirm your location, please identify yourself.'

'My name is Anne. I come from another star.'

There was a long pause, then a different voice answered. 'If you are from Ghahar, please explain your intentions.'

'I am not from Ghahar.'

'Why should I believe that? Show yourself.'

'I've taken the same shape as your people, in the hope of living among you for a while.' Anne opened a video channel and showed them her unremarkable Noudah face. 'But there's a signal being transmitted from these coordinates that might persuade you that I'm telling the truth.' She gave the location of the decoy node, twenty light-years away, and specified a frequency. The signal coming from the node contained an image of the very same face.

This time, the silence stretched out for several minutes. It would take a while for the Tirans to confirm the true distance of the radio source.

'You do not have permission to land. Please enter this orbit, and we will rendezvous and board your ship.'

Parameters for the orbit came through on the data channel. Anne said, 'As you wish.'

Minutes later, Joan's instruments picked up three fusion ships being launched from Tiran bases. When Anne reached the prescribed orbit, Joan listened anxiously to the instructions the Tirans issued. Their tone sounded wary, but they were entitled to treat this stranger with caution, all the more so if they believed Anne's claim.

Joan was accustomed to a very different kind of reception, but then the members of the Amalgam had spent hundreds of millennia establishing a framework of trust. They also benefited from a milieu in which most kinds of force had been rendered ineffectual; when everyone had back-ups of themselves scattered around the galaxy, it required a vastly disproportionate effort to inconvenience someone, let alone kill them. By any reasonable measure, honesty and cooperation yielded far richer rewards than subterfuge and slaughter.

Nonetheless, each individual culture had its roots in a biological heritage that gave rise to behaviour governed more by ancient urges than contemporary realities, and even when they mastered the technology to choose their own nature, the precise set of traits they preserved was up to them. In the worst case, a species still saddled with inappropriate drives but empowered by advanced technology could wreak havoc. The Noudah deserved to be treated with courtesy and respect, but they did not yet belong in the Amalgam.

The Tirans' own exchanges were not on open channels, so once they had entered Anne's ship Joan could only guess what was happening. She waited until two of the ships had returned to the surface, then sent her own message to Ghahar's traffic control.

'I come in peace from another star. I seek permission to land.'

3

The Ghahari allowed Joan to fly her ship straight down to the surface. She wasn't sure if this was because they were more trusting, or if they were afraid that the Tirans might try to interfere if she lingered in orbit.

The landing site was a bare plain of chocolate-coloured sand. The air shimmered in the heat, the distortions intensified by the thickness of the atmosphere, making the horizon waver as if seen through molten glass. Joan waited in the cockpit as three trucks approached; they all came to a halt some twenty metres away. A voice over the radio instructed her to leave the ship; she complied, and after she'd stood in the open for a minute, a lone Noudah left one of the trucks and walked towards her.

'I'm Pirit,' she said. 'Welcome to Ghahar.' Her gestures were courteous but restrained.

'I'm Joan. Thank you for your hospitality.'

'Your impersonation of our biology is impeccable.' There was a trace of scepticism in Pirit's tone; Joan had pointed the Ghahari to her own portrait being broadcast from the decoy node, but she had to admit that in the context her lack of exotic technology and traits would make it harder to accept the implications of that transmission.

'In my culture, it's a matter of courtesy to imitate one's hosts as closely as possible.'

Pirit hesitated, as if pondering whether to debate the merits of such a custom, but then rather than quibbling over the niceties of interspecies etiquette she chose to confront the real issue head-on. 'If you're a Tiran spy, or a defector, the sooner you admit that the better.'

'That's very sensible advice, but I'm neither.'

The Noudah wore no clothing as such, but Pirit had a belt with a number of pouches. She took a hand-held scanner from one and ran it over Joan's body. Joan's briefing suggested that it was probably only checking for metal, volatile explosives and radiation; the technology to image her body or search for pathogens would not be so portable. In any case, she was a healthy, unarmed Noudah down to the molecular level.

Pirit escorted her to one of the trucks and invited her to recline in a section at the back. Another Noudah drove while Pirit watched over Joan. They soon arrived at a small complex of buildings a couple of kilometres from where the ship had touched down. The walls, roofs and floors of the buildings were all made from the local sand, cemented with an adhesive that the Noudah secreted from their own bodies.

Inside, Joan was given a thorough medical examination, including three kinds of full-body scan. The Noudah who examined her treated her with a kind of detached efficiency devoid of any pleasantries; she wasn't sure if that was their standard bedside manner, or a kind of glazed shock at having been told of her claimed origins.

Pirit took her to an adjoining room and offered her a couch. The Noudah anatomy did not allow for sitting, but they liked to recline.

Pirit remained standing. 'How did you come here?' she asked.

'You've seen my ship. I flew it from Baneth.'

'And how did you reach Baneth?'

'I'm not free to discuss that,' Joan replied cheerfully.

'Not free?' Pirit's face clouded with silver, as if she was genuinely perplexed.

Joan said, 'You understand me perfectly. Please don't tell me there's nothing *you're* not free to discuss with me.'

'You certainly didn't fly that ship twenty light-years.'

'No, I certainly didn't.'

Pirit hesitated. 'Did you come through the Cataract?' The Cataract was a black hole, a remote partner to the Noudah's sun; they orbited each other at a distance of about eighty billion kilometres. The name came from its telescopic appearance: a dark circle ringed by a distortion in the background of stars, like some kind of visual aberration. The Tirans and Ghahari were in a race to be the first to visit this extraordinary neighbour, but as yet neither of them were quite up to the task.

'*Through* the Cataract? I think your scientists have already proven that black holes aren't shortcuts to anywhere.'

'Our scientists aren't always right.'

'Neither are ours,' Joan admitted, 'but all the evidence points in one direction: black holes aren't doorways, they're shredding machines.'

'So you travelled the whole twenty light-years?'

'More than that,' Joan said truthfully, 'from my original home. I've spent half my life travelling.'

'Faster than light?' Pirit suggested hopefully.

'No. That's impossible.'

They circled around the question a dozen more times, before Pirit finally changed her tune from *how* to *why?*

'I'm a xenomathematician,' Joan said. 'I've come here in the hope of collaborating with your archaeologists in their study of Niah artefacts.'

Pirit was stunned. 'What do you know about the Niah?'

'Not as much as I'd like to.' Joan gestured at her Noudah body. 'As I'm sure you've already surmised, we've listened to your broadcasts for some time, so we know pretty much what an ordinary Noudah knows. That includes the basic facts about the Niah. Historically they've been referred to as your ancestors, though the latest studies suggest that you and they really just have an earlier common ancestor. They died out about a million years ago, but there's evidence that they might have had a sophisticated culture for as long as three million years. There's no indication that they ever developed space flight. Basically, once they achieved material comfort, they seem to have devoted themselves to various artforms, including mathematics.'

'So you've travelled twenty light-years just to look at Niah tablets?' Pirit was incredulous.

'Any culture that spent three million years doing mathematics must have something to teach us.'

'Really?' Pirit's face became blue with disgust. 'In the ten thousand years since we discovered the wheel, we've already reached halfway to the Cataract. They wasted their time on useless abstractions.'

Joan said, 'I come from a culture of spacefarers myself, so I respect your achievements. But I don't think anyone really knows what the Niah achieved. I'd like to find out, with the help of your people.'

Pirit was silent for a while. 'What if we say no?'

'Then I'll leave empty-handed.'

'What if we insist that you remain with us?'

'Then I'll die here, empty-handed.' On her command, this body would expire in an instant; she could not be held and tortured.

Pirit said angrily, 'You must be willing to trade *something* for the privilege you're demanding!'

'Requesting, not demanding,' Joan insisted gently. 'And what I'm willing to offer is my own culture's perspective on Niah mathematics. If you ask your archaeologists and mathematicians, I'm sure they'll tell you that there are many things written in the Niah tablets that they don't yet understand. My colleague and I' – neither of them had mentioned Anne before, but Joan was sure that Pirit knew all about her – 'simply want to shed as much light as we can on this subject.'

Pirit said bitterly, 'You won't even tell us how you came to our world. Why should we trust you to share whatever you discover about the Niah?'

'Interstellar travel is no great mystery,' Joan countered. 'You know all the basic science already; making it work is just a matter of persistence. If you're left to develop your own technology, you might even come up with better methods than we have.'

'So we're expected to be patient, to discover these things for ourselves . . . but you can't wait a few centuries for us to decipher the Niah artefacts?'

Joan said bluntly, 'The present Noudah culture, both here and in Tira, seems to hold the Niah in contempt. Dozens of partially excavated sites containing Niah artefacts are under threat from irrigation projects and other developments. That's the reason we couldn't wait. We needed to come here and offer our assistance, before the last traces of the Niah disappeared for ever.'

Pirit did not reply, but Joan hoped she knew what her interrogator was thinking: *Nobody would cross twenty light-years for a few worthless scribblings. Perhaps we've underestimated the Niah. Perhaps our ancestors have left us a great secret, a great legacy. And perhaps the fastest – perhaps the only – way to uncover it is to give this impertinent, irritating alien exactly what she wants.*

4

The sun was rising ahead of them as they reached the top of the hill. Sando turned to Joan, and his face became green with pleasure. 'Look behind you,' he said.

Joan did as he asked. The valley below was hidden in fog, and it had settled so evenly that she could see their shadows in the dawn light, stretched out across the top of the fog layer. Around the shadow of her head was a circular halo like a small rainbow.

'We call it the Niah's light,' Sando said. 'In the old days, people used to say that the halo proved that the Niah blood was strong in you.'

Joan said, 'The only trouble with that hypothesis being that *you* see it around *your* head . . . and I see it around mine.' On Earth, the phenomenon was known as a 'glory'. The particles of fog were scattering the sunlight back towards them, turning it one hundred and eighty degrees. To look at the shadow of your own head was to face directly away from the sun, so the halo always appeared around the observer's shadow.

'I suppose you're the final proof that Niah blood has nothing to do with it,' Sando mused.

'That's assuming I'm telling you the truth, and I really can see it around my own head.'

'And assuming,' Sando added, 'that the Niah really did stay at home, and didn't wander around the galaxy spreading their progeny.'

They came over the top of the hill and looked down into the adjoining riverine valley. The sparse brown grass of the hillside gave way to a lush violet growth closer to the water. Joan's arrival had delayed the flooding of the valley, but even alien interest in the Niah had only bought the archaeologists an extra year. The dam was part of a long-planned agricultural development, and however tantalising the possibility that Joan might reveal some priceless insight hidden among the Niah's 'useless abstractions', that vague promise could only compete with more tangible considerations for a limited time.

Part of the hill had fallen away in a landslide a few centuries before, revealing more than a dozen beautifully preserved strata. When Joan and Sando reached the excavation site, Rali and Surat were already at work, clearing away soft sedimentary rock from a layer that Sando had dated as belonging to the Niah's 'twilight' period.

Pirit had insisted that only Sando, the senior archaeologist, be told about Joan's true nature; Joan refused to lie to anyone, but had agreed to tell her colleagues only that she was a mathematician and that she was not permitted to discuss her past. At first this had made them guarded and resentful, no doubt because they assumed that she was some kind of spy sent by the authorities to watch over them. Later it had dawned on them that she was genuinely interested in their work, and that the absurd restrictions on her topics of conversation were not of her own choosing. Nothing about the Noudah's language or appearance correlated strongly with their recent division into nations – with no oceans to cross, and a long history of migration they were more or less geographically homogeneous – but Joan's odd name and occasional *faux pas* could still be ascribed to some mysterious exoticism. Rali and Surat seemed content to assume that she was a defector from one of the smaller nations, and that her history could not be made explicit for obscure political reasons.

'There are more tablets here, very close to the surface,' Rali announced excitedly. 'The acoustics are unmistakable.' Ideally they would have excavated the entire hillside, but they did not have the time or the labour, so they were using acoustic tomography to identify likely deposits of accessible Niah writing, and then concentrating their efforts on those spots.

The Niah had probably had several ephemeral forms of written communication, but when they found something worth publishing, it stayed published: they carved their symbols into a ceramic that made diamond seem like tissue paper. It was almost unheard of for the tablets to be broken, but they were small, and multi-tablet works were sometimes widely dispersed. Niah technology could probably have carved three million years' worth of knowledge on to the head of a pin – they seemed not to have invented nanomachines, but they were into high-quality bulk materials and precision engineering – but for whatever reason they had chosen legibility to the naked eye above other considerations.

Joan made herself useful, taking acoustic readings further along the slope, while Sando watched over his students as they came closer to the buried Niah artefacts. She had learnt not to hover around expectantly when a discovery was imminent; she was treated far more warmly if she waited to be summoned. The tomography unit was almost foolproof, using satellite navigation to track its position and software to analyse the signals it gathered; all it really needed was someone to drag it along the rock face at a suitable pace.

Through the corner of her eye, Joan noticed her shadow on the rocks flicker and grow complicated. She looked up to see three dazzling beads of light flying west out of the sun. She might have assumed that the fusion ships were doing something useful, but the media was full of talk of 'military exercises', which meant the Tirans and the Ghahari engaging in expensive, belligerent gestures in orbit, trying to convince each other of their superior skills, technology, or sheer strength of numbers. For people with no real differences apart from a few centuries of recent history, they could puff up their minor political disputes into matters of the utmost solemnity. It might almost have been funny, if the idiots hadn't incinerated hundreds of thousands of each other's citizens every few decades, not to mention playing callous and often deadly games with the lives of the inhabitants of smaller nations.

'Jown! Jown! Come and look at this!' Surat called to her. Joan switched off the tomography unit and jogged towards the archaeologists, suddenly conscious of her body's strangeness. Her legs were stumpy but strong, and her balance as she ran came not from arms and shoulders but from the swish of her muscular tail.

'It's a significant mathematical result,' Rali informed her proudly when she reached them. He'd pressure-washed the sandstone away from the near-indestructible ceramic of the tablet, and it was only a matter of holding the surface at the right angle to the light to see the etched writing stand out as crisply and starkly as it would have a million years before.

Rali was not a mathematician, and he was not offering his own opinion on the theorem the tablet stated; the Niah themselves had a clear set of typographical conventions which they used to distinguish between everything from minor lemmas to the most celebrated theorems. The size and decorations of the symbols labelling the theorem attested to its value in the Niah's eyes.

Joan read the theorem carefully. The proof was not included on the same tablet, but the Niah had a way of expressing their results that made you believe them as soon as you read them; in this case the definitions of the terms needed to state the theorem were so beautifully chosen that the result seem almost inevitable.

The theorem itself was expressed as a commuting hypercube, one of the Niah's favourite forms. You could think of a square with four different sets of mathematical objects associated with each of its corners, and a way of mapping one set into another associated with each edge of the square. If the maps commuted, then going across the top of the square, then down, had exactly the same effect as going down the left edge of the square, then across: either way, you mapped each element from the top-left set into the same element of the bottom-right set. A similar kind of result might hold for sets and maps that could naturally be placed at the corners and edges of a cube, or a hypercube of any dimension. It was also possible for the square faces in these structures to stand for relationships that held between the maps between sets, and for cubes to describe relationships between those relationships, and so on.

That a theorem took this form didn't guarantee its importance; it was easy to cook up trivial examples of sets and maps that commuted. The Niah didn't carve trivia into their timeless ceramic, though, and this theorem was no exception. The seven-dimensional commuting hypercube established a dazzlingly elegant correspondence between seven distinct, major branches of Niah mathematics, intertwining their most important concepts into a unified whole. It was a result Joan had never seen before: no mathematician anywhere in the Amalgam, or in any ancestral culture she had studied, had reached the same insight.

She explained as much of this as she could to the three archaeologists; they couldn't take in all the details, but their faces became orange with fascination when she sketched what she thought the result would have meant to the Niah themselves.

'This isn't quite the Big Crunch,' she joked, 'but it must have made them think they were getting closer.' *The Big Crunch* was her nickname for the mythical result that the Niah had aspired to reach: a unification of every field of mathematics that they considered significant. To find such a thing would not have meant the end of mathematics – it would not have subsumed every last conceivable, interesting mathematical truth – but it would certainly have marked a point of closure for the Niah's own style of investigation.

'I'm sure they found it,' Surat insisted. 'They reached the Big Crunch, then they had nothing more to live for.'

Rali was scathing. 'So the whole culture committed collective suicide?'

'Not actively, no,' Surat replied. 'But it was the search that had kept them going.'

'Entire cultures don't lose the will to live,' Rali said. 'They get wiped out by external forces: disease, invasion, changes in climate.'

'The Niah survived for three million years,' Surat countered. 'They had the means to weather all of those forces. Unless they were wiped out by alien invaders with vastly superior technology.' She turned to Joan. 'What do you think?'

'About aliens destroying the Niah?'

'I was joking about the aliens. But what about the mathematics? What if they found the Big Crunch?'

'There's more to life than mathematics,' Joan said. 'But not much more.'

Sando said, 'And there's more to this find than one tablet. If we get back to work, we might have the proof in our hands before sunset.'

5

Joan briefed Halzoun by video link while Sando prepared the evening meal. Halzoun was the mathematician Pirit had appointed to supervise her, but apparently his day job was far too important to allow him to travel. Joan was grateful; Halzoun was the most tedious Noudah she had encountered. He could understand the Niah's work when she explained it to him, but he seemed to have no interest in it for its own sake. He spent most of their conversations trying to catch her out in some deception or contradiction, and the rest pressing her to imagine military or commercial applications of the Niah's gloriously useless insights. Sometimes she played along with this infantile fantasy, hinting at potential superweapons based on exotic physics that might come tumbling out of the vacuum, if only one possessed the right Niah theorems to coax them into existence.

Sando was her minder too, but at least he was more subtle about it. Pirit had insisted that she stay in his shelter, rather than sharing Rali and Surat's; Joan didn't mind, because with Sando she didn't have the stress of having to keep quiet about everything. Privacy and modesty were non-issues for the Noudah, and Joan had become Noudah enough not to care herself. Nor was there any danger of their proximity leading to a sexual bond; the Noudah had a complex system of biochemical cues that meant desire only arose in couples with a suitable mixture of genetic differences and similarities. She would have had to search a crowded Noudah city for a week to find someone to lust after, though at least it would have been guaranteed to be mutual.

After they'd eaten, Sando said, 'You should be happy. That was our best find yet.'

'I am happy.' Joan made a conscious effort to exhibit a viridian tinge. 'It was the first new result I've seen on this planet. It was the reason I came here, the reason I travelled so far.'

'Something's wrong, though, I think.'

'I wish I could have shared the news with my friend,' Joan admitted. Pirit claimed to be negotiating with the Tirans to allow Anne to communicate with her, but Joan was not convinced that he was genuinely trying. She was sure that he would have relished the thought of listening in on a conversation between the two of them – while forcing them to speak Noudah, of course – in the hope that they'd slip up and reveal something useful, but at the same time he would have had to face the fact that the Tirans would be listening too. What an excruciating dilemma.

'You should have brought a communications link with you,'

Sando suggested. 'A home-style one, I mean. Nothing we could eavesdrop on.'

'We couldn't do that,' Joan said.

He pondered this. 'You really are afraid of us, aren't you? You think the smallest technological trinket will be enough to send us straight to the stars, and then you'll have a horde of rampaging barbarians to deal with.'

'We know how to deal with barbarians,' Joan said coolly.

Sando's face grew dark with mirth. 'Now *I'm* afraid.'

'I just wish I knew what was happening to her,' Joan said. 'What she was doing, how they were treating her.'

'Probably much the same as we're treating you,' Sando suggested. 'We're really not that different.' He thought for a moment. 'There was something I wanted to show you.' He brought over his portable console, and summoned up an article from a Tiran journal. 'See what a borderless world we live in,' he joked.

The article was entitled 'Seekers and Spreaders: What We Must Learn from the Niah'. Sando said, 'This might give you some idea of how they're thinking over there. Jaqad is an academic archaeologist, but she's also very close to the people in power.'

Joan read from the console while Sando made repairs to their shelter, secreting a molasses-like substance from a gland at the tip of his tail and spreading it over the cracks in the walls.

There were two main routes a culture could take, Jaqad argued, once it satisfied its basic material needs. One was to think and study: to stand back and observe, to seek knowledge and insight from the world around it. The other was to invest its energy in entrenching its good fortune.

The Niah had learnt a great deal in three million years, but in the end it had not been enough to save them. Exactly what had killed them was still a matter of speculation, but it was hard to believe that if they had colonised other worlds they would have vanished on all of them. 'Had the Niah been Spreaders,' Jaqad wrote, 'we might expect a visit from them, or them from us, sometime in the coming centuries.'

The Noudah, in contrast, were determined Spreaders. Once

they had the means, they would plant colonies across the galaxy. They would, Jaqad was sure, create new biospheres, re-engineer stars, and even alter space and time to guarantee their survival. The growth of their empire would come first; any knowledge that failed to serve that purpose would be a mere distraction. 'In any competition between Seekers and Spreaders, it is a Law of History that the Spreaders must win out in the end. Seekers, such as the Niah, might hog resources and block the way, but in the long run their own nature will be their downfall.'

Joan stopped reading. 'When you look out into the galaxy with your telescopes,' she asked Sando, 'how many *re-engineered stars* do you see?'

'Would we recognise them?'

'Yes. Natural stellar processes aren't that complicated; your scientists already know everything there is to know about the subject.'

'I'll take your word for that. So . . . you're saying Jaqad is wrong? The Niah themselves never left this world, but the galaxy already belongs to creatures more like them than like us?'

'It's not Noudah versus Niah,' Joan said. 'It's a matter of how a culture's perspective changes with time. Once a species conquers disease, modifies their biology and spreads even a short distance beyond their home world, they usually start to relax a bit. The territorial imperative isn't some timeless Law of History; it belongs to a certain phase.'

'What if it persists, though? Into a later phase?'

'That can cause friction,' Joan admitted.

'Nevertheless, no Spreaders have conquered the galaxy?'

'Not yet.'

Sando went back to his repairs; Joan read the rest of the article. She'd thought she'd already grasped the lesson demanded by the subtitle, but it turned out that Jaqad had something more specific in mind.

'Having argued this way, how can I defend my own field of study from the very same charges as I have brought against the Niah? Having grasped the essential character of this doomed race, why should we waste our time and resources studying them further?

'The answer is simple. We still do not know exactly how and why the Niah died, but when we do, that could turn out to be the most important discovery in history. When we finally leave our world behind, we should not expect to find only other Spreaders to compete with us, as honourable opponents in battle. There will be Seekers as well, blocking the way: tired, old races squatting uselessly on their hoards of knowledge and wealth.

'Time will defeat them in the end, but we already waited three million years to be born; we should have no patience to wait again. If we can learn how the Niah died, that will be our key, that will be our weapon. If we know the Seekers' weakness, we can find a way to hasten their demise.'

6

The proof of the Niah's theorem turned out to be buried deep in the hillside, but over the following days they extracted it all.

It was as beautiful and satisfying as Joan could have wished, merging six earlier, simpler theorems while extending the techniques used in their proofs. She could even see hints at how the same methods might be stretched further to yield still stronger results. 'The Big Crunch' had always been a slightly mocking, irreverent term, but now she was struck anew by how little justice it did to the real trend that had fascinated the Niah. It was not a matter of everything in mathematics collapsing in on itself, with one branch turning out to have been merely a recapitulation of another under a different guise. Rather, the principle was that every sufficiently beautiful mathematical system was rich enough to mirror *in part* – and sometimes in a complex and distorted fashion – every other sufficiently beautiful system. Nothing became sterile and redundant, nothing proved to have been a waste of time, but everything was shown to be magnificently intertwined.

After briefing Halzoun, Joan used the satellite dish to transmit the theorem and its proof to the decoy node. That had been the deal with Pirit: anything she learnt from the Niah belonged to the whole galaxy, as long as she explained it to her hosts first.

The archaeologists moved across the hillside, hunting for more artefacts in the same layer of sediment. Joan was eager to see what else the same group of Niah might have published. One possible eight-dimensional hypercube was hovering in her mind; if she'd sat down and thought about it for a few decades she might have worked out the details herself, but the Niah did what they did so well that it would have seemed crass to try to follow clumsily in their footsteps when their own immaculately polished results might simply be lying in the ground, waiting to be uncovered.

A month after the discovery, Joan was woken by the sound of an intruder moving through the shelter. She knew it wasn't Sando; even as she slept an ancient part of her Noudah brain was listening to his heartbeat. The stranger's heart was too quiet to hear, which required great discipline, but the shelter's flexible adhesive made the floor emit a characteristic squeak beneath even the gentlest footsteps. As she rose from her couch she heard Sando waking, and she turned in his direction.

Bright torchlight on his face dazzled her for a moment. The intruder held two knives to Sando's respiratory membranes; a deep enough cut there would mean choking to death, in excruciating pain. The nanomachines that had built Joan's body had wired extensive skills in unarmed combat into her brain, and one scenario involving a feigned escape attempt followed by a sideways flick of her powerful tail was already playing out in the back of her mind, but as yet she could see no way to guarantee that Sando came through it all unharmed.

She said, 'What do you want?'

The intruder remained in darkness. 'Tell me about the ship that brought you to Baneth.'

'Why?'

'Because it would be a shame to shred your colleague here, just when his work was going so well.' Sando refused to show any emotion on his face, but the blank pallor itself was as stark an expression of fear as anything Joan could imagine.

She said, 'There's a coherent state that can be prepared for a quark-gluon plasma in which virtual black holes catalyse baryon decay. In effect, you can turn all of your fuel's rest mass into photons, yielding the most efficient exhaust stream possible.' She recited a long list of technical details. The claimed baryon decay process didn't actually exist, but the pseudo-physics under-pinning it was mathematically consistent, and could not be ruled out by anything the Noudah had yet observed. She and Anne had prepared an entire fictitious science and technology, and even a fictitious history of their culture, precisely for emergencies like this; they could spout red herrings for a decade if necessary, and never get caught out contradicting themselves.

'That wasn't so hard, was it?' the intruder gloated.

'What now?'

'You're going to take a trip with me. If you do this nicely, nobody needs to get hurt.'

Something moved in the shadows, and the intruder screamed in pain. Joan leapt forward and knocked one of the knives out of his hand with her tail; the other knife grazed Sando's membrane, but a second tail whipped out of the darkness and intervened. As the intruder fell backwards, the beam of his torch revealed Surat and Rali tensed beside him, and a pick buried deep in his side.

Joan's rush of combat hormones suddenly faded, and she let out a long, deep wail of anguish. Sando was unscathed, but a stream of dark liquid was pumping out of the intruder's wound.

Surat was annoyed. 'Stop blubbing, and help us tie up this Tiran cousin-fucker.'

'Tie him up? You've killed him!'

'Don't be stupid, that's just sheath fluid.' Joan recalled her Noudah anatomy; sheath fluid was like oil in a hydraulic machine. You could lose it all and it would cost you most of the strength in your limbs and tail, but you wouldn't die, and your body would make more eventually.

Rali found some cable and they trussed up the intruder. Sando

was shaken, but he seemed to be recovering. He took Joan aside.
'I'm going to have to call Pirit.'

'I understand. But what will she do to these two?' She wasn't
sure exactly how much Rali and Surat had heard, but it was
certain to have been more than Pirit wanted them to know.

'Don't worry about that, I can protect them.'

Just before dawn someone sent by Pirit arrived in a truck to take
the intruder away. Sando declared a rest day, and Rali and Surat
went back to their shelter to sleep. Joan went for a walk along the
hillside; she didn't feel like sleeping.

Sando caught up with her. He said, 'I told them you'd been
working on a military research project, and you were exiled here
for some political misdemeanour.'

'And they believed you?'

'All they heard was half of a conversation full of incomprehensible physics. All they know is that someone thought you
were worth kidnapping.'

Joan said, 'I'm sorry about what happened.'

Sando hesitated. 'What did you expect?'

Joan was stung. 'One of us went to Tira, one of us came here.
We thought that would keep everyone happy!'

'We're Spreaders,' said Sando. 'Give us one of anything, and we
want two. Especially if our enemy has the other one. Did you
really think you could come here, do a bit of fossicking, and then
simply fly away without changing a thing?'

'Your culture has always believed there were other civilisations
in the galaxy. Our existence hardly came as a shock.'

Sando's face became yellow, an expression of almost parental
reproach. 'Believing in something in the abstract is not the same
as having it dangled in front of you. We were never going to have
an existential crisis at finding out that we're not unique; the Niah
might be related to us, but they were still alien enough to get us
used to the idea. But did you really think we were just going to
relax and accept your refusal to share your technology? That one
of you went to the Tirans only makes it worse for the Ghahari,

and vice versa. Both governments are going absolutely crazy, each one terrified that the other has found a way to make its alien talk.'

Joan stopped walking. 'The war games, the border skirmishes? You're blaming all of that on Anne and me?'

Sando's body sagged wearily. 'To be honest, I don't know all the details. And if it's any consolation, I'm sure we would have found another reason if you hadn't come along.'

Joan said, 'Maybe I should leave.' She was tired of these people, tired of her body, tired of being cut off from civilisation. She had rescued one beautiful Niah theorem and sent it out into the Amalgam. Wasn't that enough?

'It's up to you,' Sando replied. 'But you might as well stay until they flood the valley. Another year isn't going to change anything. What you've done to this world has already been done. For us, there's no going back.'

7

Joan stayed with the archaeologists as they moved across the hillside. They found tablets bearing Niah drawings and poetry, which no doubt had their virtues but to Joan seemed bland and opaque. Sando and his students relished these discoveries as much as the theorems; to them, the Niah culture was a vast jigsaw puzzle, and any clue that filled in the details of their history was as good as any other.

Sando would have told Pirit everything he'd heard from Joan the night the intruder came, so she was surprised that she hadn't been summoned for a fresh interrogation to flesh out the details. Perhaps the Ghahari physicists were still digesting her elaborate gobbledygook, trying to decide if it made sense. In her more cynical moments she wondered if the intruder might have been Ghahari himself, sent by Pirit to exploit her friendship with Sando. Perhaps Sando had even been in on it, and Rali and Surat as well. The possibility made her feel as if she was living in a fabricated world, a scape in which nothing was real and nobody could be trusted. The only thing she was certain that the Ghaharis could not have faked was the Niah artefacts. The mathematics verified itself; everything else was subject to doubt and paranoia.

Summer came, burning away the morning fogs. The Noudah's idea of heat was very different from Joan's previous perceptions, but even the body she now wore found the midday sun oppressive. She willed herself to be patient. There was still a chance that the Niah had taken a few more steps towards their grand vision of a unified mathematics, and carved their final discoveries into the form that would outlive them by a million years.

When the lone fusion ship appeared high in the afternoon sky, Joan resolved to ignore it. She glanced up once, but she kept dragging the tomography unit across the ground. She was sick of thinking about Tiran-Ghahari politics. They had played their childish games for centuries; she would not take the blame for this latest outbreak of provocation.

Usually the ships flew by, disappearing within minutes, showing off their power and speed. This one lingered, weaving back and forth across the sky like some dazzling insect performing an elaborate mating dance. Joan's second shadow darted around her feet, hammering a strangely familiar rhythm into her brain.

She looked up, disbelieving. The motion of the ship was following the syntax of a gestural language she had learnt on another planet, in another body, a dozen lifetimes ago. The only other person on this world who could know that language was Anne.

She glanced towards the archaeologists a hundred metres away, but they seemed to be paying no attention to the ship. She switched off the tomography unit and stared into the sky. *I'm listening, my friend. What's happening? Did they give you back your ship? Have you had enough of this world, and decided to go home?*

Anne told the story in shorthand, compressed and elliptic. The Tirans had found a tablet bearing a theorem: the last of the Niah's discoveries, the pinnacle of their achievements. Her minders had not let her study it, but they had contrived a situation making it easy for her to steal it, and to steal this ship. They had wanted her to take it and run, in the hope that she would lead them to something they valued far more than any ancient mathematics: an advanced spacecraft, or some magical stargate at the edge of the system.

But Anne wasn't fleeing anywhere. She was high above Ghahar, reading the tablet, and now she would paint what she read across the sky for Joan to see.

Sando approached. 'We're in danger, we have to move.'

'Danger? That's my friend up there! She's not going to shoot a missile at us!'

'Your friend?' Sando seemed confused. As he spoke, three more ships came into view, lower and brighter than the first. 'I've been told that the Tirans are going to strike the valley, to bury the Niah sites. We need to get over the hill and indoors, to get some protection from the blast.'

'Why would the Tirans attack the Niah sites? That makes no sense to me.'

Sando said, 'Nor me, but I don't have time to argue.'

The three ships were menacing Anne's, pursuing her, trying to drive her away. Joan had no idea if they were Ghahari defending their territory, or Tirans harassing her in the hope that she would flee and reveal the nonexistent shortcut to the stars, but Anne was staying put, still weaving the same gestural language into her manoeuvres even as she dodged her pursuers, spelling out the Niah's glorious finalé.

Joan said, 'You go. I have to see this.' She tensed, ready to fight him if necessary.

Sando took something from his tool belt and peppered her side with holes. Joan gasped with pain and crumpled to the ground as the sheath fluid poured out of her.

Rali and Surat helped carry her to the shelter. Joan caught glimpses of the fiery ballet in the sky, but not enough to make sense of it, let alone reconstruct it.

They put her on her couch inside the shelter. Sando bandaged her side and gave her water to sip. He said, 'I'm sorry I had to do that, but if anything had happened to you I would have been held responsible.'

Surat kept ducking outside to check on the 'battle', then reporting excitedly on the state of play. 'The Tiran's still up there, they can't get rid of it. I don't know why they haven't shot it down yet.'

Because the Tirans were the ones pursuing Anne, and they didn't want her dead. But for how long would the Ghahari tolerate this violation?

Anne's efforts could not be allowed to come to nothing. Joan struggled to recall the constellations she'd last seen in the night sky. At the node they'd departed from, powerful telescopes were constantly trained on the Noudah's home world. Anne's ship was easily bright enough, its gestures wide enough, to be resolved from seven light-years away – if the planet itself wasn't blocking the view, if the node was above the horizon.

The shelter was windowless, but Joan saw the ground outside the doorway brighten for an instant. The flash was silent; no missile had struck the valley, the explosion had taken place high above the atmosphere.

Surat went outside. When she returned she said quietly, 'All clear. They got it.'

Joan put all her effort into spitting out a handful of words. 'I want to see what happened.'

Sando hesitated, then motioned to the others to help him pick up the couch and carry it outside.

A shell of glowing plasma was still visible, drifting across the sky as it expanded, a ring of light growing steadily fainter until it vanished into the afternoon glare.

Anne was dead in this embodiment, but her back-up would wake and go on to new adventures. Joan could at least tell her the story of her local death: of virtuoso flying and a spectacular end.

She'd recovered her bearings now, and she recalled the position of the stars. The node was still hours away from rising. The Amalgam was full of powerful telescopes, but no others would be aimed at this obscure planet, and no plea to redirect them could outrace the light they would need to capture in order to bring the Niah's final theorem back to life.

Sando wanted to send her away for medical supervision, but Joan insisted on remaining at the site.

'The fewer officials who get to know about this incident, the fewer problems it makes for you,' she reasoned.

'As long as you don't get sick and die,' he replied.

'I'm not going to die.' Her wounds had not become infected, and her strength was returning rapidly.

They compromised. Sando hired someone to drive up from the nearest town to look after her while he was out at the excavation. Daya had basic medical training and didn't ask awkward questions; he seemed happy to tend to Joan's needs, and then lie outside daydreaming the rest of the time.

There was still a chance, Joan thought, that the Niah had carved the theorem on a multitude of tablets and scattered them all over the planet. There was also a chance that the Tirans had made copies of the tablet before letting Anne abscond with it. The question, though, was whether she had the slightest prospect of getting her hands on these duplicates.

Anne might have made some kind of copy herself, but she hadn't mentioned it in the prologue to her aerobatic rendition of the theorem. If she'd had any time to spare, she wouldn't have limited herself to an audience of one: she would have waited until the node had risen over Ghahar.

On her second night as an invalid, Joan dreamt that she saw Anne standing on the hill looking back into the fog-shrouded valley, her shadow haloed by the Niah light.

When she woke, she knew what she had to do.

When Sando left, she asked Daya to bring her the console that controlled the satellite dish. She had enough strength in her arms now to operate it, and Daya showed no interest in what she did. That was naïve, of course: whether or not Daya was spying on her, Pirit would know exactly where the signal was sent. So be it. Seven light-years was still far beyond the Noudah's reach; the whole node could be disassembled and erased long before they came close.

No message could outrace light directly, but there were more ways for light to reach the node than the direct path, the fastest one. Every black hole had its glory, twisting light around it in a tight, close orbit and flinging it back out again. Seventy-four hours after the original image was lost to them, the telescopes at the node could still turn to the Cataract and scour the distorted, compressed image of the sky at the rim of the hole's black disk to catch a replay of Anne's ballet.

Joan composed the message and entered the coordinates of the node. *You didn't die for nothing, my friend. When you wake and see this, you'll be proud of us both.*

She hesitated, her hand hovering above the send key. The Tirans had wanted Anne to flee, to show them the way to the stars, but had they really been indifferent to the loot they'd let her carry? The theorem had come at the end of the Niah's three-million-year reign. To witness this beautiful truth would not destroy the Amalgam, but might it not weaken it? If the Seekers' thirst for knowledge was slaked, their sense of purpose corroded, might not the most crucial strand of the culture fall into a twilight of its own? There was no shortcut to the stars, but the Noudah had been goaded by their alien visitors, and the technology would come to them soon enough.

The Amalgam had been goaded, too: the theorem she'd already transmitted would send a wave of excitement around the galaxy, strengthening the Seekers, encouraging them to complete the unification by their own efforts. The Big Crunch might be inevitable, but at least she could delay it, and hope that the robustness and diversity of the Amalgam would carry them through it, and beyond.

She erased the message and wrote a new one, addressed to her back-up via the decoy node. It would have been nice to upload all her memories, but the Noudah were ruthless, and she wasn't prepared to stay any longer and risk being used by them. This sketch, this postcard, would have to be enough.

When the transmission was complete she left a note for Sando in the console's memory.

Daya called out to her, 'Jown? Do you need anything?'

She said, 'No. I'm going to sleep for a while.'

HOT ROCK

1

Azar turned away from her assembled friends and family and walked through the departure gate. She tried to keep her gaze fixed straight ahead, but then she paused and looked over her shoulder, as if there might yet be a chance for one more parting gesture. It was too late; there was nobody in sight. She had left her well-wishers far behind.

She managed a nervous laugh at the sheer seamlessness of the transition; she hadn't registered so much as a shift in the light. The corridor around her appeared unchanged, its walls bearing the same abstract blue-and-gold mosaics as the one she had entered, but when she walked to the far end and turned to the right, she found herself in a glass-walled observation deck, looking out into the rich blackness of space.

Doorway to the stars was the style of travel she had chosen, just one among dozens of decorative scenarios she might have wrapped around the raw, imperceptible act itself. There was no doorway; stepping through the departure gate had merely been a gesture of consent, the signal she had chosen to initiate her journey. In mid-stride, her mind had been copied from the processor that sat within her birth flesh, encoded into gamma-rays, and transmitted across fifteen hundred light-years. In a subjective instant, she had been transported from her home world of Hanuz into this scape, which mimicked a capacious habitat orbiting the planet Tallulah. She really was orbiting Tallulah, but the habitat, and the body she perceived as her own flesh, were illusory. The machine she now inhabited was scarcely larger than a grain of rice.

Azar pressed her palms to her eyes and composed herself. If she turned around and marched back through the gate it would take her home with no questions asked, but three thousand years would have passed since her departure. That price had been paid, and no second thoughts, no hasty retreat, could reverse it. All she could do now was try to make it worthwhile.

The observation deck was unlit, but a gentle glow from the floor tracked her footsteps as she crossed to the far side and looked down on Tallulah. The scape's illusory gravity almost made her feel that she was on solid ground, gazing eastwards on a cloudless night from some mountain eyrie at a rising moon: a new moon, its grey disk lit only by starlight. But she knew that however long she waited, dawn would not come creeping across the limb of this disk; no crescent, no sliver of light would appear. Tallulah had no sun; it had been an orphan for at least a billion years, drifting untethered through the galaxy. Yet distant astronomers had surmised – and the instruments here and now confirmed – that its surface was awash with running water. In the cold of inter-stellar space even its atmosphere should have been frozen down to a sludge of solid nitrogen and carbon dioxide, but instead its long night was alive with balmy breezes wafting over starlit seas.

'Salaam! You must be Azar!' A tall, smiling woman strode across the deck, stretching out her arms. 'I'm Shelma.' They embraced briefly, just as Azar would have done when meeting someone for the first time back on Hanuz. This was no more a coincidence than Shelma's human appearance and common phonetic name: for the sake of mutual intelligibility, the scape was translating every sight, every word, every gesture that passed between them.

Shelma turned to face the blank grey disk, and her eyes lit up with pleasure. 'It's beautiful!' she exclaimed.

Azar felt slightly foolish that she'd been so slow to take a proper look herself. Tallulah's surface would be emitting a far-infrared glow, but its atmosphere was virtually opaque at that frequency, so the easiest way to see any detail would be to increase her sensitivity to the usual visible spectrum. She willed the change – and the scape obliged, just as if her eyes were real.

The ocean sparkled in the starlight. Two broad continents shared the hemisphere below. Long mountain ranges, vast bare plains, and expanses of mysterious vegetation coloured the shadowless land.

'It is lovely,' she said. Every world had its own peculiar beauty, though, and Azar would not have sacrificed three thousand years just to gaze upon even the most ravishing landscape.

When Tallulah had first shown up in telescopic surveys, long before Azar's birth, people had soon realised that the best chance to visit it would come when it passed fortuitously close to an imaginary line joining the distant systems of Hanuz and Bahar. If the two worlds cooperated by launching probes that arrived simultaneously, the two spacecraft could brake against each other, sparing both of them the massive amounts of fuel needed to decelerate.

Accordingly, Mologhat 1 and 2 were sent on their way, launched in time to meet at Tallulah and merge in an intricate electromagnetic embrace. But then the news had reached Hanuz that Bahar would not be leaving the mission in the hands of insentient robots: a traveller would follow the Bahari probe, to wake inside the unified Mologhat Station and supervise the exploration of the orphan world.

No native-born traveller had left Hanuz for millennia, and Azar's people were not so crippled with pride that the absence of a representative of their own would have been intolerable. The software they had already sent with Mologhat 1 was perfectly capable of protecting their interests in the mission; they might have simply left the Bahari to their alien ways without lessening their own enjoyment of whatever discoveries followed. And yet, a ripple had spread across the planet, a shocked whisper: *One of us could go, could be there, could live through it all in person.*

'A billion years in deep space,' Shelma marvelled, 'and not an iceberg in sight.'

'It's hard to believe,' Azar replied. The endless night on Tallulah rivalled the height of summer on Hanuz. When a planet was stripped of its sun, the decay of long-lived radioisotopes could eke out enough warmth over billions of years to keep its core molten – but even with abundant greenhouse gases to trap the heat, that could not account for Tallulah's surface temperature. However warm its heart, its skin should have felt the chill by now.

Mologhat had been orbiting Tallulah for three years before their arrival, and Azar now ingested the results of its observations. No obviously artificial structures were visible on the surface, but a faint stream of neutrinos was radiating out from deep in the planet's crust. The spectrum of the neutrinos did not correspond to the decay of any known radioisotopes, natural or otherwise; nor did it match the signatures of fission or fusion. Someone had worked hard to keep this orphan warm, but it was far from clear how they had done it – and impossible to say whether or not they were still around.

'What do you think?' Azar asked Shelma. 'Is there anyone home?'

'People have been beaming signals at Tallulah for thirty thousand years,' Shelma said, 'and never raised a peep. So they're either dead, or resolute hermits.'

'If they want to be left in peace, we have no right to disturb them.' Azar hoped that this declaration was redundant, but she wanted the ground rules absolutely clear.

'Of course,' Shelma agreed. 'But if they insist on playing dead to perfection, all they'll get are the rights of the dead. Which, while not negligible, are somewhat diminished.'

Once a civilisation became extinct – not merely mutating into something new, but leaving no sentient heirs whatsoever – it was widely accepted that its history devolved into a common legacy that anyone was entitled to investigate. If sovereignty really had ceased to be an issue, Tallulah was certainly worth exploring. Tens of thousands of orphan planets had been found in the past, but only a few dozen had shown signs of habitation, and those worlds had yielded nothing but sad ruins buried beneath the permafrost. In the age of the Amalgam – the meta-civilisation that now ringed the galaxy – the extinction of an entire world was unthinkable; if a catastrophe could not be averted, people who already had a robust digital form could be evacuated in seconds, and even those who had chosen purely biological modes could be scanned in a matter of days at the most.

The people of Tallulah, it seemed, had been halfway in between. When some cosmic mishap tossed them from their stellar hearth they had been unwilling or unable to evacuate, but they had not stood by and watched the air around them fall to the ground like snow. Whether trapped by their fate or just stubbornly resolved to ride it out, they had found a way to survive it. If they had since succumbed to some other tragedy, or merely surrendered to the passage of time, Azar saw no disrespect in digging up their secrets. Their achievements had endured for a billion years; they deserved recognition and understanding.

2

Mologhat's orbit was a discreet hundred thousand kilometres from Tallulah, but it had dispatched a swarm of microprobes into smaller, faster orbits of various inclinations, providing complete coverage of the surface. If there had been any lingering suspicion that the heating of the crust might have been due to some freakish natural process, the details put that idea to rest: not only was the temperature modulated by latitude, diminishing towards the planet's rotational poles, the records showed that it cycled over a period of about three months, creating imitation seasons. These nostalgic echoes of a long-lost circumstellar orbit were so clear that Azar was surprised they'd put the heat source in the ground at all, rather than launching an artificial sun.

'Not only would that have given them light from above,' she suggested to Shelma as they strolled through Mologhat's library, 'they could have kept the old diurnal rhythm too.' Heat conduction from deep in the crust would have washed out any cycle as short as a typical planetary day.

Shelma said, 'It's a lot of extra work to make a microsun efficient – to keep it from pouring energy out into space.'

'That's true.'

'And perhaps they were insecure as well,' Shelma added, sliding out an image from the stack beside her that showed an animated model of Tallulah's weather patterns. 'They were already on the verge of losing one sun. They might have preferred to keep their energy source buried, rather than risk being parted from this one too.'

'Yeah. Still, it's interesting that they tweaked the biosphere for such a radical shift – ground heat replacing sunlight – but kept the seasons.'

Shelma smiled. 'Days, seasons, you've got to have something. People go mad without change.' Both she and Azar had chosen to retain sleep cycles, their software following the dictates of their ancestral phenotypes. But Azar knew that the Baharis' ancestors were nocturnal; what Azar perceived as the station's night would be day to Shelma, and vice versa.

Azar pulled out a map of vegetation density. Using synthetic aperture methods, the microprobes had resolved details on Tallulah's surface down to about a tenth of a metre, and even at that coarse resolution they had identified thousands of different kinds of plants. Spectroscopy could not untangle the detailed biochemistry from orbit, but the biosphere was clearly carbon-based/anaerobic, with the plants synthesising carbohydrates but releasing no free oxygen.

Shelma spread her arms to take in the whole collection of data around them. 'Everything here is open to interpretation. We're going to need to make landfall to get any further.'

'I agree.' Azar was nervous, but relieved by the verdict. She was glad she hadn't travelled this far just to find that Tallulah was clearly occupied by hermits, and there was nothing left to do but abandon them to their solitude.

'The question, then,' Shelma said, 'is how we want to do it.' She began reeling off options. They could sprinkle a few nanotech spores on the surface, then sit back and wait for the army of robot insects they built to scour the planet. Or they could leave Mologhat and travel to the surface themselves, in various ways. Of course they could always combine the two, delegating most of the exploration while still being in the thick of it.

Azar had studied all of these methods before her departure, but Shelma sounded too blasé to be merely reciting theoretical knowledge. 'You've done this kind of thing before, haven't you?'

'Dozens of times.' Shelma hesitated. 'This is your first time out-of-system?'

'Yes.' That wasn't a lucky guess; everyone knew about the dearth of travellers from Hanuz. 'It's hard for us,' Azar explained. 'Leaving everyone we know for hundreds of years. You don't mind doing that?'

'My ancestors were solitary for part of their life cycle,' Shelma said, 'and sociable for the rest. Now we're flexible: we can switch between those modes at will. What I don't understand is why you don't just travel in packs, if that would make things easier.'

Azar laughed. 'I know some people do that, but our social networks are so tangled that it's hard to find a truly self-contained group – least of all a group where everyone can agree on a single destination. And if they do, they're more likely to emigrate than to take a trip and come home again.'

'I see.'

'Anyway, forget about Hanuz. We need to make some decisions.' Azar wasn't going to sit around on Mologhat while robots had all the fun, but there were practical limits on how far she could go just to get some dirt beneath her fingernails. If she had her own standard body reconstructed down on the surface, tweaked to survive the local conditions, she'd spend all her time foraging for food. Mologhat had only a few micrograms of its original antimatter store left; the few hundred megajoules that would generate were enough for its own modest needs, but pilfering any of it to power a sixty-kilogram behemoth would be insane; she could burn up the whole lot in a month. If Tallulah had had a reasonable abundance of deuterium she could have powered her body with D-D fusion, but the isotope was rare here.

'What if we build a high-capacity processor into one of the explorer insects?' Azar suggested. 'Then we download into that. We get to see the world first-hand and make some realtime decisions, but we don't waste energy or leave a big footprint.' If Tallulah turned out to be inhabited after all, the difference between being perceived as friend or enemy might easily hang on something as simple as the amount of local resources they'd used, or how physically intrusive their presence had been.

Shelma thought it over. 'That sounds like as good a choice as any.'

3

Azar persisted with her doorway metaphor, and walked through an 'airlock' from Mologhat Station into the robot insect as if the two were docked together. Amused by the conceit, Shelma followed behind her, but she couldn't resist a mild rebuke. 'The poor balloon doesn't even rate a mention?'

Azar shuddered. 'Please, heights make me dizzy.' Only gamma-rays had the bandwidth to transmit their software in a reasonable amount of time, but gamma-rays couldn't penetrate far through a planetary atmosphere. So the nanotech on Tallulah's surface had built a small hydrogen balloon, which had risen high enough into the stratosphere to receive their transmission and transcribe the data into a densely encoded molecular memory, before deflating and descending.

The scape Azar had constructed inside the insect resembled the kind of transparent-domed flight deck found in sightseeing aircraft back on Hanuz. Shelma would be perceiving some very different furnishings, but at least the two of them shared the same view of the jungle beyond the windshield; Shelma's vision had always stretched into the far infrared, and now Azar had chosen to match her.

The insect was perched on a broad, flat leaf, one of dozens of papery structures sprouting from a slender trunk. The leaf's veins glowed with the heat of warm sap, and a hot mist wafted up from the blotchy hexagonal pores that dotted the surface. When Azar looked up into the sky, the stars were barely visible through the fog.

Scout mites had already crawled up and down this plant and begun deciphering its strange biochemistry. Sap that was cooled and concentrated by evaporation in the leaves was pumped down to the roots, where it was diluted in chambers of fresh water. The increase in entropy that the dilution entailed allowed enzymes in the sap to drive an endothermic reaction, absorbing heat from the ground while synthesising sugars from dissolved carbon dioxide.

The plant's heritable replicator was a carbohydrate polymer known as C3, which had been found on many other worlds. Once they'd built up a database of sequences from a sufficient number of species, they could start trying to construct an evolutionary tree, as well as looking for signs of technological tinkering.

Azar took hold of a joystick and flew their host across to another plant, a small bush adorned with twigs that sprouted leaves like radial cooling fins. They landed on a twig while the scout mites burrowed and sampled.

'There's not much sap in this one,' Shelma noted. 'The leaves just look like mats of fibre.' There were no pores here, no steamy exudations.

Azar watched a display of the scouts' discoveries. There were long, fibrous structures running all the way from the leaves to the tips of the roots, and they were packed with interlocking polymers. In some fibres the polymers were rich in mobile electrons; in others they had positive 'holes', electron deficits that could shuffle along the molecule's backbone from site to site.

'Thermoelectric diffusion?' she guessed. The electrons and holes would conduct heat from the ground up into the leaves, and in doing so they'd set up an electric potential, which in turn could be used to drive chemical reactions.

As the details came through, they confirmed her suspicion. The plant was a living thermocouple, with the heat-pumped currents in the polymers shuffling electrons to and from the enzymes that synthesised carbohydrates.

The thermocouple bush had no easily digestible nutrients above ground, so Azar flew back to the entropy tree and thrust the insect's proboscis into a vein, drawing out a tankful of sugary sap. There was no free atmospheric oxygen to help metabolise the sugars, but like the plant itself, their robot could make use of nitrate ions in the sap as an oxidising agent, reducing them to ammonia in the process. Scout mites were still hunting for the organisms responsible for creating the nitrates in the first place.

Shelma said, 'So where are the insects? Where are the animals?' So far, they'd seen nothing moving in the jungle.

'Maybe the Ground Heaters didn't have time to tweak any animals for the new conditions,' Azar suggested. 'If they were about to get ejected from their solar system, their priorities would have been a new form of energy, and a primary food source that could exploit it. The old animals just died out, and nobody had the heart to try to create new ones.'

'Maybe,' Shelma conceded. 'But wouldn't your first response to the prospect of losing your sun be to build a few domed arks: sealed habitats with artificial heat and light that preserved the original ambient conditions, and as much of the original biosphere as possible?'

Azar said, 'And then you'd slowly begin modifying the species from the arks to live off the new energy source. Still, they might have started with the plants but got no further.'

The scout mites collected more C3 sequences, and as the numbers reached the point where comparisons became meaningful it grew increasingly clear that these genomes were natural, not engineered. Even the genes responsible for building the gloriously technomimetic thermocouple fibres had the same messy, incrementalist, patchwork character of all the others.

Stranger still, the genetic analysis pointed to a common ancestor for all these plants just two hundred million years ago, long after Tallulah had been orphaned.

As Azar reviewed descriptions of other C3 worlds, pulling the data down from Mologhat's library, she realised that in a couple of hours the station would set below the horizon. The timelag for her queries was already ponderous, and rerouting everything around Tallulah through the limited-bandwidth microprobes would only make that worse.

'We should clone the station's library,' she suggested to Shelma. The library was far bigger than their personal software, and there was no room for it in their present insect host, but they could at least bring it down into the stratosphere, making the data far more accessible than it was from Mologhat's distant orbit.

Shelma agreed. They set the nanotech to work fitting out the balloon for a new flight, then continued exploring the jungle.

As in many communities of plants there was competition for access to the sky, but here it was all about shedding heat rather than catching sunlight. The healthiest plants had their roots deep in the ground and their leaves exposed to the darkness of space. To be caught in too warm a cranny, sentenced to uniform tepidity, was fatal. The only exceptions to that rule were parasites: vampiric vines that stretched over trunks, branches and leaves, their barbed rootlets anchoring them to their victims and drawing out nutritious sap.

As they moved through the jungle, the new sequence data that came in from the scouts only shored up their original conclusions: the life they were seeing was entirely natural, and this branch of it was relatively young.

'Suppose,' Shelma ventured, 'that the Ground Heaters didn't need to engineer anything to live this way.'

'You mean there were species that exploited thermal gradients all along?' Azar frowned. 'How do you evolve to use *that* as your energy source? A single cell can never do it alone; you need to be a certain minimum size to access a useful temperature difference.'

'I'm not saying that the very first lifeforms used it,' Shelma replied. 'They might have relied on chemosynthesis, extracting energy from volcanic gases or mineral-rich geysers.'

'Right.' That was how Azar's own ancestral lineage had begun, back on Earth; photosynthesis had come much later. 'So they grew to a certain size using chemosynthesis, then found they could switch to thermal effects. But this is all before the Ground Heaters have even evolved, so what's keeping the surface rocks so hot?'

Shelma pondered this. 'Tidal heating? What if Tallulah was orbiting close to a cool red dwarf, or even a brown dwarf? With such weak sunlight, tidal heating might have been a far more potent energy source than photosynthesis.'

'But it can't last,' Azar protested. 'Eventually the planet would end up tidally locked.' The energy used to stretch and squeeze the rock, heating it up by internal friction, would ultimately be extracted from Tallulah's spin, slowing its rotation until its day matched its year and one hemisphere faced forever sunwards.

'Eventually, yes. But what if the Ground Heaters evolved before that happened? They would have been facing a slow, predictable decline in their energy source over millennia. So instead of responding frantically to a sudden catastrophe, they could have spent centuries perfecting a replacement.'

'And the ejection from their star came much later, but by then there was nothing they needed to do. They'd already made themselves independent.' Azar laughed, delighted. The artificial seasons and the variation in heat with latitude would still make sense: tidal heating would have been strongest at the equator, and at higher latitudes it would have been affected by seasonal changes in the angle between the planet's axis and the direction of the tidal force.

What this elegant hypothesis didn't explain was why the plants here were so young. Nor did it shed any light on exactly what the Ground Heaters had done to achieve their independence.

The data-collecting balloon was in place again. Before Mologhat vanished below the horizon, Azar instructed the station to send down a copy of its library.

As she was checking the interface with the cloned library, a message arrived from the microprobes. Thousands of kilometres away, something had exploded on the ocean floor and hurled a few billion tonnes of water skywards.

Azar turned to Shelma, still watching the satellite vision with her mind's eye. 'What's happening? Some glitch with the heat source?' For a system that had survived for a billion years, this hiccup packed a mighty punch: the eruption was already high above the atmosphere, steam turning to ice like a cometary impact in reverse.

Shelma looked nervous. 'Mologhat saw no vulcanism anywhere on the planet in the last three years. Do you think we've annoyed someone?'

'If we have, why are we still alive? It's not the ground beneath our feet that's exploded.' The balloon clearly wasn't the target, nor were any of the microprobes – and though the water missile was heading roughly in Mologhat's direction, it wouldn't reach anywhere near that far. But when Azar tried to contact the station, the microprobes replied that it was not responding.

Shelma said, 'Don't jump to any conclusions. Mologhat might have imposed a communications blackout; if it thought it was under fire it would shift orbits and try not to do anything to give its position away.'

Azar felt sick. 'You think the gamma-ray transmission was mistaken for some kind of attack?' Nothing had happened when she and Shelma had arrived the same way, but that burst had been considerably shorter, and it had come down almost vertically. The second beam had come from close to the horizon, giving it a longer path through the upper atmosphere – which would have made it more noticeable, and easier to trace back to its source.

Within minutes, the microprobes had reported six more eruptions, from underwater sites scattered around the planet. It made no sense to Azar; these gigatonnes of water were rising into orbits about a thousand kilometres up, but if they were meant as weapons, who were they aimed at? The microprobes were much lower down, and Mologhat was a hundred times further away. A direct hit with a solid iceberg could have done a lot of damage to any intruder, but these glistening snowballs weren't even holding together; Tallulah was just shrouding itself with a tenuous halo of tiny ice crystals.

'This isn't warfare!' she declared. 'They don't think they're under attack. They saw the gamma-rays, and thought: *antimatter*. They're afraid they're drifting into a cloud of antimatter. The ice is to tell them if there's any more around.'

Shelma considered this. 'I think you're right. They picked up a flash of annihilation radiation, and jumped to the conclusion that it was a natural source.'

Never mind that there was no natural source of bulk antimatter anywhere in the galaxy; if you'd spent a billion years in space without encountering another civilisation, perhaps a small cloud of antihydrogen seemed like a far less extravagant hypothesis than alien visitors using proton-antiproton gamma-rays for communications.

'So they still don't even know we're here?' Azar wondered. 'All those radio messages came to nothing. What do we have to do to get noticed – tattoo the binary digits for pi across the stratosphere?'

Shelma said, 'I wouldn't advise that. But it's not even clear to me that there's anyone home; this might just be a non-sentient device that's outlived the people it's meant to be protecting.'

The water missiles had stopped; the absence of any answering flash of radiation must have made it clear that if there was antimatter around, it was far too thinly spread to pose any kind of hazard.

Azar tried calling Mologhat again, but it was still not responding. 'They must have hit it,' she said. 'Whatever they thought it was, they must have launched something small and fast, and knocked it out before the ice storm even started.' She felt numb. *So much for the doorway to the stars.*

Shelma touched her arm reassuringly. 'It might yet reply – but even if it's gone, we're not stranded.'

'No?' The microprobes had nowhere near enough power for

interstellar transmissions, or even the raw materials to build the kind of hardware they'd need. And the data-ferrying balloon couldn't send them anywhere; their return path to Mologhat would have involved a gamma-ray mirror on the balloon, modulating and reflecting radiation coming down from the station itself.

Azar slumped into her seat. *How had she ever imagined she could do this? Travel fifteen hundred light-years as if it was nothing?* There was no magic gate leading home, just fourteen quadrillion kilometres of vacuum.

Shelma said, 'We have plenty of resources down here.'

Azar rubbed her eyes and tried to concentrate. 'That's true.' Given time, the nanotech could build them almost anything – and they didn't even have to reach all the way back to Hanuz or Bahar; they just had to connect to the Amalgam's network. Still, the nearest node was seven hundred light-years away; getting a signal that far was a daunting prospect. 'Can we do this from the ground?'

'Well . . . we could build a radio dish a few hundred kilometres across,' Shelma replied, deadpan. 'Factoring in suitable error correction for the signal-to-noise ratio, it might only take two or three centuries to complete the transmission.'

Azar got the message. 'Okay: better to build a rail-gun and launch a transmitter into orbit. But even if we can power a rail-gun, how do we power the transmitter? We don't have any antimatter. There's virtually no deuterium here; are we going to try to build a hydrogen-boron fusion reactor?' The most efficient way to produce gamma-rays was from antimatter – that would certainly make for the lightest power source to loft into orbit – but trying to create even a few micrograms of antihydrogen with nothing but *plant carbohydrates* as the energy source made Shelma's giant radio dish sound like a good idea. Whatever was guarding Tallulah might be a tad obtuse, but it was difficult to imagine a particle accelerator powered by industrial-scale deforestation slipping under the radar.

'What's the point of this transmission anyway?' she said

bitterly. 'To arrive home empty-handed, with no news worth hearing? If it comes to that, I'd rather let my back-up wake.'

'So would I,' Shelma said, 'but I think you're missing something.'

'Yeah?'

'The news worth hearing,' she said, 'and the energy source we need in order to send it, are the very same thing. Whatever's keeping this planet warm is just a few kilometres beneath our feet. If we can reach it, study it, understand it and harness it, we'll have both the means to get home, and the reason.'

4

A few kilometres beneath our feet was an encouraging way of putting it; from where they stood the actual distance was twenty-seven thousand metres. The nanotech built some robot moles, powered by long thermoelectric tails, and sent them on their way. They would reach the heat source in about two hundred days.

The oceanic crust was much thinner in places. Azar did some calculations. It wasn't clear what kind of food there'd be in the water, but she thought it was worth finding out. Shelma agreed, and they set out for the coast.

The insect made good time, averaging about thirty kilometres an hour, but when they reached the edge of the jungle food became sparser and the scattered plants less nutritious. Flying across the flat, monotonously glowing savannah, Azar ached for sunrise to come and banish the interminable night. But she fought down the pang of homesickness and tried to find the beauty in this upside-down world.

Other explorer insects were already fanning out from a dozen sites where the spores had landed, building up a picture of the continent's geochemistry. A tentative analysis of the data suggested that the surface had only been above sea level for about a quarter of a billion years.

'Before that, there might have been no dry land at all,' Shelma suggested. 'That would explain why the ecosystem here is so young.'

'So where did all the water go?' Azar wondered. 'Unless their antimatter detectors have a lot of false alarms.' Even the modest amount that they'd seen thrown skywards would mostly rain back down again.

'A collision?' Shelma frowned and withdrew the suggestion. 'No, the odds would be very low out here, to hit something big enough.' The current estimate of Tallulah's galactic orbit suggested that it hadn't even crossed another system's Oort cloud in the last billion years.

They reached the shoreline. Waves lapped gently on a lifeless beach; the infrared glow of the placid ocean made Azar think of liquid metal, but if she'd been wearing her body this water would have made a luxurious warm bath.

In the waves they found only single-celled creatures, living off a very thin soup of organic debris. They flew out a kilometre and took another sample, sending scout mites a few hundred metres down. The soup was thicker here; with a little tweaking, the insect would be able to make use of it.

There was a trench some six hundred kilometres off the coast, where the mysterious neutrino source was just nine thousand metres below the ocean floor. They set out across the waves, stopping every couple of hours to dive and feed.

Each time they plunged into the water, Azar noticed Shelma tensing. She wondered about the propriety of commenting on this; if she'd been looking at Shelma's true self-image – a Bahari body with five limbs and five tails, like the rear end of a cat caught in a kaleidoscope – she would not have been able to distinguish tranquillity from terror. Still, it was not as if the scape was reading Shelma's mind; it was merely translating information that she had chosen to make public.

As they approached the trench, Azar finally spoke. 'You don't have to do this if you don't want to.' The trench was three thousand metres deep; if Shelma had retained a primal fear of drowning, Azar had no wish to see her suffer. 'We can split the processor, and you can stay up here.'

Shelma shook her head, a little puzzled by this offer. 'No, I'll go with you. But first I want to bring in as much of the library as we can fit.'

'Oh.' Azar understood now; this was nothing to do with how Baharis felt about getting their fur wet. Once they were under-water they'd lose radio contact with everything, including the balloon-borne library.

Shelma began communing with the library, trying to choose a selection of its contents that would fit inside the insect without leaving them ill-equipped in the face of some crucial problem or opportunity. 'I don't want to meet the Ground Heaters and then find we can't even make sense of their language!'

'If they're so smart,' Azar replied, 'let them make sense of ours.' Then again, if they'd spent a billion years living alone on the ocean floor, it would probably be unwise to expect too much of their communications skills.

Hanuz had sent no travellers out into the galaxy for a hundred thousand years, and that had been long enough. Though Tallulah had been an enticing destination, Azar had left home less for the sake of the orphan's secrets than for the sake of breaking the curse. As the window for joining Mologhat had approached, she'd thought: *If we don't do this now, it will only grow harder.* And she'd finally stopped waiting for someone else to volunteer.

Shelma announced that she'd completed her selection, then she changed her mind and dived back into the interface. Azar thought of her great-great-granddaughter, Shirin, struggling to pack for an overnight trip. Shirin would be ancient when Azar returned; she'd have left all her toy animals behind.

'This is it now,' Shelma declared. 'We're prepared for anything.' Her avatar wasn't quite hyperventilating, but Azar could imagine her letting a breeze of random skills and factoids play through her mind, soaking her tissues with the oxygen of information before the conduit slammed shut.

'I could always give myself amnesia, if you want a little more room,' Azar suggested. Shelma actually looked tempted for a moment, before smiling thinly at the joke.

Azar took the joystick and the insect dived beneath the waves.

Their infrared vision wasn't quite useless here; if they tuned to a wavelength a little shorter than the peak thermal emissions around them, they could see the shadows that nearby objects cast against the glow of the warmer water below. Augmented with the strobe flashes of sonar, the vague shadows became fluttering vertical ribbons, drifting in the current but maintaining their orientation. Azar sent in the scout mites, who found the ribbons to be packed with tiny buoyancy chambers that exchanged gases in a complex cycle, eking a few microwatts out of the temperature gradient. The ribbon-weed's C3 sequence made it a close cousin of the land plants; in fact, it had probably changed very little from the ancestor whose other offspring had invaded the continents.

Five hundred metres down, they saw the first animals: small, segmented worms about a millimetre long, feeding off the ribbon-weed. The scout mites grabbed a few cells from the worms' skin for analysis. As Azar watched the data coming through, she felt a sense of disorientation to rival anything since she'd stepped on to Mologhat. The worms had no C3 in their cells; they were no more related to the weed they were munching on than she was to Shelma. Their replicator was P2, a polypeptide. What's more, their genome had been the subject of some blatantly artificial modifications, probably less than a million years ago.

'Introduced?' Shelma suggested.

'They must be,' Azar replied. Colonists from a P2 world must have come to Tallulah, bringing a few species from their home planet and tweaking them in order to survive here. It was a curious strategy; almost all interstellar travellers were digital in transit, not biological, and even if – like the founders of Hanuz – they had a fetish for recreating their original biochemistry upon arrival, such travellers tended to colonise sterile worlds. But then, nobody travelled to an orphan world for the sake of its real estate value. 'It looks as if someone else came treasure-hunting long before we did.'

'Apparently,' Shelma concurred. 'But if Tallulah is such old news, why isn't the heating process known halfway around the galaxy by now?'

As they descended further the ribbon-weed grew larger, the soup of microbes thicker, and the P2 creatures more numerous and diverse. There were shrimp-like animals straining microbes from the water, floating gas bladders with poisonous tentacles, and sinuous, muscular fish of every size, feeding on each other, the ribbon-weed and the shrimp.

A vast forest came into sonar range, rising up from the ocean floor. Azar had already been impressed by the size of the free-floating ribbon-weed, but its anchored cousins were giants, fifty or sixty metres high. With convection currents in the water sweeping heat away more efficiently than air, the temperature gradient was far less steep here than on land, but the water also made it easier for taller structures to support themselves. The scout mites counted eighty species of animals in the forest's upper reaches alone; some were P2, but there were C3 species as well, the first such animals the mites had found. And some were N3, with their genome encoded in nucleic acid.

'This place really has been popular,' Shelma observed drily. 'It's enough to bring out the biograffitist in anyone. You sprinkle some N2 microbes in the water; I'll add the C1.' N2 was DNA, Azar's ancestral replicator.

The N3 species, like the P2, had been engineered, but the best estimates put the date of intervention much earlier, between two and three hundred million years ago. Azar checked their local copy of the library; there was no previous archaeological evidence for an interstellar civilisation with N3 ancestry in that epoch – and this was not one of the databases Shelma had trimmed. How could a civilisation reach such a difficult target as Tallulah, but leave no trace anywhere else?

As they descended slowly into the forest, the insect announced a discovery that had nothing to do with Tallulah's polyglot biology. The robot's mass spectrometer was constantly analysing samples from the water around them, and it had just stumbled across an extraordinary find. The object in question had a mass of 40.635 atomic units; this far from integral figure might have made sense as an average for a sample containing a mixture of calcium-40 and its heavier isotopes – but it wasn't an average, it was the mass of a single ion. Stranger still, when stripped of all its electrons the thing had a charge, not of twenty or so, but *two hundred and ten*. This was double the charge of any known stable nucleus, and ten times greater than its atomic weight implied.

'Who ordered *that*?' Azar quipped. Shelma didn't even smile; the depleted library wasn't up to providing the scape with the context for a proper translation.

'It's femtotech,' Shelma declared.

Azar hesitated, then agreed. It was a staggering notion, but what else could it be? A new fundamental particle . . . with a charge of two hundred and ten? Femtotech – the engineering of matter on the scale of atomic nuclei – was still a primitive art within the Amalgam; there had been some ingenious creations but they all had to do their job quickly, before they blew apart in a few trillionths of a second. The insect's find had endured for at least three hundred seconds, and counting.

'How do you create a femtomachine with a binding energy equal to ninety per cent of its mass?' she wondered. The most stable nuclei, nickel and iron, weighed about one per cent less than the sum of their parts, thanks to the potential energy associated with the strong nuclear force. But increasing that effect by a factor of *ninety* was almost unimaginable.

The insect measured the ion's magnetic moment. The result was orders of magnitude higher than that which a nucleus of atomic number 210 would be expected to possess if it was sitting quietly in its ground state; to generate such a strong magnetic field, it would need to be spinning at relativistic speeds. This only made the overall picture even stranger: the kinetic energy from this rotation should have added substantially to the ion's total mass, rendering the actual forty-something value even more bizarre. The one thing that made a warped kind of sense was the failure of the ion to tear itself apart from centrifugal force. How could it explode, when the fragments would need to possess ten times more energy than the whole?

Azar said, 'I take it this is ash from the heating process?'

Shelma managed a dazed smile. 'If it's not, it certainly should be. *Ninety per cent mass-to-energy conversion*. No wonder it's still going strong after a billion years!'

Tallulah's crust was generating heat at a rate of about two petawatts, stabilising the planet's temperature by replacing the energy that leaked out of the greenhouse blanket. At ninety per cent mass conversion, that would consume less than eight hundred tonnes of fuel each year, so in principle the process could continue for about ten-to-the-eighteenth years: a billion times longer than it had been running so far. Unlike fission or fusion, even if the starting point for the femtotech process had to be one particular kind of nucleus, it really didn't matter how rare it was in nature, since the energy required to synthesise it from anything else would be trivial in comparison. If each tonne of the Ground Heaters' 'gold' burnt so fiercely that it could power the transmutation of a hundred tonnes of nickel or iron into yet more fuel, then Tallulah's bonfire would easily outlive the stars.

Technology like this could transform the Amalgam. Antimatter had never been more than a wonderfully compact storage device, costing as much energy to make as it released. The most exquisitely efficient fusion systems extracted about *half a per cent* of their fuel's mass as usable energy. There were some unwieldy tricks with black holes that could do better, but they weren't very practical, let alone portable. If everyone could harness the Ground Heaters' femtotech, it would be like a magic wand that could turn nine parts in ten of *anything* into energy, leaving nothing behind but this strange spinning ash.

Azar said, 'This is a lot to conclude from one weird ion. Are we sure it's not an instrument error?'

Before the insect touched the ocean floor it picked a second speck of ash out of the water. Azar had the nanotech rebuild the relevant instruments from scratch and repeat the analysis. There had been no error; all the properties were the same.

5

The nanotech built more moles and sent them down into the rock, but even here where the crust was thinner, Azar knew she would have to be patient.

'Sixty days?' she lamented, pacing the flight deck. She didn't expect to be able to unravel the nucleon-by-nucleon details of the femtotech in a hurry, but if they could obtain a sample of the deep crust and observe the way its composition was changing as energy was released, that would at least confirm that their overall picture of the Ground Heaters' process was correct.

Until they had some of this white-hot rock to play with, the practicalities of harnessing the femtotech remained obscure, but Azar's sense of anxiety at their isolation had almost vanished. To be stranded for nothing, with little to be gained if they managed to return, had been a dismal prospect, but now that the stakes were so high the situation was exhilarating. *Prometheus, eat your heart out.*

While they waited for the moles to hit paydirt they continued to explore the ribbon forest, building up a catalogue of the three kinds of life that Tallulah's mysterious fire sustained. Perhaps unsurprisingly, the P2 animals – the newest – were by far the most numerous, having been engineered to be able to digest everything that had come before them. To the older N3s, and the even rarer C3s, the P2s were unpalatable – though not indestructible; the scouts witnessed cases of N3 fish killing off their P2 rivals, even though they were useless as food. What's more, a few of the C3 creatures were able to feed on N3 flesh; evolution had finally granted them a belated revenge on the first wave of invaders. In another hundred million years, who knew who would be eating whom?

When they first came across the colony of P2 'lizards', Azar thought that they were charming animals. Spread across a dozen square kilometres of the forest floor, their network of burrows was entwined with the giant ribbon-weeds' roots, which they tapped for food.

The lizards had two eight-clawed limbs that they used for digging and grasping objects; all their motive force came from their powerful tails. They sensed the world around them with a mixture of IR vision and sonar. Glands in their cheeks excreted complex molecular cocktails, which they squirted at each other almost constantly. Olfactory signalling within a colony of social animals was nothing surprising; the shock came when the scout mites caught some of them squirting the chemicals at inanimate objects in certain chambers within their burrows – and the inanimate objects squirted back replies. On closer examination, the devices turned out to be sophisticated chemical transceivers, linked by a fibre-optic network.

'So these are our predecessors,' Shelma said. 'They came all the way to Tallulah, in the middle of nowhere, to solve the mystery of its warmth. But they must have found the femtotech long ago, so why are they still here? Why not take the treasure home? Why not spread it across the galaxy?'

'Why leave a world that will keep you warm for a million times longer than any star?' Azar replied.

'Why not build a hundred more worlds just like it?' Shelma countered.

'Let's ask them.'

The scouts set to work sampling the chemical signals that comprised the lizards' language, and trying to correlate them with elements in the environment and the creatures' behaviour. It was an impertinent level of eavesdropping, but they had to bootstrap communications somehow, and with no culture or biology in common they couldn't simply march up to the lizards and start playing charades. Ideally the scouts would have included children as their subjects, in order to share in any lessons they received, but in the entire colony of fifty thousand there were currently no young at all – which suggested that the lizards had cut back their fertility to stabilise the population, while living more or less as long as they wished.

Fibre-optic trunk lines connected the colony to others around the planet, and all the data traffic passing through appeared to conform to a single language. If there were any intelligent N3 creatures still around, either they weren't plugged into the same network, or there'd been a radical assimilation of cultures in one direction or the other.

Fed by the forest and served by their own rudimentary nano-tech, the lizards seemed to pass the time socialising. The chemical transceivers granted them access to libraries, but most of the content being summoned appeared very similar to their habitual person-to-person exchanges, suggesting that it was closer to narrative history or fiction than anything more specialised and technical. Then again, even the most naturalistic dialogues might have encoded subtle themes that remained elusive at this stage of the analysis.

The lizards had no apparent social hierarchies, and as hermaph-rodites they exhibited no sexual dimorphism, but the scouts identified one curious form of division. Many of the lizards identified themselves as belonging to one of three groups, which were named for the actions of spiralling inwards, spiralling out-wards, and, the clear majority, following a circle. Since this was not a description of anyone's actual swimming style, it had to be a metaphor, but for what? The scouts had failed to observe anything tangible that correlated with this classification.

After thirty days Shelma declared, 'It's time to introduce ourselves.'

'Are you sure?' Azar was impatient for answers, but it seemed as if the scouts could easily spend another month piecing together further subtleties of the lizards' language.

'We've reached the point where we can greet them politely and explain who we are,' Shelma said. 'The way to get more reliable language acquisition now is through dialogue.'

Shelma instructed the nanotech to build two facsimile lizard bodies. These robots would be obvious caricatures, functional but not such perfect imitations that the lizards could mistake them for fellow colonists.

The insect communicated with the robot lizards by line-of-sight laser pulses with a range of just a few metres. Azar and Shelma kept their software on the insect's processor and operated the lizards by telepresence, monitoring the robots' points of view without becoming fully immersed in their sensoria or giving up the feeling of being located on the insect's flight deck.

With her lizard body swimming towards the edge of the colony, weaving its way between the ribbon-weeds, Azar was over-whelmed with happiness. She was more than just a traveller now; she was about to become an ambassador to a hitherto unknown culture. And however physically isolated she was at this moment, she did not feel cut off from her roots in Hanuz. In her mind's eye, she could almost see the faces of the people she hoped to regale with her adventures.

A lizard approached, seemingly unafraid. The puff of chemicals it squirted through the water was barely visible, but Azar heard the translation loud and clear. 'Who are you?'

'We come in peace from another world,' Azar announced proudly. The lizards had not been seen discussing astronomy, but they did have a word for the planet as a whole, and a general inflection for 'not this thing, but another of its kind'.

The lizard turned and fled.

On the flight deck, Azar turned to Shelma. 'What did I do wrong?' She'd half-expected her claim to be greeted with scepti-cism – their robot bodies were well within reach of the lizards' own technology, after all – but perhaps the gamma-rays that had triggered the ice halo had served as an ominous calling card.

'Nothing,' Shelma assured her. 'Summoning other witnesses is a common response.' Shelma had no prior experience of first contact, but the library confirmed her claim.

Azar said, 'What if they've forgotten that there *are* other worlds? They've been here for a million years. They might not even remember their own history.'

Shelma was not persuaded. 'There's too much technology

around; even if they fell into a dark age at some point, they would have reconstructed everything by now.' The lizards' nanotech maintained their health; it could easily have sequenced all the plants and animals around them, just as the Amalgam nanotech had done. Still, without the right context – without libraries of replicator sequences from a thousand other worlds – would they know how to interpret the data?

Azar saw bodies darting through the fronds. The first lizard had returned, with ten, twelve, fourteen friends. She could never have distinguished one from the other unaided, so she invoked software to track their features and assign phonetic names to them all.

Shelma said, 'Please accept our good wishes. We come in peace from another world.'

Omar, the first lizard they'd met, replied, 'How can that be? It's not time.'

His companion Lisa added, 'You're not taking Tallulah from us. We'll never accept that.'

Suddenly all fourteen lizards were speaking at once. Azar's robot's senses had no problem following their words; the chemical emissions were tagged with individual markers, so there was no chance of confusing one lizard's words for another's. Azar had the audio translation untangled into separate streams.

Some of the lizards were expressing surprise and scepticism, not at the notion of visitors from another world, but at the timing of their arrival. Others seemed to think that she and Shelma were the vanguard of an army of colonists who had come to seize Tallulah, and they defiantly expressed their intention to resist.

Shelma said, 'We're not colonists, we're merely explorers. We saw Tallulah and became curious.'

'Where is your own world?' a lizard dubbed Caleb demanded.

'My companion and I come from different worlds,' Shelma explained. 'Both more than a thousand light-years away.' The software would translate this into the local measure of distance, but with no units suitable for astronomical scales the number attached would be awfully large.

The lizards broke into a fresh cacophony. Such a journey was inconceivable.

Omar said, 'Please come with us.'

The crowd pressed around them from all sides, urging them forward. Shelma said privately, 'Just go where they ask, don't resist.'

The lizards seemed unaware of the tiny insect hovering between the larger robots; certainly its laser flashes were outside their visible spectrum. 'You think they're *taking us prisoner*?' Azar said. It was hard to decide which was more bizarre: the fact that someone might wish to do this, or the fact that they believed it could be done.

'More or less,' Shelma replied. 'But at this point I'd rather cooperate than escape. If we can clear up a few misunderstandings, everything should be fine.'

Azar let the pack of lizards guide her through the ribbon-weeds, then down into a burrow. Watching events through the flight deck's dome made her feel much less claustrophobic than the impression she got from her jostled robot's senses, but when the narrowing tunnels and the ever tighter crush meant the insect risked becoming conspicuous, they had it crawl inside Shelma's body. The line of sight between the two larger robots came and went, so Azar put her own lizard on autopilot, meekly complying with the flow of the crowd, and changed the insect's flight deck scape to show her an external view rather than the innards of its host.

They were taken to a small, bare chamber with a single entrance. After six of the lizards piled in with them, there was little room to spare.

Omar resumed the interrogation, his scepticism undiminished. 'Your star must be very dim,' he declared. 'We believed that we had many more years.'

Azar thought she was beginning to understand. Tallulah would not come close to another star for a very long time; the lizards had somehow fixed on that event as the most likely occasion for visitors.

'Our stars are very bright, but very distant,' she insisted. 'Why do you doubt that? Didn't your own ancestors travel far to reach this world?'

Omar said, 'Their journey took half a year.'

Half a year? Perhaps the real story had degenerated into myth, retold with cosy, domesticated numbers to replace the terrifying reality of interstellar distances.

'At the speed of light?' asked Shelma.

The chamber erupted with expressions of mirth and derision. 'Only light travels at the speed of light,' Lisa explained.

The scouts had found no evidence of the lizards digitising themselves. Had they lost that technology, or had they never possessed it? Could their ancestors really have crossed the light-years as flesh?

'So how far would they have travelled,' Azar asked, 'in that half-year?'

'Perhaps a billion kilometres,' Omar replied.

Azar said nothing, but the claim was absurd; a billion kilometres was the size of a small planetary system. The lizards had spent too long dozing away the centuries at the bottom of this warm ocean; not only had they forgotten their own history, they had forgotten the true scale of the universe around them.

Shelma persisted. 'When we follow the path of Tallulah back in time, it doesn't come that close to the path of any star for a billion years. Have you been here for a billion years?'

Omar said, 'How can you know Tallulah's path? How long have you been watching us?'

'Thirty thousand years,' Shelma replied. 'Not me personally, but people I trust.'

Mirth again. Why was this claim so laughable?

'Thirty thousand years?' Omar said. 'Why did you imagine that would tell you the whole story?'

Shelma was bewildered now. 'We've tracked your position and your speed,' she said. 'We know the motion of the stars. What else is there to account for?' Tallulah's galactic orbit was sparsely populated; chaos would eventually make retrodiction impossible, but the confidence levels over a billion years were still quite tight.

'Eight times since we arrived on Tallulah,' Omar explained, 'this world has changed course. Eight times, the heat rose from the ground to bring our path closer to our destination.'

6

An argument broke out among the lizards; they withdrew from the discussion and left the chamber, leaving their guests with only two taciturn sentries. The insect probably could have slipped past these guards, or even burrowed its way back to the surface if necessary, but Shelma insisted that it was better to try to keep the dialogue open, and on consideration Azar agreed.

'So our orphan is a tourist,' Shelma mused. 'It steered its way right into the lizards' home system, and now it's heading for a new destination. But did the Ground Heaters arrange that, or did the N3 colonists bolt on the engines later?'

'Maybe that's where the water went,' Azar suggested. The eruptions they'd seen earlier would have no longterm effect on the planet's motion, but a hotter jet that reached escape velocity would do the trick.

Shelma said, 'Water would be a strange choice of propellant. Photonic jets would be more efficient.'

'If it was the N3ers doing it,' Azar said, 'maybe they didn't have fine enough control over the femtotech.'

'Maybe. But the N3ers left no biological presence on the land, so they must have been ocean dwellers. Would ocean dwellers throw so much water into space that they lost thirty per cent of their real estate?'

'Good point,' Azar conceded. 'But why does *anyone* steer a whole planet from system to system? If it was the Ground Heaters, surely they could have made smaller, faster spacecraft using the femtotech.'

Shelma threw up her hands. 'Let's go back to the beginning.

The Ground Heaters grew up with tidal heating. When that started running down, they got lucky; they managed to devise a spectacularly good replacement. So what would they do next?'

'Some cultures would have sent out nanotech spores,' Azar said, 'followed by a wave of digitised travellers. But we know they didn't do that, or the femtotech would still be around somewhere else.'

'They didn't found colonies, but they still ended up travelling.' Shelma laughed. 'I was going to say that it must have been a deliberate choice – that they could have resisted any natural ejection from their system if they'd really wanted to – but maybe they only had fusion power then. That would explain why there's no deuterium around: they used it all up while they were developing the femtotech.'

'But either way,' Azar said, 'once they were free of their star and able to steer themselves, they decided to make the best of it. To see a few sights along the way. And where do you go, if you grew up around a dwarf star? You take a tour of other dwarf stars—'

'Until you find one with an inhabited planet,' Shelma said, 'where they're facing the same problems you faced.'

'And then what?' Azar frowned. 'I can't believe the N3ers conquered the Ground Heaters!'

'No,' Shelma agreed. 'And why would they need to? Why wouldn't the Ground Heaters simply share the femtotech, to help out their fellow thermophiles? If they weren't feeling generous and sociable, why visit an inhabited world at all? If they'd simply been looking for territory there would have been plenty of sterile worlds for them to choose from.'

Azar said, 'Maybe the Ground Heaters died out before they reached the N3 world. They'd programmed some billion-year spree for Tallulah into the femtotech, but they lost heart along the way. The ghost ship came into the N3 system, and the locals couldn't believe their luck: an empty planet, habitable for ten-to-the-eighteenth years, right on their doorstep! But they couldn't park it, they couldn't steer it, they had to go along for the ride.

And a quarter of a billion years later, the same thing happened to the lizards.'

Shelma thought for a while. 'That almost makes sense, but I can't quite believe that neither of these free-riders had any interest in turning the femtotech into a propulsion system and founding a few colonies elsewhere.'

'Maybe they did. Maybe we've missed them. Tallulah went unnoticed for a very long time.'

'We're missing something,' Shelma said. 'But perhaps our hosts will be able to enlighten us.'

Hours passed with no more contact from the lizards. The sentries were changed, but the replacements were equally determined not to engage with them.

Azar paced the flight deck. 'They must be trying to work out if we're telling the truth or not. Checking to see if Tallulah's brought them close to a very faint brown dwarf – a port of call that they failed to anticipate.'

'You'd think they'd have good enough telescopes to be sure,' Shelma said irritably, 'given what's at stake.'

'Maybe they got complacent. I mean, if you do a thorough sweep of the sky and get a very clear verdict that there's nothing to worry about for the next hundred thousand years, how motivated are you to keep repeating the search?'

'Ideally, it would all be automated,' Shelma replied. 'Motivation wouldn't come into it.'

'Well, we might not have landed on the best of all possible worlds after all.'

The lights on the flight deck were starting to soften. Ever since she'd arrived on Mologhat, Azar had been sticking scrupulously to her usual diurnal rhythm; to sleep was part of her identity. But she was too anxious now, and she willed the urge away. Her sense of self would just have to stretch to encompass an exception when she was captive to confused, paranoid lizards.

The sentries were changed again. Azar recognised them as two of the crowd who'd first appeared in the forest; her software had dubbed them Jake and Tilly, but they hadn't said much then, and she didn't bother trying to speak to them now. Let the telescopes confirm her and Shelma's honesty, and then they could all finally engage in a civilised discussion.

Jake said, 'Come with us. Quickly. We don't have much time.' He swam a short way towards his prisoners, then darted back towards the chamber's entrance.

Azar was dumbfounded.

'Come with you where?' Shelma asked.

'Out of here,' Tilly said. 'We think the Circlers are planning to kill you.'

Azar glanced at Shelma. The insect could probably defend itself against most of the lizards' technology, but it was not indestructible. They'd left back-ups in the jungle before setting out for the coast, but those snapshots of their minds were missing all the crucial discoveries they'd made since. In any case, even if they survived here, what kind of dialogue could they have with people who wanted them dead?

Shelma addressed her privately. 'So do we leave the bodies as decoys?'

Azar was unsure. The insect on its own would face technical problems communicating with the lizards – it was too small to stock the raw materials for more than a few minutes' speech – and she also found something comforting about the way it was now hidden inside a larger target.

'What if we split the difference?' she suggested. Her lizard body had enough redundancy in its engineering to allow its nanotech to make two bodies from the same materials; she instructed it to divide into a mimic of Shelma's, along with a somewhat less sturdy copy of its original form. Then she loaded both with non-sentient software that could easily pass a half-baked Turing test from their would-be executioners.

Tilly remained guarding the fake prisoners, and they followed Jake through the tunnels, leaving by a different route from the one they'd arrived by. They did not travel unobserved, but the few lizards Azar glimpsed at intersections merely watched them pass in silence; presumably they belonged to Jake's faction, and were standing lookout in aid of their escape.

On the surface the ribbon-weeds carved the forest floor into a kind of maze, and while it was possible to cheat and squeeze your way between the edges of the fronds that didn't quite touch, it certainly was faster if you knew the maze so well that you didn't have to.

After a while, Jake halted and gestured urgently at a stubby, bulbous plant in the undergrowth. Since leaving the chamber he hadn't spoken at all; words decayed quickly in the water, to the point of losing their meaning, but the residue would still be easy to track. When Shelma did nothing he ducked down, tore a bulb from the plant, and stuffed it into his mouth. Shelma took the hint and did the same. The scouts hadn't come across this plant before, but the robot's nanotech quickly analysed the bulb's contents. There were few conventional nutrients in it, but it was packed with organic azides, nitrogen-rich compounds with an extremely high energy density. The plant was C3, but its genome suggested that the lizards had modified it to produce this edible rocket fuel, and despite its modest appearance its roots probably ran deeper into the ground than the ribbon-weeds rose up into the ocean. The nanotech didn't take long to devise a pathway to metabolise the azides safely – which was lucky, because Jake was already powering ahead at five times his previous swimming speed.

As their robot body struggled to catch up with him, Shelma said, 'Now I know why they don't bother with vehicles.' Azar had once tweaked her own flesh to enable her to run non-stop across a continent – purely for the physical joy of it – but it seemed that with the right dietary supplement anyone on Tallulah could moonlight as a high-performance submarine.

As they sped through the forest, the thermal/sonar images of the ribbon-weeds on either side of them blurred together like the walls of some long, twisted canyon. 'If "the Circlers" really want to kill us,' Azar said, 'I hope that doesn't mean all of them.' References to that cryptic self-description had been present even in distant traffic coming through the fibres; the group was certainly not confined to one colony.

Shelma said, 'I'm sure this is all just a misunderstanding. They think this is the end of the line for them – that Tallulah's come within reach of another dying world, and we're its inhabitants, intent on taking over.'

'You think they have a guilty precedent in mind?' Azar suggested. 'Maybe that's what happened with them and the N3ers.'

'Maybe. But I think it's more likely that the N3ers were long gone, and that's part of the shock. The lizards weren't expecting to be around to meet their own replacements either.'

Azar said, 'So how do we convince them that there is no threat, if they refuse to believe the evidence of their own telescopes?'

'Good question. How faint is the faintest dwarf star, and how far would they be willing to believe we've come?'

The forest gave way to a dense carpet of smaller plants, but Jake still knew how to find the fuel bulbs among them. This time when they stopped, he risked talking. 'I think you're safe for now,' he declared. 'But we should keep moving. I have friends who'll shelter us, but they're still a few hundred kilometres away.'

'We don't want to put anyone's life in danger,' Azar said, borrowing Shelma's lizard body but inflecting the words with the identity tag she'd used when she'd had her own.

'You won't,' Jake assured her. 'The three philosophies have been at peace for millennia; we're not going to start killing each other now.'

'The three philosophies?' Shelma asked.

'Circlers, Spiral In, Spiral Out.'

'We've heard those phrases, but we don't know what they mean.'

Jake flexed his body like an athlete limbering up for a sprint. 'If you want to keep talking, swim close beside me and synch your tail with mine.' As he started moving, Shelma followed his advice. The layer of water trapped between them let them communicate without their words being lost in the flow.

'The Circlers,' Jake said, 'are resolved to stay. To stay on

Tallulah, and to stay as they are. They accept that we didn't build this world ourselves, that it came to us as a gift, but to the Circlers that's not the point. The Builders are gone, and now Tallulah belongs to us.'

Azar said, 'So they're ready to fight off any intruders?'

'They're willing,' Jake replied, 'but I wouldn't call them ready. They weren't expecting you. Nobody was.'

'We really don't want this place as our home,' Shelma said. 'We have worlds of our own, powered by sunlight. You believe that, don't you?'

Jake considered the question. 'I suppose it's possible for life to evolve that way, around the right kind of star. Some experts claim the radiation would be fatal, but I believe there could be a narrow habitable zone. To travel more than a thousand light-years, though . . .'

Shelma explained about Mologhat 1 and 2, meeting and cancelling their momentum against each other. About the digital forms she and Azar had taken, crossing the light-years as gamma-rays in a subjective instant.

Jake said, 'Now you're trying to tell me that Spiral In is really the same as Spiral Out.'

'Spiral Out is about travel?' Azar said. 'The idea that you should leave Tallulah and look for a new home?'

'Yes. Spiral Out is my own philosophy.'

Azar tried to frame her next question as politely as possible, and hoped the translator would be able to honour her intent. 'Then if you don't mind me asking, why are you still here?'

'Travel isn't easy,' Jake declared. 'We've been waiting for Tallulah to bring us close to an empty world that we could claim as our own. But the last time that happened – before I was born – our numbers were small and our technology was untested. The opportunity was lost.'

Shelma said, 'So what's Spiral In?'

'They aim to take the form you claim to have taken. To become pure information. But not for travel: to stay on this world. To join with this world.'

It was an odd way of putting it, but Azar thought she caught his meaning. In almost every culture with the means to go digital, there was a subculture who advocated a kind of implosion: a retreat into a universe of scapes divorced from physical reality.

'To join with this world?' Shelma pressed him.

'With the heat. With the hoops. With the Builders themselves.' Jake emitted a token of mirth that Azar heard as curt laughter. 'Some Spiral In people believe that there are ten thousand cultures under the ground.'

The ocean floor passed beneath them in a blur.

'Hoops?' Azar said.

'You haven't seen the hoops yet?' Jake replied. 'When the rock turns to heat, what's left are the hoops.'

'The ash,' Shelma said privately. 'He's talking about the ash!'

'We've seen them,' Azar said. 'But we're not quite sure what they are.'

Jake fell silent for a while, then he said, 'How much do you know about relativity?' The translator marked the final word with a cautionary footnote: the scouts hadn't heard it in use before, so the meaning was being inferred purely from its etymology.

'I understand the basics.' Azar had studied relativity as a child, but without the full library to call on she would be unwise to claim to be an expert.

'Imagine,' Jake said, 'a hoop made of something extraordinarily strong, spinning at close to the speed of light. From the hoop's point of view, it's under enormous tension. But from the point of view of a bystander watching it spin, it's moving so rapidly that some of that tension manifests itself as a decrease in its energy.'

Azar was familiar with the principle, though she was more used to thinking of the opposite effect. When you considered a gas under pressure, that pressure was due to the momentum of molecules moving from place to place. But if you were moving rapidly relative to the gas – or vice versa – then some fraction of that *momentum in motion* looked to you instead like *energy standing still*. The shift in perspective transformed pressure into energy.

Tension was simply negative pressure, so for a moving object under tension the effect changed sign: the total energy would be decreased. The quantities involved would normally be immeasurably small, though. Azar said, 'Are you telling us that these hoops are under so much tension that their energy drops to *ten per cent of their rest mass*?'

'Yes.'

'Despite the kinetic energy of rotation? Despite the energy that goes into stretching the hoop?'

'Yes,' Jake replied. 'The effect of the tension outweighs both of those increases.'

Shelma passed some calculations privately to Azar, then addressed Jake. 'I think there's a problem with your theory. If you take a hoop and spin it ever faster, the only way its energy will begin to decrease is if the speed of sound in the hoop exceeds the speed of light.'

Azar checked the calculations; Shelma was right. The total energy of the hoop depended on the precise relationship between the elasticity of the hoop material and the tension it was under. But so, too, did the speed of sound in the material. Linking the two equations showed that the total energy couldn't fall in response to an increase in tension without the speed of sound becoming greater than light-speed – which was relativity's way of telling you that no material with the necessary properties could exist.

Jake was unfazed. 'We've known that result for a long time. It doesn't change the facts.'

'What are you claiming?' Shelma asked incredulously. 'That the speed of sound *does* exceed the speed of light?'

'Of course not,' Jake said. 'I agree that you can't construct a motionless hoop and then simply spin it up to a velocity so great that its energy begins to fall. But hoops that are already rotating can change their composition – spitting out particles and transforming into a new material that can only exist under tension. So you have to approach the final state through an intermediate structure: a high-energy, low-tension hoop that decays into a high-tension, low-energy hoop, with the energy difference going into the particles that are emitted in the decay process.'

Shelma considered this. 'All right, I think I see what you're getting at. But can you explain the details of this intermediate structure, and exactly how it can be synthesised?'

'The details?' Jake said. 'We've been on Tallulah for a million years. What makes you think that we've untangled all the details?'

7

They reached an isolated burrow, far from any colony. Jake went in first, then emerged with two friends, whom Azar's software named Juhi and Rahul.

Juhi said, 'Jake tells us you came from the world of a bright star. Is that true?'

Shelma replied, 'Absolutely.'

'So your real body is not like this at all?'

Shelma sketched her ancestral, five-fold symmetric shape in the sand. Juhi said something that the translator couldn't parse.

They entered the burrow and swam together to the deepest chamber, a much larger space than the prison they'd escaped from. It contained a transceiver and some other equipment that Azar didn't recognise – and in the circumstances it seemed both discourteous and unwise to send the scouts to sniff it out.

Rahul said, 'Our friends in Jute' – the colony they'd left – 'tell us that the Circlers still think they're holding you. They're hoping to find out more about the invasion plans.'

Invasion plans was a phrase Azar associated with ancient history and broad comedy. The zombie software she'd left in the bodies would keep reciting the truth to the bitter end, but now she almost wished she'd programmed some kind of parody of a confession.

Shelma said, 'We're grateful for your help. We didn't come here to cause trouble, but before we even knew that Tallulah was inhabited we lost the means to depart.' She explained Mologhat's fate.

Jake said, 'I thought that was no coincidence. The Old Passengers' machines have blasted specks of dust before, but when you appeared so soon afterwards I knew it wasn't down to chance.'

The N3ers? 'The Old Passengers lived here after the Builders?' Azar said.

'Yes,' Juhi replied. 'A few of their animals are still around. They built thousands of machines that aim to protect Tallulah, but some of them are a bit trigger-happy.'

'So your ancestors met the Old Passengers?' Shelma asked.

'Hardly!' Rahul sounded as amused as Azar would have been by the same query in relation to trilobites or dinosaurs. 'At least, not above ground. For all we know, some of the Old Passengers might still be alive, deep in the rock. But if they are, they're not very communicative.'

Azar said, 'What exactly is going on in the crust, besides the heating process? How do the hoops connect to the Spiral In philosophy?'

Juhi said, 'Once you give up your flesh and become information, don't you look for the fastest way to process that information?'

'Not always,' Azar replied. 'In our culture most of us compromise – to stay connected to each other, and to the physical world.'

'In our culture,' Rahul said, 'there is no one coming and going over thousands of light-years. There are only your biological cousins – and to Spiral In, if your cousins don't follow you down, that's their loss.'

Shelma said, 'So the hoops can be used for information processing?'

'Some of them,' Jake replied. 'The ones you've seen up in the water, probably not. But in the ground there are a billion different varieties.'

'*A billion?*' Shelma turned to Azar so they could exchange

stunned expressions – or at least so Shelma could hallucinate a version of Azar curling her five tails in the appropriate manner.

'Maybe more,' Jake said. 'The truth is, nobody above ground really knows. But we do know that some of them can be used as computing elements. Every time Spiral In becomes serious, they study the hoops, learn how to use them . . . then disappear into the ground.'

Azar was beginning to realise that she hadn't really thought through the implications of the Ground Heaters' process; even the ash it left behind opened up avenues that the Amalgam had only dreamt of. Amalgam femtocomputers were blazingly fast while they lasted, but they decayed as rapidly as the most unstable nuclei. You then had to rebuild them from scratch, making the whole process a waste of time for all but a handful of specialised applications. If you could build complex structures on a nuclear scale that were permanently stabilised – by virtue of possessing far less energy than their individual parts – then that changed the rules of the game completely. A femtocomputer that didn't blow itself apart, that kept on computing non-stop, would run at least six orders of magnitude faster than its atomic counterparts.

She said, 'So Spiral In use the hoops to retreat into virtual reality. But why don't you use the heating process yourself, just for the energy? If you want to escape from Tallulah, why not take this process and run?'

Rahul gestured at one of the machines in the corner of the chamber, a clunky, unprepossessing structure with a dozen cables snaking out of it. 'There's a sample of deep rock in there. Do you know how much power it's generating? Less than a microwatt.'

Azar stared at the machine. Her intuition baulked at Rahul's claim, but on reflection it was entirely plausible. In bulk, buried beneath an insulating blanket of rock several kilometres thick, the miraculous fuel would be white-hot, but up here in the water a small piece would barely be warmer than its surroundings. Its power to keep the whole planet from freezing came from its sheer quantity, and its spectacular efficiency was tuned for endurance, not a fast burn.

She said, 'So in its normal state the process runs slowly. But this isn't like some radioisotope with a half-life that can't be changed.'

'No,' Rahul said, 'it's worse than that. If you take a sample of ore containing a radioisotope, you can concentrate the active ingredient. If we purify deep rock – if we remove some of the ordinary minerals it contains in the hope of producing a denser power source – the process down-regulates automatically, maintaining the same output for a given total mass. It knows what you're doing, and it cheats you out of any gain.'

'Ah.' Azar was torn between empathy for the lizards' frustration and admiration for the Ground Heaters' ingenuity. It seemed the femtotech had been designed with very strong measures to protect against accidents and weaponisation.

Shelma said, 'But in all the time you've been studying it, surely you've made some progress? You say Spiral In have learnt to use the hoops as computing devices; that must give you some insight into the whole process.'

'Using the hoops isn't the same as controlling their creation,' Juhi said. 'It's like . . . building a computer out of fish bones, compared to engineering the biology of a fish. Spiral In learn enough to embed their minds in the rock in the simplest possible way. From that starting point, perhaps they migrate to more refined modes. Who knows? They've never come back to tell us.'

'If Spiral In can migrate into the rock,' Azar said, 'why are so many of them still here, above ground?'

'After each migration the philosophy dies out,' Juhi replied, 'but every few generations it becomes popular again. It starts out as an abstract stance – an idea about what we ought to do, eventually, sometime before we find ourselves confronting the Next Passengers – but then it reaches a critical mass, with enough people taking it seriously for the practicalities to be rediscovered. Then everyone who was serious goes underground . . . and everyone who was just spouting empty rhetoric defects to a different philosophy. We're at a point in the cycle right now where there's a lot of rhetoric, but not much else.'

Azar was too polite to suggest that Spiral Out seemed to be in much the same state themselves, but in their case there was nothing cyclic about it.

Shelma turned her robot's gaze from lizard to lizard, as if searching for a crack in their pessimistic consensus. 'It must be possible to harness this process,' she said. 'To adjust it, to manipulate it. A single nuclear reaction has its rate fixed by physical laws, but this is a *system* – a flexible, programmable network of nuclear machines. If someone built this system for their own purpose – with details that they chose for themselves, that weren't forced upon them by the underlying physics – then it can be *rebuilt*. You should be able to reverse-engineer the whole thing, and put it together again any way you like.'

Jake said, 'Someone built the deep rock, that's true. And if we were willing to choose the same path as the Builders, perhaps we could match their feat. But though the Builders set Tallulah in motion, in the end their philosophy was Spiral In. To make deep rock, the Builders *became* deep rock.

'I don't believe it can be done any other way. To understand it well enough to change it, we would have to become it. And then we would have changed ourselves so much that we would no longer want the very thing that we set out to achieve.'

8

As the discussion wound its way back and forth between Tallulah's uncertain history and the competing visions of its future, Azar seized upon one piece of good news that Rahul let slip almost in passing. The lizards couldn't re-create the femtotech from scratch, or even ramp it up into a useful form of propulsion, but they did believe that there was a very good chance that they'd be able to *graft it*. Given an empty world on which to experiment, they hoped that introducing samples of the deep rock into the crust would cause the femtotech to replicate, spreading through the native rock and ultimately creating a second Tallulah.

That was a wonderful prospect, but they'd already missed at least one opportunity. Some two hundred thousand years before, Tallulah had passed through an uninhabited system, but Spiral Out had been at a low ebb and hadn't even managed to launch exploratory probes. Since then they'd simply been hanging around waiting for their next chance. The Ground Heaters had given them an extraordinary gift, rescuing them from their dying planet, but between the culture of dependency that gift had created, the constant temptations of Spiralling In and the stress of not knowing whether the next world they encountered would turn out to be the home of the Next Passengers, they had ended up paralysed.

'You should join the Amalgam,' Azar said, 'and use their network to migrate. The kind of world you're looking for is not in high demand; a frozen planet tidally locked to a faint brown dwarf is of no interest to most spacefaring cultures.'

'And it's no use to us either,' Jake replied, 'unless we can enliven it. We can't send the deep rock through your network, can we?'

'No, but if you spent a century or two manufacturing anti-matter from geothermal energy, you could build an engine to carry samples of rock at a significant fraction of light-speed. And even if for some reason you didn't have enough spare power to do that, I guarantee that you could find a partner in the Amalgam who'd trade you a few tonnes of antimatter for some deep rock samples of their own. And I mean a few tonnes on arrival at Tallulah, not a few tonnes when it left home!'

Juhi said, 'We need to be careful. It's one thing to hand Tallulah over to the Next Passengers, as the Builders intended, but we don't want a million strangers flocking here just to mine the planet.'

'Nobody's going to do that,' Shelma assured her. 'If deep rock has any value at all in the Amalgam, it will come from the ability to graft it, or the ability to reverse-engineer it. In either case, a few kilograms would be enough.'

Rahul said, 'Whether we choose to join the Amalgam or not, you need antimatter for your own journey, don't you?'

'A few micrograms would come in handy,' Shelma admitted.

The transceiver sprayed out a chemical ringtone and Rahul replied with a command for it to speak. Azar found the conversation that followed cryptic – and she suspected that parts of it were literally in code – but when it was over Rahul announced, 'Someone spotted you in the forest with Jake. The Circlers have destroyed your puppets, but they know more or less what happened now. I think we need to move from here.'

Azar was dismayed. 'Can't you talk to them? Explain the situation? None of our plans should be any threat to them.' The Amalgam would happily leave the Circlers in peace, sending no travellers and no further explorers, but the Spiral Out faction were entitled to emigrate, and to trade a few small pieces of Tallulah's exotic legacy with the wider galaxy.

Rahul said, 'They're convinced that you're the New Passengers, and that the fight to retain Tallulah has begun. In the past they've viewed Spiral Out as timid fatalists, but now that we've come to your aid we're something worse. We're traitors.'

On the flight deck Shelma muttered a string of obscenities. 'We're not going to spark a civil war,' she told the lizards. 'We'll surrender ourselves. It doesn't matter if they destroy us; we'll make back-ups.'

Jake said, 'But they understand now that you can do that. You could surrender a thousand machines to them – or one pair of living creatures, and call them your true form – but it won't be enough to convince them that they've put an end to your plans.'

Azar wanted to contest this bleak verdict, but from what she'd seen of the Circlers first-hand it rang true. Whatever the original intention of Tallulah's creators, it had sounded like a beautiful story: a chariot travelling between faint, forgotten stars, rescuing the inhabitants of dying worlds, offering them a safe, warm home for a few million years so they could build up their strength then fly from the nest – or, if they wished, dive into its depths, into a femtoscale mansion of a quadrillion rooms. In a way, she admired the Circlers for their determination to tear up the script, to scream at their long-vanished benefactors that they would make their own decisions and not just meekly come along for the ride. But the irony was that they were so intent on rebelling against the Builders that they seemed blind to anything that didn't conform to their own version of the scenario. It was chiselled in stone that one day they would fight the New Passengers for Tallulah, and they had spent so long rehearsing this play that you couldn't even tap them on the shoulder and suggest a different ending without being dragged into the plot and cast as the villain.

Shelma had their mock-lizard body destroy itself, and found a dim but agile P2 fish for the insect to parasitise and modify. A talking fish would attract suspicion, but with some help from the library they managed to engineer speech glands for it that created rapidly decaying words; if they swam up close to a chosen confidante they could emit some short-range chemical whispers with little chance of being overheard. Unfortunately, the lizards' own medical nanotech wasn't flexible enough to do the same for them, and Jake and the others recoiled from a friendly offer to let the aliens tweak their speech organs.

Shelma said privately, 'This is going to get messy.'

'So how do we fix it?' Azar replied.

'I wish I knew.'

They agreed on a place and time to rendezvous, then Jake, Rahul and Juhi scattered.

Shelma said, 'I think we should go back to the surface for a while.'

They took the fish as high as it could go, then left it parked and rode the insect alone for the last few hundred metres. When they broke the water, Azar found herself almost weeping with relief. She was still as far from home as ever, but just a glimpse of the stars after so long without them made her feel that she was back in the right universe again.

Neither the balloon nor the orbiting microprobes had experienced any form of aggression, or noticed anything else unusual. It seemed that the Circlers, for all their paranoia, had been too complacent to create a world bristling with sensors and weapons while Tallulah's next stop was still so far from sight.

Shelma said, 'We should bring the balloon down on the ground somewhere and replicate the library a few times. I think we're already carrying everything vital, but if our back-ups have to take over from us we want to be sure that they're not disadvantaged.' Their back-ups in the jungle were already receiving incremental memory updates, by radio via the microprobes.

Azar agreed, and they sent the instructions. She paced the flight deck, rubbing her eyes. She had given up the need for sleep, but there was still something irredeemably strange about the feeling of unpunctuated consciousness stretching back into the distance.

'I screwed up,' Shelma said. 'I rushed to make contact. We didn't even know what the factions' names meant.'

'And I let you do it,' Azar replied. 'We're both at fault. But I don't believe the situation's irretrievable. The Circlers have killed some alien zombies, but according to Jake the philosophies have been at peace for millennia; it could still be a step too far for them to start harming each other.'

'How do we defuse their anxiety,' Shelma said, 'when there's no invading army for them to defeat? Do we offer them the microprobes as sitting ducks? I doubt that they could hit targets that small, and even if they could they'd just assume that there were ten thousand more.'

Azar looked up at the stars again, and tried to see them as a hostile, threatening sight. 'They need some theatre. They need some catharsis.' Clearly Shelma thought the same way too, but then neither of them were exactly experts in the lizards' psychology. 'And we need to talk to Jake again.'

'What do you have in mind?'

'The microprobes are too small, and Mologhat is already gone. So maybe we should think about launching a bigger target.'

*

Only Juhi turned up at the rendezvous point in a remote stretch of ribbon-weed forest. 'Jake and Rahul are safe,' she said, 'but they're too far away at the moment.'

'What's been happening?' Azar asked her.

'We've been in contact with most of Spiral Out, and they've made a decision. They want to send a delegation with you to the closest world in the Amalgam, to make contact with this culture and report back on the possibilities for trade and migration.'

Azar was encouraged; at least Spiral Out had proved willing to break from its preconceptions.

'We're prepared to start manufacturing antimatter,' Juhi continued. 'But we should compare notes on the process first; if you have a more efficient method we should adopt that.'

Shelma said, 'What kind of power sources do you have access to?' The everyday lizard culture they'd seen was based on plant thermoelectrics.

'There are some deep-bore geothermal turbines that are used for specialised research projects,' Juhi replied. 'Obviously we can't tap the whole output, but we should be able to siphon some off discreetly.'

'What if you just built your own turbine?' Azar said. 'Would the Circlers do anything to stop you?'

'Right now,' Juhi said, 'I don't think it would be wise to find out.'

Azar turned that statement over in her mind. If people were about to begin clandestine antimatter production, what would happen to them if they were caught?

'We've had an idea,' she said, 'but I don't know if it will make sense to you. The Circlers believe we've come from a nearby planet, from a star too dim to see. What if we built a spacecraft that might have made a short journey like that . . . and then let the Circlers shoot it down?'

Juhi said, 'How are you going to power this spacecraft?'

'The azide bulbs you eat when you travel; enough of them could actually get a small craft into low orbit. The Circlers accept that we're digitised, so they don't expect the invasion force to be a fleet of thousand-tonne arks.'

'It's an interesting idea,' Juhi said, 'but the hardest part would be contriving their success in destroying the craft. Since your arrival they've been dredging up plans for weapons that our ancestors constructed for the last close approach, two hundred thousand years ago. But nobody's sure now that they still understand those designs.'

Shelma said, 'What about surveillance? Are they already monitoring what's happening in near space?'

'Yes. You can be sure of that.'

'Then the problem,' Shelma said, 'is that they'd see us taking off. It would better to convince them that something new is coming in from deep space.'

Juhi paused, the front of her body twitching from side to side, a motion that Azar now recognised as a sign of anxiety. 'I don't see how we can do that. But let me take this to the others.'

Shelma had the insect's nanotech construct a sample of a solid-state antimatter factory, and passed it to Juhi for the lizards to copy. It was the Amalgam's most efficient design, but nothing could get around the fact that it would still need thousands of times more power than any ordinary burrow consumed.

After parting from Juhi they stayed away from Jute and the other colonies, but the scout mites had placed intercepts on some of the intercolony trunk fibres long ago. The lizards had no infrastructure in place for quantum encryption, and their standard communication codes were easily cracked; clearly this wasn't a culture with an entrenched history of bitter enmities and closely held secrets. It was a culture polarised by sudden panic, and Azar clung to the hope that cooler heads would soon prevail.

The tapped conversations were discouraging, though. The idea of Spiral Out as traitors was spreading throughout the Circlers, many of whom were urging each other to keep a close watch on their treacherous neighbours and erstwhile friends. The claim that the alien visitors were benign explorers with no territorial ambitions was largely discounted; two previous examples of

Tallulah being colonised were, apparently, sufficient to render other motives unlikely. Azar began to wonder if the best course would be to lie low for a century or two and simply wait for the non-arrival of the trumpeted invasion force to leave the prophets of doom looking like fools.

Rahul met them for the next rendezvous. 'Jake's disappeared,' he said. 'I think he's been imprisoned, but nobody will admit to holding him.'

Azar was speechless. For all the bad news she'd heard from the taps, she'd never believed it would come to this.

'We can send machines to hunt for him,' Shelma said.

'If you can, please,' Rahul replied. 'But they will have moved him to another colony, so I don't know exactly where you should start.'

Azar came her to senses. She instructed the scouts that were already hovering near the fish; they would spread out and replicate, following the fibre trunk lines from colony to colony, spawning search parties as they went.

'We have an idea to placate the Circlers,' Rahul said. 'To give them the triumph they think they need.'

'Go on,' Shelma urged him.

'We can't get a craft into deep space, unseen,' he said. 'And even if we could, I doubt the Circlers could hit it. But the Old Passengers' machines are still working very well after all this time – as you know, to your cost. If they were seen to repel the would-be New Passengers, I think the Circlers would treat that victory as their own.'

Shelma said, 'But how do we get the target up there? And how do we guarantee that the machines strike it?'

'We cheat,' Rahul said. 'We hack into the Old Passengers' network, and make it respond with as much sound and fury as possible to something that isn't really there.'

Azar said, 'Do you know how to do that?'

'Not quite,' Rahul admitted. 'This is where we need your help.'

The lizards had mapped parts of the Old Passengers' network long ago. It was bioengineered from native C3 plants, and used a modified form of the conductive polymers that Azar had first seen in the thermocouple bush. There were sensors of various kinds scattered across the continents, processing hubs on land and in the water, and dozens of geothermal cannons on the ocean floor.

Every thousand years or so someone had tried tapping into the network, but the protocols had always eluded them. There had been talk of trying to decommission the whole eccentric, unpredictable system, but the contrary view – that the Old Passengers had known what they were doing, and always had the interests of Tallulah at heart – had prevailed. Certainly the system had been benign enough to allow the lizards themselves to cross from their home world unmolested, and if the cannons sometimes spat steam and ice at phantoms that was a small price to pay.

Armed with Rahul's map, Azar and Shelma returned to the surface and sent instructions to the other explorer insects, which had now reached every continent. As the insects tapped into the network, the microprobes monitored the flashes of Cerenkov radiation that incoming cosmic rays created in the upper atmosphere. Whatever else might elicit a response from the system, radiation was a proven irritant.

As they waited for the data to accumulate, Azar couldn't stop thinking about Jake. What would his captors do? *Torture him?* While the lizards had engineered senescence away, and pumped their bodies full of medical nanotech that could combat the subtlest toxins and parasites, a simple metal blade could still be as painful, or as fatal, as it would have been for their earliest ancestors.

In three days, the insects had cracked the protocol: they knew how the Old Passengers' network represented the atmospheric flashes, and how the data was cross-checked and confirmed. Though the system was moderately robust against errors, if the lizards' anecdotes meant anything it was prone to the occasional false positive, and it certainly hadn't been designed with resistance to tampering as a high priority. Azar was beginning to suspect that the Old Passengers had never actually contemplated an invasion; all of their concerns had revolved around natural hazards.

Would the Circlers understand as much, and know that they were being had? Or would they seize upon the evidence as vindication of their fantasies?

They dived to meet Rahul again, and Shelma told him that the network was now in their hands.

'Make it happen,' he said. 'Shoot down the invaders.'

Azar communed with the scout mites. There was still no news of Jake.

9

The insect glided in a gentle helix a few metres above the ocean, but Azar locked the flight deck scape to the stars, banishing the perceived rotation. She fixed her gaze on the horizon and waited.

Data was being fed into the Old Passengers' network, painting an elaborate mirage: a cloud of antihydrogen heading straight for Tallulah, three million kilometres away and closing fast. Interstellar gas and dust colliding with the cloud was creating highly energetic gamma-rays; in turn, these gamma-rays were striking nitrogen molecules in Tallulah's stratosphere and generating particle-antiparticle pairs. None of this exotic radiation would be getting close to the ground, so the whole hallucination was being played out in terms of flashes of light from high in the atmosphere.

Shelma said, 'Given their proclivities, you'd think they would have put satellites in orbit: gamma-ray telescopes at least.'

'Maybe they did,' Azar replied, 'but the orbits were destabilised when Tallulah entered the lizards' system. Or maybe they were just corroded away.' A quarter of a billion years was a long time; deep rock in the satellites might have provided a constant trickle of power, and nanotech could have carried out repairs, but if they lost material to abrasive dust or cosmic ray ablation, however slowly, nothing could have kept them intact for ever.

'There she blows!' Shelma cried out happily; with the full library now accessible to the scape, the translations Azar heard of her speech were much more evocative. In infrared, the distant column of superheated steam glowed like an electric arc, rising out of the ocean and stretching into the sky. The ascending tip grew dim and faded into the distance, but when Azar added an overlay with visible frequencies amplified she could see the end of the icy spear glistening in the starlight as it hurtled into space.

This time there was no planet-shrouding halo needed to flush out the danger; the target was all too clear. The microprobes were tracking the ice missiles, and would feed their interaction with the imaginary antimatter cloud into the models that were generating the hoax atmospheric light show for the network, ensuring that all the data continued to reflect a consistent scenario. Of course, if the Circlers also happened to be looking for atmospheric flashes they would see no such thing, but that shouldn't matter, since they had no way of knowing exactly what the Old Passengers' defences thought they were firing at.

Azar said, 'If someone had told me that I'd be faking a battle for Tallulah between an extinct species and an imaginary invader, I would never have walked through that gate.'

'Oh, this is nothing,' Shelma scoffed. 'One day I'll tell you about the time—'

A message from the microprobes half a world away cut off the boast in mid-sentence. Something was emerging from the middle of a continent on the other side of the planet, and it wasn't a fountain of steam. A narrow beam of gamma-rays was rising up from the ground, just millimetres thick but energetic enough to have wrapped itself in a radiant cylinder of plasma as it punched its way out of the atmosphere.

Azar let out an anguished moan. 'What have we done now?' Her skin crawled as one alarming possibility crossed her mind: someone could be messing with the microprobes, feeding them a vision of nonexistent radiation. But that was just paranoid; who would gain anything from hoaxing the hoaxer? Perhaps the insects had screwed up their analysis of the Old Passengers' protocols and inadvertently injected a second phantom target into the data – one that had elicited a far harsher response.

For several long seconds Shelma was frozen, either in shock or in contemplation. Then she declared, 'It's a photonic jet. *We've triggered an unscheduled course correction.'*

'What?'

'The steam jet is exceeding escape velocity, which means it's pushing Tallulah off course, very slightly. So the Builders, the Ground Heaters, are compensating.'

Azar wasn't sure yet what she believed, but she hoped the Circlers reached the same conclusion as Shelma; they'd have no reason, then, to question their interpretation of the steam jet as a defensive measure. The photonic jet was just a technical detail, an anti-recoil device for Tallulah's big guns. In any case, the Old Passengers' network seemed to know that such a response was only to be expected; it wasn't treating it as yet another interstellar hazard that needed to be dispelled by its own separate fire hose.

But assuming it wasn't a counter-hoax, this beam of radiation was infinitely more substantial than the nonexistent hazard that *was* being pummelled. 'There are now real gamma-rays blasting through the atmosphere,' Azar said. 'Hitting nuclei, undergoing pair production. *The photonic jet will be surrounded by antimatter.'*

Shelma said, 'I believe you're right.'

They instructed the closest insects to fly up near the beam and investigate. The central cylinder of plasma was rich in antiprotons, and though they weren't lasting long before annihilating, the annihilation gamma-rays themselves were in turn striking nitrogen nuclei and creating more proton-antiproton pairs, giving rise to a long cascade before the energy was converted into heat, or escaped into space at the top of the beam.

Nanotech in the insects took just minutes to construct the necessary magnetic harvesters, which plucked the slowest antiprotons from the relatively cool margins of the plasma. There were only a few dozen insects in range, and they could only sip from a small part of the beam, but the bounty here dwarfed the travellers' needs. The task that might have taken their Spiral Out accomplices months of furtive, dangerous work would now be complete in less than an hour.

Azar felt an intense surge of relief. The Amalgam was almost within reach now, and no one else would need to put themselves at risk to make the journey possible.

Shelma said, 'I think I know where the water went.'

'Yeah?'

'When Tallulah came into the Old Passengers' system, the Ground Heaters were nowhere in sight; they were either dead or they'd gone femto. So the Old Passengers had no one to negotiate with, no one to learn from, no one to spell out the rules. They'd simply found this luxurious abandoned lifeboat, and they wanted to take control. But it takes a long time to evacuate a planet physically, building and launching thousands of spacecraft; it's possible that there were still millions of people who wanted to make the crossing even as Tallulah was going out of range of their ships.'

'So they built the geothermal cannons,' Azar said, 'to try to bring it back in range. They were so desperate to let the stragglers come on board that they were willing to pump half the ocean into the sky.'

'To no avail. The ghosts of the Ground Heaters – or some insentient navigation system – fought them every step of the way. The femtotech couldn't shut off the cannons; even if it switched off the heating process locally, the rocks would have stayed hot for thousands of years. But the photonic jets it already used for steering could easily compensate for the momentum of the steam.' Shelma hesitated, then added, 'That could also explain why the Old Passengers ended up allergic to antimatter. An ordinary course change would have taken Tallulah clear of any debris from its own jets, but after a series of long, complicated tussles, there might have been clouds of antimatter lying around that really were worth sweeping aside.'

Azar said, 'What drives me crazy is that if the deep rock can be grafted, it was all for nothing. The Old Passengers could have brought a sample back to their own world and solved all their problems without anyone leaving.'

'That was probably the Ground Heaters' original plan,' Shelma said. 'To travel the galaxy handing out deep rock, to reheat dying worlds. But to the Old Passengers, *grafting rock* would probably have sounded as ridiculous as trying to reignite a dead star with a spoonful of lukewarm helium. By the time they understood the first thing about the femtotech it would have been too late.'

Azar watched the column of luminous steam, still rushing into the sky. 'Now we've thrown away a few more gigatonnes of water, just to deceive the lizards.'

Shelma said, 'If you want it to sound slightly less tawdry when you tell your great-great-grandchildren, I recommend the version where we were doing it for the antimatter all along.'

'I don't mind lying if it saves people's lives,' Azar replied, 'but I'd like to return to Hanuz with some prospect that we're not leaving behind a civil war.'

'Yeah. We need to find out how far this charade has gone in cleaning up our mess.' Shelma inhaled deeply. 'Let's dive.'

At the rendezvous point, Rahul explained that the Circlers were still debating the significance of the steam jet. The ice halo had been written off as a false alarm until Azar and Shelma had introduced themselves, but this time nobody doubted that such an intense, sustained effort from the Old Passengers' machines had something to do with encroaching aliens.

When Azar told him that they'd now harvested enough anti-matter to make a transmission, Rahul confessed that the photonic jet hadn't taken him entirely by surprise. 'Some people have always believed that the Old Passengers fought against the Builders to control Tallulah's path. That's been enough to keep the Circlers from trying to do the same thing themselves; they take it as given that they can't steer the world, and their only choice is to fight to defend it.'

Shelma said, 'Why not trade to defend it? Why not offer any would-be invaders a few kilograms of deep rock grafts?'

'Because grafting is unproven,' Rahul replied. 'We've done a thousand experiments with different minerals at various temperatures and pressures, and it *looks* as if there's a balance we can exploit between the hoop system's ability to spread and the safety mechanism that stops it running amok . . . but the only real proof will come when we try it on a completely new world. Until then, what is there to trade? A handful of warm pebbles that might turn your planet into a fireball, or might do nothing at all.'

As they spoke, a wave of scout mites swam inside the camouflage fish and docked with the insect. They had found Jake; he was being held in an isolated burrow, almost three thousand kilometres away.

Azar gave Rahul the position. He said, 'We have no one close. Do you know how many Circlers are guarding him?'

'Our machines saw twenty.'

'Then I don't know how to help him,' Rahul confessed. 'When he broke you out it was easier, everything was still in a state of confusion. Half the people around you had no declared allegiance; Jake and Tilly were not known as Spiral Out before, it was your presence that forced them to take sides. But all twenty people with Jake now will be resolute Circlers, committed to that philosophy for centuries.'

Shelma said, 'The invasion has been repelled! What would the Circlers have to gain now by harming him?'

'It would set an example for future collaborators.'

They swam together to the closest intercept point on the trunk line; the scouts were piggybacking their own data onto the fibre, using methods too subtle for the lizards to detect. Azar and Shelma watched through the scouts' senses and passed on the Circlers' chemical conversation to Rahul. Jake was in one chamber, along with four guards; in a nearby chamber the other Circlers had gathered to discuss the latest news and plan their next move.

Shelma spoke to Azar privately. 'I've got the nanotech primed to go in and digitise him, if it comes to that. But if we wait for them to kill him it might be too late; if they mutilate the body or use corrosive chemicals we won't have time to capture him properly.'

Jake hadn't given them explicit consent to do anything, but Azar swallowed her objections. According to Juhi he had wanted to be part of a delegation to the Amalgam, and if he turned out to be displeased about being snatched into the infosphere without warning, they could always write him back into ordinary flesh once they'd smuggled his software to safety. The real danger here was jumping in too soon or too late. Too soon and they risked re-igniting tensions with an unmistakable alien intervention. Too late and Jake would be dead.

Among the Circlers in the other chamber were two that Azar recognised from their first encounter: Omar and Lisa. Most of the talk here so far had been petty squabbling, but now the subject turned to Jake.

'We should release him,' Omar insisted. 'The fleet has been destroyed or turned back; it doesn't matter what he does now.'

'Spiral Out need to know what happens to traitors,' Lisa replied. 'He set New Passengers free among us. He put everyone in danger.'

Another Circler, Silas, said, 'You saw their technology; they could have escaped anyway. Whatever Spiral Out do, we're never going to be sure that we're safe, that we're alone. That's the reality now, and we need to find a way to live with it.'

Half a dozen other Circlers responded to this angrily, swimming around the chamber in tight, anxious loops. 'We need to kill him,' Judah declared. 'We need to draw a clear boundary between the right of Spiral Out to make their plans to leave Tallulah, and our right to live here safely and defend our own world.'

Omar said, 'If we kill him we'll start another war. Do you know how many people died in the last one?'

'Better a million die than we lose the whole world to the New Passengers,' Lisa replied.

'Better *nobody dies*,' Omar retorted, 'and we spend our efforts on something that can help us all. We've been living like fools. We don't deserve to feel safe, and killing our own people won't change that. We don't even know with certainty where the closest world really lies! And we have no idea what kind of life there might be around the bright stars; I doubt that the aliens were telling us the truth, but none of us really know what's possible.'

'We've been caught sleeping,' Judah conceded. 'That much is our fault. But what do you suggest we do about it?'

Omar said, 'We need to work together with Spiral Out to explore the nearest worlds, before any more of their inhabitants reach us themselves. If we send out small robots to gather information, the results can serve everyone: defenders of Tallulah, and those who want to leave.'

Lisa was scornful. 'After this, you're going to trust Spiral Out as our allies?'

'Jake freed two aliens that you were threatening to kill,' Omar replied. 'They had done us no harm, and we don't even know for sure that they were lying. Because of that, we should slaughter all of Spiral Out? Or treat them all as our enemies? If everything that's happened wakes them from their sleep the way it should wake us, we can benefit from each other's efforts.'

Azar looked to Rahul for a reading of the situation, but he was motionless, his posture offering no verdict. Jake's fate could go either way.

After forty minutes of discussion with no clear consensus, Omar said, 'I'm releasing him.' He paused for a few seconds, then left the chamber. Lisa squirted wordless, dissatisfied noise, but nobody moved to stop him.

Omar entered the chamber where Jake was being held and spoke with the Circlers who were standing guard.

'I don't agree,' said Tarek. 'You've come alone to demand this. Who else is with you?'

Omar and Tarek went together to the other Circlers. Omar said, 'I repeat, I'm releasing Jake. If anyone here wants a war, I will be an enemy of the warmongers, so you'd better kill me now.'

Judah said, 'No one's going to kill you.' He swam with Omar to Jake's chamber and spoke with the remaining guards. Then all five of them departed, leaving Jake alone.

Jake circled the chamber nervously a few times, then headed out of the burrow. Azar sent a swarm of scouts after him, but they had no data channel back to the fibre, and Jake was soon out of sight.

Almost an hour later, a message came through from the scouts; Jake had reached a nearby colony where the scouts could tap into the fibre again. Azar told Rahul their location.

Rahul said, 'He's safe, he's with friends. It's over for now.'

Azar sat on the flight deck weeping, hiding her tears even from Shelma.

10

Launched from a rail-gun on Tallulah's highest mountain, Mologhat 3 spent six seconds ploughing through the atmosphere before attaining the freedom of space. Its heat shield glowed brightly as it ascended, but if the Old Passengers' machines noticed it they found no reason to molest this speck of light as it headed out of harm's way. When it reached an altitude of a thousand kilometres it fired its own tiny photonic jet, but the radiation was horizontal and highly directional; nothing on Tallulah had a hope of detecting it.

Jake, Tilly, Rahul, Juhi and a fifth delegate, Santo, swam across the flooded observation deck, looking down on their world for the first time. Azar swam among them, but not as a lizard in anyone's eyes. Her words would come to them as familiar chemicals, but they could cope with the sight of her as she really was.

As Azar gazed upon Tallulah, she dared to feel hope. There would be no war, no pogrom, but there was still a daunting task ahead for the millions of Spiral Out who remained. They would need to prepare the Circlers for the truth: for the eventual return of this secret delegation, for trade with the Amalgam, for a galaxy that was not what they'd imagined at all. For a future that didn't follow their script.

Jake said, 'Do you think we'll ever meet Shelma again?'

Azar shrugged; Jake wouldn't recognise the gesture immediately, but he'd soon learn. 'She once told me that she could choose for herself between solitude and a connection with her people. If she wants to come back, she'll make those connections as strong as she can.'

'No one's ever returned before,' Jake said.

'Did Spiral In ever really want to?'

When the moles finally hit paydirt beneath the ocean floor, their mass spectrometers had detected more than a hundred billion variants of the hoop, and that was only counting the stable forms. The deep rock was more complex than most living systems; no doubt much of that complexity was fixed by the needs of the heating process, but there was still room for countless variations along the way – and room for a new passenger hitching a ride on the hoops as they turned iron and nickel into heat.

If you had to become deep rock in order to understand it, Shelma had decided, she would become it, and then come back. She'd drag the secrets of the hoops out of the underworld and into the starlight.

'What if you can't?' Azar had asked her. 'What if you lose your way?'

'There's room in there for a whole universe,' Shelma had replied. 'If I'm tempted into staying, don't think of me as dead. Just think of me as an explorer who lived a good life to its end.'

Jake said, 'Tell me more about your world. Tell me about Hanuz.'

'There's no need,' Azar replied. She gestured at the departure gate. 'If you're ready, I'll show it to you.'

'Just like that?' Jake twitched anxiously.

'It's fourteen quadrillion kilometres,' she said. 'You won't be back for three thousand years. You can change your mind and stay, or you can gather your friends and swim it with me. But I'm leaving now. I need to see my family. I need to go home.'

OCEANIC

1

The swell was gently lifting and lowering the boat. My breathing grew slower, falling into step with the creaking of the hull, until I could no longer tell the difference between the faint rhythmic motion of the cabin and the sensation of filling and emptying my lungs. It was like floating in darkness: every inhalation buoyed me up, slightly; every exhalation made me sink back down again.

In the bunk above me, my brother Daniel said distinctly, 'Do you believe in God?'

My head was cleared of sleep in an instant, but I didn't reply straight away. I'd never closed my eyes, but the darkness of the unlit cabin seemed to shift in front of me, grains of phantom light moving like a cloud of disturbed insects.

'Martin?'

'I'm awake.'

'Do you believe in God?'

'Of course.' Everyone I knew believed in God. Everyone talked about Her, everyone prayed to Her. Daniel most of all. Since he'd joined the Deep Church the previous summer, he prayed every morning for a kilotau before dawn. I'd often wake to find myself aware of him kneeling by the far wall of the cabin, muttering and pounding his chest, before I drifted gratefully back to sleep.

Our family had always been Transitional, but Daniel was fifteen, old enough to choose for himself. My mother accepted this with diplomatic silence, but my father seemed positively proud of Daniel's independence and strength of conviction. My own feelings were mixed. I'd grown used to swimming in my older brother's wake, but I'd never resented it, because he'd always let me in on the view ahead: reading me passages from the books he read himself, teaching me words and phrases from the languages he studied, sketching some of the mathematics I was yet to encounter first-hand. We used to lie awake half the night, talking about the cores of stars or the hierarchy of transfinite numbers. But Daniel had told me nothing about the reasons for his conversion, and his ever-increasing piety. I didn't know whether to feel hurt by this exclusion, or simply grateful; I could see that being Transitional was like a pale imitation of being Deep Church, but I wasn't sure that this was such a bad thing if the wages of mediocrity included sleeping until sunrise.

Daniel said, 'Why?'

I stared up at the underside of his bunk, unsure whether I was really seeing it or just imagining its solidity against the cabin's ordinary darkness. 'Someone must have guided the Angels here from Earth. If Earth's too far away to see from Covenant . . . how could anyone find Covenant from Earth, without God's help?'

I heard Daniel shift slightly. 'Maybe the Angels had better telescopes than us. Or maybe they spread out from Earth in all directions, launching thousands of expeditions without even knowing what they'd find.'

I laughed. 'But they had to come *here*, to be made flesh again!' Even a less-than-devout ten-year-old knew that much. God prepared Covenant as the place for the Angels to repent their theft of immortality. The Transitionals believed that in a million years we could earn the right to be Angels again; the Deep Church believed that we'd remain flesh until the stars fell from the sky.

Daniel said, 'What makes you so sure that there were ever really Angels? Or that God really sent them Her daughter, Beatrice, to lead them back into the flesh?'

I pondered this for a while. The only answers I could think of came straight out of the Scriptures, and Daniel had taught me years ago that appeals to authority counted for nothing. Finally, I had to confess: 'I don't know.' I felt foolish, but I was grateful that he was willing to discuss these difficult questions with me. I wanted to believe in God for the right reasons, not just because everyone around me did.

He said, 'Archaeologists have shown that we must have arrived about twenty thousand years ago. Before that, there's no evidence of humans, or any co-ecological plants and animals. That makes the Crossing older than the Scriptures say, but there are some dates that are open to interpretation, and with a bit of poetic licence everything can be made to add up. And most biologists think the native microfauna could have formed by itself over millions of years, starting from simple chemicals, but that doesn't mean God didn't guide the whole process. Everything's compatible, really. Science and the Scriptures can both be true.'

I thought I knew where he was headed, now. 'So you've worked out a way to use science to prove that God exists?' I felt a surge of pride; my brother was a genius!

'No.' Daniel was silent for a moment. 'The thing is, it works both ways. Whatever's written in the Scriptures, people can always come up with different explanations for the facts. The ships might have left Earth for some other reason. The Angels might have made bodies for themselves for some other reason. There's no way to convince a non-believer that the Scriptures are the word of God. It's all a matter of faith.'

'Oh.'

'Faith's the most important thing,' Daniel insisted. 'If you don't have faith, you can be tempted into believing anything at all.'

I made a noise of assent, trying not to sound too disappointed. I'd expected more from Daniel than the kind of bland assertions that sent me dozing off during sermons at the Transitional church.

'Do you know what you have to do to get faith?'

'No.'

'Ask for it. That's all. Ask Beatrice to come into your heart and grant you the gift of faith.'

I protested, 'We do that every time we go to church!' I couldn't believe he'd forgotten the Transitional service already. After the priest placed a drop of seawater on our tongues, to symbolise the blood of Beatrice, we asked for the gifts of faith, hope and love.

'But have you received it?'

I'd never thought about that. 'I'm not sure.' I believed in God, didn't I? 'I might have.'

Daniel was amused. 'If you had the gift of faith, you'd *know*.'

I gazed up into the darkness, troubled. 'Do you have to go to the Deep Church to ask for it properly?'

'No. Even in the Deep Church, not everyone has invited Beatrice into their hearts. You have to do it the way it says in the Scriptures: "like an unborn child again, naked and helpless".'

'I was Immersed, wasn't I?'

'In a metal bowl, when you were thirty days old. Infant Immersion is a gesture by the parents, an affirmation of their own good intentions. But it's not enough to save the child.'

I was feeling very disoriented now. My father, at least, approved of Daniel's conversion . . . but now Daniel was trying to tell me that our family's transactions with God had all been grossly deficient, if not actually counterfeit.

Daniel said, 'Remember what Beatrice told Her followers, the last time She appeared? "Unless you are willing to drown in My blood, you will never look upon the face of My Mother." So they bound each other hand and foot, and weighted themselves down with rocks.'

My chest tightened. 'And you've done that?'

'Yes.'

'*When?*'

'Almost a year ago.'

I was more confused than ever. 'Did Ma and Fa go?'

Daniel laughed. 'No! It's not a public ceremony. Some friends of mine from the Prayer Group helped; someone has to be on deck to haul you up, because it would be arrogant to expect Beatrice to break your bonds and raise you to the surface like She did with Her followers. But in the water, you're alone with God.'

He climbed down from his bunk and crouched by the side of

my bed. 'Are you ready to give your life to Beatrice, Martin?' His voice sent grey sparks flowing through the darkness.

I hesitated. 'What if I just dive in? And stay under for a while?' I'd been swimming off the boat at night plenty of times, there was nothing to fear from that.

'No. You have to be weighted down.' His tone made it clear that there could be no compromise on this. 'How long can you hold your breath?'

'Two hundred tau.' That was an exaggeration; two hundred was what I was aiming for.

'That's long enough.'

I didn't reply. Daniel said, 'I'll pray with you.'

I climbed out of bed, and we knelt together. Daniel murmured, 'Please, Holy Beatrice, grant my brother Martin the courage to accept the precious gift of Your blood.' Then he started praying in what I took to be a foreign language, uttering a rapid stream of harsh syllables unlike anything I'd heard before. I listened apprehensively; I wasn't sure that I wanted Beatrice to change my mind, and I was afraid that this display of fervour might actually persuade Her.

I said, 'What if I don't do it?'

'Then you'll never see the face of God.'

I knew what that meant: I'd wander alone in the belly of Death, in darkness, for eternity. And even if the Scriptures weren't meant to be taken literally on this, the reality behind the metaphor could only be worse. Indescribably worse.

'But . . . what about Ma and Fa?' I was more worried about them, because I knew they'd never climb weighted off the side of the boat at Daniel's behest.

'That will take time,' he said softly.

My mind reeled. He was absolutely serious.

I heard him stand and walk over to the ladder. He climbed a few rungs and opened the hatch. Enough starlight came in to give shape to his arms and shoulders, but as he turned to me I still couldn't make out his face. 'Come on, Martin!' he whispered. 'The longer you put it off, the harder it gets.' The hushed urgency of his voice was familiar: generous and conspiratorial, nothing like an adult's impatience. He might almost have been daring me to join him in a midnight raid on the pantry – not because he really needed a collaborator, but because he honestly didn't want me to miss out on the excitement, or the spoils.

I suppose I was more afraid of damnation than drowning, and I'd always trusted Daniel to warn me of the dangers ahead. But this time I wasn't entirely convinced that he was right, so I must have been driven by something more than fear and blind trust.

Maybe it came down to the fact that he was offering to make me his equal in this. I was ten years old, and I ached to become something more than I was; to reach, not my parents' burdensome adulthood, but the halfway point, full of freedom and secrets, that Daniel had reached. I wanted to be as strong, as fast, as quick-witted and widely read as he was. Becoming as certain of God would not have been my first choice, but there wasn't much point hoping for divine intervention to grant me anything else.

I followed him up onto the deck.

He took cord, and a knife, and four spare weights of the kind we used on our nets from the toolbox. He threaded the weights onto the cord, then I took off my shorts and sat naked on the deck while he knotted a figure-eight around my ankles. I raised my feet experimentally; the weights didn't seem all that heavy. But in the water, I knew, they'd be more than enough to counteract my body's slight buoyancy.

'Martin? Hold out your hands.'

Suddenly I was crying. With my arms free, at least I could swim against the tug of the weights. But if my hands were tied, I'd be helpless.

Daniel crouched down and met my eyes. 'Ssshh. It's all right.'

I hated myself. I could feel my face contorted into the mask of a blubbering infant.

'Are you afraid?'

I nodded.

Daniel smiled reassuringly. 'You know why? You know who's doing that? Death doesn't want Beatrice to have you. He wants you for himself. So he's here on this boat, putting fear into your heart, because he *knows* he's almost lost you.'

I saw something move in the shadows behind the toolbox, something slithering into the darkness. If we went back down to the cabin now, would Death follow us? To wait for Daniel to fall asleep? If I'd turned my back on Beatrice, who could I ask to send Death away?

I stared at the deck, tears of shame dripping from my cheeks. I held out my arms, wrists together.

When my hands were tied – not palm to palm as I'd expected, but in separate loops joined by a short bridge – Daniel unwound a long stretch of rope from the winch at the rear of the boat and coiled it on the deck. I didn't want to think about how long it was, but I knew I'd never dived to that depth. He took the blunt hook at the end of the rope, slipped it over my arms, then screwed it closed to form an unbroken ring. Then he checked again that the cord around my wrists was neither so tight as to burn me, nor so loose as to let me slip. As he did this, I saw something creep over his face: some kind of doubt or fear of his own. He said, 'Hang onto the hook. Just in case. Don't let go, no matter what. Okay?' He whispered something to Beatrice, then looked up at me, confident again.

He helped me to stand and shuffle over to the guard rail, just to one side of the winch. Then he picked me up under the arms and lifted me over, resting my feet on the outer hull. The deck was inert, a mineralised endoshell, but behind the guard rails the hull was palpably alive: slick with protective secretions, glowing softly. My toes curled uselessly against the lubricated skin; I had no purchase at all. The hull was supporting some of my weight, but Daniel's arms would tire eventually. If I wanted to back out, I'd have to do it quickly.

A warm breeze was blowing. I looked around, at the flat horizon, at the blaze of stars, at the faint silver light off the water. Daniel recited: 'Holy Beatrice, I am ready to die to this world. Let me drown in Your blood, that I might be redeemed, and look upon the face of Your Mother.'

I repeated the words, trying hard to mean them.

'Holy Beatrice, I offer You my life. All I do now, I do for You. Come into my heart, and grant me the gift of faith. Come into my heart, and grant me the gift of hope. Come into my heart, and grant me the gift of love.'

'And grant me the gift of love.'

Daniel released me. At first, my feet seemed to adhere magically to the hull, and I pivoted backwards without actually falling. I clung tightly to the hook, pressing the cold metal against my belly, and willed the rope of the winch to snap taut, leaving me dangling in midair. I even braced myself for the shock. Some part of me really did believe that I could change my mind, even now.

Then my feet slipped and I plunged into the ocean and sank straight down.

It was not like a dive – not even a dive from an untried height, when it took so long for the water to bring you to a halt that it began to grow frightening. I was falling through the water ever faster, as if it was air. The vision I'd had of the rope keeping me above the water now swung to the opposite extreme: my acceleration seemed to prove that the coil on the deck was attached to nothing, that its frayed end was already beneath the surface. *That's what the followers had done, wasn't it? They'd let themselves be thrown in without a lifeline.* So Daniel had cut the rope, and I was on my way to the bottom of the ocean.

Then the hook jerked my hands up over my head, jarring my wrists and shoulders, and I was motionless.

I turned my face towards the surface, but neither starlight nor the hull's faint phosphorescence reached this deep. I let a stream of bubbles escape from my mouth; I felt them slide over my upper lip, but no trace of them registered in the darkness.

I shifted my hands warily over the hook. I could still feel the cord fast around my wrists, but Daniel had warned me not to trust it. I brought my knees up to my chest, gauging the effect of the weights. If the cord broke, at least my hands would be free, but even so I wasn't sure I'd be able to ascend. The thought of trying to unpick the knots around my ankles as I tumbled deeper filled me with horror.

My shoulders ached, but I wasn't injured. It didn't take much effort to pull myself up until my chin was level with the bottom of the hook. Going further was awkward – with my hands so close together I couldn't brace myself properly – but on the third attempt I managed to get my arms locked, pointing straight down.

I'd done this without any real plan, but then it struck me that even with my hands and feet tied, I could try shinning up the rope. It was just a matter of getting started. I'd have to turn upside down, grab the rope between my knees, then curl up – dragging the hook – and get a grip with my hands at a higher point.

And if I couldn't reach up far enough to right myself?

I'd ascend feet first.

I couldn't even manage the first step. I thought it would be as simple as keeping my arms rigid and letting myself topple backwards, but in the water even two-thirds of my body wasn't sufficient to counterbalance the weights.

I tried a different approach: I dropped down to hang at arm's length, raised my legs as high as I could, then proceeded to pull myself up again. But my grip wasn't tight enough to resist the turning force of the weights; I just pivoted around my centre of gravity – which was somewhere near my knees – and ended up still bent double, but almost horizontal.

I eased myself down again and tried threading my feet through the circle of my arms. I didn't succeed on the first attempt, and then on reflection it seemed like a bad move anyway. Even if I managed to grip the rope between my bound feet – rather than just tumbling over backwards, out of control, and dislocating my shoulders – climbing the rope *upside down with my hands behind my back* would either be impossible, or so awkward and strenuous that I'd run out of oxygen before I got a tenth of the way.

I let some more air escape from my lungs. I could feel the muscles in my diaphragm reproaching me for keeping them from doing what they wanted to do; not urgently yet, but the knowledge that I had no control over when I'd be able to draw breath again made it harder to stay calm. I knew I could rely on Daniel to bring me to the surface on the count of two hundred. But I'd only ever stayed down for a hundred and sixty. Forty more tau would be an eternity.

I'd almost forgotten what the whole ordeal was meant to be about, but now I started praying. *Please Holy Beatrice, don't let me die. I know You drowned like this to save me, but if I die it won't help anyone. Daniel would end up in the deepest shit . . . but that's not a threat, it's just an observation.* I felt a stab of anxiety; on top of everything else, had I just offended the Daughter of God? I struggled on, my confidence waning, *I don't want to die. But You already know that. So I don't know what You want me to say.*

I released some more stale air, wishing I'd counted the time I'd been under; you weren't supposed to empty your lungs too quickly – when they were deflated it was even harder not to take a breath – but holding all the carbon dioxide in too long wasn't good either.

Praying only seemed to make me more desperate, so I tried to think other kinds of holy thoughts. I couldn't remember anything from the Scriptures word for word, but the gist of the most important part started running through my mind.

After living in Her body for thirty years, and persuading all the Angels to become mortal again, Beatrice had gone back up to their deserted spaceship and flown it straight into the ocean. When Death saw Her coming, he took the form of a giant serpent, coiled in the water, waiting. And even though She was the Daughter of God, with the power to do anything, She let Death swallow Her.

That's how much She loved us.

Death thought he'd won everything. Beatrice was trapped inside him, in the darkness, alone. The Angels were flesh again, so he wouldn't even have to wait for the stars to fall before he claimed them.

But Beatrice was part of God. Death had swallowed part of God. This was a mistake. After three days, his jaws burst open and Beatrice came flying out, wreathed in fire. Death was broken, shrivelled, diminished.

My limbs were numb but my chest was burning. Death was still strong enough to hold down the damned. I started thrashing about blindly, wasting whatever oxygen was left in my blood, but desperate to distract myself from the urge to inhale.

Please Holy Beatrice—

Please Daniel—

Luminous bruises blossomed behind my eyes and drifted out into the water. I watched them curling into a kind of vortex, as if something was drawing them in.

It was the mouth of the serpent, swallowing my soul. I opened my own mouth and made a wretched noise, and Death swam forward to kiss me, to breathe cold water into my lungs.

Suddenly, everything was seared with light. The serpent turned and fled, like a pale, timid worm. A wave of contentment washed over me, as if I was an infant again and my mother had wrapped her arms around me tightly. It was like basking in sunlight, listening to laughter, dreaming of music too beautiful to be real. Every muscle in my body was still trying to prise my lungs open to the water, but now I found myself fighting this almost absent-mindedly while I marvelled at my strange euphoria.

Cold air swept over my hands and down my arms. I raised myself up to take a mouthful, then slumped down again, giddy and spluttering, grateful for every breath but still elated by something else entirely. The light that had filled my eyes was gone, but it left a violet after-image everywhere I looked. Daniel kept winding until my head was level with the guard rail, then he clamped the winch, bent down and threw me over his shoulder.

I'd been warm enough in the water, but now my teeth were chattering. Daniel wrapped a towel around me, then set to work cutting the cord. I beamed at him. 'I'm so happy!' He gestured to me to be quieter, but then he whispered joyfully, 'That's the love of Beatrice. She'll always be with you now, Martin.'

I blinked with surprise, then laughed softly at my own stupidity. Until that moment, I hadn't connected what had happened with Beatrice at all. But of course it was Her. I'd asked Her to come into my heart, and She had.

And I could see it in Daniel's face: a year after his own Drowning, he still felt Her presence.

He said, 'Everything you do now is for Beatrice. When you look through your telescope, you'll do it to honour Her creation. When you eat, or drink, or swim, you'll do it to give thanks for Her gifts.'

I nodded enthusiastically.

Daniel tidied everything away, even soaking up the puddles of water I'd left on the deck. Back in the cabin, he recited from the Scriptures, passages that I'd never really understood before, but which now all seemed to be about the Drowning and the way I was feeling. It was as if I'd opened the book and found myself mentioned by name on every page.

When Daniel fell asleep before me, for the first time in my life I didn't feel the slightest pang of loneliness. The Daughter of God was with me: I could feel Her presence, like a flame inside my skull, radiating warmth through the darkness behind my eyes.

Giving me comfort, giving me strength.

Giving me faith.

2

The monastery was almost four milliradians north-east of our home grounds. Daniel and I took the launch to a rendezvous point and met up with three other small vessels before continuing. It had been the same routine every tenth night for almost a year – and Daniel had been going to the Prayer Group himself for a year before that – so the launch didn't need much supervision. Feeding on nutrients in the ocean, propelling itself by pumping water through fine channels in its skin, guided by both sunlight and Covenant's magnetic field, it was a perfect example of the kind of legacy of the Angels that technology would never be able to match.

Bartholomew, Rachel and Agnes were in one launch and they travelled beside us while the others skimmed ahead. Bartholomew and Rachel were married, though they were only seventeen, scarcely older than Daniel. Agnes, Rachel's sister, was sixteen. Because I was the youngest member of the Prayer Group, Agnes had fussed over me from the day I'd joined. She said, 'It's your big night tonight, Martin, isn't it?' I nodded, but declined to pursue the conversation, leaving her free to talk to Daniel.

It was dusk by the time the monastery came into sight, a conical tower built from at least ten thousand hulls, rising up from the water in the stylised form of Beatrice's spaceship. Aimed at the sky, not down into the depths. Though some commentators on the Scriptures insisted that the spaceship itself had sunk for ever, and Beatrice had risen from the water unaided, it was still the definitive symbol of Her victory over Death. For the three days of Her separation from God, all such buildings stood in darkness, but that was half a year away, and now the monastery shone from every porthole.

There was a narrow tunnel leading into the base of the tower; the launches detected its scent in the water and filed in one by one. I knew they didn't have souls, but I wondered what it would have been like for them if they'd been aware of their actions. Normally they rested in the dock of a single hull, a pouch of boatskin that secured them but still left them largely exposed. Maybe being drawn instinctively into this vast structure would have felt even safer, even more comforting, than docking with their home boat. When I said something to this effect, Rachel, in the launch behind me, sniggered. Agnes said, 'Don't be horrible.'

The walls of the tunnel phosphoresced pale green, but the opening ahead was filled with white lamplight, dazzlingly richer and brighter. We emerged into a canal circling a vast atrium and continued around it until the launches found empty docks.

As we disembarked, every footstep, every splash echoed back at us. I looked up at the ceiling, a dome spliced together from hundreds of curved triangular hull sections, tattooed with scenes from the Scriptures. The original illustrations were more than a thousand years old, but the living boatskin degraded the pigments on a timescale of decades, so the monks had to constantly renew them.

'Beatrice Joining the Angels' was my favourite. Because the Angels weren't flesh, they didn't grow inside their mothers; they just appeared from nowhere in the streets of the Immaterial Cities. In the picture on the ceiling, Beatrice's immaterial body was half-formed, with cherubs still working to clothe the immaterial bones of Her legs and arms in immaterial muscles, veins and skin. A few Angels in luminous robes were glancing sideways at Her, but you could tell they weren't particularly impressed. They'd had no way of knowing, then, who She was.

A corridor with its own smaller illustrations led from the atrium to the meeting room. There were about fifty people in the Prayer Group – including several priests and monks, though they acted just like everyone else. In church you followed the liturgy; the priest slotted in his or her sermon, but there was no room for the worshippers to do much more than pray or sing in unison and offer rote responses. Here it was much less formal. There were two or three different speakers every night – sometimes guests who were visiting the monastery, sometimes members of the group – and after that anyone could ask the group to pray with them, about whatever they liked.

I'd fallen behind the others, but they'd saved me an aisle seat. Agnes was to my left, then Daniel, Bartholomew and Rachel. Agnes said, 'Are you nervous?'

'No.'

Daniel laughed, as if this claim was ridiculous.

I said, 'I'm not.' I'd meant to sound loftily unperturbed, but the words came out sullen and childish.

The first two speakers were both lay theologians, Firmlanders, who were visiting the monastery. One gave a talk about people who belonged to false religions, and how they were all – in effect – worshipping Beatrice, but just didn't know it. He said they wouldn't be damned, because they'd had no choice about the cultures they were born into. Beatrice would know they'd meant well, and forgive them.

I wanted this to be true, but it made no sense to me. Either Beatrice *was* the Daughter of God, and everyone who thought otherwise had turned away from Her into the darkness, or . . . there was no 'or'. I only had to close my eyes and feel Her presence to know that. Still, everyone applauded when the man finished, and all the questions people asked seemed sympathetic to his views, so perhaps his arguments had simply been too subtle for me to follow.

The second speaker referred to Beatrice as 'the Holy Jester', and rebuked us severely for not paying enough attention to Her sense of humour. She cited events in the Scriptures which she said were practical jokes, and then went on at some length about 'the healing power of laughter'. It was all about as gripping as a lecture on nutrition and hygiene; I struggled to keep my eyes open. At the end, no one could think of any questions.

Then Carol, who was running the meeting, said, 'Now Martin is going to give witness to the power of Beatrice in his life.'

Everyone applauded encouragingly. As I rose to my feet and stepped into the aisle, Daniel leant towards Agnes and whispered sarcastically, 'This should be good.'

I stood at the lectern and gave the talk I'd been rehearsing for days. Beatrice, I said, was beside me now whatever I did: whether I studied or worked, ate or swam, or just sat and watched the stars. When I woke in the morning and looked into my heart, She was there without fail, offering me strength and guidance. When I lay in bed at night, I feared nothing, because I knew She was watching over me. Before my Drowning, I'd been unsure of my faith, but now I'd never again be able to doubt that the Daughter of God had become flesh, and died, and conquered Death, because of Her great love for us.

It was all true, but even as I said these things I couldn't get Daniel's sarcastic words out of my mind. I glanced over at the row where I'd been sitting, at the people I'd travelled with. What did I have in common with them, really? Rachel and Bartholomew were married. Bartholomew and Daniel had studied together, and still played in the same dive-ball team. Daniel and Agnes were probably in love. And Daniel was my brother . . . but the only difference that seemed to make was the fact that he could belittle me far more efficiently than any stranger.

In the open prayer that followed, I paid no attention to the problems and blessings people were sharing with the group. I tried silently calling on Beatrice to dissolve the knot of anger in my heart. But I couldn't do it; I'd turned too far away from Her.

When the meeting was over and people started moving into the adjoining room to talk for a while, I hung back. When the others were out of sight I ducked into the corridor and headed straight for the launch.

Daniel could get a ride home with his friends; it wasn't far out of their way. I'd wait a short distance from the boat until he caught up; if my parents saw me arrive on my own I'd be in trouble. Daniel would be angry, of course, but he wouldn't betray me.

Once I'd freed the launch from its dock, it knew exactly where to go: around the canal, back to the tunnel, out into the open sea. As I sped across the calm, dark water, I felt the presence of Beatrice returning, which seemed like a sign that She understood that I'd had to get away.

I leant over and dipped my hand in the water, feeling the current the launch was generating by shuffling ions in and out of the cells of its skin. The outer hull glowed a phosphorescent blue, more to warn other vessels than to light the way. In the time of Beatrice, one of her followers had sat in the Immaterial City and designed this creature from scratch. It gave me a kind of vertigo, just imagining the things the Angels had known. I wasn't sure why so much of it had been lost, but I wanted to rediscover it all. Even the Deep Church taught that there was nothing wrong with that, so long as we didn't use it to try to become immortal again.

The monastery shrank to a blur of light on the horizon, and there was no other beacon visible on the water, but I could read the stars and sense the field lines, so I knew the launch was heading in the right direction.

When I noticed a blue speck in the distance, it was clear that it wasn't Daniel and the others chasing after me; it was coming from the wrong direction. As I watched the launch drawing nearer I grew anxious; if this was someone I knew and I couldn't come up with a good reason to be travelling alone, word would get back to my parents.

Before I could make out anyone on board, a voice shouted, 'Can you help me? I'm lost!'

I thought for a while before replying. The voice sounded almost matter-of-fact, making light of this blunt admission of helplessness, but it was no joke. If you were sick, your diurnal sense and your field sense could both become scrambled, making the stars much harder to read. It had happened to me a couple of times, and it had been a horrible experience – even standing safely on the deck of our boat. This late at night, a launch with only its field sense to guide it could lose track of its position, especially if you were trying to take it somewhere it hadn't been before.

I shouted back our coordinates, and the time. I was fairly confident that I had them down to the nearest hundred microradians and few hundred tau.

'That can't be right! Can I approach? Let our launches talk?'

I hesitated. It had been drummed into me for as long as I could remember that if I ever found myself alone on the water, I should give other vessels a wide berth unless I knew the people on board. But Beatrice was with me, and if someone needed help it was wrong to refuse them.

'All right!' I stopped dead, and waited for the stranger to close the gap. As the launch drew up beside me, I was surprised to see that the passenger was a young man. He looked about Bartholomew's age, but he'd sounded much older.

We didn't need to tell the launches what to do; proximity was enough to trigger a chemical exchange of information. The man said, 'Out on your own?'

'I'm travelling with my brother and his friends. I just went ahead a bit.'

That made him smile. 'Sent you on your way, did they? What do you think they're getting up to, back there?' I didn't reply; that was no way to talk about people you didn't even know. The man scanned the horizon, then spread his arms in a gesture of sympathy. 'You must be feeling left out.'

I shook my head. There was a pair of binoculars on the floor behind him; even before he'd called out for help he could have seen that I was alone.

He jumped deftly between the launches, landing on the stern bench. I said, 'There's nothing to steal.' My skin was crawling, more with disbelief than fear. He was standing on the bench in the starlight, pulling a knife from his belt. The details – the pattern carved into the handle, the serrated edge of the blade – only made it seem more like a dream.

He coughed, suddenly nervous. 'Just do what I tell you, and you won't get hurt.'

I filled my lungs and shouted for help with all the strength I had; I knew there was no one in earshot, but I thought it might still frighten him off. He looked around, more startled than angry, as if he couldn't quite believe I'd waste so much effort. I jumped backwards, into the water. A moment later I heard him follow me.

I found the blue glow of the launches above me, then swam hard, down and away from them, without wasting time searching for his shadow. Blood was pounding in my ears, but I knew I was moving almost silently; however fast he was, in the darkness he could swim right past me without knowing it. If he didn't catch me soon he'd probably return to the launch and wait to spot me when I came up for air. I had to surface far enough away to be invisible – even with the binoculars.

I was terrified that I'd feel a hand close around my ankle at any moment, but Beatrice was with me. As I swam, I thought back to my Drowning, and Her presence grew stronger than ever. When my lungs were almost bursting, She helped me to keep going, my limbs moving mechanically, blotches of light floating in front of my eyes. When I finally knew I had to surface, I turned face up and ascended slowly, then lay on my back with only my mouth and nose above the water, refusing the temptation to stick my head up and look around.

I filled and emptied my lungs a few times, then dived again.

The fifth time I surfaced, I dared to look back. I couldn't see either launch. I raised myself higher, then turned a full circle in case I'd grown disoriented, but nothing came into sight.

I checked the stars, and my field sense. The launches should *not* have been over the horizon. I trod water, riding the swell, and tried not to think about how tired I was. It was at least two milliradians to the nearest boat. Good swimmers – some younger than I was – competed in marathons over distances like that, but I'd never even aspired to such feats of endurance. Unprepared, in the middle of the night, I knew I wouldn't make it.

If the man had given up on me, would he have taken our launch? When they cost so little, and the markings were so hard to change? That would be nothing but an admission of guilt. *So why couldn't I see it?* Either he'd sent it on its way, or it had decided to return home itself.

I knew the path it would have taken; I would have seen it go by, if I'd been looking for it when I'd surfaced before. But I had no hope of catching it now.

I began to pray. I knew I'd been wrong to leave the others, but I asked for forgiveness, and felt it being granted. I watched the horizon almost calmly – smiling at the blue flashes of meteors burning up high above the ocean – certain that Beatrice would not abandon me.

I was still praying – treading water, shivering from the cool of the air – when a blue light appeared in the distance. It disappeared as the swell took me down again, but there was no mistaking it for a shooting star. *Was this Daniel and the others – or the stranger?* I didn't have long to decide; if I wanted to get within earshot as they passed, I'd have to swim hard.

I closed my eyes and prayed for guidance. *Please Holy Beatrice, let me know.* Joy flooded through my mind, instantly: it was them, I was certain of it. I set off as fast as I could.

I started yelling before I could see how many passengers there were, but I knew Beatrice would never allow me to be mistaken. A flare shot up from the launch, revealing four figures standing side by side, scanning the water. I shouted with jubilation, and waved my arms. Someone finally spotted me, and they brought the launch around towards me. By the time I was on board I was so charged up on adrenalin and relief that I almost believed I could have dived back into the water and raced them home.

I thought Daniel would be angry, but when I described what had happened all he said was, 'We'd better get moving.'

Agnes embraced me. Bartholomew gave me an almost respectful look, but Rachel muttered sourly, 'You're an idiot, Martin. You don't know how lucky you are.'

I said, 'I know.'

Our parents were standing on deck. The empty launch had arrived some time ago; they'd been about to set out to look for us. When the others had departed I began recounting everything again, this time trying to play down any element of danger.

Before I'd finished, my mother grabbed Daniel by the front of his shirt and started slapping him. 'I trusted you with him! *You maniac!* I trusted you!' Daniel half-raised his arm to block her, but then let it drop and just turned his face to the deck.

I burst into tears. 'It was my fault!' Our parents never struck us; I couldn't believe what I was seeing.

My father said soothingly, 'Look . . . he's home now. He's safe. No one touched him.' He put an arm around my shoulders and asked warily, 'That's right, Martin, isn't it?'

I nodded tearfully. This was worse than anything that had happened on the launch, or in the water; I felt a thousand times more helpless, a thousand times more like a child.

I said, 'Beatrice was watching over me.'

My mother rolled her eyes and laughed wildly, letting go of Daniel's shirt. 'Beatrice? *Beatrice?* Don't you know what could have happened to you? You're too young to have given him what he wanted. He would have had to use the knife.'

The chill of my wet clothes seemed to penetrate deeper. I swayed unsteadily, but fought to stay upright. Then I whispered stubbornly, 'Beatrice was there.'

My father said, 'Go and get changed or you're going to freeze to death.'

I lay in bed listening to them shout at Daniel. When he finally came down the ladder I was so sick with shame that I wished I'd drowned.

He said, 'Are you all right?'

There was nothing I could say. I couldn't ask him to forgive me.

'Martin?' Daniel turned on the lamp. His face was streaked with tears; he laughed softly, wiping them away. 'Fuck, you had me worried. Don't ever do anything like that again.'

'I won't.'

'Okay.' That was it; no shouting, no recriminations. 'Do you want to pray with me?'

We knelt side by side, praying for our parents to be at peace, praying for the man who'd tried to hurt me. I started trembling; everything was catching up with me. Suddenly, words began gushing from my mouth – words I neither recognised nor understood, though I knew I was praying for everything to be all right with Daniel, praying that our parents would stop blaming him for my stupidity.

The strange words kept flowing out of me, an incomprehensible torrent somehow imbued with everything I was feeling. I knew what was happening: *Beatrice had given me the Angels' tongue.* We'd had to surrender all knowledge of it when we became flesh, but sometimes She granted people the ability to pray this way, because the language of the Angels could express things we could no longer put into words. Daniel had been able to do it ever since his Drowning, but it wasn't something you could teach, or even something you could ask for.

When I finally stopped, my mind was racing. 'Maybe Beatrice

planned everything that happened tonight? Maybe She arranged it all, to lead up to this moment!'

Daniel shook his head, wincing slightly. 'Don't get carried away. You have the gift; just accept it.' He nudged me with his shoulder. 'Now get into bed, before we're both in more trouble.'

I lay awake almost until dawn, overwhelmed with happiness. Daniel had forgiven me. Beatrice had protected and blessed me. I felt no more shame, just humility and amazement. I knew I'd done nothing to deserve it, but my life was wrapped in the love of God.

3

According to the Scriptures, the oceans of Earth were storm-tossed, and filled with dangerous creatures. But on Covenant, the oceans were calm, and the Angels created nothing in the ecopoiesis that would harm their own mortal incarnations. The four continents and the four oceans were rendered equally hospitable, and just as women and men were made indistinguishable in the sight of God, so were Freelanders and Firmlanders. (Some commentators insisted that this was literally true: God chose to blind Herself to where we lived, and whether or not we'd been born with a penis. I thought that was a beautiful idea, even if I couldn't quite grasp the logistics of it.)

I'd heard that certain obscure sects taught that half the Angels had actually become embodied as a separate people who could live in the water and breathe beneath the surface, but then God destroyed them because they were a mockery of Beatrice's death. No legitimate church took this notion seriously, though, and archaeologists had found no trace of these mythical doomed cousins. Humans were humans, there was only one kind. Free-landers and Firmlanders could even intermarry – if they could agree where to live.

When I was fifteen, Daniel became engaged to Agnes from the Prayer Group. That made sense: they'd be spared the explanations and arguments about the Drowning that they might have faced with partners who weren't so blessed. Agnes was a Freelander, of course, but a large branch of her family, and a smaller branch of ours, were Firmlanders, so after long negotiations it was decided that the wedding would be held in Ferez, a coastal town.

I went with my father to pick a hull to be fitted out as Daniel and Agnes's boat. The breeder, Diana, had a string of six mature hulls in tow, and my father insisted on walking out onto their backs and personally examining each one for imperfections.

By the time we reached the fourth I was losing patience. I muttered, 'It's the skin underneath that matters.' In fact, you could tell a lot about a hull's general condition from up here, but there wasn't much point worrying about a few tiny flaws high above the waterline.

My father nodded thoughtfully. 'That's true. You'd better get in the water and check their undersides.'

'I'm not doing that.' We couldn't simply trust this woman to sell us a healthy hull for a decent price; that wouldn't have been sufficiently embarrassing.

'Martin! This is for the safety of your brother and sister-in-law.'

I glanced at Diana to show her where my sympathies lay, then slipped off my shirt and dived in. I swam down to the last hull in the row, then ducked beneath it. I began the job with perverse thoroughness, running my fingers over every square nanoradian of skin. I was determined to annoy my father by taking even longer than he wanted – and determined to impress Diana by examining all six hulls without coming up for air.

An unfitted hull rode higher in the water than a boat full of furniture and junk, but I was surprised to discover that even in the creature's shadow there was enough light for me to see the skin clearly. After a while I realised that, paradoxically, this was because the water was slightly cloudier than usual, and whatever the fine particles were, they were scattering sunlight into the shadows.

Moving through the warm, bright water, feeling the love of Beatrice more strongly than I had for a long time, it was impossible to remain angry with my father. He wanted the best hull for Daniel and Agnes, and so did I. As for impressing Diana . . . who was I kidding? She was a grown woman, at least as old as Agnes, and highly unlikely to view me as anything more than a child. By the time I'd finished with the third hull I was feeling short of breath, so I surfaced and reported cheerfully, 'No blemishes so far!'

Diana smiled down at me. 'You've got strong lungs.'

All six hulls were in perfect condition. We ended up taking the one at the end of the row, because it was easiest to detach.

Ferez was built on the mouth of a river, but the docks were some distance upstream. That helped to prepare us; the gradual deadening of the waves was less of a shock than an instant transition from sea to land would have been. When I jumped from the deck to the pier, though, it was like colliding with something massive and unyielding, the rock of the planet itself. I'd been on land twice before, for less than a day on both occasions. The wedding celebrations would last ten days, but at least we'd still be able to sleep on the boat.

As the four of us walked along the crowded streets, heading for the ceremonial hall where everything but the wedding sacrament itself would take place, I stared uncouthly at everyone in sight. Almost no one was barefoot like us, and after a few hundred tau on the paving stones – much rougher than any deck – I could understand why. Our clothes were different, our skin was darker, our accent was unmistakably foreign . . . but no one stared back. Freelanders were hardly a novelty here. That made me even more selfconscious; the curiosity I felt wasn't mutual.

In the hall, I joined in with the preparations, mainly just lugging furniture around under the directions of one of Agnes's tyrannical uncles. It was a new kind of shock to see so many Freelanders together in this alien environment, and stranger still when I realised that I couldn't necessarily spot the Firmlanders among us; there was no sharp dividing line in physical appearance, or even clothing. I began to feel slightly guilty; if God couldn't tell the difference, what was I doing hunting for the signs?

At noon we all ate outside, in a garden behind the hall. The grass was soft, but it made my feet itch. Daniel had gone off to be fitted for wedding clothes, and my parents were performing some vital task of their own; I only recognised a handful of the people around me. I sat in the shade of a tree, pretending to be oblivious to the plant's enormous size and bizarre anatomy. I wondered if we'd take a siesta; I couldn't imagine falling asleep on the grass.

Someone sat down beside me and I turned.

'I'm Lena. Agnes's second cousin.'

'I'm Daniel's brother, Martin.' I hesitated, then offered her my hand; she took it, smiling slightly. I'd awkwardly kissed a dozen strangers that morning, all distant prospective relatives, but this time I didn't dare.

'Brother of the groom, doing grunt work with the rest of us.' She shook her head in mocking admiration.

I desperately wanted to say something witty in reply, but an attempt that failed would be even worse than merely being dull. 'Do you live in Ferez?'

'No, Mitar. Inland from here. We're staying with my uncle.' She pulled a face. 'Along with ten other people. No privacy. It's awful.'

I said, 'It was easy for us. We just brought our home with us.' *You idiot. As if she didn't know that.*

Lena smiled. 'I haven't been on a boat in years. You'll have to give me a tour sometime.'

'Of course. I'd be happy to.' I knew she was only making small talk; she'd never take me up on the offer.

She said, 'Is it just you and Daniel?'

'Yes.'

'You must be close.'

I shrugged. 'What about you?'

'Two brothers. Both younger. Eight and nine. They're all right, I suppose.' She rested her chin on one hand and gazed at me coolly.

I looked away, disconcerted by more than my wishful thinking about what lay behind that gaze. Unless her parents had been awfully young when she was born, it didn't seem likely that more children were planned. So did an odd number in the family mean that one had died, or that the custom of equal numbers carried by each parent wasn't followed where she lived? I'd studied the region less than a year ago, but I had a terrible memory for things like that.

Lena said, 'You looked so lonely, off here on your own.'

I turned back to her, surprised. 'I'm never lonely.'

'No?'

She seemed genuinely curious. I opened my mouth to tell her about Beatrice, but then changed my mind. The few times I'd said anything to friends – ordinary friends, not Drowned ones – I'd regretted it. Not everyone had laughed, but they'd all been acutely embarrassed by the revelation.

I said, 'Mitar has a million people, doesn't it?'

'Yes.'

'An area of ocean the same size would have a population of ten.'

Lena frowned. 'That's a bit too deep for me, I'm afraid.' She rose to her feet. 'But maybe you'll think of a way of putting it that even a Firmlander can understand.' She raised a hand goodbye and started walking away.

I said, 'Maybe I will.'

The wedding took place in Ferez's Deep Church, a spaceship built of stone, glass and wood. It looked almost like a parody of the churches I was used to, though it probably bore a closer resemblance to the Angels' real ship than anything made of living hulls.

Daniel and Agnes stood before the priest, beneath the apex of the building. Their closest relatives stood behind them in two angled lines on either side. My father – Daniel's mother – was first in our line, followed by my own mother, then me. That put me level with Rachel, who kept shooting disdainful glances my way. After my misadventure, Daniel and I had eventually been allowed to travel to the Prayer Group meetings again, but less than a year later I'd lost interest, and soon after I'd also stopped going to church. Beatrice was with me, constantly, and no gatherings or ceremonies could bring me any closer to Her. I knew Daniel disapproved of this attitude, but he didn't lecture me about it, and my parents had accepted my decision without any fuss. If Rachel thought I was some kind of apostate, that was her problem.

The priest said, 'Which of you brings a bridge to this marriage?'

Daniel said, 'I do.' In the Transitional ceremony they no longer asked this; it was really no one else's business – and in a way the question was almost sacrilegious. Still, Deep Church theologians had explained away greater doctrinal inconsistencies than this, so who was I to argue?

'Do you, Daniel and Agnes, solemnly declare that this bridge will be the bond of your union until death, to be shared with no other person?'

They replied together, 'We solemnly declare.'

'Do you solemnly declare that as you share this bridge, so shall you share every joy and every burden of marriage – equally?'

'We solemnly declare.'

My mind wandered; I thought of Lena's parents. Maybe one of the family's children was adopted. Lena and I had managed to sneak away to the boat three times so far, early in the evenings while my parents were still out. We'd done things I'd never done with anyone else, but I still hadn't had the courage to ask her anything so personal.

Suddenly the priest was saying, 'In the eyes of God, you are one now.' My father started weeping softly. As Daniel and Agnes kissed, I felt a surge of contradictory emotions. I'd miss Daniel, but I was glad that I'd finally have a chance to live apart from him. And I wanted him to be happy – I was jealous of his happiness already – but at the same time, the thought of marrying someone like Agnes filled me with claustrophobia. She was kind, devout and generous. She and Daniel would treat each other, and their children, well. But neither of them would present the slightest challenge to the other's most cherished beliefs.

This recipe for harmony terrified me, not least because I was afraid that Beatrice approved, and wanted me to follow it myself.

Lena put her hand over mine and pushed my fingers deeper into her, gasping. We were sitting on my bunk, face to face, my legs stretched out flat, hers arching over them.

She slid the palm of her other hand over my penis. I bent forward and kissed her, moving my thumb over the place she'd shown me, and her shudder ran through both of us.

'Martin?'

'What?'

She stroked me with one fingertip; somehow it was far better than having her whole hand wrapped around me.

'Do you want to come inside me?'

I shook my head.

'Why not?'

She kept moving her finger, tracing the same line; I could barely think. *Why not?* 'You might get pregnant.'

She laughed. 'Don't be stupid. I can control that. You'll learn, too. It's just a matter of experience.'

I said, 'I'll use my tongue. You liked that.'

'I did. But I want something more now. And you do, too. I can tell.' She smiled imploringly. 'It'll be nice for both of us, I promise. Nicer than anything you've done in your life.'

'Don't bet on it.'

Lena made a sound of disbelief, and ran her thumb around the base of my penis. 'I can tell you haven't put this inside anyone before. But that's nothing to be ashamed of.'

'Who said I was ashamed?'

She nodded gravely. 'All right. Frightened.'

I pulled my hand free, and banged my head on the bunk above us. Daniel's old bunk.

Lena reached up and put her hand on my cheek.

I said, 'I can't. We're not married.'

She frowned. 'I heard you'd given up on all that.'

'All what?'

'Religion.'

'Then you were misinformed.'

Lena said, 'This is what the Angels made our bodies to do. How can there be anything sinful in that?' She ran her hand down my neck, over my chest.

'But the bridge is meant to . . .' *What?* All the Scriptures said was that it was meant to unite men and women, equally. And the Scriptures said God couldn't tell women and men apart, but in the Deep Church, in the sight of God, the priest had just made Daniel claim priority. So why should I care what any priest thought?

I said, 'All right.'

'Are you sure?'

'Yes.' I took her face in my hands and started kissing her. After a while, she reached down and guided me in. The shock of pleasure almost made me come, but I stopped myself somehow. When the risk of that had lessened, we wrapped our arms around each other and rocked slowly back and forth.

It wasn't better than my Drowning, but it was so much like it that it had to be blessed by Beatrice. And as we moved in each other's arms, I grew determined to ask Lena to marry me. She was intelligent and strong. She questioned everything. It didn't matter that she was a Firmlander; we could meet halfway, we could live in Ferez.

I felt myself ejaculate. 'I'm sorry.'

Lena whispered, 'That's all right, that's all right. Just keep moving.'

I was still hard; that had never happened before. I could feel her muscles clenching and releasing rhythmically, in time with our motion, and her slow exhalations. Then she cried out, and dug her fingers into my back. I tried to slide partly out of her again, but it was impossible, she was holding me too tightly. This was it. There was no going back.

Now I was afraid. 'I've never—' Tears were welling up in my eyes; I tried to shake them away.

'I know. And I know it's frightening.' She embraced me more tightly. 'Just feel it, though. Isn't it wonderful?'

I was hardly aware of my motionless penis any more, but there was liquid fire flowing through my groin, waves of pleasure spreading deeper. I said, 'Yes. Is it like that for you?'

'It's different. But it's just as good. You'll find out for yourself, soon enough.'

'I hadn't been thinking that far ahead,' I confessed.

Lena giggled. 'You've got a whole new life in front of you, Martin. You don't know what you've been missing.'

She kissed me, then started pulling away. I cried out in pain, and she stopped. 'I'm sorry. I'll take it slowly.' I reached down to touch the place where we were joined; there was a trickle of blood escaping from the base of my penis.

Lena said, 'You're not going to faint on me, are you?'

'Don't be stupid.' I did feel queasy, though. 'What if I'm not ready? What if I can't do it?'

'Then I'll lose my hold in a few hundred tau. The Angels weren't completely stupid.'

I ignored this blasphemy, though it wasn't just any Angel who'd designed our bodies – it was Beatrice Herself. I said, 'Just promise you won't use a knife.'

'That's not funny. That really happens to people.'

'I know.' I kissed her shoulder. 'I think—'

Lena straightened her legs slightly and I felt the core break free inside me. Blood flowed warmly from my groin, but the pain had changed from a threat of damage to mere tenderness; my nervous system no longer spanned the lesion. I asked Lena, 'Do you feel it? Is it part of you?'

'Not yet. It takes a while for the connections to form.' She ran her fingers over my lips. 'Can I stay inside you until they have?'

I nodded happily. I hardly cared about the sensations any more; it was just contemplating the miracle of being able to give a part of my body to Lena that was wonderful. I'd studied the physiological details long ago, everything from the exchange of nutrients to the organ's independent immune system – and I knew that Beatrice had used many of the same techniques for the bridge as She'd used with gestating embryos – but to witness Her ingenuity so dramatically at work in my own flesh was both shocking and intensely moving. Only giving birth could bring me closer to Her than this.

When we finally separated, though, I wasn't entirely prepared for the sight of what emerged. 'Oh, that is disgusting!'

Lena shook her head, laughing. 'New ones always look a bit . . . encrusted. Most of that stuff will wash away, and the rest will fall off in a few kilotau.'

I bunched up the sheet to find a clean spot, then dabbed at my – her – penis. My newly formed vagina had stopped bleeding, but it was finally dawning on me just how much mess we'd made. 'I'm going to have to wash this before my parents get back. I can put it out to dry in the morning, after they're gone, but if I don't wash it now they'll smell it.'

We cleaned ourselves enough to put on shorts, then Lena helped me carry the sheet up onto the deck and drape it in the water from the laundry hooks. The fibres in the sheet would use nutrients in the water to power the self-cleaning process.

The docks appeared deserted; most of the boats nearby belonged to people who'd come for the wedding. I'd told my parents I was too tired to stay on at the celebrations; tonight they'd continue until dawn, though Daniel and Agnes would probably leave by midnight. To do what Lena and I had just done.

'Martin? Are you shivering?'

There was nothing to be gained by putting it off. Before whatever courage I had could desert me, I said, 'Will you marry me?'

'Very funny. Oh—' Lena took my hand. 'I'm sorry, I never know when you're joking.'

I said, 'We've exchanged the bridge. It doesn't matter that we weren't married first, but it would make things easier if we went along with convention.'

'Martin—'

'Or we could just live together, if that's what you want. I don't care. We're already married in the eyes of Beatrice.'

Lena bit her lip. 'I don't want to live with you.'

'I could move to Mitar. I could get a job.'

Lena shook her head, still holding my hand. She said firmly, '*No*. You knew, before we did anything, what it would and wouldn't mean. You don't want to marry me, and I don't want to marry you. So snap out of it.'

I pulled my hand free and sat down on the deck. *What had I done?* I'd thought I'd had Beatrice's blessing, I'd thought this was all in Her plan . . . but I'd just been fooling myself.

Lena sat beside me. 'What are you worried about? Your parents finding out?'

'Yes.' That was the least of it, but it seemed pointless trying to explain the truth. I turned to her. 'When could we—?'

'Not for about ten days. And sometimes it's longer after the first time.'

I'd known as much, but I'd hoped her experience might contradict my theoretical knowledge. *Ten days*. We'd both be gone by then.

Lena said, 'What do you think, you can never get married now? How many marriages do you imagine involve the bridge one of the partners was born with?'

'Nine out of ten. Unless they're both women.'

Lena gave me a look that hovered between tenderness and incredulity. 'My estimate is about one in five.'

I shook my head. 'I don't care. We've exchanged the bridge, we have to be together.' Lena's expression hardened, then so did my resolve. 'Or I have to get it back.'

'Martin, that's ridiculous. You'll find another lover soon enough, and then you won't even know what you were worried about. Or maybe you'll fall in love with a nice Deep Church boy, and then you'll both be glad you've been spared the trouble of getting rid of the extra bridge.'

'Yeah? Or maybe he'll just be disgusted that I couldn't wait until I really *was* doing it for him!'

Lena groaned and stared up at the sky. 'Did I say something

before about the Angels getting things right? Ten thousand years without bodies, and they thought they were qualified—'

I cut her off angrily, 'Don't be so fucking blasphemous! Beatrice knew exactly what She was doing. If we mess it up, that's our fault!'

Lena said, matter-of-factly, 'In ten years' time, there'll be a pill you'll be able to take to keep the bridge from being passed, and another pill to make it pass when it otherwise wouldn't. We'll win control of our bodies back from the Angels and start doing exactly what we like with them.'

'That's sick. That really is sick.'

I stared at the deck, suffocating in misery. *This was what I'd wanted, wasn't it? A lover who was the very opposite of Daniel's sweet, pious Agnes?* Except that in my fantasies, we'd always had a lifetime to debate our philosophical differences, not one night to be torn apart by them.

I had nothing to lose now. I told Lena about my Drowning. She didn't laugh; she listened in silence.

I said, 'Do you believe me?'

'Of course.' She hesitated. 'But have you ever wondered if there might be another explanation for the way you felt in the water that night? You were starved of oxygen—'

'People are starved of oxygen all the time. Freelander kids spend half their lives trying to stay underwater longer than the last time.'

Lena nodded. 'Sure. But that's not quite the same, is it? You were pushed beyond the time you could have stayed under by sheer willpower. And . . . you were cued, you were told what to expect.'

'That's not true. Daniel never told me what it would be like. I was *surprised* when it happened.' I gazed back at her calmly, ready to counter any ingenious hypothesis she came up with. I felt chastened, but almost at peace now. This was what Beatrice had expected of me before we'd exchanged the bridge: not a dead ceremony in a dead building, but the honesty to tell Lena exactly who she'd be making love with.

We argued almost until sunrise; neither of us convinced the other of anything. Lena helped me drag the clean sheet out of the water and hide it below deck. Before she left, she wrote down the address of a friend's house in Mitar, and a place and time we could meet.

Keeping that appointment was the hardest thing I'd ever done in my life. I spent three solid days ingratiating myself with my Mitar-based cousins, to the point where they would have had to be openly hostile to get out of inviting me to stay with them after the wedding. Once I was there, I had to scheme and lie relentlessly to ensure that I was free of them on the predetermined day.

In a stranger's house, in the middle of the afternoon, Lena and I joylessly reversed everything that had happened between us. I'd been afraid that the act itself might rekindle all my stupid illusions, but when we parted on the street outside, I felt as if I hardly knew her.

I ached even more than I had on the boat, and my groin was palpably swollen, but in a couple of days, I knew, nothing less than a lover's touch or a medical examination would reveal what I'd done.

In the train back to the coast, I replayed the entire sequence of events in my mind, again and again. *How could I have been so wrong?* People always talked about the power of sex to confuse and deceive you, but I'd always believed that was just cheap cynicism. Besides, I hadn't blindly surrendered to sex; I'd thought I'd been guided by Beatrice.

If I could be wrong about that—

I'd have to be more careful. Beatrice always spoke clearly, but I'd have to listen to Her with much more patience and humility.

That was it. That was what She'd wanted me to learn. I finally relaxed and looked out the window at the blur of forest passing by, another triumph of the ecopoiesis. If I needed proof that there was always another chance, it was all around me now. The Angels had travelled as far from God as anyone could travel, and yet God had turned around and given them Covenant.

4

I was nineteen when I returned to Mitar, to study at the city's university. Originally, I'd planned to specialise in the ecopoiesis – and to study much closer to home – but in the end I'd had to accept the nearest thing on offer, geographically and intellectually: working with Barat, a Firmlander biologist whose real interest was native microfauna. 'Angelic technology is a fascinating subject in its own right,' he told me. 'But we can't hope to work backwards and decipher terrestrial evolution from anything the Angels created. The best we can do is try to understand what Covenant's own biosphere was like before we arrived and disrupted it.'

I managed to persuade him to accept a compromise: my thesis would involve the impact of the ecopoiesis on the native microfauna. That would give me an excuse to study the Angels' inventions alongside the drab unicellular creatures that had inhabited Covenant for the last billion years.

'The impact of the ecopoiesis' was far too broad a subject, of course; with Barat's help, I narrowed it down to one particular unresolved question. There had long been geological evidence that the surface waters of the ocean had become both more alkaline and less oxygenated as new species shifted the balance of dissolved gases. Some native species must have retreated from the wave of change, and perhaps some had been wiped out completely, but there was a thriving population of zooytes in the upper layers at present. So had they been there all along, adapting *in situ*? Or had they migrated from somewhere else?

Mitar's distance from the coast was no real handicap in studying the ocean; the university mounted regular expeditions, and I had plenty of library and lab work to do before embarking on anything so obvious as gathering living samples in their natural habitat. What's more, river water, and even rainwater, was teeming with closely related species, and since it was possible that these were the reservoirs from which the 'ravaged' ocean had been recolonised, I had plenty of subjects worth studying close at hand.

Barat set high standards, but he was no tyrant, and his other students made me feel welcome. I was homesick, but not morbidly so, and I took a kind of giddy pleasure from the vivid dreams and underlying sense of disorientation that living on land induced in me. I wasn't exactly fulfilling my childhood ambition to uncover the secrets of the Angels – and I had fewer opportunities than I'd hoped to get sidetracked on the ecopoiesis itself – but once I started delving into the minutiae of Covenant's original, wholly undesigned biochemistry, it turned out to be complex and elegant enough to hold my attention.

I was only miserable when I let myself think about sex. I didn't want to end up like Daniel, so seeking out another Drowned person to marry was the last thing on my mind. But I couldn't face the prospect of repeating my mistake with Lena; I had no intention of becoming physically intimate with anyone unless we were already close enough for me to tell them about the most important thing in my life. But that wasn't the order in which things happened here. After a few humiliating attempts to swim against the current, I gave up on the whole idea and threw myself into my work instead.

Of course, it *was* possible to socialise at Mitar University without actually exchanging bridges with anyone. I joined an informal discussion group on Angelic culture, which met in a small room in the students' building every tenth night – just like the old Prayer Group, though I was under no illusion that this one would be stacked with believers. It hardly needed to be. The Angels' legacy could be analysed perfectly well without reference to Beatrice's divinity. The Scriptures were written long after the Crossing by people of a simpler age; there was no reason to treat them as infallible. If non-believers could shed some light on any aspect of the past, I had no grounds for rejecting their insights.

'It's obvious that only one faction came to Covenant!' That was Céline, an anthropologist, a woman so much like Lena that I had to make a conscious effort to remind myself, every time I set eyes on her, that nothing could ever happen between us. 'We're not so homogeneous that we'd all choose to travel to another planet and assume a new physical form, whatever cultural forces might drive one small group to do that. So why should the Angels have been unanimous? The other factions must still be living in the Immaterial Cities, on Earth, and on other planets.'

'Then why haven't they contacted us? In twenty thousand years, you'd think they'd drop in and say hello once or twice.' David was a mathematician, a Freelander from the southern ocean.

Céline replied, 'The attitude of the Angels who came here wouldn't have encouraged visitors. If all we have is a story of the Crossing in which Beatrice persuades every last Angel in existence to give up immortality – a version that simply erases everyone else from history – that doesn't suggest much of a desire to remain in touch.'

A woman I didn't know interjected, 'It might not have been so clear-cut from the start, though. There's evidence of settler-level technology being deployed for more than three thousand years after the Crossing, long after it was needed for the ecopoiesis. New species continued to be created, engineering projects continued to use advanced materials and energy sources. But then in less than a century, it all stopped. The Scriptures merge three separate decisions into one: renouncing immortality, migrating to Covenant and abandoning the technology that might have provided an escape route if anyone changed their mind. But we *know* it didn't happen like that. Three thousand years after the Crossing, something changed. The whole experiment suddenly became irreversible.'

These speculations would have outraged the average pious Freelander, let alone the average Drowned one, but I listened calmly, even entertaining the possibility that some of them could be true. The love of Beatrice was the only fixed point in my cosmology; everything else was open to debate.

Still, sometimes the debate was hard to take. One night, David joined us straight from a seminar of physicists. What he'd heard from the speaker was unsettling enough, but he'd already moved beyond it to an even less palatable conclusion.

'Why did the Angels choose mortality? After ten thousand years without death, why did they throw away all the glorious possibilities ahead of them, to come and die like animals on this ball of mud?' I had to bite my tongue to keep from replying to his rhetorical question: because God is the only source of eternal life, and Beatrice showed them that all they really had was a cheap parody of that divine gift.

David paused, then offered his own answer – which was itself a kind of awful parody of Beatrice's truth. 'Because they discovered that they weren't immortal, after all. They discovered that *no one can be*. We've always known, as they must have, that the universe is finite in space and time. It's destined to collapse eventually: "the stars will fall from the sky". But it's easy to *imagine* ways around that.' He laughed. 'We don't know enough physics yet, ourselves, to rule out anything. I've just heard an extraordinary woman from Tia talk about coding our minds into waves that would orbit the shrinking universe so rapidly that we could think *an infinite number of thoughts* before everything was crushed!' David grinned joyfully at the sheer audacity of this notion. I thought primly: what blasphemous nonsense.

Then he spread his arms and said, 'Don't you see, though? If the Angels *had* pinned their hopes on something like that – some ingenious trick that would keep them from sharing the fate of the universe – *but then they finally gained enough knowledge to rule out every last escape route*, it would have had a profound effect on them. Some small faction could then have decided that since they were mortal after all, they might as well embrace the inevitable, and come to terms with it in the way their ancestors had. In the flesh.'

Céline said thoughtfully, 'And the Beatrice myth puts a religious gloss on the whole thing, but that might be nothing but a *post hoc* reinterpretation of a purely secular revelation.'

This was too much; I couldn't remain silent. I said, 'If Covenant really was founded by a pack of terminally depressed atheists, what could have changed their minds? Where did the desire to impose a *"post hoc reinterpretation" come from?* If the revelation that brought the Angels here was "secular", why isn't the whole planet still secular today?'

Someone said snidely, 'Civilisation collapsed. What do you expect?'

I opened my mouth to respond angrily, but Céline got in first. 'No, Martin has a point. If David's right, the rise of religion needs to be explained more urgently than ever. And I don't think anyone's in a position to do that yet.'

Afterwards, I lay awake thinking about all the other things I should have said, all the other objections I should have raised. (And thinking about Céline.) Theology aside, the whole dynamics of the group was starting to get under my skin; maybe I'd be better off spending my time in the lab, impressing Barat with my dedication to his pointless fucking microbes.

Or maybe I'd be better off at home. I could help out on the boat; my parents weren't young any more, and Daniel had his own family to look after.

I climbed out of bed and started packing, but halfway through I changed my mind. I didn't really want to abandon my studies. And I'd known all along what the antidote was for all the confusion and resentment I was feeling.

I put my rucksack away, switched off the lamp, lay down, closed my eyes, and asked Beatrice to grant me peace.

I was woken by someone banging on the door of my room. It was a fellow boarder, a young man I barely knew. He looked extremely tired and irritable, but something was overriding his irritation.

'There's a message for you.'

My mother was sick, with an unidentified virus. The hospital was even further away than our home grounds; the trip would take almost three days.

I spent most of the journey praying, but the longer I prayed, the harder it became. I *knew* that it was possible to save my mother's life with one word in the Angels' tongue to Beatrice, but the number of ways in which I could fail, corrupting the purity of the request with my own doubts, my own selfishness, my own complacency, just kept multiplying.

The Angels created nothing in the ecopoiesis that would harm their own mortal incarnations. The native life showed no interest in parasitising us. But over the millennia, our own DNA had shed viruses. And since Beatrice Herself chose every last base pair, that must have been what She intended. Ageing was not enough. Mortal injury was not enough. Death had to come without warning, silent and invisible.

That's what the Scriptures said.

The hospital was a maze of linked hulls. When I finally found the right passageway, the first person I recognised in the distance was Daniel. He was holding his daughter Sophie high in his outstretched arms, smiling up at her. The image dispelled all my fears in an instant; I almost fell to my knees to give thanks.

Then I saw my father. He was seated outside the room, his head in his hands. I couldn't see his face, but I didn't need to. He wasn't anxious, or exhausted. He was crushed.

I approached in a haze of last-minute prayers, though I knew I was asking for the past to be rewritten. Daniel started to greet me as if nothing was wrong, asking about the trip – probably trying to soften the blow – then he registered my expression and put a hand on my shoulder.

He said, 'She's with God now.'

I brushed past him and walked into the room. My mother's body was lying on the bed, already neatly arranged: arms straightened, eyes closed. Tears ran down my cheeks, angering me. Where had my love been when it might have prevented this? When Beatrice might have heeded it?

Daniel followed me into the room, alone. I glanced back through the doorway and saw Agnes holding Sophie.

'She's with God, Martin.' He was beaming at me as if something wonderful had happened.

I said numbly, 'She wasn't Drowned.' I was almost certain that she hadn't been a believer at all. She'd remained in the Transitional church all her life – but that had long been the way to stay in touch with your friends when you worked on a boat nine days out of ten.

'I prayed with her, before she lost consciousness. She accepted Beatrice into her heart.'

I stared at him. Nine years ago he'd been certain: you were Drowned, or you were damned. It was as simple as that. My own conviction had softened long ago; I couldn't believe that Beatrice really was so arbitrary and cruel. But I knew my mother would not only have refused the full-blown ritual; the whole philosophy would have been as nonsensical to her as the mechanics.

'Did she say that? Did she tell you that?'

Daniel shook his head. 'But it was clear.' Filled with the love of Beatrice, he couldn't stop smiling.

A wave of revulsion passed through me; I wanted to grind his face into the deck. *He didn't care what my mother had believed.* Whatever eased his own pain, whatever put his own doubts to rest, had to be the case. To accept that she was damned – or even just dead, gone, erased – was unbearable; everything else flowed from that. *There was no truth in anything he said, anything he believed. It was all just an expression of his own needs.*

I walked back into the corridor and crouched beside my father. Without looking at me, he put an arm around me and pressed me against his side. I could feel the blackness washing over him, the helplessness, the loss. When I tried to embrace him he just clutched me more tightly, forcing me to be still. I shuddered a few times, then stopped weeping. I closed my eyes and let him hold me.

I was determined to stay there beside him, facing everything he was facing. But after a while, unbidden, the old flame began to glow in the back of my skull: the old warmth, the old peace, the old certainty. Daniel was right, my mother was with God. *How could I have doubted that?* There was no point asking how it had come about; Beatrice's ways were beyond my comprehension. But the one thing I knew first-hand was the strength of Her love.

I didn't move, I didn't free myself from my father's desolate embrace. But I was an impostor now, merely praying for his comfort, interceding from my state of grace. Beatrice had raised me out of the darkness, and I could no longer share his pain.

5

After my mother's death, my faith kept ceding ground, without ever really wavering. Most of the doctrinal content fell away, leaving behind a core of belief that was a great deal easier to defend. It didn't matter if the Scriptures were superstitious nonsense or the Church was full of fools and hypocrites; Beatrice was still Beatrice, the way the sky was still blue. Whenever I heard debates between atheists and believers, I found myself increasingly on the atheists' side – not because I accepted their conclusion for a moment, but because they were so much more honest than their opponents. Maybe the priests and theologians arguing against them had the same kind of direct, personal experience of God as I did – or maybe not, maybe they just desperately needed to believe. But they never disclosed the true source of their conviction; instead, they just made laughable attempts to 'prove' God's existence from the historical record, or from biology, astronomy or mathematics. Daniel had been right at the age of fifteen – you couldn't prove any such thing – and listening to these people twist logic as they tried made me squirm.

I felt guilty about leaving my father working with a hired hand, and even guiltier when he moved onto Daniel's boat a year later, but I knew how angry it would have made him if he thought I'd abandoned my career for his sake. At times that was the only thing that kept me in Mitar: even when I honestly wanted nothing more than to throw it all in and go back to hauling nets, I was afraid my decision would be misinterpreted.

It took me three years to complete my thesis on the migration of aquatic zooytes in the wake of the ecopoiesis. My original hypothesis, that freshwater species had replenished the upper ocean, turned out to be false. Zooytes had no genes as such, just families of enzymes that resynthesised each other after cell division, but comparisons of these heritable molecules showed that, rather than rain bringing new life from above, an ocean-dwelling species from a much greater depth had moved steadily closer to the surface, as the Angels' creations drained oxygen from the water. That wouldn't have been much of a surprise, if the same techniques hadn't also shown that several species found in river water were even closer relatives of the surface-dwellers. But those freshwater species weren't anyone's ancestors; they were the newest migrants. Zooytes that had spent a billion years confined to the depths had suddenly been able to survive (and reproduce and mutate) closer to the surface than ever before, and when they'd stumbled on a mutation that let them thrive in the presence of oxygen, they'd finally been in a position to make use of it. The ecopoiesis might have driven other native organisms into extinction, but the invasion from Earth had enabled this ancient benthic species to mount a long overdue invasion of its own. Unwittingly or not, the Angels had set in motion the sequence of events that had released it from the ocean to colonise the planet.

So I proved myself wrong, earned my degree, and became famous among a circle of peers so small that we were all famous to each other anyway. Vast new territories did not open up before me. Anything to do with native biology was rapidly becoming an academic cul-de-sac; I'd always suspected that was how it would be, but I hadn't fought hard enough to end up anywhere else.

For the next three years, I clung to the path of least resistance: assisting Barat with his own research, taking the teaching jobs no one else wanted. Most of Barat's other students moved on to better things, and I found myself increasingly alone in Mitar. But that didn't matter; I had Beatrice.

At the age of twenty-five, I could see my future clearly. While other people deciphered – and built upon – the Angels' legacy, I'd watch from a distance, still messing about with samples of seawater from which all Angelic contaminants had been scrupulously removed.

Finally, when it was almost too late, I made up my mind to jump ship. Barat had been good to me, but he'd never expected loyalty verging on martyrdom. At the end of the year a bi-ecological (native and Angelic) microbiology conference was being held in Tia, possibly the last event of its kind. I had no new results to present, but it wouldn't be hard to find a plausible excuse to attend, and it would be the ideal place to lobby for a new position. My great zooyte discovery hadn't been entirely lost on the wider community of biologists; I could try to rekindle the memory of it. I doubted there'd be much point offering to sleep with anyone; ethical qualms aside, my bridge had probably rusted into place.

Then again, maybe I'd get lucky. Maybe I'd stumble on a fellow Drowned Freelander who'd ended up in a position of power, and all I'd have to do was promise that my work would be for the greater glory of Beatrice.

Tia was a city of ten million people on the east coast. New towers stood side by side with empty structures from the time of the Angels, giant gutted machines that might have played a role in the ecopoiesis. I was too old and proud to gawk like a child, but for all my provincial sophistication I wanted to. These domes and cylinders were twenty times older than the illustrations tattooed into the ceiling of the monastery back home. They bore no images of Beatrice; nothing of the Angels did. But why would they? They predated Her death.

The university, on the outskirts of Tia, was a third the size of Mitar itself. An underground train ringed the campus; the students I rode with eyed my unstylish clothes with disbelief. I left my luggage in the dormitory and headed straight for the conference centre. Barat had chosen to stay behind; maybe he hadn't wanted to witness the public burial of his field. That made things easier for me; I'd be free to hunt for a new career without rubbing his face in it.

Late additions to the conference programme were listed on a screen by the main entrance. I almost walked straight past the display; I'd already decided which talks I'd be attending. But three steps away, a title I'd glimpsed in passing assembled itself in my mind's eye, and I had to backtrack to be sure I hadn't imagined it.

Carla Reggia: 'Euphoric Effects of *Z/12/80* Excretions'

I stood there laughing with disbelief. I recognised the speaker and her co-workers by name, though I'd never had a chance to meet them. If this wasn't a hoax . . . what had they done? Dried it, smoked it, and tried writing that up as research? *Z/12/80* was one of 'my' zooytes, one of the escapees from the ocean; the air and water of Tia were swarming with it. If its excretions were euphoric, the whole city would be in a state of bliss.

I knew, then and there, what they'd discovered. I knew it, long before I admitted it to myself. I went to the talk with my head full of jokes about neglected culture flasks full of psychotropic breakdown products, but for two whole days, I'd been steeling myself for the truth, finding ways in which it didn't have to matter.

Z/12/80, Carla explained, excreted among its waste products an amine that was able to bind to receptors in our Angel-crafted brains. Since it had been shown by other workers (no one recognised me; no one gave me so much as a glance) that *Z/12/80* hadn't existed at the time of the ecopoiesis, this interaction was almost certainly undesigned and unanticipated. 'It's up to the archaeologists and neurochemists to determine what role, if any, the arrival of this substance in the environment might have played in the collapse of early settlement culture. But for the past fifteen to eighteen thousand years, we've been swimming in it. Since we still exhibit such a wide spectrum of moods, we're probably able to compensate for its presence by down-regulating the secretion of the endogenous molecule that was designed to bind to the same receptor. That's just an educated guess, though. Exactly what the effects might be from individual to individual, across the range of doses that might be experienced under a variety of conditions, is clearly going to be a matter of great interest to investigators with appropriate expertise.'

I told myself that I felt no disquiet. Beatrice acted on the world through the laws of nature; I'd stopped believing in supernatural miracles long ago. The fact that someone had now identified the way in which She'd acted on *me*, that night in the water, changed nothing.

I pressed ahead with my attempts to get recruited. Everyone at the conference was talking about Carla's discovery, and when people finally made the connection with my own work their eyes stopped glazing over halfway through my spiel. In the next three days, I received seven offers – all involving research into zooyte biochemistry. There was no question, now, of sidestepping the issue, of escaping into the wider world of Angelic biology. One man even came right out and said to me: 'You're a Freelander, and you know that the ancestors of Z/12/80 live in much greater numbers in the ocean. Don't you think *oceanic* exposure is going to be the key to understanding this?' He laughed. 'I mean, you swam in the stuff as a child, didn't you? And you seem to have come through unscathed.'

'Apparently.'

On my last night in Tia, I couldn't sleep. I stared into the blackness of the room, watching the grey sparks dance in front of me. (Contaminants in the aqueous humour? Electrical noise in the retina? I'd heard the explanation once, but I could no longer remember it.)

I prayed to Beatrice in the Angels' tongue; I could still feel Her presence, as strongly as ever. The effect clearly wasn't just a matter of dosage, or transcutaneous absorption; merely swimming in the ocean at the right depth wasn't enough to make anyone feel Drowned. But in combination with the stress of oxygen starvation, and all the psychological build-up Daniel had provided, the jolt of zooyte piss must have driven certain neuro-endocrine subsystems into new territory – or old territory, by a new path. *Peace, joy, contentment, the feeling of being loved* weren't exactly unknown emotions. But by short-circuiting the brain's usual practice of summoning those feelings only on occasions when there was a reason for them, I'd been 'blessed with the love of Beatrice'. I'd found happiness on demand.

And I still possessed it. That was the eeriest part. Even as I lay there in the dark, on the verge of reasoning everything I'd been living for out of existence, my ability to work the machinery was so ingrained that I felt as loved, as blessed, as ever.

Maybe Beatrice was offering me another chance, making it clear that She'd still forgive this blasphemy and welcome me back. But why did I believe that there was anyone there to 'forgive me'? You couldn't reason your way to God; there was only faith. And I knew now that the source of my faith was a meaningless accident, an unanticipated side-effect of the ecopoiesis.

I still had a choice. I could, still, decide that the love of Beatrice was immune to all logic, a force beyond understanding, untouched by evidence of any kind.

No, I couldn't. I'd been making exceptions for Her for too long. Everyone lived with double standards – but I'd already pushed mine as far as they'd go.

I started laughing and weeping at the same time. It was almost unimaginable: all the millions of people who'd been misled the same way. All because of the zooytes and . . . what? One Freelander, diving for pleasure, who'd stumbled on a strange new experience? Then tens of thousands more repeating it, generation after generation – until one vulnerable man or woman had been driven to invest the novelty with meaning. Someone who'd needed so badly to feel loved and protected that the illusion of a real presence behind the raw emotion had been impossible to resist. Or who'd desperately wanted to believe that – in spite of the Angels' discovery that they, too, were mortal – death could still be defeated.

I was lucky: I'd been born in an era of moderation. I hadn't killed in the name of Beatrice. I hadn't suffered for my faith. I had no doubt that I'd been far happier for the last fifteen years than I would have been if I'd told Daniel to throw his rope and weights overboard without me.

But that didn't change the fact that the heart of it all had been a lie.

I woke at dawn, my head pounding, after just a few kilotaus' sleep. I closed my eyes and searched for Her presence, as I had a thousand times before. *When I woke in the morning and looked into my heart, She was there without fail, offering me strength and guidance. When I lay in bed at night, I feared nothing, because I knew She was watching over me.*

There was nothing. She was gone.

I stumbled out of bed, feeling like a murderer, wondering how I'd ever live with what I'd done.

6

I turned down every offer I'd received at the conference and stayed on in Mitar. It took Barat and me two years to establish our own research group to examine the effects of the zooamine, and nine more for us to elucidate the full extent of its activity in the brain. Our new recruits all had solid backgrounds in neurochemistry, and they did better work than I did, but when Barat retired I found myself the spokesperson for the group.

The initial discovery had been largely ignored outside the scientific community; for most people, it hardly mattered whether our brain chemistry matched the Angels' original design, or if it had been altered fifteen thousand years ago by some unexpected contaminant. But when the Mitar zooamine group began publishing detailed accounts of the biochemistry of religious experience, the public at large rediscovered the subject with a vengeance.

The university stepped up security, and despite death threats and a number of unpleasant incidents with stone-throwing protesters, no one was hurt. We were flooded with requests from broadcasters – though most were predicated on the notion that the group was morally obliged to 'face its critics', rather than the broadcasters being morally obliged to offer us a chance to explain our work, calmly and clearly, without being shouted down by enraged zealots.

I learnt to avoid the zealots, but the obscurantists were harder to dodge. I'd expected opposition from the Churches – defending

the faith was their job, after all – but some of the most ı.
tually bankrupt responses came from academics in other ̆
ciplines. In one televised debate, I was confronted by a Deep
Church priest, a Transitional theologian, a devotee of the ocean
god Marni, and an anthropologist from Tia.

'This discovery has no real bearing on any belief system,' the
anthropologist explained serenely. 'All truth is local. Inside every
Deep Church in Ferez Beatrice *is* the daughter of God, and we're
the mortal incarnations of the Angels, who travelled here from
Earth. In a coastal village a few milliradians south, Marni is the
supreme creator, and it was She who gave birth to us, right here.
Going one step further and moving from the spiritual domain to
the scientific might appear to "negate" certain spiritual truths . . .
but equally, moving from the scientific domain to the spiritual
demonstrates the same limitations. We are nothing but the
stories we tell ourselves, and no one story is greater than another.'
He smiled beneficently, the expression of a parent only too
happy to give all his squabbling children an equal share in some
disputed toy.

I said, 'How many cultures do you imagine share your definition of "truth"? How many people do you think would be content to worship a God who consisted of literally nothing but the
fact of their belief?' I turned to the Deep Church priest. 'Is that
enough for you?'

'Absolutely not!' She glowered at the anthropologist. 'While
I have the greatest respect for my brother here,' she gestured at
the devotee of Marni, 'you can't draw a line around those people
who've been lucky enough to be raised in the true faith, and then
suggest that *Beatrice's* infinite power and love is confined to that
group of people . . . like some collection of folk songs!'

The devotee respectfully agreed. Marni had created the most
distant stars, along with the oceans of Covenant. Perhaps some
people called Her by another name, but if everyone on this planet
were to die tomorrow, She would still be Marni: unchanged, undiminished.

...ologist responded soothingly, 'Of course. But in
...ith a wider perspective—'

...ly happy with a God who resides within us,' offered
...nal theologian. 'It seems . . . *immodest* to expect
...nstead of fretting uselessly over these ultimate questions, ...ould confine ourselves to matters of a suitably human
scale.'

I turned to him. 'So you're actually indifferent as to whether an
infinitely powerful and loving being created everything around
you, and plans to welcome you into Her arms after death . . . or
the universe is a piece of quantum noise that will eventually
vanish and erase us all?'

He sighed heavily, as if I was asking him to perform some
arduous physical feat just by responding. 'I can summon no
enthusiasm for these issues.'

Later, the Deep Church priest took me aside and whispered,
'Frankly, we're all very grateful that you've debunked that awful
cult of the Drowned. They're a bunch of fundamentalist hicks,
and the Church will be better off without them. But you mustn't
make the mistake of thinking that your work has anything to do
with ordinary, civilised believers!'

I stood at the back of the crowd that had gathered on the beach
near the rock pool to listen to the two old men who were standing
ankle-deep in the milky water. It had taken me four days to get
here from Mitar, but when I'd heard reports of a zooyte bloom
washing up on the remote north coast, I'd had to come and see
the results for myself. The zooamine group had actually recruited
an anthropologist for such occasions – one who could cope with
such taxing notions as the existence of objective reality, and a
biochemical substrate for human thought – but Céline was only
with us for part of the year, and right now she was away doing
other research.

'This is an ancient, sacred place!' one man intoned, spreading
his arms to take in the pool. 'You need only observe the shape of

it to understand that. It concentrates the energy of the stars, and the sun and the ocean.'

'The focus of power is there, by the inlet,' the other added, gesturing at a point where the water might have come up to his calves. 'Once, I wandered too close. I was almost lost in the great dream of the ocean when my friend here came and rescued me!'

These men weren't devotees of Marni, or members of any other formal religion. As far as I'd been able to tell from old news reports, the blooms occurred every eight or ten years, and the two had set themselves up as 'custodians' of the pool more than fifty years ago. Some local villagers treated the whole thing as a joke, but others revered the old men. And for a small fee, tourists and locals alike could be chanted over, then splashed with the potent brew. Evaporation would have concentrated the trapped waters of the bloom; for a few days, before the zooytes ran out of nutrients and died *en masse* in a cloud of hydrogen sulphide, the amine would be present in levels as high as in any of our laboratory cultures back in Mitar.

As I watched people lining up for the ritual, I found myself trying to downplay the possibility that anyone could be seriously affected by it. It was broad daylight, no one feared for their life, and the old men's pantheistic gobbledegook carried all the gravitas of the patter of streetside scam merchants. Their marginal sincerity, and the money changing hands, would be enough to undermine the whole thing. This was a tourist trap, not a life-altering experience.

When the chanting was done, the first customer knelt at the edge of the pool. One of the custodians filled a small metal cup with water and threw it in her face. After a moment, she began weeping with joy. I moved closer, my stomach tightening. *It was what she'd known was expected of her, nothing more. She was playing along, not wanting to spoil the fun – like the good sports who pretended to have their thoughts read by a carnival psychic.*

Next, the custodians chanted over a young man. He began swaying giddily even before they touched him with the water;

when they did, he broke into sobs of relief that racked his whole body.

I looked back along the queue. There was a young girl standing third in line now, looking around apprehensively; she could not have been more than nine or ten. Her father (I presumed) was standing behind her, with his hand against her back, as if gently propelling her forward.

I lost all interest in playing anthropologist. I forced my way through the crowd until I reached the edge of the pool, then turned to address the people in the queue. 'These men are frauds! There's nothing mysterious going on here. I can tell you exactly what's in the water: it's just a drug, a natural substance given out by creatures that are trapped here when the waves retreat.'

I squatted down and prepared to dip my hand in the pool. One of the custodians rushed forward and grabbed my wrist. He was an old man, I could have done what I liked, but some people were already jeering, and I didn't want to scuffle with him and start a riot. I backed away from him, then spoke again.

'I've studied this drug for more than ten years, at Mitar University. It's present in water all over the planet. We drink it, we bathe in it, we swim in it every day. But it's concentrated here, and if you don't understand what you're doing when you use it, that misunderstanding can harm you!'

The custodian who'd grabbed my wrist started laughing. 'The dream of the ocean is powerful, yes, but we don't need your advice on that! For fifty years, my friend and I have studied its lore, until we were strong enough to *stand* in the sacred water!' He gestured at his leathery feet; I didn't doubt that his circulation had grown poor enough to limit the dose to a tolerable level.

He stretched out his sinewy arm at me. 'So fuck off back to Mitar, Inlander! Fuck off back to your books and your dead machinery! What would you know about the sacred mysteries? *What would you know about the ocean?'*

I said, 'I think you're out of your depth.'

I stepped into the pool. He started wailing about my unpurified body polluting the water, but I brushed past him. The other custodian came after me, but though my feet were soft after years of wearing shoes, I ignored the sharp edges of the rocks and kept walking towards the inlet. The zooamine helped. I could feel the old joy, the old peace, the old 'love'; it made a powerful anaesthetic.

I looked back over my shoulder. The second man had stopped pursuing me; it seemed he honestly feared going any further. I pulled off my shirt, bunched it up, and threw it onto a rock at the side of the pool. Then I waded forward, heading straight for the 'focus of power'.

The water came up to my knees. I could feel my heart pounding, harder than it had since childhood. People were shouting at me from the edge of the pool – some outraged by my sacrilege, some apparently concerned for my safety in the presence of forces beyond my control. Without turning, I called out at the top of my voice, 'There is no "power" here! There's nothing "sacred"! There's nothing here but a drug—'

Old habits die hard; I almost prayed first. *Please, Holy Beatrice, don't let me regain my faith.*

I lay down in the water and let it cover my face. My vision turned white; I felt like I was leaving my body. The love of Beatrice flooded into me, and nothing had changed: Her presence was as palpable as ever, as undeniable as ever. I *knew* that I was loved, accepted, forgiven.

I waited, staring into the light, almost expecting a voice, a vision, detailed hallucinations. That had happened to some of the Drowned. How did anyone ever claw their way back to sanity after that?

But for me, there was only the emotion itself, overpowering but unembellished. It didn't grow monotonous; I could have basked in it for days. But I understood, now, that it said no more about my place in the world than the warmth of sunlight on skin. I'd never mistake it for the touch of a real hand again.

I climbed to my feet and opened my eyes. Violet after-images danced in front of me. It took a few tau for me to catch my breath and feel steady on my feet again. Then I turned and started wading back towards the shore.

The crowd had fallen silent, though whether it was in disgust or begrudging respect I had no idea.

I said, 'It's not just here. It's not just in the water. It's part of us now; it's in our blood.' I was still half-blind; I couldn't see whether anyone was listening. 'But as long as you know that, you're already free. As long as you're ready to face the possibility that everything that makes your spirits soar, everything that lifts you up and fills your heart with joy, *everything that makes your life worth living* . . . is a lie, is corruption, is meaningless – then you can never be enslaved.'

They let me walk away unharmed. I turned back to watch as the line formed again; the girl wasn't in the queue.

I woke with a start, from the same old dream.

I was lowering my mother into the water from the back of the boat. Her hands were tied, her feet weighted. She was afraid, but she'd put her trust in me. 'You'll bring me up safely, won't you, Martin?'

I nodded reassuringly. But once she'd vanished beneath the waves, I thought: What am I doing? I don't believe in this shit any more.

So I took out a knife and started cutting through the rope—

I brought my knees up to my chest and crouched on the unfamiliar bed in the darkness. I was in a small town on the railway line, halfway back to Mitar. Halfway between midnight and dawn.

I dressed and made my way out of the hostel. The centre of town was deserted, and the sky was thick with stars. Just like home. In Mitar, everything vanished in a fog of light.

All three of the stars cited by various authorities as the Earth's sun were above the horizon. If they weren't all mistakes, perhaps I'd live to see a telescope's image of the planet itself. But the prospect of seeking contact with the Angels – if there really was a faction still out there, somewhere – left me cold. I shouted silently up at the stars: *Your degenerate offspring don't need your help! Why should we rejoin you? We're going to surpass you!*

I sat down on the steps at the edge of the square and covered my face. Bravado didn't help. Nothing helped. Maybe if I'd grown up facing the truth, I would have been stronger. But when I woke in the night, knowing that my mother was simply dead, that everyone I'd ever loved would follow her, that I'd vanish into the same emptiness myself, it was like being buried alive. It was like being back in the water, bound and weighted, with the certain knowledge that there was no one to haul me up.

Someone put a hand on my shoulder. I looked up, startled. It was a man about my own age. His manner wasn't threatening; if anything, he looked slightly wary of me.

He said, 'Do you need a roof? I can let you into the Church if you want.' There was a trolley packed with cleaning equipment a short distance behind him.

I shook my head. 'It's not that cold.' I was too embarrassed to explain that I had a perfectly good room nearby. 'Thanks.'

As he was walking away, I called after him, 'Do you believe in God?'

He stopped and stared at me for a while, as if he was trying to decide if this was a trick question – as if I might have been hired by the local parishioners to vet him for theological soundness. Or maybe he just wanted to be diplomatic with anyone desperate enough to be sitting in the town square in the middle of the night, begging a stranger for reassurance.

He shook his head. 'As a child I did. Not any more. It was a nice idea . . . but it made no sense.' He eyed me sceptically, still unsure of my motives.

I said, 'Then isn't life unbearable?'

He laughed. 'Not all the time.'

He went back to his trolley and started wheeling it towards the Church.

I stayed on the steps, waiting for dawn.

ACKNOWLEDGEMENTS

'Lost Continent' was first published in *The Starry Rift*, edited by Jonathan Strahan; Viking Penguin, 2008.

'Dark Integers' was first published in *Asimov's Science Fiction*, October/November 2007.

'Crystal Nights' was first published in *Interzone 215*, April 2008.

'Steve Fever' was first published in *Technology Review*, November/December 2007.

'Induction' was first published in *Foundation 100*, edited by Farah Mendlesohn and Graham Sleight; Science Fiction Foundation, Summer 2007.

'Singleton' was first published in *Interzone 176*, February 2002.

'Oracle' was first published in *Asimov's Science Fiction*, July 2000.

'Border Guards' was first published in *Interzone 148*, October 1999.

'Riding the Crocodile' was first published in *One Million A.D.*, edited by Gardner Dozois, Science Fiction Book Club, 2005.

'Glory' was first published in *The New Space Opera*, edited by Gardner Dozois and Jonathan Strahan; HarperCollins, 2007.

'Hot Rock' was first published in *Godlike Machines*, edited by Jonathan Strahan; Science Fiction Book Club, 2009.

'Oceanic' was first published in *Asimov's Science Fiction*, August 1998.

Turn the page for a sneak preview of the new Greg Egan novel

Zendegi

Coming soon from Gollancz

ONE

Martin stared anxiously at the four crates full of vinyl LPs in the corner of the living room. A turntable, amplifier and speakers sat on the floor beside them, their cables draped in dust; it had been three weeks since he'd sold the shelving unit that had housed the components. The records would be far too heavy to take with him on the plane to Iran, and he didn't think much of their chances if he sent them separately as surface freight. He'd contemplated putting them in storage, as he'd done when he'd gone to Pakistan, but having already spent a month selling furniture and throwing out junk he was determined to complete the process: to reach the point where he could fly out of Sydney with no keys in his pocket, leaving nothing behind.

He squatted beside the crates and did a quick count. There were two hundred and forty albums; it would cost more than two thousand dollars to replace them all with downloads. That seemed like an extravagant price to pay in order to end up exactly where he'd started, give or take a few minor scratches and crackles. He could always just replace his favourites, but he'd been lugging these crates around for decades without discarding anything. They were part of his personal history, a diary written in track lists and sleeve notes; there were plenty of bizarre and embarrassing choices, but he didn't want to forget them, or disown them. Whittling the collection down would feel like a kind of revisionism; he knew that he'd never part with money again for Devo, The Residents or The Virgin Prunes, but he didn't want to tear those pages from his diary and pretend that he'd spent his youth entirely in the exalted company of Elvis Costello and The Smiths. The more obscure, the more dubious, the more down-right cringe-inducing the album, the more he'd have to lose by excising it from his past.

Martin knew what he had to do, and he cursed himself for not facing up to it sooner. Normally he would have scoured the web for the pros and cons of different methods, then spent another week mulling over the choices, but he had no time to waste. The crates held almost seven days' worth of continuous music, and he was flying out in a fortnight. It was not impossible, but he'd be cutting it fine.

He left his apartment and walked two doors down the hall.

At the sound of his knocking, Alice called out grumpily, 'I'm coming!' Half a minute later she appeared at the door, wearing a wide-brimmed hat, as if she was about to brave the afternoon sun.

'Hi,' Martin said, 'are you busy?'

'No, no. Come in.'

She ushered him into the living room and motioned for him to sit. 'Would you like some coffee?'

Martin shook his head. 'I won't take your time; I just wanted some advice. I'm going to bite the bullet and put my vinyl on computer—'

'Audacity,' Alice replied.

'Sorry?'

'Download *Audacity*; that's the best software to use. Plug your turntable preamp into your sound card, record every-thing you want and save it as WAV files. If you want to split each album side into individual tracks, you'll have to do that manually, but it's pretty easy.' She took a small notepad from the coffee table and scribbled something, then handed him the page. 'If you use these settings it will make life simpler if you decide to burn CDs at some point.'

'Thanks.'

'Oh, and make sure you get the recording level right.'

'Okay.' Martin didn't want to appear rude, picking her brains and then rushing away, but since she hadn't taken her hat off he assumed she was itching to get moving herself. 'Thanks for your help.' He rose to his feet. 'It looks like you were going somewhere—'

Alice frowned, then understood. 'You mean this?' She took hold of the hat by the brim and pulled it off, revealing a mesh of brightly coloured wires tangled in her short dark hair. 'I didn't know who was at the door, and it takes me ten minutes to stick all the electrodes back on.' Though it didn't look as if any hair had been shaved off, irregular partings revealed patches of white skin to which small metal disks adhered. Martin had a disconcerting flashback to his childhood: grooming the family cat in search of ticks.

He said, 'Can I ask what they're for?'

'There's a Swiss company called Eikonometrics who want to see if they can classify images by flashing them on a monitor subliminally and looking at the viewer's brain activity. I signed up for one of their trials. You just sit and work normally; you don't even notice the pictures.'

Martin laughed. 'Are they paying you?'

'One cent per thousand images.'

'That'll catch on.'

Alice said, 'I expect they'll replace the micro-payments with some kind of privileges scheme. Maybe give people free access to games or movies if they're willing to wear the electrodes while they watch. In the long run they're hoping to get it working with a standard gamer's biofeedback helmet instead of all this DIY-neurologist crap, but off-the-shelf models don't have the resolution yet.'

Martin was intrigued. 'So what's your angle?' Alice earned her living as a website designer, but she seemed to spend most of her spare time on mildly nefarious projects, like the 'Groundhog Cage' she'd constructed that made thirty-day free-trial software think it was always on the first day of the trial. Apparently this was harder than simply lying to the software about the true date; there were exchanges with distant servers to be faked as well.

'I'm still analysing the system,' she said, 'trying to figure out how to game it.'

'Right.' Martin hesitated. 'But if the experts can't write software that classifies images as well as a human brain can, how are you going to write a program to simulate your own responses?'

'I don't have to,' Alice replied. 'I just have to make something that *passes for* human.'

'I don't follow you.'

'People aren't all going to react identically,' she said. 'There might or might not be a clear majority response to each class of image, but you certainly won't get the same signal from everyone. Some participants – through no fault of their own – won't be pulling their weight; that's a statistical certainty. But the company wouldn't dare discriminate against people whose brains don't happen to go *aaah* every time they see a fluffy kitten; they'll still get the same rewards. I want to see if I can ride the coattails of the distribution.'

'So you'd be satisfied with passing as a low-affect psychopath, just so long as you don't actually come across as brain-dead?'

'That's about it.'

Martin rubbed his eyes. Though he admired her ingenuity, there was something about her obsessive need to prove that she could milk the system that felt every bit as crass as the brain-farming scheme itself.

'I'd better go,' he said. 'Thanks for the tips.'

'No problem.' Alice smiled, suddenly self-conscious. 'So when are you flying out?'

'Two weeks.'

'Right.' Her smile stayed awkwardly frozen, and Martin

realised that it wasn't her eccentric head-ware that was making her embarrassed. 'I'm really sorry about you and Liz,' she said.

'Yeah.'

'How long were you together?'

'Fifteen years,' he said.

Alice looked stunned; she'd been their neighbour for almost a year, but the subject had probably never come up before. Alice was in her mid-twenties; fifteen years would sound like a lifetime.

Martin said, 'I think Liz decided that Islamabad was the last hardship post she was willing to put up with.' He couldn't blame her; Pakistan and Iran were not the most appealing locations for Western women with no reason of their own to be there. Liz worked in finance, for a company that didn't mind where she lived so long as she had an internet connection, but Martin suspected that somewhere in the back of her mind she'd imagined that the years in Purgatory were going to be rewarded with Paris or Prague. Martin's employers reasoned instead that his time in Pakistan was the ideal preparation for their new Tehran correspondent, and after twelve months slacking off as an online news editor in Sydney, a return to the field was long overdue.

'I'm sorry,' Alice repeated.

Martin waved her crib-notes in thanks and replied with a parody of a honey-toned late-night DJ from the eighties, 'I'd better go spin some disks.'

Martin started with the Eurythmics' *Touch*. He fussed over the cables and the software settings, checking and rechecking every option, and when he'd finished the recording he played back the entire album to be sure that everything had worked properly.

Annie Lennox's voice still gave him goose-bumps. He'd only seen her performing live once, in a muddy field in the countryside north of Sydney in January 1984. Talking Heads, The Cure and The Pretenders had all played at the same festival. Unseasonal downpours had drenched the camp-grounds and he could still remember queuing in the rain to use the unspeakable toilets, but it had all been worth it.

Martin had been eighteen years old then; he would not meet Liz for more than a decade. In fact, all of his vinyl predated her; by the time they moved in together he'd bought a CD player and now the soundtrack to their entire relationship was already on his hard drive, safely out of sight. These crate-loads of old music would carry him back to the era before her – and with the possible exception of Ana Ng, you couldn't miss someone you hadn't even met yet.

It was an appealing idea, and for a few hours he lost himself in Talking Heads, drinking in their strange, naïve optimism. But by late evening he'd started on Elvis Costello and the mood was turning darker. He could have hunted through the crates for something cheerier – there was a Madness com-pilation in there somewhere – but he was tired of steering his emotions. Even when the music simply made the years melt away, the time-tripping itself was beginning to leave him maudlin. If he kept this up for two weeks he'd be a wreck.

He continued with the recording marathon, flipping and changing the albums like pancakes, but he turned down the playback volume so he wouldn't have to listen anymore. Better to start thinking of the imminent future; Martin opened his browser and began catching up on the news from Iran.

The opposition group that had garnered the most attention in the run-up to the impending parliamentary election was Hezb-e-Haalaa, literally the 'Party of Now'. Tongue-tied for-eigners occasionally pronounced this almost indistinguishably from Hezbollah, 'Party of God' (not to mention confusing the Iranian Hezbollah with the Lebanese group of the same name), but the two could not have been more different. Among other things, Hezb-e-Haalaa had announced a policy of recognising Israel; as Dariush Ansari, the party's founder, put it: 'Iraq killed a million of our people in the war, but we now have normal diplomatic relations with them. In proposing the same with Israel, I am not giving my blessing to anything that nation has done, any more than our esteemed leaders who sent their ambassador to Baghdad were giving theirs to the invasion of our territory and the slaughter of our people.'

Ansari travelled with a bodyguard to discourage freelance zealots from physically rebuking him for this line of reasoning – and there was still a chance that his big mouth would get him sent to Evin Prison – but his positions on economic, legal and social reform were far less controversial and received substantial support in opinion polls. Even in a perfectly fair and open ballot, Hezb-e-Haalaa probably would not have won a majority in the Majlis – a body that had only limited power, in any case – but in combination with other reformists it could still have embarrassed the conservative president.

However, the final say on eligibility fell to the twelve-member Guardian Council, who had just declared every candidate who happened to belong to Hezb-e-Haalaa unfit to stand in the election. There would be no need to engineer the results to keep them out of the Majlis – risking fresh cries of 'Where's my vote?' – now that they had been pre-emptively wiped right off the ballot.

The flight to Singapore left Sydney at the very civilised hour of nine a.m., but Martin had been up for forty-eight hours dealing with a plethora of last-minute tasks and his biological clock no longer recognised the distinction between good and bad times to travel. He spent the journey drifting fitfully in and out of sleep. Eight hours later as he strode through Changi Airport he still felt like a pared-down version of himself, an automaton with tunnel vision ignoring everything but signs that promised to take him closer to the right gate for Dubai.

He actually had a ninety-minute layover, but he could never relax until he knew exactly where he had to be at departure time.

On the flight to Dubai the mental fog began to lift. He knew he'd have a headache for the next few days, but at least he was sure that he'd ticked everything off his list and wouldn't have to send a stream of emails back to Sydney begging people to tie up loose ends for him. If the plane went down over the Indian Ocean he could drown in peace, with no fear of real estate agents blacklisting him in the afterlife for failing to dryclean his curtains.

The passenger in the seat beside him was a telecommunications engineer named Haroun who was headed for Abu Dhabi. When Martin explained that he was going to be covering the Iranian election, Haroun replied good-naturedly that he doubted it would be as newsworthy as the previous, presidential vote. Martin couldn't argue with that prognosis; after the turmoil of 2009 this was likely to be the most tightly managed poll in decades. Still, no one believed that the fire beneath the ashes had been extinguished.

In his present state it was pointless re-reading his background notes on the election; he slipped on his headphones and started up iTunes. The music library software had provisions for storing cover art and he'd started out taking photos of each album himself, but it had been hard to get the lighting and the angles right, so he'd ended up grabbing images off the net instead. Many of the sleeves had also included lyrics, notes or extra artwork, but he hadn't had time to digitise any of that. The day before he'd flown out he'd taken the crates to a charity shop in Glebe, but they'd told him that unless he had collectors' items, vinyl wasn't worth their shelf space. By now, it would all be landfill.

Martin flipped through the cover art. It was certainly a richer cue for memory than a mere list of names, but though the images had been endowed with perspective and reflections in some imagined glossy shelf-top, the faux-3D effects made it look like a museum exhibit trying too hard.

No matter; he had the music itself, and that was the main thing. He'd even diligently backed up everything to an external drive; his laptop could fry itself and these memories would still survive intact.

He wanted to hear something by Paul Kelly, but he couldn't make up his mind where to start so he let the software choose. 'St Kilda to King's Cross' filled the headphones; Martin closed his eyes and leant back in the seat, beaming nostalgically. Next came 'To Her Door', a song about a break-up and reconciliation. Martin kept smiling, focusing on the power and simplicity of the lyrics, refusing to countenance any connection to his own life.

Something made a loud crackling noise. He tugged off the headphones, wondering if he was missing an emergency announce>ment by the pilot. But the plane was silent, save for the engines' monotonous drone, and he could see a flight attendant chatting calmly with a passenger. Perhaps it had been some kind of electrical interference.

Halfway through the next song, 'You Can't Take It With You', he heard the crackling sound again. He paused the song, skipped back a few seconds and replayed the same section. The noise was there again, as if it was part of the recording itself. But it didn't sound like dust on the stylus, a scratch on the vinyl, or some random electronic pollution that had snuck into the circuitry from a mobile phone or fluorescent light. As Kelly's voice surged it *became* the noise, as if something mechanical inside the headphones might be scraping against its housing when the sound became too loud. But when Martin replayed the track with the volume turned down two notches, the noise was still there.

He started playing other tracks at random. His heart sank; about a third of them had the same problem, as if someone had gone through his record collection with a piece of sandpaper. He pictured Liz flipping through the crates in the dark, urged on by the ghost of Peter Cook from *Bedazzled*. But petty vindictiveness wasn't her style.

Haroun said, 'You seem very angry with that machine. You're welcome to borrow my laptop if it's any help.'

Martin wondered nervously if the obscenities that had been running through his head had remained entirely unvocalised; it didn't take much erratic behaviour for an overzealous flight marshal to pump you full of horse tranquilliser and lock you in the toilet. 'That's very kind of you,' he replied, 'but it's nothing urgent. And I don't think the problem's with this laptop.' He explained what he'd done with his music collection. 'I checked the first seven or eight albums and everything sounded perfect.'

'May I listen?'

'Sure.' Martin cued up an example of the strange blemish and passed Haroun the headphones.

After a moment Haroun gave a smile of grim satisfaction. 'That's wave shaping. I'm afraid you're right: there's nothing wrong with your playback, it's part of the recording.'

'Wave shaping?'

'You set the recording level too high.'

'But I checked that! I adjusted the level when I did the first album, and it was fine for at least six more!'

Haroun said, 'The signal strength would vary from album to album. Getting the right level for the first few would be no guarantee for all the others.'

No doubt that was true, but Martin still didn't understand why the effect was so ruinous. 'If the level from the turntable was too high for the computer, why doesn't the recording just . . . fail to be as loud as the original? Just lose some dynamic range?'

'Because when the level is too high,' Haroun explained patiently, 'you're not shrinking the waveform, you're decapitating it. Once the voltage exceeds the highest value the sound card can represent as data, it can't take it upon itself to re-scale everything on the fly. It just hits the maximum and draws a plateau there, in place of the true signal's complicated peaks. And when you truncate a wave like that, not only do you lose detail from the original, you generate noise right across the spectrum.'

'I see.' Martin accepted the headphones back from him and tried to laugh off the setback. 'It seems I'll be paying these starving musicians a few more cents after all. I just can't believe I wasted so much time and made such a bad job of it.'

Haroun was silent for a moment, then he said, 'Let me show you something.' He booted up his own laptop and summoned a website from his browser's offline cache. 'This book is a translation into English of a story in Arabic; it was published in the nineteenth century, so it's now in the public domain. An American company obtained a copy and scanned it, making it available to the world. Very generous of them, no?'

'I suppose so.' Martin couldn't see the screen clearly from where he was sitting, but the title bar read *The Slave Girl and the Caliph*.

'Optical character recognition isn't perfect,' Haroun said. 'The software can sometimes recognise that there's been a problem and call on human help to patch things up, but that process isn't perfect, either. This story is obscure, but my grandfather gave me a copy when I was ten, so I know that the heroine is named Mariam. This digital version, scanned from the English translation, has turned the "r" and "i" in her name into an "n" throughout. Mariam has become *Manam* – which, other than being an island off the coast of Papua New Guinea, so far as I know means nothing in any language.'

Martin said, 'That doesn't sound like a mistake the translator would have made. Not unless he was in the middle of an opium-smoking competition with Richard Burton.'

Haroun closed his laptop. 'I'm sure no human was involved, beyond feeding the book down a chute, along with ten thousand others.' He was smiling, but Martin could see the frustration in his eyes. He'd probably tried emailing these custodians of culture to put them straight, to no avail, while the grating error had seeped into mirror sites, multiplying irreversibly.

He gestured at Martin's own damaged library. 'With time and care everything could be preserved, but no one really has the patience.'

'I was about to leave the country,' Martin explained defensively. 'I had a lot of things to do.'

Haroun inclined his head understandingly. 'And why wouldn't any traveller want to turn their fragile music into something robust and portable? But so many processes are effortless and automatic now that it's easy to forget that most things in the world still play by the old rules.'

'Yeah.' Martin had to concede that; having treated the first few albums with care, he'd let himself imagine that the rest would follow as easily as if he'd merely been copying files from one hard drive to another.

'We're at the doorway to a new kind of world,' Haroun said. 'And we have the chance to make it extraordinary. But if we spend all our time gazing at the wonders ahead without remembering where we're standing right now, we're going to trip and fall flat on our faces, over and over again.'